THE GOLDILOCKS GAME

Peter Strongbear

THE GOLDILOCKS GAME

This novel is entirely a work of fiction. Names, characters, incidents or places are either the product of the author's imagination or they are used fictitiously. Any resemblance to actual events or locales, persons, living or dead, is purely coincidental. Furthermore, while minor edits have been made to the work in 2007, the entire essence of the story was completed in 2005. As such, any actual occurrences that mirror events in the story since then have also been purely coincidental.

Cover illustration by Peter Strongbear

Published by Kaleidodream Press

ISBN: 978-0-6151-6365-9

www.thegoldilocksgame.com

Acknowledgements

With thanks to my parents, Daniel and Elizabeth for their help, support and feedback while writing this novel. Special thanks goes to my brother Patrick for all the encouragement, suggestions, additional research and other work involved. Thanks also to my sister Beth and her husband Alex for their feedback, Alyssa and Jayden for being a bundle of fun, Carine for her feedback, Gim See for the Chinese translations, Irishka for the Russian translations and Russian cultural aspects, Montana Jade for lending me her eye, David Tran for his photos of the Pierrepont Building, and to anyone else I may have forgotten.

I also wish to thank Louis Bacon of *Moore Capital Management*, Anita Infante of and the engineers at *Carter Aviation Technologies* for their technical assistance, and Cindy Barshop and Hana Curanovic of the *Completely Bare Spa*.

I am also indebted to the various books, publications, brochures and websites from which I gleaned much valuable geographical, political and technical information – particularly to *The New Great Game: Blood and Oil in Central Asia* by Lutz Kleveman; the *Insight Guide* series of books for Moscow and Beijing; *The Companion Guide to St Petersburg* by Zinovieff and Hughes; *Beijing & Shanghai: China's Hottest Cities* by Hibbard, Mooney and Schwankert, The Kamov Company, the CIA website, Systema UK, BMW C1 Owners Forum, Diabolo Tricks, and the expertise of members of Siberian Siren who were of indirect help to me.

Finally, thanks to my muse for being a constant inspiration throughout this project.

PETER STRONGBEAR

Peter Strongbear lives in London, United Kingdom. He has a Masters Degree in Systematic Theology, a Bachelor's Degree in Law and has also been called to the Bar. Between writing, he runs his own internet business. His passions include tennis, Russian history and culture, spy thrillers, painting, and writing music. He is also an administrator of the popular tennis site, Siberian Siren (www.siberiansiren.com).

Peter loves to hear from his readers. You can contact him and find out more information about the book and learn more about the characters and the world of Goldilocks at www.thegoldilocksgame.com.

"There are those who know they are in the game, those who don't, and those who have unwittingly become the game themselves."
- Louis Bacon, Moore Capital Management.

"You have to learn the rules of the game. And then you have to play better than anyone else."
- Albert Einstein.

Prologue

Like a discarded rag doll, Tatiana Likamolova crumpled into a heap at the foot of the massage bed, almost sobbing as the immediate threat abated. Still choking and gasping for air, her pulse rate began to return to normal.

Realising her immodesty, she grabbed the towel still strung across the bed. She wrapped it around her body and tied a knot in front. Hardly the ideal thing with which to cover herself, but in the heat of the moment, it was all that was available.

Her attacker was still clutching his arm, trying to stop the bleeding. He swore under his breath.

"Who are you?" she spluttered, still coughing as she tried to crawl away.

The man did not answer. Instead, he rose defiantly, ready to renew his attack.

She struggled to her feet. As she stood upright, it was then, for the first time, she became aware of his size. While she was by no means a small girl at six feet tall in her bare feet, the razor-short-haired, hulking man in front of her stood a good six or seven inches taller and was built like a bulldozer. The blonde Russian beauty's supple, sylph-like frame looked positively skinny by comparison.

"Why are you trying to kill me?" she demanded.

Again, her muscular nemesis did not answer.

Was his assault sexually motivated? Clad in nothing but a towel, she allowed her eyes to glance downward for a second to ensure she was properly covered up. *No need to provide an unnecessary peep show.*

However, in that split second of distraction, her attacker lunged towards the massage bed where her phone still lay. Believing he was about to bore into her, she slammed the bed into him in her panic. Still moving, his momentum carried him forward, straight into it with an almighty crash. The bed toppled to the ground under his weight, while her phone went sliding across the floor.

It was then that it occurred to her that the masseur might in fact be after that object, and not her.

What was so special about it?

As she dropped to her feet to retrieve it, she felt his huge hands grabbing her ankle. She gasped, startled. The man was anchoring her in, dragging her across the floor towards him as if he were mooring a boat, while she watched helplessly as the phone slipped from her grasp.

Another feeling of dread shot through her as her towel began to loosen, little by little.

"*Góspadi!*" she gasped in Russian. "Oh God!"

She clasped a hand around the knot to ensure it stayed in place. But that was the least of her concerns. Like an animal hunted for game, it was as if her foot were caught in a rabbit trap, and the more she struggled, the more it tightened around her...

Chapter 1

One day earlier, Wednesday evening.

It has been rightly said that there are those who know they are in the game, those who don't, and those who have unwittingly become the game themselves.

In the case of Russian tennis sensation, Tatiana Likamolova, she was the golden girl of the game. Most definitely in, and she knew it. How could she not? If she was the game at all, it was because she was currently the most sought-after sports celebrity in the world.

Tonight, however, she found herself face-to-face with each one of these three scenarios, all in one go. Would she still be in the game against her formidable opponent, Natalya Shikolenko, as she trailed 2-4 in the final set of the US Open quarter-finals? Or would she be left uncertain whether she could cut it as a player if Natalya blasted her off the court in one thunderous, blink-and-you'll-miss-it serve to take a 5-2 lead? Worse still, even if Tatiana survived, would she immediately find herself hunted down while her opponent closed out this epic gladiatorial contest?

Naturally, Tatiana, or Tania for short, preferred the first scenario. But at the moment, things weren't entirely in her hands. The game had gone to deuce five times now, while the final points see-sawed between an advantage in Natalya's favour and a break point in hers. So far, both had failed to convert.

Tania waited like a prisoner before a firing squad as Natalya launched her next onslaught, a huge, booming projectile set for maximum damage. Unimpressed, the plucky Russian blonde rifled a powerful, lightning-fast backhand return, bruising the white line at the edge of the court, too fast and too low for her opponent to reach.

"GAME: MISS LIKAMOLOVA."

The Arthur Ashe Stadium erupted in an explosion of excitement as she breathed a huge sigh of relief. All eyes were magnetised on her willowy figure and endlessly long legs as she catwalked gracefully across the floodlit, royal blue court to her chair with feline steps.

Tania breathed a huge sigh of relief as she sat herself down. The strains of *Girls Just Wanna Have Fun* by Cyndi Lauper began blaring over the loudspeakers around the stadium. How ironic. This match was anything but fun. As defending US Open Champion, the pressure was squarely on her shoulders, especially against her older and more experienced opponent. But this big game cat still had a few lives left. Tania wasn't going down that easily. At least not without a fight, Russian-style, to the death.

Two ice maidens on court. The only thing threatening to thaw them out was the stifling humidity and the unbearable temperature that had soared well over 110 degrees. New York was on the tail end of a scorching Indian summer, and this evening, the sultry, suffocating air in Flushing Meadows made playing conditions almost impossible.

Impossible, at least for the champion, as she sat, lost deep in her thoughts.

Wow. It's like a sauna out here tonight.

She took a sip of her bottled water as she adjusted her visor, and brushed aside a few strands of her usually-shiny, long cornfield-coloured blonde hair that was pulled back into a ponytail. It felt disgusting. A matted mop caked with sweat, even though she had just washed it earlier. Tania sponged herself down with her towel. A lot of help that did. The perspiration that had formed on her well-tanned skin made her entire body glisten a warm, golden colour as though she had been rubbed from head to toe in baby oil. It made her elegant cream and white dress with gold trimmings - thoroughly damp from the workout - cling to her like adhesive.

Crud. I bet I look like crap right now.

She didn't. She possessed a natural Slavic beauty that ensured that, even without any makeup and her hair a mess, she could still manage to look positively radiant.

At least one particular person in the crowd thought so.

Jonah Bull sat restlessly in the stands waiting for the players to commence once more. The sight of this flaxen-haired warrior on court had not been lost on him. She was even more beautiful in person than he had imagined. Her mere presence and fighting spirit seemed to fill the stadium, larger-than-life. Perhaps this evening wasn't such a waste of time as he had initially thought.

It wasn't that he didn't welcome the opportunity to tear away from his desk for a few hours, but he originally reasoned that his time could be better spent in more productive activities compared to what appeared to be a rather mundane assignment: go to Flushing Meadows and observe Tania Likamolova, find out all he can about her, and use her to get close to the actual intended target.

Bull had never even heard of the Russian beauty before his mission, let alone seen her play. He was not a fan of tennis, considering it to be nothing more than a frivolous activity. His interest was naturally piqued, however, when his boss, Director John Abraham Hassall, called him into his office a few days earlier.

"I'm sure you're aware of the raid on the *Chang Yudong Chem* petroleum research facility in the Xinjiang Autonomous Region three weeks ago?" Hassall announced. This was more a formality than an inquiry. The Director knew very well that Bull had been involved in various related intelligence gathering on the matter, as part of his job at IRIS – the International Reconnaissance and Intelligence Service.

"Yes, sir," Bull replied. "A breakthrough bacteria for treating oil spills was stolen from their vaults. I know. I wrote up a report about it."

"I want you to have a look into this," came the Director's reply, somewhat economical and brief. Hassall was a strong, charismatic, but no-nonsense leader in his mid-fifties with silver-grey hair and an athletic build.

Two other IRIS agents were also present in the room. The first was a bookish, young, but slightly rotund Chinese man with an innocent-looking face, wearing a sleeveless cardigan and spectacles. Bull knew him by sight, but had barely had a chance to socialise with him. The other was a tall, granite-faced man in his late-forties with greying hair - Hassall's second-in-command, Deputy Director for Operations, Wendell Krennick - with whom Jonah was already very familiar.

"I believe you know, Mr Xiu, our technical wizard," Hassall said, pointing at the Chinese man with an open hand.

"I've seen you around," Bull remarked, giving a welcoming smile. "Elvin, is it?"

"Please, call me Elf," Xiu chuckled nervously. "Although some people call me the Shoemaker. Get it? Xiu-maker. Xiu in Chinese also means fixer or builder or..."

"I'm sure he gets the picture, Mr Xiu." Hassall sounded slightly impatient as he cut in.

Bull grinned inwardly. This Elvin Xiu seemed full of enthusiasm and optimism. A refreshing change from his other colleagues in this stuffy organisation.

As the others sat down, Krennick walked over to a screen and clicked the remote control in his hand, bringing up an enlarged photograph of a Slavic-looking man with sand-coloured hair. "Our intel has led us to this individual, Piotr Volkov, a member of RISK, whose cover is as a media consultant for OAO Red Gold, the Russian company that produces *Zolot* Vodka. We believe he and an accomplice are responsible for the theft, and plan to sell the bacteria to an organisation I'm sure you already know - The Three Bears?"

The Three Bears.

Bull nodded in acknowledgement, running a hand through his short, dark-brown hair. That name was becoming somewhat notorious around here.

"We need to find out more about his plans - when and where the sale is going down," Krennick continued.

Bull studied the image of Volkov carefully. He appeared to be a man in his mid-to-late twenties, not much older than himself. Bull often felt he himself was too young and too green to be doing this kind of work, and far too prone to doing things by the book. But what else was there to do? Clean-cut and typically all-American-looking, he was a bit of a boy scout, as Krennick sometimes referred to him. Yet Bull's superiors evidently had confidence in his abilities. Or was it his apparent innate sense of responsibility and willingness to follow orders that made him easily malleable?

"You're planning to assign me to track him?" he inquired.

"Not exactly," Hassall replied. "We're opting for a more indirect approach. Our sources indicate he is currently dating the Russian tennis player, Tatiana Likamolova, affectionately known to the public as Tania."

"Sir, I believe she pronounces it *Tarnia* not *Tan-ya*," Elf corrected him.

Hassall grumbled begrudgingly. "Thank you for pointing that out, Mr Xiu."

"I've never heard of her before," Bull stated categorically. He was definitely not up to date with the latest tennis starlets.

"You don't know her?" Elf's tone of voice suggested he was unable to come to terms with such an apparently gross oversight. "Where have you been all this time? She's only the current World Number Two and the latest 'It'-girl of tennis."

"I'm afraid I don't follow the game at all." Bull replied flatly, naturally failing to share his colleague's enthusiasm for the subject.

"You're missing out, man." Elf handed Bull a small, pocket-sized publicity photograph of Tania.

Bull's eyes widened as he studied the alluring photo of the Russian tennis player for a moment. *She's beautiful. Maybe I should pay closer attention to this sport.*

"She's a real looker and can play too," Elf added. "In fact, they're calling her the next…"

"Well I didn't call you gentlemen in here to discuss tennis," Hassall interrupted, somewhat irritated, as he brought the discussion back on track. "Agent Bull, I want you to head over to the *USTA Billie Jean King National Tennis Center* in Flushing Meadows and establish contact with her."

"That's my assignment?" Bull had to double-check he had heard correctly. It sounded rather mundane on the surface.

"Try to contain your enthusiasm, Mr Bull," Hassall said with a hint of sarcasm in his voice.

"I'm sorry, sir. It's just… may I ask what exactly I'm meant to be doing there?"

"We need someone to acquire the information that Volkov possesses, someone he wouldn't suspect. Likamolova already has a close relationship with him. She could find out information and feed it back to us."

Krennick spoke up, making an objection. "Abraham, with all due respect, if you're suggesting using Likamolova as some kind of informer, I'm uneasy with this approach you're taking. We aren't even sure at the moment where her loyalties lie?"

"I agree we do need to proceed cautiously with Likamolova," Hassall said. "But we also have to weigh our options, and at the moment there aren't many open to us. We'll discuss this in more detail once we've made contact with her. In the meantime, I need to know that you're going to back me up on this, Wendell."

Krennick nodded silently, indicating he was, in agreement, if only reluctantly.

"Now as for your assignment, Mr Bull," Hassall continued. "Likamolova is playing her quarter-final match in a couple of days against another Russian, Natalya Shikolenko, whom we're also observing for reasons I'm sure you're familiar with."

"Is Shikolenko's involvement in this confirmed?"

"You've read the intelligence reports yourself. This could be our chance to kill two birds with one stone, figuratively speaking, of course. But your primary focus should be Likamolova. Your ticket is booked for Wednesday."

He rose to his feet at the same time as Bull, who stood there silently, hesitant and unsure of himself. Looking him straight in the eye, Hassall asked, "Are there any problems?"

"Hey," Elf chimed in eagerly. "If he doesn't want to go, I'd be more than happy to take his place. I've always wanted to…"

"I believe he was talking to Agent Bull," Krennick interjected, curbing his excitement like a damp towel. "You're here merely to assist with the technical aspects of the operation, Mr Xiu, unless you've suddenly developed a taste for field work without anyone noticing."

Elf looked somewhat disappointed, his rising hopes suddenly dashed.

Sensing this, Bull spoke up. "To be honest sir, I'm not exactly what you'd call field-ready either."

"You're a fully-trained agent," Hassall replied.

"Maybe so, but let's not forget why I requested a transfer for a desk job here at IRIS. I'm not ready to go back out in the field."

"I disagree with you," the Director chided him. "You can't spend the rest of your time here at IRIS avoiding working with others again just because of one incident. You have to make a start somewhere. This is just the sort of easy assignment to get you back out there."

"But…"

"My mind is settled on the matter. Trust me. It will be good for you."

Bull was more than a little sceptical of the task Hassall had assigned him. But at least it was not too far away from the IRIS headquarters in Manhattan. He was to pose as a member of the press, where he would raise as little suspicion as possible.

"Genette Zetterling will give you the relevant files on Likamolova," Hassall informed him before he left. "I trust you'll do the appropriate reading on her and any other details involved. And make sure you keep your eyes open for anything unusual."

Bull was certainly keeping his eyes fully open at the moment. Although tennis was not his cup of tea, he nevertheless watched in utter fascination.

The Russian blonde galvanised herself into action, determined to see this match through to the end. There was no room for error, or her opponent could break her again. Then the next thing she'd know, she could kiss her title goodbye.

However, such thoughts of potential defeat or victory may have been premature, as a mysterious female figure observed the game on a miniature, palm-held screen somewhere outside the stadium, but within the grounds of Flushing Meadows, determined that it would not play out to the last point.

"Time?" another female inquired, clutching a remote-control device in her hand.

"Not yet," the first one with the TV screen replied. "A few more minutes. It's not ready yet."

Tania bounced the ball at her feet, ready to serve, as the roaring sound of an overhead jet from LaGuardia airport shuttled past. Waiting until it had passed, she launched a thunderous cannon down the centre with a rip-roaring, semi-orgasmic scream.

"Fault," a voice blurted out, as if conspiring to deny her the point.

Tania scowled at the linesman intensely, with a look of petulance, before collecting her thoughts. Her brow furrowed as she studied carefully where to place the next ball. Salty streams trickled down her forehead onto her nose, and into her large, lime-green eyes, limpid so you could see the fire inside. She couldn't afford to bludgeon her second serve in the same way. Every point counted. Pin-point accuracy.

Focus.

"Is it time now?" the same shadowy figure with the remote control asked once again."

"Almost. You'll know when the little red light goes off in a second."

Everything seemed to be moving in slow motion. The thud of the ball bouncing off the baseline resonated deafeningly in rhythm with Tania's pounding heart. Before her, the royal blue court had transformed into a vast ocean surrounded by a distant shore of green. She was walking on water. 'In the zone', as many would call it - that dream-like tennis state, where mind and body were perfectly synchronised, where every shot was child's play.

Around her, the champion's world grew deathly silent. Encased in a bubble of her own. Tania tossed the ball high above her head. It had swelled to resemble one of those oversized tennis balls that players usually signed at the end of a match. The racquet had become an extension of her long arms. She only had but to visualise the shot in her mind, and then thought became deed. In a single motion of balletic grace combined with a flurry of tremendous power, her racquet struck the ball violently. The ball coursed through the air, seemingly creating a shimmer of heat, as she traced its trajectory from its launch pad to the other side of the court.

She was ready for anything. Anything that is, except for what was about to happen next.

A short distance away, a red light began blinking, as a finger pressed down on a button.

Natalya stuck her weapon out for a double-handed backhand. She might as well have been waving a white flag instead as the ball rocketed towards her, leaving her looking more like she was attempting to swat an evasive fly than returning her opponent's fire.

Suddenly, in mid-swing, as the ball connected with her racquet strings, Natalya let out an ear-splitting, agonising scream that filled the entire stadium from top to bottom, as if someone had plunged a hot knife into her body. Eyes wrenched tight like screws, her face began contorting in agony. Unable to let go of the racquet handle, she began to shake uncontrollably, convulsing in acute shock.

This game had taken an unexpected turn of events.

Chapter 2

The crowd was stunned, while the USTA staff stood by hesitantly like statues, temporarily paralysed by indecision. Yet from the other side of the court, Tania saw everything. She had to act. Now. Without a moment's thought, she executed a move which she had performed hundreds of times before. Only now, it was not a simple hit-or-miss affair in which, if she were inaccurate, she would simply be faulted. This time she required deadly, bull's-eye precision.

Like a sharpshooter, the champion served a bullet again. Dead on target. The ball clipped the edge of Natalya's racquet with such force that it tore it out of her hands, sending it tumbling across the outer green border of the court.

The Russian blonde glanced over at her opponent, bewilderment setting in as the medical trainers rushed onto the scene. As Natalya crumpled to the ground in a frazzled heap, she looked down at her hands. Steam. Wafting from them like a red hot iron doused with water.

Tania skipped to the other side of the court, where her opponent sat, the jolt she received from her racquet having clearly unsettled her. "Are you okay?" the blonde Russian asked. Her voice rang with genuine concern.

The older Russian looked up. "I will be fine," she replied coolly, without a word of thanks. Her face had returned to its previous icy demeanour.

Tania was slightly taken aback by Natalya's abrupt response and stand-offish attitude. Then again, when had her compatriot ever spoken a word to her? Although Tatiana Likamolova barely knew her opponent, she had heard reports from other players on the women's tour that it was difficult to strike up a conversation with her. Raven-haired and beautiful with dark, haunting eyes, Natalya Shikolenko was equally a dark horse who seemed to relish her own privacy. Quite understandable though. Many players preferred to keep to themselves between matches rather than striking up friendships. After all, they were competing at the top level against each other on court. One needed to be ruthless against one's opponent. Forget any notion of friendship that may exist.

Tania chose not to make anything of it. Perhaps her older Russian compatriot was simply in shock and wanted some additional space to recover. Tania moved back to allow the US Open security staff to do a quick sweep of the area, while the trainer attended to her opponent. In the meantime, as she began flexing her long, supple limbs in an attempt to avoid cooling down, she noticed that Svetlana's expression had become an unsettled mixture of grave concern and paranoia. The dark-haired beauty was gazing around the stadium into the packed stands, scrutinising each person closely, one by one.

Her own curiosity aroused, Tania made a quick surveillance of her own. *Who or what is she looking at?* All she saw was a sea of colours. Maybe it was that man up there with the huge floppy hat? Or that woman over there whose face was painted with the stars and stripes? She gave up. This was the largest tennis stadium in the world. Four tiers of over twenty-two thousand people. She was hardly going to check out all the faces. There didn't seem to be anything particularly unusual. Besides, it was perfectly normal to see people strangely attired.

"You appear to have some serious burns on your hands," the trainer informed Natalya, remarking on the fact that they were red, blistered and leathery. "I've never seen anything like this happen before."

Neither had the injured Russian, but she had her own theories on how precisely this had happened. Of course, sharing it with any of the officials here would only cause unnecessary alarm.

She swore under her breath in her native tongue, too faint for the trainer to hear. "They have found me and plan to kill me."

After fifteen or twenty minutes had passed, the US Open security indicated that everything appeared to be in order. The trainer helped

Natalya to her feet, whereupon she marched immediately over to the umpire like a wounded soldier, indicating that she was retiring from the match. The crowd was generally sympathetic, although a few boos and hisses were clearly audible. Then, the wounded Russian strode off the court without so much as a word to her opponent nor a wave to the crowd, leaving behind a dark cloud of gloom in her wake.

And there Tania stood, a lone figure, but the default winner of the match. A bittersweet victory.

She was perplexed by this odd behaviour. Almost as if Natalya had more pressing matters to attend to, and both this match and her injury were simply minor annoyances disrupting a busy schedule. But what else could be more important than the tournament?

***

In the stands, Jonah Bull watched with growing intrigue. Perhaps this assignment wasn't going to be as mundane after all.

He moved away from the crowd and placed a call on his cell phone. "I haven't made contact with Likamolova yet," he whispered. "But Hassall also asked me to keep my eyes open for anything unusual. There've been some interesting developments today, as you may well have seen on the TV concerning Natalya Shikolenko."

"Yes, Mr Xiu brought it to my attention, being the avid tennis fan that he is," Deputy Director Krennick replied.

"What do you make of it, Elvin… er…*Elf?*" Bull asked.

Elvin Xiu shared his thoughts. "The sports commentators thought she might've suffered some kind of electric shock."

"It certainly looked that way," Bull agreed. "But from a racquet?"

"Weird huh?"

"How would that even be possible?"

"I'll have to do some research," Elf replied. "I'll let you know what I find."

Krennick showed a measure of concern in his voice. "What's your opinion on it, Agent Bull?"

"Maybe someone was trying to scare her, sir," Bull replied. "Give her some sort of warning."

Krennick paused for a moment, deciding on the next course of action. "Very well. I'll have Mr Xiu look further into this and get back to you shortly. Meanwhile, you're going to have your hands doubly full, tracking both Likamolova and keeping tabs on Shikolenko. Keep us up to date on your progress."

"Will do, sir," Bull replied.

"And while you're at it," Elf interjected, "see if you can get me Tania Likamolova's autograph. Just say it's for a friend."

***

Normally, Tania found the dazzling photographers' flashes to be intrusive. This time they went unnoticed. Caught up in her own thoughts, she strolled over to her equipment bag, hurriedly threw on a top, and began to head off court toward the locker room, stopping only briefly to sign autographs for a long line of admirers.

Walking down a turquoise-painted corridor decorated with pictures of past US Open winners, her trance-like state was broken by the sound of her cell phone ringing - a bright, musical tune that reflected her personality. She pulled it out of her bag and placed it to her ear. "Hello?" Her voice was soft, inquisitive.

"Hello Tatya…" the voice began.

"Piotr", Tania exclaimed cheerfully. Her face lit up suddenly, beaming with delight.

Like all Russians, Tania Likamolova had several forms of her name. Her compatriots formally referred to her by her patronymic, Tatiana Ulyanovna. To the rest of the world, she was Tania, while the more affectionate form of her name, 'Tatya', was used by those closest to her. Piotr Volkov was one such person in that last category - he had the enviable privilege of being her first real boyfriend, as well as the Head of Global Marketing for *Zolot*, the new top-selling super-premium brand of Vodka produced by Russia's largest beverage distributor, Red Gold. Tania preferred to keep her private life out of the media glare, but rumours were constantly fuelled whenever she was seen with a guy, whether that guy was another tennis player or a celebrity.

"I'm sorry I missed the match," he apologised profusely. "You know how busy I can be?"

"That's okay," she replied. "It's been crazy here actually." Tania proceeded to summarise the evening's events as vividly as she could. "I'm okay really, Piotr," she assured him eventually.

"Are you sure?" he continued on the other end.

She nodded firmly. "Positive. I'm just a bit shaken. But I'm surprised you haven't heard anything about it on the news."

"I've been finalising arrangements for a commercial shoot in Xi'an next Tuesday," he replied simply.

"Xi'an," Tania mused. "That's in China, isn't it?"

"Yes. Not too far from Beijing where you'll be playing soon. We're trying something different as part of our new marketing campaign to reach a broader audience. We want to appeal to a more global audience by shooting a bunch of supermodels in various exotic locations around the world."

"It sounds like there's dance music playing in the background," Tania remarked. "Where exactly are you?"

"In the VIP room of *The Vogue Café*," he answered. "A Moscow nightclub - it's business."

She frowned. "Hold on a second. If you're in Moscow, then will I still get to see you this weekend?"

"Yes. You're going to the Ball aren't you?"

"I should think so," Tania replied archly. "Isn't that one of the objectives of tennis? To go to the ball?"

Failing to see the humour, Piotr continued. "I thought you meant the Imperial Ball hosted by Oleg Korsakov at the Catherine Palace in St Petersburg - the one we've both been invited to, remember?"

"Oh that again?" Tania shook her head. "I told you already I'm not going. It's the Ladies' Final on Saturday, remember?"

Piotr cleared his throat, suggesting he was about to deliver some bad news which, by now, Tania had learned to detect. "Unfortunately I will have to miss it."

"What?" Her heart shrank inside her instantly. "Why? You know it's important to me."

"Because I've already made plans to be in St Petersburg." His voice was firm, his answer definite.

"But it's only on Sunday evening," she protested.

"Well let's not jump ahead of ourselves. We don't even know if you'll be playing on Saturday yet."

Tania felt her hackles rising. She wasn't generally that way, but when it came to tennis, her sense of passion rose as easily as her on-court decibel level. "Don't say that. I don't want to think negatively about it at this point. What's so special about this Oleg Korsakov that you have to be there and not with me?"

"Tatya, relax," he encouraged her, speaking in a sedate tone of voice that was evidently meant to calm her down, but instead had the opposite effect. "He is my boss and the CEO of Red Gold after all. And he's invited everyone who is anyone from Russia. All the Russian jet-set, models and dancers, you name it. I must therefore attend. It's business. But why don't you come along to the Ball? That way I can make it up to you? Besides, there'll be other matches."

Other matches my ass. Tania was smouldering silently. This conversation was taking a more serious turn, which was something with which she was not entirely happy. She shook her head, debating the issue in her mind. *The final's at eight on Saturday, so even if I flew straight out afterwards I would never make it to the Ball on time. But even if I lose before then, I still can't commit to anything else at this point.*

"Well, think about it," he advised her. "Don't say yes or no just yet. I *have* to go with or without you, but if you do reconsider, it's never too late. So just say the word."

"Whatever," Tania sighed indifferently, trying her best to hide the disappointment in her voice.

"Well I'll talk to you later okay?" Piotr assured her. "There's someone else waiting to speak to me on the other line."

Tania stashed her cell phone away and began to walk to the locker room, determined to change out of her tennis outfit. One interruption was acceptable, but another would be pushing it. Her sweat-drenched clothing was drying icy cold, leaving her with a distinct chill as marked as the final few frosty words between her and her boyfriend.

***

In the locker room, Natalya mopped her brow with her towel. She glanced around. The slightest squeak would set her on edge. It didn't help that the TV was on in there, but at present, she was unable to find the remote control to switch it off. Checking that the coast was clear, she punched a few buttons on her cell phone and began to speak, exchanging vital information in Russian.

"You could've thrown the match earlier," the voice on the other end of the phone chided her. "There's a greater priority here than tennis. We don't need this kind of publicity."

"I was unable to get out of it as planned," she stated.

"I'm just concerned for you. Your life could be in danger now."

"It goes without saying," Natalya replied coldly. "My life *is* in danger now. I will have to take more care, especially now I know they are probably onto me."

Natalya sat herself down on a nearby bench while she endured a tense moment of silence from the speaker on the other end. During those few seconds of uncertainty, she spotted a copy of *Tennis* magazine lying there, with its cover turned face down. She picked it up and, with it still facing downwards, began thumbing casually through the pages, noting all the familiar faces from both the women's and men's tour. Names old and new. Young hopefuls and experienced veterans. They were all there.

After what seemed like an eternity, the voice on the other end finally broke through. "What about the information - is it safe?"

She nodded. "Of course."

"Then get yourself out of there. Maintain a low profile until we make contact again. But remember, your first priority is to the file. The information you've gathered on there is of the utmost importance."

Summoning her resolve, Natalya took a deep breath, while simultaneously flipping the magazine over so that it was facing the right way up. "You needn't remind me, Piotr. If necessary, I will do whatever is required to ensure its safety or to get it into your hands." Then, sensing someone was coming, she ended the phone call with a few last words of assurance. "And I think I know how."

She peered down at the glossy front cover of the publication in her hands. Staring her in the face was a glamorous photo of the darling of the tennis world, Tania Likamolova.

Yes. Exactly how.

***

Tania's last conversation had cast a deep shadow over her as she arrived inside the players' locker room. She tried to shake it off. *No use dwelling on the negative.*

Such thoughts didn't last long however, as she was distracted by the TV that had been left on in there, with images from the CNN news headlines playing:

"*...Onto business news now, technical analysts at Goldman Sachs speculate that if crude oil prices continue to climb over $120 a barrel, the bear could be in for the long haul... In other news around the world, Russian President Dmitry Zolkin continues talks for Russia and the Chinese province of Xinjiang to unite with ex-Soviet States, including Azerbaijan, Kazakhstan and Turkmenistan, in an OPEC-like Eurasian cartel of oil and gas... Meanwhile, the long-discussed pipeline near Sakhalin Island and Japan...*"

Tania found the remote control over to one side beneath a pile of towels, and hit the off button. "Enough of that," she muttered. "As Piotr would say: 'it's business.'"

She tiptoed over the jungle of shoes, clothing, bags and other belongings strewn all over the floor. Whoever was in here last had left it looking like the place had been ransacked. With all the various iPods and the odd cell phone lying around, perhaps someone was searching for something of vital importance?

Scratch that. What was she thinking? This room was always a mess.

She placed her own cell phone down on the bench, stripped off her tennis shoes and socks, and walked over to her locker in her bare feet. They were noticeably lighter in shade than the rest of her legs, and bore a distinct but inevitable sock tan line just below her ankles from being covered up during her many sun-drenched matches. She was looking forward to changing out of her tennis outfit and taking a long shower to cool off. With a post-match interview scheduled with the press in an hour's time, Tania wanted to make sure she looked her best. That wouldn't be difficult. Her statuesque, slender build, more akin to a swimmer than an athlete, always ensured that whatever she wore, whether on-court or off, she would look fantastic.

As Tania turned the combination on her locker, she sensed the presence of someone else in the room. She spun around instantly.

It was Natalya.

Tania smiled at her politely in acknowledgement. The moment was filled with both uncertainty and awkwardness, leading her to break the silence. "*Zdrástvuitye.* Hello." She was unsure whether to greet her in Russian or English.

"*Zdrástvuitye,*" Natalya replied.

Unlike Tania, whose faint Russian tones lightly peppered her mostly-American accent, there was no mistaking where Natalya was from. The dark-haired Russian's accent was very pronounced and deliberate. She brimmed with a self-assurance and authority that could sometimes come across as imperious. By contrast, the blonde's own confidence came from hours of interviews answering questions from the press or chat show hosts, but she still sounded very much like a girl.

Even Natalya's appearance was more that of a seasoned pro. With her strong nose, high sculpted cheekbones and a pair of icy-cold eyes that looked like two shards of charcoal whose embers had gone out, she held Tania's gaze unflinchingly. Professional at something, that was for sure.

Tania felt compelled to ask her former opponent about her state of well-being. She continued in English. "Are you okay? You must be quite shaken up after tonight's events." She glanced down to see that Natalya's hand was heavily bandaged.

"I will be fine, thank you," she answered inscrutably, attempting to appear nonchalant. "It was nothing."

Nothing or not, Tania felt obliged to show further concern. "Well, if you ever need anything…"

The older Russian's response was swift and unexpected. "Perhaps you can be of assistance."

Tania perked up, her face suddenly inquisitive. "Sure. How?"

Natalya extended a long, bony finger towards the object on the bench next to Tania's tennis shoes. "I need to make an important phone call, but my phone is not working properly. May I borrow yours for a few minutes?"

Tania glanced behind her. "Oh, sure, that's no problem." She stepped over a pile of shoes, nearly tripping on them as she went to fetch the cell, then directed her toes nimbly over them again on the journey back. "By the way, this place is a mess."

"*Da*," Natalya agreed, smoothing that black, silky mane of hers with those long, pointed fingers. "And I thought the men's locker room was bad."

"Um… yeah," Tania laughed, deciding she was better off not asking how her compatriot would know that unless she had been in there herself.

Natalya took the phone from Tania and studied it, slightly amused. "Bright pink!"

"Don't mind that." Tania giggled, wrinkling her nose as she shrugged her shoulders. "It's my favourite colour. Well I'll just be over there, okay? So whenever you finish…"

The Russian blonde sauntered back over to her locker and removed her belongings. She saw Natalya move some distance away, past the massage tables, and out of her immediate line of vision.

She probably just wants some privacy.

That much was true. The ebony-haired dark horse had what she needed, and that naïve girl had handed it over so willingly. She took a second to glance back over at the ingénue who had been so unwittingly generous. *So young and innocent. I hate to do this to her, but I am left no other choice.*

***

Jonah Bull was attempting to navigate his way through the vast grounds of the Tennis Center, so far with little success. His destination was the press room, where Tania would be having an interview shortly. Unfortunately, he had completely lost his bearings and now his frustration was boiling slowly inside him like a kettle, threatening to match the sweltering temperature in New York.

His cell phone began to ring, interrupting his thoughts. He answered it promptly.

"Bull," the voice spoke. "Elf here."

"Elf," Bull replied. "That was quick. What have you found?"

"I did some research into the way tennis racquets are made. Lots of them now utilise nanoparticles or piezoelectric crystals as part of the new racquet technology. These millions of microscopic crystals each emit a small electrical charge, and collectively they power special magnets hidden inside the head of the racquet to give it a solid feel without making it heavy. Now, normally when the ball strikes the racquet, it can cause the frame to deform a bit. What these crystals do is power up the magnets, forcing it back into shape, giving the ball much more speed, precision and accuracy when hit."

"I'm sure that's fascinating," Bull replied, "but I don't need a lesson on the composition of tennis racquets right now. What I want to know is can these crystals produce an electric current strong enough to give someone a shock?"

"Well theoretically," Elf began, "certain crystals such as quartz can generate thousands of volts. If the racquet had been modified to release a much greater electrical current than normal - say, a nano-sized capacitor was inserted to store the electrical charge generated from its kinetic energy each time it struck the ball - then once it had built up sufficient charge, the electric shock could be triggered via a remote-controlled device."

"It sounds like a trap, if you ask me," Krennick's voice spoke up suddenly over the speaker phone.

"A trap sir?" Bull inquired, surprised that his mentor was listening in on the conversation. "How so?"

"Well the attack was completely unexpected and yet it happened so quickly that Shikolenko was powerless to do anything about it. As I've often instructed you, surprise is an important strategy: an action must be so indiscernible that it cannot be anticipated, so swift that it cannot be outmanoeuvred, and so overwhelming that it cannot be repelled. Surprise can be far more effective than a full-frontal assault, and far more deadly. And by using what is unexpected in the mind of your opponent, you can manoeuvre them into weakness."

Bull nodded silently, acknowledging his mentor's words. He had heard him say something to this effect many times in the past, as the Deputy Director of IRIS was skilled in the art of conflict and surprise tactics.

"So, someone could have intended to kill her," Bull concluded.

"Yeah, that's possible," Elf agreed. "But who?"

"Perhaps someone who sees tennis as more than just a game."

***

Natalya had previously inspected the few cell phones that were lying around on the locker room floor. Tania's one, although not as high-spec as her own, was the best that she could manage under the circumstances.

She wrestled her own smartphone out from her pocket. Unlike the brightly-coloured cell that her young compatriot owned, Natalya's was stainless steel. No frills or fancy extras. Simply a very business-like design to match her equally business-like personality. The mysterious Russian began playing around on the keypad in order to access an encrypted section.

Within seconds, a message appeared on the screen in Cyrillic: ACCESS SECURE FILES: YES OR NO.

Natalya pressed YES and waited. The screen took her to a file labelled "3B". Natalya selected it.

Next, she held Tania's phone beside her own. She noticed that, as on her own phone, Tania's had Cyrillic letters beneath the standard western alphabet on the keypad. She began tapping a few keys, calling up a few hundred songs stored there on Tania's MP3 player. Natalya bulk-deleted them without a second thought.

Moving back to her own phone, the screen read: FILE TRANSFER: YES OR NO?

Again, she pressed YES. A file was sent across and began uploading onto Tania's phone.

Natalya glanced over at Tania, double-checking to see whether she was growing suspicious. No. Everything was fine. That poor, clueless girl was still getting changed, oblivious to anything that was going on.

The transfer took almost three minutes. As soon as it was complete, she walked over to the Russian blonde and placed it firmly in her hand.

"Oh, you've finished already?" Tania remarked, looking up in surprise.

"Yes. *Spasiba*," Natalya said gratefully, allowing herself the grace to smile. "Thank you, Tatiana Ulyanovna. And good luck in your next match. *Udachi*."

"*Spasiba*," the young Russian replied. She shoved the phone into her bag, ready to walk into the shower, but then spun around quickly, as if something else had come to mind. "Well, maybe I'll see you around. *Dosvidaniya*."

But Natalya was gone. And Tania stood all alone in an empty locker room, naïvely unaware that she now carried something of vital importance on her cell phone.

Chapter 3

An hour or so later, a tangle of journalists and photographers bustled impatiently in their seats in the press room, waiting for the glamorous tennis star to arrive. With her model looks, the press were like hungry gold diggers eager to grab any photos of the Russian Klondike, no matter what the occasion, and cash in on the ensuing gold rush.

Among those seated was Jonah Bull, tucked away indiscreetly, albeit near the front of the room where he would be afforded a good view. Having decided beforehand that he neither knew enough about tennis nor about Likamolova to ask any informed questions, he opted to remain silent and simply observe. He had never seen the girl up close before, and waited in eager expectation like everyone else.

As soon as Tania walked in and sat herself down, any chatter was instantly drowned out by her presence. She gave a gentle wave of her hand, and a broad smile for the cameras. Her hair, still damp from her shower, was now worn loose and tumbled gracefully around her shoulders. She wore little make-up to hide the light dusting of freckles on her face, and her skin had a fresh, luminous quality about it that made it seem as if it was illuminated from within. Her casual attire - consisting of a running top, a white mini-skirt and flip-flops - gave her more a girl-next-door appearance than a multi-million-dollar tennis superstar, and thus could have allowed her to pass easily for any regular, albeit trendy college student.

Bull was pleasantly surprised. She was a refreshingly natural and down-to-earth beauty, with the sweetest face and most enchanting smile he'd seen in a long time.

As always, before any conference, Tania mentally prepped herself for another round of questions, both in English and Russian. She had been uneasy at first with all the publicity and attention she had gained over the past year, but having given a slew of endless interviews, she now handled herself with aplomb, even if her answers of late sometimes had the distinct ring of sounding slightly rehearsed and less spontaneous. Still, the press seemed to be wrapped around her finger, mesmerised by her delectable charm as they hung onto every word uttered by the girl with the golden tongue.

"Ladies and gentlemen," the moderator began, "Tania Likamolova for you. We'll take questions for her first in English."

The microphones bobbed up and down amid the little firefly sparks of the camera flashes. Then a hand shot up. A well-dressed man in his late-twenties for the *New York Post*. "Tania…" he began.

"It's *Tarnia* actually," she interrupted him, drumming her long, slender fingers on the desktop and fiddling with her name plate.

The reporter looked blank with surprise. "I'm sorry?"

"My name." A gamine grin flickered across her face. "You said *Tan-ya*, like 'can ya'. I prefer it pronounced *Tarnia* - almost like it rhymes with Narnia – you know, like in 'the Chronicles of…'?"

The reporter bit his lip. "I'm sorry about that, *Tarnia*! Was that okay?"

"Yeah, sorry." Tania tinkled with a girlish, melodious giggle which proved infectious. The whole press room burst into simultaneous laughter. To them, she must have seemed overly-meticulous. She rolled her shoulders upwards, slightly self-consciously as she began to blush - something she seemed to do without much difficulty. She decided she would qualify her correction. "It's just a pet peeve I have when people incorrectly pronounce my name. I'm a bit of a perfectionist as you've probably guessed."

"That's okay," the reporter assured her, raising the flat of his hand out in surrender. "*Tarnia* it is. Any tips on pronouncing your last name?"

Not this again.

Tania rolled her eyes, before letting out a faint laugh. Pronunciations ranged from the more-correct, Russian *Lika-MOL-ova* to the Americanised *Lika-mol-OVA*, and everything else in between. The problem was that, having grown up in the US, she had virtually settled on the Americanised version herself, at least whenever she was out in public. It certainly had a more stellar ring to it, even though it encouraged countless jokes at her expense, especially when said quickly. Having blossomed into a poised and confident young woman however, its suggestive nature didn't seem to bother her anymore. On the contrary, she now considered it an asset that added to her appeal.

She screwed up her lips, trying to think of a suitable response. Then her mouth broke into a cheeky, Cheshire Cat grin, causing her to dimple sweetly as she answered the question. "Uh, what cats do when giving their litter a bath! Does that help?"

The press roared with laughter at her artful reply. Tania joined them, scrunching up her nose as she broke into a semi-embarrassed giggle, making a sound as if she were sucking air inwards while chirping higher and higher. Her cheeks were now flushed with a maddening red, giving her a glowing, ruddy complexion that lit up her countenance, and made her even more adorable than usual. Part of the reason they all loved her was that she could poke fun of herself.

The stone-faced moderator decided to move things back on topic.

"I'm sorry," Tania said to the reporter, still grinning. "You were about to ask me a question?"

"Yes. Many people are saying you were quite the heroine out there tonight, the way you came to Natalya Shikolenko's aid when she seemed to go into shock with her racquet. How do you feel about that and do you know what was happening at all?"

Tania smiled modestly. "Yeah, I hadn't heard people saying that. But I would've done that for anyone else. I just saw she was in pain so I knocked it out of her hand with a serve. Nothing heroic about that. I don't know what that was about though. There just seemed to be something wrong with her racquet. I guess it was just some kind of accident, so I'm as much in the dark about this as you guys."

***

The earlier incident was no accident. Natalya knew it. She allowed her eyes to ping-pong back and forth as she made her way frantically through the vast grounds of the *USTA Billie Jean King National Tennis Center*. The severe shock she received during the match had served as an unmistakable wake-up call that someone was after her. She had to get out of there.

Immediately.

She glanced around furtively at her surroundings. The low hum of movement and the guests' geese-like gabble filled the air. The Tennis Center's grounds were still bustling with activity, with visitors swarming like ants scattered in every direction, some hoping to catch one last glimpse of their favourite tennis stars before they left for the day. The light was fading rapidly, with the sky now a deep, dusky blue that matched the colour of the courts. In the distance, visible for all to see, was the monumental, stainless steel globe known as the Unisphere, looming above the stadium grounds. The structure - a remnant from the 1964 World Fair - had now become the most well-known symbol of Corona Park where tourists would frequently gather.

Such trivialities mattered little to the enigmatic Russian. Her only concern was escaping to a more secure location. With so many unknown faces around, anyone here in the crowd could set her paranoia over the edge.

***

In the press room, the questions continued like rapid fire. A thirty-something female reporter from the *New York Times* spoke. "Now you are through to the next round, do you feel that there is an immense pressure on you to win here as defending champion?"

Tania nodded. "Obviously there's a lot more pressure to win. That can sometimes mean not playing as freely as I'd like, but of course I don't want to become too relaxed either. Pressure can be good – it's just a matter of conditions being neither too hot nor too cold."

The press looked somewhat bemused by that statement.

"Is that your general philosophy in life?" a reporter from the *Evening Tribune* quizzed her. "Being neither too hot nor too cold but having everything 'just right'?"

Tania giggled sheepishly. "I don't know where that came from. I just thought of that on the spot. Maybe I've been reading too many fairy tales before bedtime."

Someone from the *Daily Sentinel* spoke up. "Generally speaking, are things 'just right' for you in your life at the moment?"

Where were they going with this?

"Boy, you guys are really sticking with this 'just right' theme aren't you?" Tania laughed. "I'm pretty happy with where things are at this stage, but I'm always trying to outdo myself and stay on top. I guess what I'm saying is that what might be 'just right' at this moment might not be in six months' time. Maybe that means I'm restless and always seeking something else. But that's me. Does that make sense?"

She reflected upon her own words for a moment. *Wow. Did I really say that? Am I so easily discontented that this so-called just-right-fix only lasts that long?*

The moderator chimed in again. "Could we have a different type of question please, again in English before we take questions in Russian?"

A hand from the back of the room shot up. "Back to this evening's match," a reporter began. "I know it's been suggested that there are frosty relations between you and the other Russians, so I was wondering how you felt about what happened to Natalya tonight."

Tania shook her head. "I don't know what you're getting at. Of course I wouldn't want anything to happen to Natalya or any of the other players. As for the 'frosty relations' you mention, well we aren't exactly sorority sisters, but we don't have punch-ups or anything like that. We all just do our own thing in between matches. As I'm sure you're aware, it's hard to be friends with someone you have to be completely ruthless with on court. But if you must know, Natalya did actually talk to me after the match today in the girls' locker room."

"What did she say?"

"Oh, nothing much. Girl stuff. Just the usual few words between players. I'm sure she's fine though. She's probably relaxing somewhere right now!"

***

Natalya was doing anything but relaxing. She continued through the grounds with increased urgency.

The tournament officials had insisted that she be accompanied by bodyguards, or at least the US Open security. She stubbornly declined. If someone was after her, they would get to her regardless of any added protection. Still, the men in the yellow security T-shirts loitered around in case she should change her mind.

No chance of that.

She froze in her tracks. In the distance she could've sworn she spotted two figures approaching, heading straight in her direction.

As the two figures drew nearer, Natalya could make out that they were two women garbed in what appeared to be traditional Romani dress. One was clad in a white, basque-like outfit with long, thigh-length boots. She had dark blonde hair and innocent, Lolita-like eyes. The second woman was attired in a corseted outfit of scarlet with lace trimmings, but she had rich olive skin and her hair was a deep red, almost auburn shade. When it caught the floodlights at certain angles, it looked like she wore a halo of fire on her head. Both women were statuesquely built and exotically attractive in a vampish sort of way.

As a native of Moscow, Natalya had to remind herself that this was New York - one big melting pot and a city where, many have suggested, one could truly belong. The Russian neither fitted in, nor did she have any desire to do so. But the two figures? They could be anyone. It was hard to tell. The Tennis Center was surrounded by Corona Park, where people could easily be dressed in an assortment of bizarre costumes for the myriad of activities that took place over the summer. This certainly held true at the moment. Were they simply one of the fire-eaters, jugglers or acrobats?

The two women seemed to be holding something that could easily suggest that was the case, and from the looks of other visitors around, no-one gave them a second glance. They had probably been performing in the park earlier.

Natalya shook her head, disgusted with herself for letting her paranoia get the better of her.

Her instincts told her otherwise.

Natalya began jogging a few steps to test out their intentions. She watched as they matched her pace in response, as if to ensure that she did not escape. That was confirmation enough for her.

Regardless of who they were, Natalya knew they spelled danger. Whoever was after her had found her. And this time, they would be sure to finish the job properly.

Natalya bolted.

Like greyhounds chasing a bait at a racetrack, the two women charged after her.

Natalya raced down one of the cone-shaped, tree-lined avenues within the Tennis Center's grounds that led away from the Arthur Ashe Stadium. She had walked this route on many an occasion. Now she viewed everything from a different perspective. Everywhere was a potential escape route or hiding place. Or a potential obstacle.

Behind her, she heard them shouting something as she sprinted, pumping her legs to accelerate. She dared not look back. Fortunately, she was used to running.

Emerging from the other end of the avenue, she dashed into an area where there were a number of display booths, the owners of which were packing up for the night. Suddenly, one of the display attendants walked in front of her, blocking her path. Unable to stop, her momentum carried her forward as she collided straight into him, knocking him to the ground with considerable force, while she herself nearly toppled over.

"Hey what do you think you're doing?" he cried angrily, before seeing the familiar tennis star hurtling past. Almost about to forgive her for her offence, he was swiftly knocked back down to the ground by Natalya's pursuers.

Having regained her balance, Natalya pressed on frantically. Was that her heart pounding inside or was it her pursuers' footsteps on the ground as they gained on her? To confuse her further, she could hear the distant rhythm of drums outside the stadium in Corona Park beating away, as she raced towards the food court area. There were still a number of stragglers hanging around near the spread of tables and chairs, little suspecting that one of their much-vaunted tennis stars would suddenly come hurtling through their midst like a bullet.

The Russian leapt over a couple of chairs as the two women followed her, carving their own path. Natalya overturned a few tables as she passed them, much to the dismay of the customers who had not yet finished eating. This merely slowed the two women down but did not stop them, as they dodged around the obstacles. They were both extremely fit, as well as fiercely determined and relentless in pursuit of their quarry. They shoved startled visitors out of the way, creating a wave of mayhem as they knocked a few more to the ground.

Darting her head from side to side as she ran, Natalya examined her options. She could either try to fight them off or keep running. But if they caught up with her, she would probably have to fight them anyway. She was reluctant to draw any further publicity to herself, having endured her share of the media spotlight for one day.

Natalya looked around. From here, she could see the glare of the floodlights from the nearby Grandstand stadium. She knew the Tennis Center like the back of her hand. But where could she go? Her best bet was to lead her pursuers away to a place where she could more effectively deal with them. On her terms.

***

At the press room, the journalists were filing out as Tania was finishing off her interviews in Russian.

As soon as the last question had been answered, and before she had a chance to tear away, she heard a voice next to her. It was her publicity agent, Samuel Kurtzberg.

"Gah. I thought those poor schmucks would never finish," he moaned.

Tania turned to face him.

A dark-haired man in his late thirties, Kurtzberg's stress level always seemed to be set on a low boil, as if the pressure of being her agent was getting to him. But then, he was like that before they had even met.

"It's cool," she said evenly. "I don't mind the interviews."

"Hmm, well good for you," he said curtly. "By the way Tania, you're a difficult girl to keep up with."

"I'm sorry," she replied. "I haven't been avoiding you."

"Yeah, yeah. So you've told me." He gave a dismissive gesture of his hand. "We need to talk. Seriously."

"What, right now?" Her posture tightened. And here she thought that maybe he was simply coming to chat, not digging for more gold when the mine had already been excavated today. "I'm exhausted and just want to hit the sack. Can't this wait until morning?"

"Save the perennial excuses and listen. It won't take long."

Tania sighed in resignation. "Okay, you've got my attention. What's up?"

Kurtzberg wasted little time outlining his plans. He took pride in the fact that he had managed to secure the Russian tennis star a number of lucrative endorsements. "I've got you lined up for a big promotional campaign in Beijing where you'll be playing the week after next," he said. "You're effectively the public face of the China Open this year - huge billboards, merchandise, the works, all with your image."

"Hmm, I don't know about that," Tania replied, still not entirely at home with all the attention she was getting.

Kurtzberg did not like the uncertain tone of her voice. "Hey, I hope you're not planning on pulling out of Beijing like you've done with a number of your other tournaments this year. I had to work my ass off to make sure your image came off in tip-top condition among the tournament officials and sponsors."

Tania cut him short. "Don't worry, I haven't forgotten. I'll definitely be in Beijing to defend my title and the points I gained last year. Nothing's going to stop me. Besides, what could possibly go wrong between now and then?

***

Natalya headed into the Grandstand Stadium. This was far more intimate than the breathtaking four-tiered venue she had been playing on earlier. She was amazed that, at this late hour, it was still open. Shouldn't it have been closed to the public? No matter. It worked to her advantage, and that was all that counted.

She ran into the tennis court with her two pursuers following close behind, shadowing her relentlessly like ravenous wolves.

It was here, for the first time, that she turned and faced her pursuers. "Who are you?" she demanded, panting for air as she paused to catch her breath.

The red-head spoke, her voice seductive but deadly. "She's Snow White, and I'm Rose Red."

Natalya saw the woman calling herself Rose Red remove a cloth sling from over her shoulder and pull something out. In her hands, she was brandishing a pair of sticks around which was tied a long piece of string, and what looked like two metal bowls joined end-to-end on an axle, in the shape of an hourglass. Natalya gasped. She recognised it as a diabolo - a spool-like juggling prop that could be whirled and tossed high in the air like a giant yo-yo, using the sticks to perform a huge variety of spectacular tricks. The diabolos were often fashioned from materials such as rubber, wood or metal. The metal ones could be set on fire using a wick and some fuel. Whatever it was made of, if it connected with the diaboloist or another person, the prop could cause serious and permanent damage.

Natalya had only seen it used as a prop. Rose Red was using it as a weapon.

The Russian did not plan to stick around for a demonstration. She pushed her legs again as she began to run once more, this time heading towards the stands. Perhaps she could lose them up there.

Suddenly, the diabolo came flying through the air, spinning furiously as it hurtled towards her like a missile. Natalya narrowly dodged this lethal projectile as it crashed into one of the seats. Shaken, the Russian continued to run, hoping that, in the time it took the red-haired woman to retrieve her weapon, it would buy her a few precious minutes to get a head start.

Good idea in theory, but in her haste to avoid Rose Red's offence, she had forgotten about Snow White. The blonde assassin pulled out what looked like an elaborately-decorated, oriental-looking fan with razor-sharp blades and arrowheads on the tips. She tossed it like a Frisbee with one sudden flick of the wrist. It whizzed through the air before Natalya could react. The Russian attempted to duck out of the way again, but the bladed weapon sliced her arm and stuck in. Crying in pain as blood started gushing out, she gritted her teeth and attempted to yank the fan out of her arm. But the arrowheads were firmly embedded.

The red-head renewed her attack, as the diabolo rolled skilfully along the string between each twirling stick. With no other choice, Natalya broke off the end of the fan, with the blades still implanted in her arm. The pain was excruciating, but she would have to bear it. Clutching her arm, she thought for a moment. She needed to formulate a plan if she were to survive. Perhaps she could separate the two, and fight them off individually. She was no match for both of them together. But alone, perhaps she might stand a chance.

She lunged at Snow White, who was temporarily deprived of a weapon. She began to attack her. No holds barred. However, Snow White was an expert in both Brazilian Jiu-jitsu and Capoeira and easily held her own, quickly shifting from a defensive position to one of offence while dancing around her. The blonde let loose a barrage of high kicks which Natalya, with her loss of blood, was at pains to deflect. Snow White stunned her with a blow to the face, striking her squarely on her cheekbone below her eye. Then, while she was still momentarily distracted, the blonde kicked her from behind, knocking Natalya to the ground, face forward. Immediately, the assassin pinned her arm in an aikido-like hold, so that she was locked in position. She had to find a way to break free.

Suddenly, the Russian heard a whirring noise and looked up. What was she doing? *Oh no.* Rose Red had flung her diabolo over thirty feet into the air, right over the spot where Snow White had trapped Natalya. To make matters worse, the blonde assassin was holding her firmly in position for the death blow of that spinning weapon. She struggled, but it was too late. Rose Red's diabolo came crashing down on the back of Natalya's head with an almighty thud, before she even knew what had hit her.

The last thing she remembered was the taste of dull metal permeating through her skull and mixing in with the blood in her mouth as she slipped into complete darkness.

"She's dead." Snow White announced, examining the beautiful Russian's lifeless body and feeling her pulse. "Check her phone."

Rose Red reached down and flipped it open. She placed it into a special mobile phone reader which cradled it tightly and began emitting a light source. A message on the screen read: VERIFYING BIOMETRIC SCAN.

A few seconds later it read: IDENTITY CONFIRMED.

Rose Red tapped some other buttons on the reader. It began to scan for files. She was searching for one in particular.

"It's no longer here," she exclaimed.

Within minutes, Snow White placed a call to her superior and explained everything. "It looks like it's been transferred somehow. Shikolenko must've known we'd be after it."

"If you hadn't bungled your attempt to dispose of her earlier, you would not have alerted her," the voice on the other end of the phone scolded.

"There was a malfunction," Snow White explained.

"I don't wish to hear your excuses," the voice said. "You have already drawn enough attention for one day. Too many people will have seen you and could make the connection back to us. I cannot take that risk. There is too much at stake here. I will send someone else to deal with the situation."

"You're reassigning us?"

There was a long silence on the other end of the phone. When the caller finally spoke again, his voice was cold and matter-of-fact. "For the moment, yes. Now dispose of the body and then pull all the news footage tapes and interviews with any other player. Once you've acquired this information, report back immediately and hand it to your replacements who'll be waiting. I want to know who else had contact with her."

"But there could be hundreds of people. Journalists, other tennis players, sports staff."

"Then you'd better get started right now. This information is far too important to fall into the wrong hands. I don't care who it is. If Shikolenko has passed it on to someone else, that person needs to be eliminated. Immediately."

Chapter 4

Thursday morning.

Tatiana's interview footage often made fascinating viewing. Sooner or later, even the most casual tennis fan found that the often-tedious press conferences roared to life at the winsome charm of the Russian ingénue. Once the tone had been set, the delightful banter was thoroughly engaging and entertaining to watch. This morning, however, the recording was being observed closely by two men whose sole purpose was for reasons far more sinister. They pricked up their ears as the relevant portion replayed over a large screen.

"... if you must know, Natalya did actually talk to me after the match today in the girls' locker room."

"What did she say?"

"Oh, not much. Just the usual few words between players. I'm sure she's fine. She's probably relaxing somewhere right now"

"There," the first man named Fahad pointed out, pausing the playback. "Shikolenko did make contact with someone else. Tania Likamolova."

The second man named Kluge looked uncertain, and sought to challenge that assumption. "There's no way of knowing for sure whether the exchange was anything significant," he said, speaking with a distinct German accent.

"Then we need to observe her, monitor her conversations."

"And if she's heavily surrounded by bodyguards, then what? It won't be easy to plant a bug."

"We don't need a bug," Fahad assured his colleague. "We can use her own cell phone to act as a microphone and transmitter to listen in on anything she says."

Kluge was sceptical. "How is that possible?"

"Simple," he explained. "We'll be using the same sort of scanning technology that phone hackers use. We have it right here. By transmitting a maintenance command to her cell phone via the control channel, it will put it into diagnostic mode, allowing her phone to pick up all nearby sounds which can be monitored over the voice channel until she actually places a call."

"Where is she right now?"

"Probably off practising somewhere. But we can listen in on her at this very moment as soon as she has her phone within earshot. Seeing as she is just a girl, that shouldn't be too long at all. They're always on the phone. If she spoke to Natalya Shikolenko, we'll know for sure soon enough."

***

Tania's workout routine, although hardly unvaried, was mostly hard work. It involved, among other things, a range of yoga stretching exercises, jumping the heavy rope, and kickboxing using a punch bag, and weight-training with Russian kettle bells before she even walked on court. Then she began a curious mixture of eye-hand coordination drills with the tennis balls followed by drill after drill of serving, eliminating any niggling problems, and brushing up on her techniques, particularly volleying. She spent too much time on the baseline and really needed to come forward more in a match. She would have to work on that too. Yes, her routine was indeed mostly hard work.

This morning would have been no different, except that a most unusual element had been added to today's session. Set up on one end of the court was a portable dunk tank, of all things, similar to those seen in carnivals and fundraisers. It was sure to attract a number of bystanders - if they could find their way to the private, almost inaccessible court where the young Russian chose to practise.

"This is crazy," Tania exclaimed, staring wide-eyed at the tank. "Who would ever think to do this?"

"It's called target practice," her coach, Igor informed her. "One day everything might depend on you serving completely accurately."

"I can't believe they actually allowed you to set this thing up here," she said, shaking her head in amazement.

"I pulled a few strings here and there. It's entirely for your benefit."

"I hope so," said an extremely pretty, continental-looking girl dressed in a white halter-neck top sitting inside the tank, grinning broadly at the blonde. She spoke with a sensuous French accent that lilted musically. "Only a really good friend like me would willingly volunteer to do this for you. Just be glad I have the time to do this, now I'm already out of the singles tournament."

Tania gave a ghost of a smile, sighing in frustration. For some reason today, her aim seemed strangely off. Dressed in high-cut shorts and a tight-fitting, baby-pink T-shirt, cut off at the navel, she had been serving one erroneous shot after another across the court. The balls skewed either into the net, or inches wide of the baseline, as though they were specially weighted in such a way as to thwart her every attempt at precision. What was wrong with her?

It was after almost an hour of racquet-induced teeth-pulling that Igor finally brought out his ace-in-the-hole. With its large, emergency-stop-style target, the dunk tank would not only provide Tania with some practice at accuracy in order to hit the bull's-eye, but also some fun and added incentive, by getting her best friend and some-time doubles partner, Isabelle Dumond, entirely wet.

Of course, that was all in theory. Both Isabelle's clothes and long, chestnut-coloured hair were still completely dry.

"Don't hit so hard," Igor hollered across the court. "It's not just about power." Most of the time it was a joy to oversee his student's progress, but there were days when she seemed positively erratic, particularly in recent months. Was the strain of being a celebrity starting to get to her?

Igor Rokovsky was a medium-built man in his late forties with thinning grey hair and a beard, he had known her since she was a little girl. Over the years, he had watched her develop into a striking, graceful and self-possessed young woman before his eyes. And a champion at that – one who was usually deferential to his wise counsel and words of advice.

However, these words seemed to fall on deaf ears today, as Tania continued serving in the same hapless manner. The more she served, the greater the chance it would go astray. These types of shots she could normally execute, but on this occasion every ball went either too deep or fell short, often bouncing off the protective chain-link enclosure a few feet from the top of the tub, or onto the heavy-duty plastic curtain hanging behind the target. She breathed a heavy sigh and threw her arms up in semi-defeat.

"Having trouble with your game?" Isabelle teased her from behind the cage as she splashed the water with her bare feet. "You didn't have any trouble at all yesterday when you knocked Natalya's racquet out of her hand."

"Yeah. I'm afraid I'm not very accurate today," Tania said ruefully, as she walked towards her, swinging her racquet. "I'm having a problem serving."

"I can see that," Isabelle remarked as her laughter danced through the air. "The trick is not to hit it too hard or too softly. You need to focus."

"Thank you, Miss Dumond," Igor grumbled mirthlessly. "As usual, you make pointing out the obvious a skill unto itself. Unfortunately, what you say is more or less correct. She's been far too distracted lately."

Isabelle rolled her large, smouldering green eyes skyward. "Well what else do you expect with young love?" she said, climbing out of the tank, while flashing a broad, mischievous smile. "I'm tempted to say I'm jealous."

"What do you mean?" Tania inquired.

"Well not of Piotr," she clarified, as she towelled off her feet. "He's not really my type. And I didn't think he was yours either. But all those sleepless nights..."

Without blinking, Tania gave her an innocent look, moving her shoulders about coyly, in a circular motion as her face went a damask shade. "What 'sleepless nights' are you talking about?"

Isabelle wouldn't let it go that easily. "You know? You two having plenty of fun. It can be quite distracting."

Caught off guard, she gave a sheepish reply. "We haven't slept together yet Isabelle, if that's what you're suggesting." She began to wave her hand in a fanning motion in front of her face, the pink still vividly colouring her cheeks.

"After all this time?" the French flirt exclaimed, finding that somewhat hard to believe. Determined to keep the thermostat on full, she continued. "Come on, Tania. Don't try to avoid the question. You can tell me. We confide everything in each other."

Tania giggled nervously, her cheeks now burning with a colour almost as deep as her T-shirt. She shrugged her shoulders apologetically, as if shy to admit it. "I'm saving myself. I'm not entirely sure if he's the one."

"Don't worry my dear," Isabelle assured her, giving a wry smile as she relented with her teasing. "With looks like yours, someday your prince will come."

"Well you know what they say about needing to kiss a few frogs before finding your prince?" Tania said, giving her friend a knowing wink.

"Hey, I'll gladly help you out in any way I can."

"Your 'Prince' is right here," Igor growled, pointing to his protégée's *Prince Sports* tennis racquet, as he turned to look her in the eye. "And that's what you should be concentrating on. Your forehand really needs work too. We need to change that odd lasso motion of yours you've got going there. It's going to be your Achilles' heel one day. Everyone thinks so."

"Works for me," Tania replied. "And my dad doesn't have a problem with it."

"Well, maybe so, but your father asked me to keep a watch over you and ensure you practise diligently."

"Where is your dad anyway," Isabelle inquired.

"He's flown home with my mom to visit my grandmother," Tania replied.

Home? The town of *Nikolayevsk-on-Amur* in the Russian Far East had long since ceased to be that since she moved to the States as a child. Located near the Amur River and Sakhalin Island off the East Coast of Siberia, for Tania, it was too out of sync with her modern, hectic lifestyle and too out of step with her values. Home to *Nikolayevsk*? What was she talking about? Her home was here in the US, or wherever she could hit a tennis ball.

"Don't forget you have your *other* training later on today," Igor interrupted her.

"Other training?" Isabelle arched her perfectly plucked eyebrows. "Don't tell me. That funky Russian martial arts thing you do, supposedly to assist your overall routine? Between that and the dunk tank today, your coach really has you doing some strange things."

Tania giggled amusedly. "I'm afraid so. I frequently wonder about that myself."

"There is nothing 'funky' about Systema, as you put it," Igor hastened to clarify. "While it's most similar to the eclectic style of Jeet Kune Do, if you wanted to compare it to anything, it is simply of practical benefit to her to give Tania that overall fitness she requires. Its philosophy is just the sort of thing that helps her to acquire that tough and positive mental state that people refer to as her 'match toughness', and to enable her to relax in stressful situations - playing the big points in a tournament, for example. Then of course, there are all the other physical benefits from that particular discipline such as helping her to move more freely and gain athletic ability, especially for a girl of her height."

"Yeah?" Isabelle looked rather sceptical. "So how come I don't know of many other tennis players doing that particular kind of martial arts training?"

"'Different strokes for different folks' I guess," Tania surmised.

"Except that it's your groundstrokes that the rest of us folks have to contend with," she said endearingly.

Tania smiled sweetly. That much was true, or so the other players frequently reported. "Igor actually recommended I also take it up for breath control reasons when playing a match," she elaborated.

"Because you normally run round with an oxygen tank on your back, no doubt?" Isabelle offered, her voice having a hint of playful sarcasm.

"No, it's uh… you know… because people say I make too much noise on court." Tania blushed again. She didn't want to admit it might be true. The truth was, however, that when she was on court, she barely paid any attention to those so-called shrill sounds.

"Hmm. Whoever said that 'silence is golden' obviously hadn't met you. Personally I wouldn't change a thing. Who cares what others think? If critics want to up the noise level they make about your screams, I say up yours."

Tania giggled modestly. "Well thank you for the vote of confidence."

"You're welcome my dear," came the reply, as Isabelle puckered her sultry lips to blow a light kiss in Tania's direction. Still curious, she inquired further about this strange training method her friend frequently employed. "So have you ever used it on anyone to kick some ass?"

"Systema? Goodness, no," Tania exclaimed. "It's meant only as a form of training. And you know me, I hate violence. I only even use the kickboxing for sports. I doubt I'd even ever get to use it in a real combat situation."

"Well," Isabelle added. "If it helps you with your game, then go for it."

Tania smiled gratefully. "Maybe you should try it."

Isabelle winced, shaking her head. "No thanks. It's not my cup of tea."

"Oh well. If you ever do…"

"Speaking of do's," Isabelle said, deftly changing the subject, "I almost forgot. I came here to remind you of my birthday party next week, on Tuesday, before I got suckered into taking a dip in the dunk tank."

"Thanks," Tania replied, grinning. "I'm really looking forward to it. I'm sorry I missed it last year."

"Well that's okay," Isabelle assured her. "I've told you before that I understand. You had all that publicity surrounding you after your win, and it was a big opportunity for you. Just be there this time though - it's a big one."

"I'll definitely be there," Tania said emphatically. "No doubt about it."

Tania walked over to her sports bag at the other end of the court and removed her cell phone. With the touch of a few buttons, she entered a reminder as one of the alerts in the organiser section.

"Well, it's time to get back to your practice," her coach said. "You've spent more than enough time already in frivolous conversation."

"You know," Tania began, still holding her phone, as she walked back towards him. The tentativeness in her voice suggested she had other ideas which were contrary to his. "I'm feeling kinda tight, like my muscles are rather tense right now. They've been feeling that way all morning. Maybe that's why my aim is so off today."

"Maybe you're tired after the match yesterday," Isabelle suggested. "You should go for a massage. Pamper yourself."

"Ugh. In the players' locker room?" Tania cringed at the thought, if that was indeed what her friend was advocating. "Do you know that I was in there yesterday and the place was a total mess?"

"And you thought the men's locker room was bad."

Tania laughed spiritedly. "You know, Natalya Shikolenko said the same thing. What, has everyone been in there except for me?"

Isabelle shrugged her shoulders evasively. "I dunno. I thought it was a well known fact. So you spoke to Natalya after the match?"

"Yes. Well, briefly. She was there when I was getting changed and just wished me luck in the next round. Oh, and she borrowed my phone too."

"Well that's odd, coming from the ice queen," Isabelle concluded. "But I wasn't suggesting you go to the locker room. There's this great spa I know in downtown Manhattan called *Completely Bare* on Fifth Avenue. It's one of the trendiest places in town, and apparently a fan favourite with celebrities and models. I usually use them for bikini waxes but they offer massages too. It's just your sort of thing."

Igor was, again, less than enthusiastic, indicating his contempt at such an idea. "I really don't think that she should be going there, Miss Dumond. She needs to practise. She hasn't been playing anywhere near her best."

"Igor Rokovsky," Isabelle chided him playfully. "You've got to lighten up a bit. Don't be such a party pooper."

"She's right," Tania said to her coach. "I mean, about the massage. Besides, it will be great for relaxing."

Igor shook his head wearily. "I can see you're not going to listen to me. Well at least take some bodyguards with you."

Tania waved her hand dismissively, shirking his advice. "Pooh, what can happen?"

As Tatiana and Isabelle walked away, the last fragments of their conversation were replayed over monitoring equipment inside in a silver-grey SUV, by the same two men who had been watching the Russian's interview footage from earlier that morning.

"Did you hear that?" Fahad said, speaking to a disembodied voice on the phone who was quite obviously his superior. "We know now that, not only did she make contact with Natalya Shikolenko, but she allowed her to borrow her phone."

The voice on the other end answered coldly. "We have to assume that Shikolenko may have either given it to her or transferred it to her phone without her knowledge."

"So now what do you want us to do?"

"Deal with her accordingly," the voice instructed. "Retrieve the information by whatever means necessary, but do it without attracting any attention. Contact me when you're done." The phone call ended abruptly.

Kluge turned to his colleague. "Do you think she might have the file?"

"We need to follow her and find out," Fahad replied. "She's heading to the *Completely Bare* spa on Fifth Avenue."

"Well, our boss said to deal with it accordingly, and we don't want to let him down. Let's make sure she gets a massage she'll never forget."

Chapter 5

Thursday afternoon.

The *Completely Bare* spa on the fourth floor of the Pierrepont Building on Fifth Avenue was not somewhere Tania had visited before. If she usually required some form of physiotherapy before or after a match, there was an abundance of massage therapists on site at the National Tennis Center. However, the women's locker room was not exactly a state-of-the-art beauty salon. By contrast, the prospect of being completely pampered with a peppermint foot rub and a full-body massage at *Completely Bare* proved simply too irresistible for the Russian tennis star.

The spa was known more for its extensive permanent hair removal treatment using photo-epilation, but from time to time whenever they had a massage therapist available, other services such as massages could be offered.

The inside of the spa was a 2,500 square-foot estate consisting of French antique-style furnishings based around a cream and gold palette scheme. The spa receptionist directed Tania from the parlour-like reception to one of the treatment rooms.

"Someone will be with you shortly," the attractive, short-haired, brunette employee said, as she left the tennis star to get undressed. "The rooms are pretty well insulated so no-one will disturb you."

Tania made a quick survey of her surroundings. The room was elegantly decorated with pastel-shaded curtains and white leather armchairs, while the diffused lighting created a gentle, soothing atmosphere. On one wall was a large mirror, while stacked away to the side on shelves were various massage accessories and oils. Slightly above her, plasma screen monitors were broadcasting the latest news.

Tania lay face forward on the bed, clad only in a white towel, waiting for the massage therapist to arrive. To pass the time, she decided to check her cell phone for text messages. There were at least five to which she had been too busy to respond. And so she began, keying away industriously on her phone, sending even the briefest of messages to ensure she kept in touch with her friends.

Once she had finished replying to a backlog of texts, she pulled out a pair of earphones, plugged them into a socket at the bottom of the phone, and slipped them carefully into her ears. She scrolled down the screen on her phone to access the MP3 player. There was a large collection of music on the drive to listen to whenever she was on the move.

Or at least, there was normally.

Tania was mystified. There were only twenty songs remaining. Hardly the vast store she remembered. She began to double-check, scrolling down to see if she had misread it. *No. Only twenty. No mistake.*

She frowned. Where were they? Had she somehow misplaced them, moved them around? She couldn't remember doing that.

She began to search on other sections of her phone.

Pictures? No. Besides, what would it be doing in there?

Ring tones?

After a few minutes, she saw something that caused her to blink as if she had been dazzled by a camera flash. Memory full.

That's so weird. How can that be?

Eventually she located a file on her hard drive that she did not recognise. It was several hundred megabytes in size.

Tania clicked on it, attempting to gain access.

A message came up on the screen: ACCESS DENIED. PLEASE ENTER CORRECT CODE.

She scratched her head and blinked again. *I've never seen that sort of message before. That's not supposed to happen.*

She tried it again. No luck. She received the same message.

Very odd. She shrugged her shoulders. Something was definitely wrong. But at the moment, it was too much of a bother to figure out what. She would simply have to make do with the songs she had, even if they were fewer than she had hoped for. With one slender finger, she selected her play list and the music began.

***

The female receptionist outside was sitting at her desk thumbing quietly through the pages of *Elle*, the front cover of which was graced by a glamorous image of the Russian tennis star. She looked up briefly as she saw the massage therapist disappearing into one of the rooms to prepare himself for the session.

The receptionist smiled faintly as she thought about the celebrity customer that awaited him. *He's sure to get a pleasant surprise. It's not every day we're graced by such distinguished company.*

She buried her head in her magazine again like a book worm, until a small noise over to the right caught her attention. She took a cursory peek, but it was nothing. False alarm. Only the cleaner.

She shook her head, then seeing that she needed to put out a fresh batch of bathrobes for the customers, went off to the stock room to fetch a trolley, failing to notice that this so-called cleaner crept stealthily into the very same room where the massage therapist had entered minutes before.

The cleaner, upon entering the preparation room, saw that the masseur had his back turned, and was busy rinsing his hands in a wash basin. He did not notice anything until it was too late. Before he could even make a sound, the cleaner placed a hand over the masseur's mouth to muffle any noise, while simultaneously using his other arm to choke him to death.

The masseur's body went limp, and crumpled to the floor in a heap.

Stashing the body to one side, the cleaner got dressed into a massage therapist's uniform, then placed a phone call.

"Kluge here," he said. "I'm ready."

***

Jonah Bull had been tracking Tania since earlier that morning. He was determined to establish contact with her, bring her into the loop and be done with this assignment as quickly as possible.

He had noticed that, shortly after she climbed into a black Mercedes that escorted her from the Tennis Center to Manhattan, a dark silver-grey Ford Escapade SUV appeared to be following her. It could be nothing, but it was probably best to look into it. From her file, Bull had read that she was known for using bodyguards from time to time, but would sometimes dispense with them altogether when she wanted to roam freely. Bull gave this some thought. If they were on duty today, wouldn't they travel in the same car? Of course, there was always the possibility they had decided to follow behind separately.

Well, anything was possible. But better to be safe than sorry.

He frowned as he considered the kind of lifestyle she must lead. It must be rather constricting at times. Everyone always around you, crowding you in. No room to breathe.

Bull had pulled up in his Chrysler Crossfire across the street from the Pierrepont Building, several cars away from the SUV. He had watched Tania clamber out of the Mercedes and stroll briskly towards a greyish-light-brown stone office-block building. No bodyguards around. At least none he had seen. She had stood outside the entrance alone, buzzed the intercom and waited. Within a few seconds, the wooden doors had opened and she had disappeared inside.

Bull sat where he was. He had chosen not to follow her earlier. She might not appreciate him showing up there, and besides, what excuse would he have for explaining his presence? That he wanted to book an appointment?

While he was waiting, Bull tried not to imagine what might happen in there while she was receiving her massage treatment. Best not to go down that route, even though entertaining such thoughts might be perfectly natural.

He looked around as he sat in his car. In order to pass the time, he began to observe the various activities taking place around him. A small group of tourists were loitering nearby, having emerged from the *Barnes & Noble* bookshop, while a vagrant was closely inspecting his shopping cart in the background. Across the street, at the *Gap Kids* store, a couple of fashionably-dressed women fully laden with their shopping trophies were pushing strollers. He gazed over his shoulder. Looming in the distance was the limestone façade of the Empire State Building towering over the city. As boredom began to set in, he recalled those accelerated time-lapse photography animations he had seen on many an occasion. Wouldn't it be nice if he could experience that for himself right now? It would surely enable him to fast forward to a more interesting point than sit here waiting for things to unfold at a snail's pace. So far, everything was quiet. Maybe Tania Likamolova wasn't in any danger.

***

Back in the therapy room, Tania lay on the bed, overcome by a distinct feeling of lethargy, as the music continued to play through her headphones. Rather than simply lie there idly, she took out a steel nail file which she had brought along with her, and began to buff her finger nails, kept short for the practicalities of competitive tennis.

After a few minutes, she registered the presence of someone entering the room. She barely allowed her eyes to glance upwards for very long. It was only the 'masseur'.

"Hi," she mumbled languidly. "Be gentle with me, okay?"

"Don't worry," came the reply. "This will be quick and painless."

With the music drowning out his voice, Tania couldn't hear him, so she assumed he understood her request.

The assassin known as Kluge, dressed as the masseur, rubbed the palms of his hands with peppermint oil, and walked over to where Tania was lying. He stood over her for a few seconds, eyes lingering lasciviously on those extraordinarily long limbs, the exquisite contours of her statuesque body and the tantalising sea of silky-smooth, golden skin. He decided he might as well take the opportunity to enjoy himself before killing her. He pulled her towel gently downwards from her back so that only her lower half was covered, and began to work the muscle on either side of her spine with his thumbs and the heels of his hands.

Without turning, she motioned to him. "Could you start with my feet first? They're killing me."

The pseudo-masseur obliged. Naturally. "I'm sure that won't be the only thing." He moved down to the bottom of the bed and cradled her right foot in his hand. It was atypically soft and delicate for a tennis player, as if she had made a conscious effort to keep them in immaculate condition. Her toenails were painted with a splash of gold that perfectly complemented her auric-blonde hair.

Oiling her feet one by one, Kluge began to massage them with surprising skill, first rotating her ankles and pulling out each toe individually, then stroking his thumbs across her soles, from the base of her toes up to her ankles.

Tania flinched, biting her lip to stifle a giggle, as she was extremely ticklish. However, she let out a gentle, sensuous sigh as she began to relax. She continued to buff her fingernails, oblivious to any impending danger, as the music played on through her headphones while the masseur pressed his knuckles into the ball of each foot.

After a few minutes, the heavily-built German massaged her thighs, before moving over to her back again as he began to work the area adeptly like a baker kneading dough. Tania was in good hands, simply enjoying the sensation of being pampered. What more could she ask for?

Cupping her head in one hand, he began to stroke the back of her neck with the other, easing the tension out of her muscles gently. Tania moaned again contentedly, for what would be the last time in this session.

Suddenly, massive hands clamped around her, tightly and firmly like a monkey wrench. Her supply of air was instantly cut off.

She gasped. "Hey... what... what are you doing?"

The ruthless German squeezed harder, wringing her neck like a wet towel for every precious last drop of life.

Eyes watering. Her breath rapidly choked out of her. Tania's airway was constricted, as if a knot had been tied around her throat and pulled tight. Her pulse was racing off the chart. Her face, now as red as a beetroot, began streaming with perspiration. Arms were flailing frantically. Everywhere! Yanking away the earphones. Trying to grab his hands. Anything that she could find. Her feet were kicking wildly as she struggled. Every part of her body was thrashing about as the horror of the situation set in. The golden-haired beauty was traversing the spectrum of the rainbow, from blood red to sickening yellow to death black.

A blanket of darkness began to wash over her, wafting like a heavy fog. Tania was slipping away into oblivion. The room was spinning around her, her eyes losing focus. She had to do something. Quickly. In her frenzied state, she managed to reach towards the pillow and made a grab for the nail file lying in front of her which she had dropped in her panic. With one last ounce of strength, she plunged the pointed edge of the metal manicure tool into her attacker like an ice pick, hoping, no, praying that it would be enough.

Kluge howled in pain, flinching away instinctively as the sharp instrument caused a deep gash in his forearm. It was sufficient time for Tania to break free of his deadly hold. Wrestling herself out from under him, she rolled off the bed and onto the floor. Like a discarded rag doll, she crumpled into a heap at the foot of the massage bed, almost sobbing as the immediate threat abated. Still choking and gasping for air, her pulse rate began to return to normal.

Realising her immodesty, Tania grabbed the towel still strung across the bed. She wrapped it around her body and tied a knot in front. Hardly the ideal thing with which to cover herself, but in the heat of the moment, it was all that was available.

Her attacker was still clutching his arm, trying to stop the bleeding. He swore under his breath.

"Who are you?" she spluttered, still coughing as she tried to crawl away.

The man did not answer. Instead, he rose defiantly, ready to renew his attack.

Tania struggled to her feet. As she stood upright, it was then, for the first time, she became aware of his size. While she was by no means a small girl at six feet tall in her bare feet, the razor-short-haired, hulking man in front of her stood a good six or seven inches taller and was built like a bulldozer. The blonde Russian beauty's supple, sylph-like frame looked positively skinny by comparison.

"Why are you trying to kill me?" she demanded.

Again, her muscular nemesis did not answer.

Was his assault sexually motivated? Clad in nothing but a towel, she allowed her eyes to glance downward for a second to ensure she was properly covered up. *No need to provide an unnecessary peep show.*

However, in that split second of distraction, her attacker lunged towards the massage bed where her phone still lay. Believing he was about to bore into her, Tania slammed the bed into him in her panic. Still moving, his momentum carried him forward, straight into it with an almighty crash. The bed toppled to the ground under his weight, while her phone went sliding across the floor.

It was then that it occurred to her that the masseur might in fact be after that object, and not her.

What was so special about it?

As Tania dropped to her feet to retrieve it, she felt his huge hands grabbing her ankle. She gasped, startled. The man was anchoring her in, dragging her across the floor towards him as if he were mooring a boat, while she watched helplessly as the phone slipped from her grasp.

Another feeling of dread shot through her as her towel began to loosen, little by little.

"*Góspadi!*" she gasped in Russian. "Oh God!"

She clasped a hand around the knot to ensure it stayed in place. But that was the least of her concerns. Like an animal hunted for game, it was as if her foot were caught in a rabbit trap, and the more she struggled, the more it tightened around her.

In a fit of panic, Tania swung her free leg in the air in a circular scissor motion towards her captor's head. The sole of her foot struck him squarely in the face, sending him reeling backwards. Stunned, he released his grip, allowing the Russian to slip her slender leg away.

Tania knotted her towel again as she stood up, making sure not to turn her back on him. For the moment, she had managed to keep the brute at bay.

Suddenly, in a flash, Kluge rose to his feet again and charged directly towards her. Tania had to respond immediately. Her Systema training, which she had used for all-round tennis fitness, was about to come in handy right now. Perhaps even save her life. There was no particular stance or routine she had learnt. It was all about improvisation. Whatever worked in the heat of the moment. On top of that, maybe, just maybe her kickboxing might work too. If she could hold her nerves together.

As her assailant bore in, she pivoted on her left foot, swinging her right leg in a roundhouse kick which caught him hard in his ribs. He buckled slightly as she punched outward towards his face. Her arm was loose and relaxed while it moved towards its target, but her muscles tensed at the last possible moment upon approaching the point of contact. The effect was like a sudden, elliptical whipping motion. Her fist cracked against his face. Then a second quick jab to his jaw.

Kluge's head snapped backwards, staggering him. But he had a broad, rounded head that seemed built to withstand impact, and so he quickly shook it off. Tania swung her leg up for another kick, but he blocked her, grabbed her foot and spun her off balance. As she sought to recover, he seized her by the throat, using the element of surprise to throw her backwards through the air.

Tania landed hard against the shelves, knocking some of the accessories onto the floor, and the wind out of her.

***

In the stockroom, the receptionist had just finished placing a number of folded bathrobes onto the trolley and was about to wheel it back into the reception area when she heard a huge crash that shook the walls violently. She looked up, startled. "What the hell was that?"

***

Tania grimaced in pain, somewhat bruised. She was still in one piece. Inwardly, she chided herself. Systema advised against using high kicks common in kickboxing, as that could leave her vulnerable to the sort of counterattack she just experienced.

She lay on the floor, slightly dazed. The German jammed a kick towards her head. Seeing it heading towards her, she gasped. It spurred her back into action. Instead of rolling out of the way, she parried his leg with her forearm while simultaneously raising her elbow to lead his leg over her head towards her other arm. Then, she pushed his foot up with one hand while pushing down on his knee in the opposite direction with the other. One swift motion. It sent him off balance and reeling in pain.

Tania scrambled hastily to her feet. But her opponent had recovered too. Before she had time to launch another offence, he swept towards her, lifting her off her feet. She found herself wrapped in a vice-like grip. His brutal hands were clasped firmly around her slender waist in a bear hug, threatening to snap her in half like a brittle twig. Tania struggled to break free, kicking her feet about helplessly. As he swung her around effortlessly, her body arched, her arms flailing everywhere. It was no use. He was as strong as a rhino and just as relentless.

Tania slammed the palms of her hands into the thick mass of her assailant's neck, padded with muscle, shoving his head backwards. This merely had the effect of angering him as he applied an equal resisting force with his head in the opposite direction. It became a battle of wills to see which was strongest: the German's head or the Russian's hands. Both pushed against each other, straining for dominance.

In desperation, Tania head-butted the man, hoping to stun him into releasing her. The top of her forehead connected with his, sending a minor shock through her brain. However, this merely proved to be a minor irritation like a mosquito sting. Kluge flinched, but did not yield, and Tania remained firmly in his clutches.

Damn. That was a stupid move. That would probably give her more of a concussion than it would him. The sharp pain knifed through her skull like hot metal, as her eyes began to water involuntarily. She had no intention of using her head as a battering ram again.

He was overwhelming her. No way could she match his animal strength. She would have to defeat him using some other method. At the corner of her eye, Tania spotted a glass jug of massage oil sitting on a table. Her own strength was fading. The masseur's grip was tightening around her. The jug was her only chance. She stretched out her arm to reach it while Kluge focused on crushing the Russian nymph's delicate body.

Tania's fingers brushed the edge of the massage jug. She squirmed, panting heavily for breath. The jug seemed to move from being almost virtually within her grasp to being torn hopelessly away. Meanwhile, the knot on her towel had loosened itself fully. The whole thing was about to come open. It was held in place purely by the fact that she was being held so tightly in his constrictor-like arms.

One last burst of energy. Tania made a supreme effort to seize the jug. Her fingers miraculously found the handle. It was now or never. In one swift motion, she swung the glass jug with all her might. The jug collided hard with the big man's head, shattering in his face. Shards of broken glass and splashes of oil flew everywhere.

The muscle-bound German roared in pain, releasing his grip on her as she fell to the floor. While her attacker tended to his wounds, she used this temporary distraction to fix her towel, retrieve her phone from the floor and make a dash for the door. No time to think about her clothes, or to see whether her attacker was unconscious either. Her only concern was getting the heck out of there.

As she raced outside, she passed the receptionist who was returning from the stock room with the trolley full of folded bathrobes. The receptionist stepped out of the way, startled by the tennis star's sudden appearance. "What's going on?" she inquired. "What was that crash?"

"Your masseur was too rough," Tania answered quickly, sidestepping the truth about the fracas.

Her towel was unravelling itself again. There was no way she was going to run around like this. Certainly not once she hit the streets. Besides, if the paparazzi were around, they would have a field day photographing her in this barely-there attire.

And wouldn't they like that?

Spotting the trolley, she grabbed the first bathrobe on top and slipped it over her body as she let the towel drop to the floor simultaneously. It wasn't a perfect fit. A little on the short side, leaving her slightly self-conscious with her legs almost fully exposed. But it was better than what she was wearing before.

Back in the treatment room, Kluge had picked himself up from the floor.

The receptionist emerged at the doorway, her mouth agape. "What the hell happened?" she demanded, seeing the destruction everywhere.

But Kluge did not answer. Instead, he shoved her rudely from his path, whilst pulling out a cell phone from his pocket. "Likamolova is getting away. Meet me out front and stop her when she gets outside."

Tania heard the pounding of footsteps behind her as she hurtled out of the reception towards the stairwell, her bare feet slapping on the floor as she fled the scene.

Chapter 6

Bull sat in his Chrysler Crossfire, watching the traffic on Fifth Avenue creep by with an incessant mechanisation.

The group of tourists and the vagrant he had seen earlier were still hanging around outside at the foot of the Pierrepont Building. Meanwhile, a casually-dressed man in his twenties had left his yellow BMW C1 200 Scooter temporarily unattended as he had popped into the *Fossil Watch* store a few minutes earlier to buy a gift. Those C1 Scooters always looked rather bizarre - a strange cross between a two-wheeled car and a motorcycle with a roof over the top. Bull saw the man emerge again carrying a couple of coloured bags. He appeared to be checking his receipts, and was therefore not concentrating on his vehicle.

Suddenly, the striking blonde burst out of the wooden entrance of the *Completely Bare* spa, and onto the street outside, past the tourists and crashing straight into the *Fossil Watch* customer.

"Hey, watch it," the man yelled. But when he looked up, he saw who it was. He stood there, stunned. "Hey you're that tennis player…" he exclaimed, loudly enough for the tourists to hear.

The tourists looked up, seeing the blonde dressed only in her bathrobe. "Hey it's Tania Likamolova," they screamed, whipping out their digital cameras immediately in the hope of catching a shot of the scantily-clad Russian tennis ace.

Tania's heart rose up into her throat as she burned a bright shade of red.

Oh great, that's the last thing I need.

Ignoring them, her eyes darted around for some kind of vehicle in which she could make her escape. She caught sight of the man's C1 scooter.

At that very moment, the SUV that had been following her that morning pulled out from the other side of the road with a screech. There were probably more people after her.

No time to think. The BMW C1 was her best bet. After all, how different could it be from other mopeds she'd ridden before?

"I need to borrow your scooter," she shouted.

"What?" The man looked at her for a split second, amazed by her request.

"I'm late for a tennis match," she said urgently. It was the first thing that popped into her head.

Staring at her in disbelief, he appeared unsure whether he should oblige.

Meanwhile, Kluge had reached the street level. He emerged from the wooden entrance. *Bang!* Straight into the star-struck tourists. With his way barred, he shoved them to the side ruthlessly to cries of angry protests, only to collide straight into the vagrant who had pushed his shopping cart into the German's path. Kluge slammed into it and flew straight over onto the ground, knocking the contents of the cart everywhere.

The vagrant began kicking up a storm, shaking an angry fist at the German and ranting loudly.

Tania caught sight of Kluge and gasped with alarm. "Please," she said, pressing the *Fossil Watch* customer in desperation. "I need your bike."

"Who are you running from?" he inquired, seeing the huge, imposing meat-head struggling to pick himself off the ground while the vagrant was threatening to start a fight with him.

"Paparazzi," Tania lied. "No time to explain."

"Here, take it," he replied, handing her the keys.

The Russian blonde climbed onto the bike, swung her leg over and sat down. She began fumbling around at the controls in the cockpit. She had ridden a scooter on several occasions before, but never one of these machines. She tried to start the bike, but to her consternation, it wouldn't budge.

"What's wrong with this?" she wailed, as she saw Kluge finally getting up.

The owner pointed to a small message which was appearing on a screen on the dashboard prompting her to fasten her seatbelt before it could move. As if she needed to know about safety procedures right now.

Tania sighed in frustration as she stretched the seatbelt rapidly across her chest and lap. There. All buckled up. Then, reaching for the controls once more, she revved the engine, opening up the throttle. The engine roared to life with a deep sound as the C1 exploded out of there just as the German was about to catch up with her.

She screeched to a rapid halt several feet ahead. What the heck? She nearly collided with the SUV, flinging her forward ever so slightly before she regained her balance. She gasped. She was so inadequately protected that if she were to crash unexpectedly, she could be seriously hurt. No helmet. No leathers. Only a blasted bathrobe.

Bull's Crossfire braked next to her. He had observed everything. Now he needed to get over there as quickly as possible and come to the tennis star's rescue.

The Russian was cornered between the two cars. Where did they come from? Seeing her difficulty, Bull backed up to allow her space to move. He had planned to offer her a ride, but she appeared to have already arranged transportation of her own.

She navigated the scooter quickly around the two vehicles and was off again like a shot. *Thank God.*

Kluge climbed into the moving SUV, driven by his partner Fahad, as it reversed. The tyres squealed, and the vehicle burst out of there, leaving a trail of exhaust and the smell of burning rubber. Bull followed closely behind, flooring the pedal as he tried to stay close to the action.

Tania raced along Fifth Avenue, her heart pounding like a pneumatic drill. The C1 was more awkward to handle than a conventional scooter. What possessed her to pick this? The size and weight of it was much heavier than she was accustomed to, while the design of the seat meant that she was forced to sit more upright than normal. As a result, Tania had some difficulty maintaining her balance. If that wasn't enough, she wasn't used to being completely encapsulated by a bubble windshield roof while riding a bike. But it wasn't like she had much of a choice. This wasn't some leisurely ride through the city. There were assassins on her tail who were trying to kill her, and if she wanted to survive, she would have to adapt quickly.

Tania glanced into the mirror. She could see the SUV speeding along behind her, gaining rapidly.

Come on. Got to accelerate.

She zoomed past *The Body Shop* on the corner of 20th Street and beyond the dome-roofed, layer-cake-shaped Merchants Central Building at the corner of 21st.

It was late afternoon, and the onset of rush hour traffic seemed to be building slowly, together with an escalating sense of frustration. The SUV, unable to make much headway on the streets, swerved out of its lane and onto the sidewalk, ploughing through the crowds of unsuspecting pedestrians as they leapt frantically out of the way.

The SUV was gaining on her, unconstrained by the other cars in the street. Oh no. She yanked the bike to the left, weaving in and out of the speeding cars around her, from lane to lane, as if she were on a slalom obstacle course. She gritted her teeth tightly, forcing herself forward.

Tania headed towards the corner of Broadway near Madison Square Park. Separating the traffic, where Broadway crossed Fifth Avenue, there stood the unmistakable triangular Flatiron building. Unusually-proportioned in the shape of an iron, and elaborately-carved in a French Renaissance style, the limestone and terra-cotta edifice was one of New York's best loved structures.

At this point, Tania couldn't care less. All she wanted to do was get away, and she saw a route ahead of her leading onto Broadway. Although she was doubling back on herself, maybe she could shake them loose if she headed towards Times Square.

Tania's scooter accelerated, the engine revving furiously now. She began exhaling, trying to take deep breaths to calm herself down. She had never been in this sort of situation before, and a repeat performance was definitely not on the cards.

Suddenly, the traffic lights at the intersection began to change.

No. Now what?

At one side of the intersection was a policeman sitting in his patrol car, sitting in traffic, having come from the nearby 10th Precinct in West 20th Street. It had been a slow day for him so far. He was about to get a piece of the action.

The lights turned red.

With no choice, the Russian hurtled forward frantically, past the stationary cars, as the oncoming traffic from one of the other intersections began roaring to life, threatening to mow her down.

The policeman swore. "Someone's just jumped the lights." He radioed for backup and pulled out, switching on his siren. "All units. We have a Code 505 in progress between Fifth Avenue and Broadway. In pursuit of a silver-grey SUV chasing a blonde female Caucasian on a yellow BMW C1 scooter. Heading down Broadway towards Times Square."

As Tania picked up speed, a hoard of frustrated drivers began beeping at her, creating a cacophony of honking horns and angry voices as they shouted at her to get out of the way. The SUV followed in her wake, also jumping the lights and ignoring the drivers' vehement protests.

A yellow taxi cab darted forward into her path out of nowhere. Tania gasped. Where did that come from? There was sure to be a collision. But no. She narrowly dodged it as, miraculously, she swerved to the right. *That was close.* The taxi driver, also desperate to avoid a crash, slammed his foot on the brake. He came to an abrupt halt. But behind it, a green Jetta was still accelerating. *Crash!* It rammed straight into the back. The impact sent the taxi forward, straight into the path of the SUV.

The next few moments were a blur.

The SUV narrowly averted a collision. But then a second crash followed by another! An oncoming Chevy smashed into the front left wing of the taxi, automatically sending it spinning nearly 180 degrees clockwise into the path of a navy blue Dodge Neon on its right.

Still skidding furiously in a circle, the taxi was struck by the Neon on the front right wing, carrying it almost to the other side of the intersection. There was the distinctive crunching of metal and the shatter of glass flying everywhere, creating a terrible sound. Another car, a black Toyota, which was in the left lane next to the yellow taxi cab, skidded forcefully into the right side of the Chevy, spinning it 90 degrees clockwise. As a result, both cars nearly ended up at the other side of the intersection where the cars were still stationary. It was like a stock-car pile-up.

Tania glanced behind her shoulder for a second, gasping in shock. *Oh God.* What had just happened? She scrunched her face in horror, apologising inside. She could easily have been in that. She ushered those thoughts out of her mind. Then she was off again, hurtling down the theatre district of New York.

With its path temporarily blocked, the SUV careered off onto the sidewalk with a wheel spin and shot after the Russian blonde.

The chase was on again.

Bull followed behind, seeing what had happened with the pile up in the Flatiron District. He slalomed past the wreckage and raced forward after the police cars, the assassins and Tania on the scooter.

The BMW C1 screeched past the souvenir shop, *Memories of New York* on Broadway. Today was one memory Tania could do without. She would rather forget this whole affair. And hope everyone else would likewise.

Up ahead was a delivery truck for the *House of Perfume* at the corner of Broadway and West 28th Street. Two men were unloading cases full of perfume bottles, stacking it on the road before transporting them to the store. Tania hurtled past them. They jumped back in surprise. The SUV brushed past, smashing into the cases. The sound of breaking bottles could be heard as glass went flying everywhere.

Tania raced on along the vast stretch of Broadway. The police siren was screaming behind her. Another police car joined in the chase, skidding round the corner before slamming into the SUV. However, because of the angle in which the SUV was travelling, combined with the momentum it had gathered, the police car was sent spinning into the path of an Acura. Fortunately for Fahad and Kluge, the airbag of the SUV did not open, or else it would have hindered their pursuit.

At the corner of West 32nd Street and Broadway, a man on bicycle was waiting as a baby buggy had finished crossing. The SUV skidded towards it, knocking the cyclist off his bike. He shook an angry fist at them. But they were gone.

Tania headed up towards the busy expanse of Times Square. High above her, adorning one of the billboards in the distance was a huge image of her, advertising for a mobile phone company. Imagine what her fans would think if they could see her right now? She did a double-take as she passed *ESPN Sports Zone*, the sports-themed restaurant bar at the corner of West 42nd Street. Hanging in its window, among the other unusual artwork, was a specially-made stained glass picture of her dressed in her tennis outfit from last year's US Open.

A huge, articulated military truck was moving out from the nearby Army Recruiting Office, leaving a marginal gap between it and another van. She ploughed through the space, narrowly missing both of them. *That was close.*

The SUV wasn't so lucky. Unable to stop, it went straight into the path of the military truck. Tania glanced around quickly. Then a crash! The increasingly familiar sounds of metal being demolished. The squashed SUV was sent straight through the window-pane of *ESPN Sports Zone*, shattering the glass and destroying the famous US Open image of her immediately.

Tania breathed a sigh of relief. She was free. However, having temporarily lost concentration, she did not notice the woman pushing a stroller in front of her until it was too late. She turned around and gasped. *Oh no. Not a baby.* The thought of hitting either of them was too much for her. She swerved abruptly out of the way to avoid them. The scooter skidded out of control, lost balance and collided with a stationary pick-up truck.

The airbag of the C1 inflated immediately, cushioning the impact, while the frame of the scooter protected her from serious injury. Nevertheless, Tania was knocked unconscious by the force of the rapidly-expanding bag slamming her head backwards against the frame, and engulfing her completely.

Bull's Crossfire screeched to a halt. He jumped out. Scrambling towards her, he pulled out his Emerson folding combat knife to puncture the bag, and free her from the scooter. Cradling her in his arms, he dragged her limp body out, and carried the tennis star to his car just in time before more police arrived on the scene.

Tania was safe. For now.

Chapter 7

Time: unknown.

Like a carousel grinding slowly to a halt, the spinning room was winding down around her as Tania entered the initial stages of regaining consciousness.

Her head was pounding, while her body, heavy as lead, was unresponsive. Her eyes flickered open slowly, but the glare of the lights overhead was blinding, compelling her to want to close them again until she could brace herself properly to return to the land of the living.

Where was she and for how long had she been unconscious?

She wiggled her toes about to get a feel for her surroundings. Her feet were bare, but they were resting on something soft. In fact, everything around her was of a similar nature. *Some kind of bed!* But it wasn't her own.

Feeling braver, she allowed her eyes to open again slightly, this time peering through slits. With strained senses, she noted that she was in what appeared to be a stark white room with no windows, preventing her from determining her exact location. Definitely no place she recognised. There was also someone else present in the room. A male. But the details of his face were too blurry to make out. Should she be alarmed or relieved? At this point, seeing as she was too confused to decide, she remained neutral.

Still disorientated, she groaned wearily. "Where am I? What...what happened?"

"It's okay, Miss Likamolova," the man assured her, his voice was unfamiliar. "You're in safe hands now."

She took a deep breath. Could she trust his words? Her eyelids flickered, and she opened her eyes fully to see the face of the person in the room with her. Though groggy, she took a moment to examine him. Tall and square-jawed, he was athletically-built, and filled his suit nicely, as if he regularly worked out. His dark brown hair was closely cropped, but not so short that it was a crew cut. More like he kept it of a suitable length that he could wear it stylishly.

Nice. At least a friendly face.

"It's okay, I'm not going to hurt you," he said. "My name's Jonah Bull. You took a bit of a bump on your head earlier today."

His piercing, intelligent blue-grey eyes seemed fixed intently upon her as they exchanged glances. He was staring. *Well, let him stare.* She was used to it by now. Sometimes it was disconcerting, other times, flattering. This time?

Wait a minute! What did he say about earlier today? She sat up abruptly, remembering. She had been chased by unknown assailants through the streets of Manhattan. When she finally thought she had escaped, the scooter skidded out of control, followed by a collision. Then she blacked out. She could try to dismiss it all as a bizarre dream, but she was still dressed in the same bathrobe she wore from the *Completely Bare* spa.

No doubt about it, this was quite real.

Bull walked over to her. "I know this must seem alarming to you, but all will be explained in good time."

Alarming? He had that right. As if she was going to wait around for any explanation. She threw the covers aside and swung her legs over the edge of the bed. Her superbly conditioned body, normally full of energy, was still lethargic. But the lethargy quickly wore off as a surge of adrenaline coursed through her veins, spurring her into action.

"Now wait a second," Bull began, trying to restrain her.

"No," she screamed, shoving him out of the way. "Let me go. I have to get out of here."

He tried to grab her wrist, but she fended him off with a side-kick to his stomach, sending him crashing into the bed. Tania bolted for the door.

It was unlocked. *Thank God.* She swung it open and burst out of the room, desperate to be out of there.

"Wait," he yelled after her.

Tania ran out into a vast open-plan area full of faces of every race and colour, busily moving about like worker drones engaged in all sorts of activity, and seemingly oblivious to the tennis star's presence.

However, that initial lack of acknowledgement lasted but a few seconds as Bull called out after her. "Stop her."

With their attention drawn, those same worker drones began swarming around, surrounding her from every angle.

Cornered. Nowhere to escape.

Tania darted around nimbly on the balls of her feet to evade capture, but ran smack into a jovial-looking African man with short-cropped dreadlocks in a white shirt and loud red braces. He was eating a jar full of jelly beans.

"Oi, oi, steady on there, love," he said, in a distinctive cockney accent, while making a bungled attempt to restrain her wrists.

She kneed him in the groin, causing him to keel over in agony.

"Oh bloody 'ell," he swore.

In the scuffle, more people joined in to assist him, overwhelming her by sheer numbers. She began screaming hysterically. Kicking. Struggling to break free.

"Let me go," she demanded. "You can't do this."

"Sorry, love," the African man groaned, still writhing in pain, "but it's for your own good."

Suddenly a calm, commanding voice cut through the commotion, instantly stilling the storm. "We'll let you go, Miss Likamolova, as long as you promise not to try to run."

Tania glanced over at where the voice originated from. A tall, solidly-built man, probably in his fifties, stood there. Commanding respect from the others, he seemed like he might be in charge.

She wasn't promising anything.

"Miss Likamolova," the man began, as he approached her. "I realise this must be quite traumatic for you, but I assure you that, not only are you not a prisoner here, but we have no intention to harm you."

Tania didn't believe him. Why should she?

As a show of good faith, the man ordered the others to release her.

After a few minutes, Tania finally calmed down, and for the first time, noticed that everyone there was wearing a security ID badge.

The man who had ordered her release spoke. "I apologise for the somewhat rough treatment there, Miss. I'm Abraham Hassall, and I'm in charge of this operation here." Seeing Bull emerging on the scene, he pointed to him. "I believe you've already met Jonah Bull?"

Tania nodded. "We just ran into each other, yeah."

"You seem to make an 'abit of that," another voice spoke up. "Running into people that is."

Hassall turned around to the African man who had now recovered from Tania's earlier retaliation. "And this unfortunate fellow is Mr Dare-Brown."

"Chauncey's my name, Miss," Dare-Brown announced, breathing a heavy sigh. "Chauncey from Chelsea. That's Chelsea in London, not New York. Sorry about restraining you there."

"And so you should be," Tania murmured. But then, seeing the man's genuinely penitent demeanour, decided that she wasn't going to kick up a fuss. "Okay, apology accepted. I'm sorry about kneeing you back there."

"No problem, love," he replied. "Just try tackling your problems differently in future. None of this 'knees-up' business."

"I'll keep that in mind next time I'm confronted by a bunch of strange men."

Tania noticed he was ogling her. She began to turn a scarlet colour, pressing her lips together to hide a nervous smile.

"Well, Mr Dare-Brown," Hassall huffed impatiently. "Had a good stare? Because if you're quite done drooling now, we'd like to ask Miss Likamolova some questions."

"Oh, sorry about that, Mr 'Assall," he apologised. "But you know, as Mae West once said, 'it's better to be looked over than overlooked'."

Tania rolled her eyes. "So immature," she muttered, shaking her head in resignation, before following Hassall and Bull through a vast central atrium area with metallic sloping walls, still clad only in her bathrobe. The marble floor felt cold beneath her bare feet. Looking down, she gazed across towards a huge, circular blue shield with a gold edge, about fifteen feet in diameter, emblazoned with a map of the world. At the centre of the circle, was the symbol of an eye with a multi-coloured iris, with a golden compass superimposed over it and the letters I.R.I.S in place of the standard points of the compass. At the bottom was the motto *"Keeping an eye on the world"*.

What is this place? Things were growing stranger by the minute.

She was led into a dark, high-tech conference room lined with monitors, presentation screens and blinking lights. In the centre of the room was a large, shiny black table upon which terminals were positions at several points for personal use.

Joining them in the conference room was another man with a chiselled face and swarthy complexion - Wendell Krennick. He quickly introduced himself.

"Okay, who are you all?" Tania asked, taking a seat in one of the leather chairs around the table.

"We'll answer your questions and more, if you'll just be patient," Hassall assured her. "We need to ask you a few of our own."

"What kind of questions?" Tania was perplexed. "Hey, you're not a bunch of journalists trying to get an exclusive interview, are you?" But deep down, she knew the possibility of that was highly unlikely, judging from what she had seen outside.

"No," Hassall replied. "Please, Miss Likamolova. Just try to contain your curiosity for the moment."

"I'm sorry, but until you tell me who you are, I'm not cooperating."

"Fine," he conceded. "This will take some explaining. Can I get you something to drink first?"

"Well I'd kind of like something to wear instead of parading about in this glorified facecloth."

Hassall glanced briefly at her bathrobe. "I'll have my assistant, Mrs Zetterling find you some clothes. In the meantime, what can I get you?"

"Water will be fine." Her throat was parched from the sweltering heat, and having not had anything to drink since earlier that afternoon, she desperately needed something to quench her thirst.

Hassall motioned to Bull to fetch a cup of water from the water cooler over in the corner. Filling it up, he handed it to her, which she accepted gratefully.

After allowing her a few sips, Hassall began to explain. "Miss Likamolova, we belong to an organisation called IRIS."

"IRIS?" Tania exclaimed, remembering the letters she had seen on the shield on the floor outside. "What are you? Eye specialists?"

"No."

"A division of the IRS? Let me guess, I haven't paid my taxes. Is that it? Is that why I'm here?"

"IRIS stands for International Reconnaissance and Intelligence Service. We're a global intelligence agency established by the International Intelligence Community. We exist to keep an eye on the rest of the world to ensure that information gathered by specific countries can be objectively and comprehensively assessed by an international and impartial third party."

"Keeping an eye on the world huh? Hmm," Tania mused. "Kind of big-brotherish, aren't you? Watching everyone like that?"

Bull spoke up. "Well as Chauncey Dare-Brown put it earlier, it's better to be looked over than overlooked."

"So this Chauncey character was just doing his job earlier when he was having a good stare?"

"Well practice makes perfect," Bull muttered wryly.

Hassall brought the discussion back on course. "Miss Likamolova, to answer your question, we're not some all-seeing eye as you might think. We function more as a global network between various organizations in order to put an end to the need for complete dependency on country-specific ones like the CIA for intelligence. We gather up-to-the-minute information by monitoring current world events and long-term trends using sophisticated surveillance technology and then act upon it to prevent potential terrorist attacks and other asymmetric threats. And we ensure that members of the various national intelligence communities can be held accountable in the event of a failure or an abuse of power."

"Okay." Tania nodded, accepting his explanation. "So how come I've never heard of you before?"

"Only a small number of people have. We prefer to keep a low profile. We originally started life as a covert strategic support branch specifically proposed by the Pentagon to complement the Central Intelligence Agency - hence our somewhat similar structure to the CIA. However, we developed beyond that rather narrow vision. We now have a much more world-wide scope since the International Intelligence Community was interested in setting up a department of the United Nations to maintain international peace and security."

Tania frowned. "So what on earth does an intelligence agency want with a girl like me? I mean, kidnapping me like this…"

Hassall seemed to take offence at such a suggestion. "I think we'd better get one thing clear. We haven't kidnapped you."

"But you're holding me against my will."

"You're not being held prisoner, Miss Likamolova. We - or rather, Jonah Bull here - rescued you from your pursuers."

Tania raised an eyebrow. "Okay, well let's say that's true. Then who were they?"

"First things first," Hassall interrupted her. "We've answered your initial questions, now we have a few of our own."

"Fine. What do you want to know?"

The three IRIS operatives started questioning her. "I understand from your press conference yesterday that you spoke with Miss Shikolenko after your match with her?" Krennick began.

"We exchanged a few words in the locker room," Tania said. "A few minutes at most. What's this all about?"

"Miss Likamolova, please," Hassall entreated. "Let us ask the questions. What was the nature of your conversation with Miss Shikolenko?"

"Nothing really. I just thought it was polite to speak to her since she was injured in the match."

"That was all?" Krennick seemed sceptical.

"Well, mostly, although she did borrow my phone."

"Your phone?"

"She said hers wasn't working properly. She wanted to borrow mine to make a call."

"What was the phone call about?" Bull inquired.

"I don't know," Tania groaned. "I don't make it a habit of eavesdropping on other people's conversations."

Bull proceeded to his next question. "How long did she speak for?"

Her eyebrows knit together for a second. "I'm not sure. A minute. Maybe less."

"Where were you at the time?"

"Just there in the same room getting changed."

"And that didn't strike you as unusual?" he asked tersely.

"No. Why should it? It's not like she doesn't see that sort of stuff every day in the mirror."

"Not that," Bull quickly corrected her. "The phone call. You didn't think anything of it?"

"Well, you know, lots of people borrow my phone. It's not something out of the ordinary."

"Did she give you anything else?"

"No. She didn't give me *anything* at all."

"Are you certain of that?"

"Yes." Tania began to feel very uneasy. "Look, if you want to know all this information, why don't you just ask Natalya herself?"

"You don't know?" Hassall asked.

"Know what?"

Hassall paused for a moment to break the news to her. "I'm afraid Natalya Shikolenko was found dead this afternoon."

"What?" Tania went white with shock. This was the last thing she expected to hear. "How?"

"We haven't confirmed the cause of death yet, but preliminary findings suggest her skull was fractured with a blunt object. Our Chief Medical Examiner, Dr de Silva, is performing an autopsy right now."

She drew in a deep, shuddering breath. "Are you saying someone killed Natalya?"

Hassall nodded. "We think so."

Tania was speechless. "When... when did she die?"

"We believe it was around 10.00 or 10.30 pm last night."

"That's terrible," she gasped. "Do you know who did it?"

"We have our suspicions," Krennick stated economically, without elaborating any further.

"Why are you guys examining her body anyway, instead of the police forensics team? Isn't this just a normal homicide?"

Krennick shook his head. "No. And our authority trumps that of the police in this matter."

Tania thought for a moment. "Wait a minute. Does this have something to do with the shock she received during our match?"

"Perhaps." He was being decidedly vague.

This was like drawing blood from a stone. Tania probed further. "You mean someone did that on purpose?"

"Yeah, most likely," Bull said, getting a word in. "And it would have probably killed her if you hadn't intervened to save her."

"But who would want to do such a thing?" Tania asked, her voice still betraying her shock.

"That's what we're trying to find out," Hassall announced. "Now think, Miss Likamolova. Did you notice anything unusual afterwards?"

She gave him a blank look. "Like what?"

"Anything at all. For example, with your phone."

Tania screwed up her lips as she considered the possibility. "You know, come to think of it, I did notice something odd. Earlier today, when I was at the spa, I was trying to access certain tunes stored on my phone's MP3 player. I couldn't find them. I began to search my phone to see if I had accidentally moved the songs, but instead I came across a very large file I didn't recognise."

"And then what?"

"I tried to access it, but I couldn't. Before I could do anything else I was attacked by that brute of a masseur. I thought Onan the Barbarian there was merely some creep trying to get off on some fanboy fix of testosterone-filled excitement, but believe it or not, he actually appeared to be after my phone."

"Hmm. That's interesting," Hassall mused. He pressed a button on an intercom and spoke. "Mr Xiu, could you come in here for a moment?"

"Does it have something to do with Natalya," Tania asked. "And if so what do I have to do with it? Who were those people after me?"

Before anyone could answer her, another IRIS operative entered the room. It was Elvin Xiu.

"Sir," Elf began. "You wanted to see me?"

Hassall decided introductions were in order. "Miss Likamolova, this is our resident techie, Elvin Xiu, our Chief Science, Technology and Weapons Analyst."

"Uh, hi," the Chinese man greeted her reverentially. "Pleased to meet you Miss Likamolova. Call me Elvin, or 'Elf' for short."

Tania smiled back gently. "Please, call me Tania."

Elf turned to Hassall, beaming with a cherub-like expression. "Sir, this is very kind of you introducing me like this. You know I'm a big fan of Tania Likamolova. I watch all her matches."

"I didn't call you in here for that," Hassall snapped irritably.

"Sorry sir," he apologised. "It's just that every time she serves me one of her looks, she leaves me in love."

"Mr Xiu," Hassall growled irascibly. "I expect awkward teenagers in the first throes of young love to get googly-eyed, not grown men who left behind the last shreds of puberty over a decade ago, and most certainly not experienced IRIS operatives. Now I want you to analyse Miss Likamolova's phone - see if there's anything stored on it. Apparently, a large file has been uploaded onto her phone's memory."

"Oh, oh right," Elf stammered. "I'll get on it straight away." He turned back towards Tania. "By the way, I meant what I said about being a fan of yours. I'm eager to see how you'll do in Beijing this year. I've calculated the number of WTA points you need…"

"Xiu," Hassall interrupted. "I meant *now*."

Elf nodded, and then quickly left the room with Tania's phone.

"I'm sorry about that," Hassall apologised.

"Am I free to go now?" Tania asked.

"Well there are a few things we need to discuss with you."

"You still haven't answered my question," Tania interrupted. "Who were those guys chasing me?"

"Tania," Hassall began, "those people chasing you today were operatives working for a group known as The Three Bears."

Chapter 8

"**T**hree Bears?" As a child, she had read about them. As an adult, she fondly remembered them. Now, as a rising tennis star, she had now been roughed up by them. Tania pinched her forearm to give herself a quick reality-check. "You're kidding me, right?"

"I'm afraid we're not," Hassall replied flatly.

"So who are these Three Bears?" She inquired. "Patrons of the Teddy Bears' Society?"

"Unfortunately, they are not an innocuous organisation," Hassall explained. "We know relatively little about their identities at this stage, but using ASAP technology we've been able to establish that they are an alliance or coalition whose activities and agenda with regard to world economic conditions might best be described as anti-Goldilocks."

"Anti-Goldilocks?" The Russian star looked bemused.

"If you remember in the Goldilocks story, Goldilocks wanted porridge that was neither too hot nor too cold, but just right. Well, a Goldilocks economy is one whose growth is neither too hot - ie too fast, nor too cold - ie too slow, but just right. Such an economy avoids both inflation and unemployment. Compare China and Russia with the US respectively, for an example. By contrast, The Three Bears - the real Three Bears that is, and not the ones in the fairy tale - appear to want to bring about something that is the exact opposite: a 'bear economy' – one that is characterised either by high inflation and/or recession, and high oil prices. Hence, anti-Goldilocks."

"Okay," Tania replied tentatively. Economics wasn't her strong point, so she simply accepted his explanation. "Well that doesn't sound good. Why do they want to do that?"

"That's what we're trying to find out."

"And you say Natalya is somehow mixed up in this?"

"More than merely 'somehow'."

Tania bit her lip. "Why? What did she ever do?"

"We suspect that Natalya transferred classified information to your phone. Information which The Three Bears are after."

Tania was at a loss. "What kind of classified information could Natalya possibly have? Secret WTA stats?"

"It was much more dangerous information than that I'm afraid, especially if it was worth killing her over. We believe that she somehow learnt the identity of one of The Three Bears. When Elf comes back with the analysis, we should have a better idea. Once they realised she was no longer in possession of it, and that you inadvertently made contact with Natalya, they pursued you."

"Great. So now I'm a target as well."

"Well," Hassall assured her, "although we can't guarantee that more of The Three Bears' operatives won't come after you, we've taken care of those chasing you today."

"Gee, that's swell of you. I feel so much better now." She shook her head in resignation. "But why on earth would Natalya know their identity? She was just a tennis player wasn't she?"

Hassall thought for a moment, gauging how to explain everything to her. "This might sound hard to believe but Natalya Andreevna Shikolenko was actually a covert intelligence operative."

"A what?"

"In other words, a spy," Bull interjected, not wishing to beat about the bush.

"Pfft! A spy?" Tania nearly choked on her water. Had she heard correctly?

"Well I wouldn't have put it quite so bluntly as Mr Bull here," Hassall added. "But yes, that's essentially what she was."

Tania burst into a fit of musical giggles. "You mean, like a sort of *tennis* spy?"

Hassall sat there with a straight face. He didn't appear to be joking.

Tania sighed heavily. "This is utterly ridiculous!"

"I know how it must sound," Hassall began, "but I'm afraid what we've told you about Natalya's clandestine career is all true."

"*Okay*." She acknowledged him provisionally, knowing full well that this was all just a little too weird. She decided she should play along, at least delve deeper, until the auspicious moment where she could find the loose thread on this theory and unravel the whole thing at the seams. "So who was Natalya working for?"

"She was an operative for a covert Russian organisation called RISK."

Tania cocked her head slightly. "RISK?" The name didn't register with her. Not that it should.

"*Raslyedavaiya I Sluzhba Kontrrazvedki* or Investigations and Counter-Intelligence Service," Hassall explained.

"Wouldn't that strictly be *Sluzhba Kontrrazvedki I Raslyedavanyi?*" Tania pointed out.

"Hey, it's just an acronym," Bull interjected. "Otherwise they would be SKIR."

"Thank you, Mr Bull." Hassall resumed, "RISK is an elite, clandestine division of the FSB. The *Federal'naya Sluzhba Bezopasnosti*. I assume you at least know about them?"

"Of course," Tania replied. "What Russian doesn't? The Federal Security Service - the successor to the old KGB."

"Yes. However, RISK operates almost independently of the FSB with its own agenda, using unconventional methods and somewhat questionable ethics. Although RISK specialises mainly in counter-espionage, the organisation is wide enough that some of its investigation activities include undertaking covert espionage and reconnaissance operations that are not strictly authorised by the Federal Security Service and would be politically or diplomatically risky - hence their acronym. They're effectively a Black Ops division of the FSB if you like. It's rumoured that the organisation is so secretive that RISK's existence is denied by the Kremlin, while it remains highly classified from all but a few of the most senior-ranking officers within the FSB. Of course, we know about them because it's our business to know."

Tania leaned forward, trying to comprehend everything she was hearing. "So let me get this straight, you expect me to believe that, while everyone thought she was a tennis player, Natalya was really some kind of secret agent?

"Well, more like a cross between a sleeper agent and an agent of influence."

Tania frowned. "I'm not familiar with those terms."

"It's not something new. During the Cold War, the West was rife with them. KGB agents were often sent overseas to integrate themselves fully into society where they would not be suspected, and could simply lie dormant for years, until they needed to be activated as and when necessary. In the meantime, they would establish all sorts of contacts with eminent figures such as politicians or scientists while obtaining secrets for their own country. In certain cases, these agents would be successful enough to place themselves in positions of influence. Natalya Shikolenko was like these agents, except that she was an agent in the tennis world."

"But how?"

"Well as you know, tennis as a sport was mostly neglected under the former Soviet regime, until it was restored as a medal Olympic sport after the 1988 games. From that time on, it slowly found support among the Russians, who began to reserve special coaches for high-ranking members of the Communist Party in addition to spies and diplomats in order to help them develop sources and make contacts in the West. Tennis was also made compulsory for cosmonauts as part of their training programme, because it was considered the only game that could completely relax one's brain. However, after the fall of the Soviet Union, tennis received a massive breakthrough in terms of popularity. You may recall that tennis was one of the former Russian President Boris Yeltsin's passions in life while he was still alive?"

"Not really... I was a bit too young. I've read about it though."

"Well let me try this. I'm sure the name Shamil Tarpishev would mean something to you?"

"Yes." Tania nodded. "Former president of the Russian Tennis Federation, as well as former Davis Cup and Fed Cup Captain. He's retired now."

"Right. Tarpishev was both Yeltsin's coach and a close confidant, having previously served as head of the State Committee on Sport and Tourism within the Kremlin. Both he and Yeltsin used to play a lot of tennis together and were an unbeaten doubles pair in the Kremlin for almost a decade in the early 1990's. After Yeltsin was photographed playing on a tennis court in his shorts, the popularity of tennis soared, and everyone from poor Russian people to businessmen saw an incredible golden goose at their disposal. Tennis proved to be a lucrative industry. Tarpishev founded the National Sports Foundation in 1992, which was granted lucrative exemptions on import tax by Yeltsin. Over the next four years, several billion dollars of revenue were mysteriously diverted from the NSF funds, until 1996 when it was discovered and a scandal broke. It was uncertain who was behind this at the time, although intelligence reports now suggest it may have been RISK."

Tania looked stunned. Surely this couldn't be true? Had this clandestine Russian agency really been around that long?

The IRIS director continued. "The glamour of the sport made tennis a convenient and more respectable way to invest dirty money both in tennis courts and prestigious clubs instead of simply hiding it away somewhere. RISK acquired some of these funds anonymously, initially using them to finance the tennis training of Russian spies who still operated in the background. However, this wouldn't have been ideal as payments could still be traced from certain agents to their sponsors, and therefore at this point the idea of a 'tennis spy' had not yet taken off."

"So what happened?"

"Well, it was really the Russian revolution in tennis in the early-to-mid-2000's, where many of the top twenty female players in the world consisted of Russian women. Inspired by these role models, hundreds of Russian parents signed their children up to the sport, hoping they would be the bright young stars of tomorrow. Eventually, rather than teaching spies to play tennis, it naturally became easier to train tennis prodigies to become spies. Natalya Shikolenko was one such prodigy who was trained in the skills of espionage and counter-intelligence and then formally recruited into RISK when the time was right to activate her. Because she really was a professional tennis player, Natalya would have been the ideal agent since she would earn enough money from tournaments to finance herself in order to avoid any traceable payments from abroad. Furthermore, since she was 'recruited' as a child, before even officially joining RISK, she could move around the world easily without any counter-intelligence agencies ever suspecting her of being a spy, since she was already established in the West as a celebrity. And of course, her celebrity status would naturally have placed her in a position of great influence."

Tania was grappling with this concept, trying to decide whether she could accept it as true or not. There was one particular question that loomed large in her mind. "When would she ever have had time for spying? It's not like tennis leaves room for much else."

"Any intel gathering was largely based around all the various world locations travelled to as part of the tennis circuit. She could spend most of her time playing tennis, and then would be called into service if the situation warranted it."

She sighed. "I guess you never really do know your opponents."

"Perhaps not," Hassall agreed. "But it's better if you do."

"So wait a second." A piercing thought shot through her like an electric current. "Are you also saying that there are other spies out there in the tennis world operating secretly?"

"It's a distinct possibility. This information is only really coming to light now."

Tania paused for a moment to think. "So where do I fit in? This seems like fairly top secret material. Why would she give it to me? Don't tell me it was just a coincidence."

"I don't think it was coincidental at all. Natalya Shikolenko probably realised the importance of this file and knew precisely what she was doing when she made the transfer. She was a trained agent. If she was doing her best to prevent it falling into the wrong hands, then it's highly unlikely that she would have selected any person at random, even in an emergency. She would've singled you out specifically."

"But what's special about me? Is there something you're not telling me?"

"You happen to be Piotr Volkov's girlfriend."

"Piotr?" The mention of the name startled her. "What does he have to do with all this? And how do you know about us? It's not exactly public."

"Well, as to how, that's not important. As for his involvement - I know this is going to be hard to accept, but Piotr Volkov is also a member of RISK, and was working in conjunction with Shikolenko."

"What?" she gasped. "That can't be true. He's Head of Global Marketing for Red Gold."

"I'm afraid that's only his cover identity he has used to operate without suspicion and form numerous high-profile contacts since *Zolot* Vodka is widely distributed in many countries around the world. As I mentioned earlier, RISK develop agents not only in the tennis world but within all walks of life. RISK planted Volkov as a media consultant within the company. However, he began his own operation, independent of his superiors at RISK Directorate."

"What kind of operation?"

"Several weeks ago, samples of bacteria for treating oil spills were stolen from the *Chang Yudong Chem* oil research facility in Xinjiang, China. Although we know little about it at this stage, our intel reveals that, when normally applied, the bacteria has the ability to chemically alter the properties of oil. We aren't sure of its intended purpose at the moment, but we have learnt that both Shikolenko and Volkov were behind the theft and are planning to sell the bacteria to The Three Bears. And if that's the case, we can be certain that The Three Bears' goals are less than benevolent."

Tania shook her head doubtfully. "I don't believe you about Piotr," she snapped.

"Well, how well do you really know him?"

"I know him as well as two people in a relationship would know each other."

"Do you?" Hassall walked over to his desk and picked up an A4 manila folder. He placed it in her hands. "See for yourself."

Tania began to thumb through the dossier. It contained a number of photos of him, as well as an extensive biographical sketch detailing various activities she knew nothing about. Piotr Sergeyevich Volkov, also known as Piotr Sergeyevich Vasiliev/Vanko/Volsky, and a host of other alternate identities. Which name was real and which was simply an alter ego?

She read on. After completing his military service, Volkov served briefly in OMON or *Otryad Militsii Osobogo Naznacheniya*, more commonly known as the Black Berets. Volkov himself had been stationed in Chechnya, where he was first approached to work for RISK as a counter-intelligence specialist. He later took on the identity of a top media expert for *Zolot* Vodka since it provided him with ample opportunities to establish international contacts as part of the alcoholic beverage industry.

The Russian shook her head in disbelief, tears forming in her eyes. Page after page confirmed her worst fears.

It's true.

But wait a minute. So Piotr was an agent for his country. But what was so bad about that? Perhaps he was acting under orders to steal from the *Chang Yudong* research facility. Tania read on, learning of the cold-blooded way in which both Volkov and Natalya disposed of the security guards in Xinjiang. He was a murderer.

As if that wasn't bad enough, a final revelation struck her heart like an arrow. Piotr had a five-year-old daughter named Sasha from a previous relationship, who was currently hidden away in a RISK safe house somewhere in Russia with the mother. Tania had no idea. Piotr had said nothing all this time. Not a word.

Her mouth was agape in stunned silence. She didn't know her boyfriend at all. Could it be that she had been such a poor judge of character? She hoped this was all some huge, practical joke. Maybe Piotr would come through the door at any moment and surprise her. They would laugh about it later on, that is, after she had finished wringing his neck for putting her through this ordeal. But no. The evidence was there.

Overwhelmingly there.

Nevertheless, she had to ask, "How do I know you didn't just make this up?"

"It *is* true," Hassall said emphatically. "We have no reason to make this sort of thing up."

Tania pondered that for a moment. She had to admit that he might be right. At least she couldn't think of any reason off the top of her head.

"We've spent months collecting data and gathering evidence to build up that file," Hassall continued. "It's what we do as an international intelligence agency, pooling resources from different sources around the world. It's not simply the findings of one particular country without any sense of accountability on our part. We don't operate like that. You can rest assured that we have an accurate picture of the state of affairs."

Not that his assurance helped. But she had nothing with which to counter these accusations.

"You said you needed my help," Tania reminded him. "I don't see how."

"Volkov is planning to sell the oil spill bacteria to The Three Bears shortly. We don't know when or where. We need you to acquire this information."

"And how am I supposed to do that?"

"We understand that both you and Volkov have been invited to an Imperial Ball at the Catherine Palace in *Tsarkoye Selo*, St Petersburg this weekend, hosted by Oleg Korsakov."

"Well, yes. But I already said that I can't go there anyway. I have a match to play on Saturday, in case you didn't realise."

"Unfortunately, your own plans will have to wait," Hassall informed her. "It looks like you *will* be going to the Ball after all."

Tania gave a pout of childish petulance. "What are you now? My Fairy Godmother? What am I supposed to do there anyway?"

"Volkov is meeting a contact there named Konstantin Chernovsky, another RISK agent working undercover within The Three Bears organization," Hassall explained. "Chernovsky will have the information on his smartphone, which doubles as a PDA. When they are in range, he will transfer the information to Volkov's phone by a short-distance wireless link which leaves no trace of the transfer. Once the transfer is complete, we need you to get close to Volkov to find out when this sale is taking place, what the components are being used for and whether it is being manufactured anywhere. Find out all you can and report back on anything that can lead us to The Three Bears."

"What are you saying?" She gave him a quizzical look. "You want me to be, like… a spy?"

Chapter 9

If someone had told her before that she would one day be a famous tennis star, Tania might've laughed. But given her background, it still seemed within the realms of possibility. If, however, someone had told her she would be involved in some kind of espionage, never in her wildest dreams could she ever have imagined it would be like this.

But had she heard him correctly? More to the point, had she arrived at the right conclusion? Or had there been some faulty reasoning somewhere along the way? She blinked in surprise, hoping she had misunderstood, and that this time she would be let off the hook.

Any such hopes were dashed as her doubts were clarified immediately.

"Think of it more as a simple undercover reconnaissance mission," Hassall answered, having failed to notice the look of surprise that had been flickering across the faces of both Bull and Krennick for the past minute. "You've already been invited to the Ball, now all you need to do is stick close to him and feed back to us all you've learnt."

"What makes you think I'm even vaguely qualified for this?"

"Well for starters," Hassall began, "we all know you're in excellent physical condition and have superb fitness and stamina as a world-class athlete. You're used to dealing with pressure and intense situations. Our file on you also shows that you're currently studying for an online degree in Psychology and Languages, and you are, in fact, already fluent in several languages. You're also familiar with various cultures and used to adjusting to different time zones from all your globe-trotting around the world as a tennis player. And then let's not forget you've trained in Systema, among other things."

"Well you certainly seem to have done your homework on me. But although I might know a few moves, as far as I'm concerned that's mostly been fitness training for my tennis."

"Well that's the official line," Hassall responded.

Tania gave him a blank stare. "What are you talking about?"

Hassall paused for a moment before answering, somewhat evasively. "All I mean is that you've learnt these skills, but they are easily transferable to another field."

"And exactly what am I supposed to be finding out? I could be reporting back something you already know."

"We will explain all of that to you, but we need to be certain you are on board with us first."

"Well why not someone else?" Tania was still unconvinced, and she would need far more persuasion than that to even consider such a request.

Before Hassall could explain, Wendell Krennick pulled him to one side. "I think we should talk before this goes any further."

"Not now," Hassall dismissed him. "We're in the middle of something."

"Director," Krennick persisted, "it's important."

Seeing that his right-hand man was adamant in his stance, he relented. "Okay," Hassall whispered. "Go ahead."

"Privately," Krennick added.

"You'll have to excuse us for a moment," Hassall informed Tania, as he motioned to Bull to escort her outside into the open-plan area. "In the meantime, if there's anything you need, my operations manager, Mrs Genette Zetterling will see to it."

***

"Okay, what is it Wendell?" Abraham Hassall demanded, slightly irritated that the briefing had been interrupted.

As part of his duties as the Deputy Director for Operations, Krennick usually supervised the recruitment of IRIS officers. He was damned if he was going to let anyone on a mission without the compulsory training. He got straight to the point, dropping the formalities with his friend. "Abe, my understanding was that you were going to use her as an informer. Now, am I to believe that you seriously want her as some amateur undercover agent? We never discussed actually sending her out to St Petersburg. Isn't that going against standard IRIS protocol? The DII would never authorise it."

"Why don't you let me clear things with the head?" Hassall suggested. "I think once I explain the situation, the Director of International Intelligence is likely to agree with me."

"Really?" Krennick challenged him. "Don't you think Director d'Aulnoy will see this as a rather cavalier attitude you're taking to this whole operation?"

"Wendell, what's this about?" Hassall asked, taken aback by the fact that they suddenly seemed to be at loggerheads with each other. "You know that we've been friends for ages and you've never had a problem with my methods. Is it something to do with the fact that d'Aulnoy placed me in charge here over you when Southey resigned as Director?"

"Abraham, don't even let that cross your mind," Krennick assured him. "You know you have my full support in what you do, but I'm merely questioning the wisdom of your current decision. After all, am I not here as someone you can be accountable to? Your friend? All I'm saying is that by letting Tania in on all of this confidential information in the first place, that alone is taking a terrible risk. Was it wise to reveal that we knew about Volkov? What if she relays a message that we are onto him and it gets back to The Three Bears?"

"And how else do you propose we go about this?" Hassall replied. "As I've said before, we have to weigh our options carefully, and all things considered, this is the best one available. Sometimes you have to use the enemy's spies to work for you so you can win without any loss inflicted on your side."

Bull arrived back in the room, overhearing the last shreds of the conversation. He was not convinced as to Hassall's approach either and gave his own opinion on the matter. "She's not a spy, sir. That's the whole point. She's a civilian. And using a civilian - that's extremely risky as we've already seen several times before. Likamolova could endanger our whole mission and everything we've accomplished so far. Why not train someone else?"

Krennick added his own thoughts, trying to appeal to a different side of Hassall. "I'm inclined to agree with Agent Bull here, Abe. Likamolova's just a young girl. Southey would never have thought of sending out anyone that young."

"Well I'm not Director Southey," Hassall said categorically. "And I do things differently to him."

Krennick sighed. "Yes, you can't wear another man's armour. I understand that. I'm just saying she lacks the experience. She could get herself killed."

"Wendell, I share your concern," Hassall replied. "I really do. After all, I have a daughter her age. I also fully realise what you're saying, all of you. But while I too am hesitant to send her out into the field, we may not have any other choice. There's no one else who has Volkov's confidence, or has her abilities. I think that definitely gives her an edge over any normal tennis player we could train, or any agent we could use."

Krennick was determined not to let this go without a fight. "So she's multi-lingual and knows a few fighting techniques. Good for her. But that still doesn't qualify her as an operative. What if she's captured? Then what? Will she break? Will she spill the beans on our operation? She hasn't even been tested in that way. When it comes to carrying out operations, that's an entirely different matter to possessing certain skills or playing in a tennis match. All our field agents require extensive training from anywhere between three months to a year. You of all people should know that."

"Wendell, your objections are noted," Hassall replied. "And I fully realise that. That's why she won't be alone here. I'm planning to send Agent Bull in with her."

"What?" Bull exclaimed. "You're kidding, right?"

"No, Jonah. I'm quite serious."

"I thought my role in all of this was just to approach Likamolova and bring her in so we could use her, not to babysit her."

"There's nothing 'babysitting' about this. You both would have a job to do, each your part to play. Think of it as if you were acting as her more experienced partner on a mission."

"There must be a dozen other IRIS agents who would be better qualified."

"But there's no-one more familiar with this case than you. You've already suggested that it's a risky move to send someone like Likamolova on this mission, so to that end, I'm placing her under your care. I know you will do everything by the book and make sure that she does everything in the way she should. That's why I'm relying on you for this operation."

"Sir, I don't need this right now."

"I disagree with you. Our Force Multiplier Office has reviewed your dossier and has concluded you're not currently working to your full potential. Based on their recommendations, that's another reason why I'm assigning you this."

"With all due respect, sir, the FMO doesn't understand my situation."

"Agent Bull, you can't spend the rest of your time here at IRIS avoiding working with others again or going through life doubting everything, wondering 'what if?' We have to live in the present, learn from our mistakes but not keep looking in the rear view mirror. You know the story of your namesake, Jonah the prophet, in the Old Testament, don't you?"

"Of course."

"You remember how he tried to run away from his duties when God sent him on a mission, and he ended up being washed up and swallowed by a whale?"

"What's your point, sir?"

"You can't keep a good man down. And you can't stay washed up forever. This mission is just the sort of thing to help you rediscover your sea legs - or flying wings in your case."

Bull sighed ruefully. Those coveted flying wings were gathering dust in his desk. "You said something similar before, sir, when you told me to watch Likamolova."

"And my reasoning still stands. I don't have to order you to do this, do I?"

"No sir," Bull muttered reluctantly.

"Good. Now, I need to know that the rest of you are going to back me up on this. Are we all clear?"

No-one said anything, but their silent expressions indicated they were in agreement, if only reluctantly.

"Well, I think it's time we get back to Miss Likamolova," Hassall continued. "She's waiting for us. Hopefully we can make her understand."

***

"Miss, are you okay there?"

Tania was sitting alone outside, musing over the recent revelations, when she heard the distinct cockney tones coming from above her. She looked up. It was Chauncey Dare-Brown, standing there with Elvin Xiu.

"I'm okay, thanks," she replied flatly. "But again, I'm sorry about kneeing you in the groin earlier."

"Say no more," he assured her, guffawing heartily. "All is forgiven. Although it does kind of bring a different meaning to the phrase 'new balls please'."

Tania rolled her eyes and groaned. She had heard them all before.

"By the way, here's your phone back," Elf said, offering it to her.

"Thanks," she replied. "Have you got everything you need from it?"

Elf nodded. "For the time being."

Chauncey spoke up again. "Are you sure I can't get you anything, Miss? Jelly beans perhaps?" He waved a jar of the candy in front of her face.

"It's okay, thanks," she replied.

"I think Genette Zetterling is looking after her," Elf said.

"That's right," Tania confirmed, hoping they would both go away. "She's just gone to get me a drink of water and some clothes." She was in no mood to socialise with anyone.

"Zetterling eh?" Chauncey scratched his head as he continued to stand there, insensitive to Tania's present state of mind.

Geneviève 'Genette' Zetterling was a full-figured, middle-aged woman of Swedish descent who resembled a severe school-marm. A former curator at the Stockholm City Museum, she was a long-serving staff member who had been there before Hassall's appointment as Director. Although she was extremely efficient at her job, other IRIS agents regarded the irascible and indomitable operations manager as overly protective of what she regarded as her own personal office territory. As such, they secretly enjoyed poking fun at her expense, despite the fact that Zetterling considered such behaviour morally reprehensible.

"So tell me, Elf," Chauncey continued. "'ow come in the movies, spies get these attractive assistants, but all we get is this frumpy old bat like 'er?"

"Too true," Elf agreed, joining in with the laughter.

"Ah, but you gotta love 'er," he chuckled merrily. "The old girl cracks me up at times. She's like Phyllis Diller - the typical ugly 'ousewife who doesn't even realise it."

Elf smiled nervously, but did not answer. He merely cleared his throat, indicating that it might be in his friend's best interests if he were to take a gander behind him.

Chauncey did not pick up on the hint. "Of course, when she's in a foul mood, she can be a bit of a dragon too. I'm surprised she doesn't 'ave 'orns growing out of 'er 'ead."

"Horns growing out of my head, huh?" an angry voice thundered from seemingly out of nowhere.

Chauncey whipped round, his jaw dropping immediately as he saw Genette Zetterling standing there, arms folded, her face black as pitch, and shaking her head disapprovingly at what she had overheard.

"Oh, speak of the devil," was the first thing he blurted out, before biting his tongue.

He had put his foot in it. Yet again.

Zetterling raised her voice indignantly. "This 'ugly housewife', as you so blatantly put it, also has the power to see that your pay-cheque is the very last one processed, especially if you keep up these facially-discriminating remarks like that."

Feeling belittled, like a chastised schoolboy, Chauncey tried to extricate himself from the delicate situation. "Now Genette, darling, don't get your dander up. When I compared you to an 'ousewife, I meant that in the best possible way. Your administrative skills are tip-top, especially for an old girl like you."

"Stuff it," she replied abruptly. "I know what you meant. And don't you 'old girl' me. I may not be as young or sprightly as you kids, but I'm hardly in need of a Zimmer frame either."

"Hey, love," he said, raising the flat of his palm upwards in the hope of appeasing her. "No need to take it all so *au sérieux*."

"*Au sérieux?*" she repeated.

"Yes," he explained, inwardly gloating at the thought that this phrase had seemingly gone over her head. "*Au sérieux*. You know, French for…"

"I'm well aware of its actual meaning, Mr Dare-Brown," came the scolding reply. Her voice was terse and condescending.

"Well then - what I said. No need to be so *au sérieux*."

"Chauncey Dare-Brown," she huffed vehemently. "The use of the French language on your lips is as ill-fitting as one of Miss Likamolova's tight tennis dresses would be on me."

Still seated, having observed the curious exchange, Tania raised an eyebrow in silent amusement. If she weren't in so sombre a mood, she might actually have giggled at the absurdity of such a prospect, especially when she took a good hard look at the prim and fussy matronly figure hovering above her. She tried to imagine this amply-proportioned, sensibly-dressed woman with her greying hair squeezing into one of her girlish, elegant bright pink outfits with a low-cut décolletage. She shuddered. *Perish the thought.*

"Don't you all have something better to do?" a voice resounded suddenly. It was Director Hassall, having emerged from his private conference with Jonah Bull and Wendell Krennick. "Xiu," he continued in the same irritated tone. "Have you finished analysing Miss Likamolova's phone already?"

"Yes. I mean, no sir," Elf replied. "I've uploaded the contents of her hard drive to our computers but there's an encrypted file on it that still needs to be broken."

"And what about you, Agent Dare-Brown?"

"Er… yeah, Director 'Assall," Chauncey stammered. "I'm running our latest findings through ASAP."

"Then I suggest you get back to work a.s.a.p.," Hassall growled. "The same goes for the rest of you with your bickering."

"Now hold your horses, sir," Genette snorted. "It was Mr Dare-Brown who started this."

Hassall was astounded. "I beg your pardon? Hold my horses, Mrs Zetterling?"

"I'm sorry, sir," she relented. "I meant…"

"That will be enough," Hassall snapped. "The two of you will need to take your recriminations elsewhere, or do I have to send you both to stand in a corner?"

They nodded in understanding, with Genette muttering under her breath. "Things were never like this under Director Southey."

Seeing that she still carried some resentment, Hassall stopped her. "Genette. Listen to me. I need you here. You've been here longer than I have, and you're able to manage this office better than anyone I know. I realise Southey had a different style, but we're all trying to fit in with each other here, and that's going to take some time."

Genette nodded, her demeanour softening. Then, turning back towards Tania, she held up a bundle of spare clothing. "Here you go dear, you can put these on. You look like a salad without dressing at the moment."

Tania thanked her, as the small crowd that had gathered around the young Russian dispersed quickly in separate directions, leaving her to change.

"Now, Miss Likamolova," Hassall began, once Tania was fully dressed, "it's time we talk seriously."

Seriously? What had they been doing all this time? Her eyebrows furrowed. "There's something I don't understand. Even if Piotr may be up to no good, why would he invite me along to join him in St Petersburg if he's conducting his own secret business? Don't tell me he just wanted to bring a date?"

"Let's just say your celebrity status far outshines anyone else's in Russia," Hassall said. "As one of your country's biggest superstars, any contacts you would've made would be another contact for him and ultimately for RISK. Since you had already been invited, he wanted to use that to his advantage. You would've been there, unwittingly doing some of his reconnaissance work for him without ever realising it."

"Well, you won't have to worry about me making any contacts on his behalf, because as I said, I'm not going."

"Look, before you make your decision…"

Tania shook her head resolutely. "No. I'm just a tennis player. I'm not cut out for this line of work. Surely there must be someone else?"

"It's not a matter of finding other operatives," Hassall explained. "That part is easy enough. We have plenty of trained field agents. But since we don't have much time, we need someone who is both close enough to Volkov to find out information from him directly, and can at least handle themselves in these sorts of situations should anything go wrong. In the circumstances, you are the *only* person qualified."

"The answer is still no."

"If we could do this without you, we would. There isn't another way."

"I don't believe that. The intelligence world has managed perfectly fine on its own without the likes of me. I'm sure it will get by once again. What if there wasn't someone like me - another tennis player who fits your profile? Then what would you do?"

"That isn't the case though. We do have you."

"No. You don't." There was no question about that. Not even for a moment.

"Well, you need to think long and hard about this before giving me your final answer. At least grant us that much. Tell me you'll consider it."

Tania sighed, knowing he was not going to let up that easily. "I can't decide right now," she said, her voice non-committal as she stalled for time. "It's all too much for me to take in. And I have a semi-final match to play tomorrow. I've been out far longer than I intended today. I've barely been able to practise and work on my game."

"Well don't wait too long," Hassall answered. "You have twenty-four hours in which to reach your decision. Remember, at the moment, with The Three Bears still out there, *you* are the game."

Chapter 10

Friday.

For a fraction of a second, when Tania awoke the following morning, she simply imagined she had experienced a bizarre dream. The sunlight streaked through her bedroom window, giving little hint of the previous day's events. Then, reality hit her like a bullet, and a torrent of anguish came flooding back. Head buried in her pillow again, she breathed a huge sigh of frustration before crawling wearily out of bed, one foot at a time.

The ominous start to the morning continued to loom over her like a dark cloud, well into the next few hours such that, by the time her semi-final match rolled around, she was plagued by a persistent nagging feeling that today might not be her day. She tried to empty herself of these negative thoughts as she entered the Arthur Ashe Stadium, but they continued to linger in the back of her mind, even as she began her warm-up exercises. Understandably distrait, she was nevertheless determined to give a feisty performance even if she wasn't feeling quite one hundred percent.

Not quite one hundred percent? Ha! That would be an understatement.

The night before had been spent in a state of utter restlessness. She had tossed and turned for hours, mentally replaying everything she had learnt from IRIS, trying to find a way around the demand made of her to act as a spy. Hassall would've preferred she forfeit the match. But come on. This was her tennis he was talking about. She had worked too hard all year for this. Visualised herself on more than one occasion lifting that precious trophy again. She was not about to turn her back on her dreams just like that.

But Tania's mind was not on the game, but on other ruminations. *Can it really be true about everything I was told? Was I so blind? Was Piotr really lying to me all this time? I can't believe he never told me about that previous relationship or his daughter.*

Tania shook her head. If she kept this up, she would lose this match all on her own. Of course, even if she managed to cast aside all her concerns, her opponent this afternoon would have put paid to any notions of victory: Asteria Hunter of the USA - originally from Zanzibar - standing at nearly six-foot-ten, muscularly built like an Amazon and wearing her hair in a Mohawk. Dressed in black, she was an awesome, imposing figure who struck fear into the hearts of every player on the women's circuit. Correction. Make that every player on *both* the men's and women's circuit. She could probably go five sets with the entire Davis Cup team at once and still outgun them.

Tania was sure that Asteria was secretly one of those mythical she-warriors who wouldn't have given a second thought to removing her right breast so as not to interfere with her serve.

With the fastest one on record in both the men's and women's game at 168.3 mph, Asteria had no need for that.

Today was no exception. Ripped like a bodybuilder, every vein and sinew was on display as Asteria employed a combination of lightning-fast serves and ruthless, aggressive tactics to rout her opponent. The number four seed would win game after game to claim the first set 6-0 without the Russian even being able to get a touch on the ball. Tania soon found herself in dire trouble in the second, down at 0-3.

To make matters worse, what was up with that crowd? Talk about fickle. In her quarter-final match on Wednesday, everyone was cheering for the Russian sensation. Now, as soon as an American was in the picture, Tania had the distinct impression that all that support had given way to patriotism. If she did have any fans left in the stadium, they were keeping awfully quiet. The crowd was clearly on her opponent's side.

Traitors!

Tania slapped her thigh, forcing herself to snap out of her internalisation that was ticking away like a time bomb, ready to completely destroy any chance she had left of remaining in the match.

Come on. Focus. Forget about them. You just need to hold and then break, hold and then break.

Easier said than done. Tania served to her opponent's forehand. Big mistake. Her opponent blasted a return so powerful that all that Tania could do was get her racquet on the ball and try to keep it in play. No way to play her own game. Just pure defensive tennis. Survival of the strongest.

Damn. 0-4.

Moving like quicksilver, the amazon was continually charging towards the net like an express train, forcing the young Russian to make error after error. For Tania, coming forward to the net wasn't the most natural thing for her, even though she had worked hard on that area of her game. Today she seemed glued to the baseline. The pressure of the constant hammering upon her was relentless and insurmountable. Her enemy clubbed the ball so hard that by the time it arrived on the other side of the net it was like a squashed tomato, useless for any sort of constructive point.

In direct proportion to the pressure, Tania's screams were getting louder and louder, but it was doing her no good. To cap it off, where was Tania's accuracy? Her forehand, with its unusual lasso motion her coach had suggested needed changing, was spraying balls all over the place. Everywhere but in the court. Maybe he was right after all. Maybe it was her Achilles' heel. To make matters worse, an intended drop shot was trapped at the net, foiling her attempts to vary her game. *0-5.*

Perhaps she should've stayed and practised like her coach had suggested, instead of wrangling her way out of it and heading for the spa. Perhaps then, she might not be in this most desperate of situations.

Those blasted internalisations began bubbling up in her mind again, like a cooker on a stove. *Piotr's last name is Volkov. Now that I think about it, it sounds almost like Volk - Russian for wolf. Was he just a wolf in sheep's clothing? No, that can't be. Volkov isn't an uncommon Russian name. I'm just being paranoid.*

It was as though someone were stoking the fire under her pot, determined for it to boil over and spill out into her game. The fight and the talent had all but left this so-called prodigy from Russia.

She served a half-hearted ball, hoping to take the pace off it so that her opponent would have to generate her own.

No good.

Another projectile catapulted over the net with such force that Tania had to duck out of the way to avoid injury.

Forget recovering that. Save yourself.

A loud crack was heard. The ball collided with one of the linesmen who cried out sharply in pain as he had failed to dodge quickly enough.

The crowd gasped in shock at the amazon's awesome power to inflict that kind of damage.

The Russian served another. Her opponent bludgeoned it back at her. Miraculously, Tania managed to get her racquet on the ball this time. She chipped it down the line, hoping to put it out of play. But to her chagrin, Asteria magically appeared there again, and Tania, in no position to recover, was completely wrong-footed as the amazon pelted it back, sealing the point with a sizzling cross-court winner. *Match point.*

In less than forty-five minutes, it was all over. All she had managed to scrounge up were a few measly crumbs. The distinct smell of bagels filled the air.

Not even a single game!

With no more aces up her sleeve, Tania served up one last-ditch attempt, knowing in her heart that her reign as champion was over. Her opponent stunned her with a deep return which the Russian could only sink into the net.

And there she stood - a lonely, disconsolate figure - completely broken but holding back the flood of tears. The fierce tigress had been lured down from the mountain and tamed into a harmless paper version. Mellowed into regular girl once again. One who looked completely devastated and crushed. And as if to rub salt into her wounds, her opponent paraded around the stadium triumphantly, gloating with a haughty stare and an air of arrogance. The media's Golden Delicious was left dejected like a rotten apple, with the anguish of having been lambasted in so humiliating a way now rocking her to the core.

***

Once out of the intrusive glare of the public eye, the tears came quickly like a rushing stream, as Tania sat in the locker room crying. She wasn't usually this lachrymose, but under the circumstances, how could she do otherwise? Head hung low, she failed to notice her coach enter until his words interrupted her.

"Are you okay?" he asked, his voice full of concern.

"I don't want to talk about it right now," Tania sobbed. Her fragile, vulnerable expression suggested she was presently encumbered with the weight of the world on her shoulders. She simply wanted to forget about today's debacle and hide her head in the sand, lick her wounds, and shed her own tears in private.

Respecting her need for space, Igor turned around to leave. "If you'd rather be alone…"

Tania looked up. Perhaps she would. The truth was that she had been completely distracted today. At the worst possible moment, tennis had been the last thing on her mind, but how could she possibly reveal that to her coach? Even if, in the event she told him, he did believe her, there was no way she wanted to place him in danger by making him a party to that knowledge. No. She would have to keep it to herself.

When he was almost out the door, Tania choked back her tears and spoke up. "It's over, isn't it? The fairy tale is over."

Igor sat down beside her and curled a comforting arm around her shoulder. He looked into her eyes which were filled with moisture and spoke earnestly. "I know this meant a lot to you. But you've been through a big loss before. This is no different. The period you enjoyed as reigning champion was always going to come to an end eventually."

Tania's head bobbed up and down in acknowledgement, if not in agreement. "I know."

Her poor coach. So dedicated to the sport. So single-minded. He had no idea what happened to her yesterday. How could he? It wasn't just her reign as champion that had ended.

"I just hoped it would be later rather than sooner," she added.

"You're tough enough to overcome this and survive in the real world, to handle life's ups and downs. Just remember: Moscow wasn't built in a day. Learn from this defeat and become a better player. Learn to play the game."

Tania gave him a diffident look, suggesting she wasn't entirely clear what he was talking about. "In what way do I do that?"

Had things become so bad that Igor had now resorted to dispensing such seemingly trite advice? Perhaps even insulting her by suggesting she didn't know how to play? But what if he was right? What if it was simply due to her own weakness that she couldn't pull herself together when it mattered? Perhaps ice didn't really flow through her veins on court as everyone had believed. Perhaps she was still merely a girl, unable to still the torrent of nerves under pressure.

Igor placed his hand on her forearm and spoke sagely. "Tatya, let me tell you something I've never taught you before. Don't play another person's game. It puts you at a disadvantage. You do not know their rules or they may change the rules without telling you. Since it's their game, they probably know how to play it better than you do. So instead, make them play your game. But if you have no choice but to play another person's game, learn the rules of that game fully, including how to change them to your advantage. Be clever enough to play the game better than that person. If the game is one you cannot afford to lose, delay playing it until you've acquired the skill and experience to win, or you have worn out your opponent. However, if the game is one you can afford to lose, play the game to learn the skill and gain the experience."

She dwelled upon his words for a few seconds. What did he mean by all that double talk? Surely not tennis? For she knew the rules of that game well, and would have little choice as to the time or opponent of her next match. He knew that. Or was he in fact alluding to something deeper, unrelated to the match and her ignominious defeat?

"Remember," he repeated. "Play your own game."

Igor left the former champion shortly afterwards to reflect upon his counsel. At least the parts which seemed to refer to the non-tennis aspects of her life. It was a long and hard decision. One that weighed heavily on her mind for hours after her coach's words had faded to silence.

Tania teetered on the brink of the decision that could change her life forever. What would she choose? Would she help IRIS?

No. Who was she kidding? She wasn't ready to go out into the field. Let someone else play hero.

Play your own game? To her, that was tennis. Not spying.

***

Saturday morning.

"May I have your passport please?" the airport attendant requested. She smiled warmly at the Russian tennis star standing before her at the first class passengers' check-in desk at the departures terminal of the John F Kennedy International Airport, the city's international hub.

Tania handed it over, giving her an equally warm smile that barely betrayed her true state of mind. Eager to be on her way, she was getting out of New York which, after yesterday's fiasco and the events directly preceding it, had proved to be a place of anguish. Take a few days off, maybe even visit her family in Siberia before heading over to Beijing.

Having arrived about half an hour earlier, she was sure that a car had been following her for at least part of the way to the airport. However, when she emerged with her bodyguards from the back of the limousine to remove her luggage, the car remained some distance away. Perhaps it was her own imagination. She hadn't even associated with IRIS for more than a day, and yet some of that spy paranoia was already rubbing off onto her.

While the check-in girl called up the relevant details on the computer, Tania gazed around at her surroundings. The terminal was crowded, with thousands of travellers shuffling about, slowly overheating with frustration, as they waited in line at the economy class check-in desks. There also appeared to be a fair bit of construction going on, which delayed things further. Fortunately, people barely noticed her today. She was dressed in casual attire, consisting of an orange Nike T-shirt and blue jeans, topped off with dark glasses and a baseball cap. Unfortunately, however, those who did pay her constant attention were a few men in suits patrolling the area, peering intermittently in her direction while attempting to make themselves as inconspicuous as possible. The way they kept turning away whenever she glanced back at them seemed to make them all the more obvious. They were probably those IRIS agents again.

Within a few moments, the attendant had finished checking in her baggage, leaving Tania free to wander, while her bodyguards fanned out and followed at a distance.

She sauntered past the collection of shops and towards a magazine stand where she began to browse through their selection. Perhaps she could pick something up to read on the plane. Her attention was drawn to a copy of *Sports Illustrated*, with her image adorning the front cover. Underneath was a caption: 'Tania Likamolova - US Open Champion. Will she give her opponents a good licking this year?'

She shook her head sadly, feeling a pang of regret inside. *So much for that.* The cover served to remind her of all that she had lost. US Open Champion? That was yesterday's news now. Completely passé.

The call of nature beckoned, and she headed to the restroom. At least in there, she could think what to do about those suits who, as she strolled over to the entrance, seemed to be on the move once again, heading her way. This was getting preposterous. Were they planning to come in too? Or perhaps they were waiting for her until she came out?

Perhaps she could pass herself off as an air stewardess? That was a thought. Yeah. Maybe one might waltz into the restroom and she could cunningly persuade her to trade clothes. All she needed to do was wait for one who was the correct height. She could walk out of there in disguise and lose those creeps on her tail.

Wait a minute? What was she saying? That was a ridiculous idea. For one thing, she would probably get into trouble for impersonating a flight attendant, and secondly, she was easily recognisable with her face being plastered all over the magazines and billboards. It didn't help either, that there was a huge poster of her hanging up in the terminal for all to see.

Tania exited the restroom and headed for the security checkpoints, emptied her pockets, and left her hand luggage on the conveyor belt for screening. Hopefully, this would be straightforward enough since she was a celebrity. As the security guard began to frisk her, she noticed another one speaking on his walkie-talkie. The guard looked her way, then walked over and asked her to remove her shoes. She made nothing of it, considering it nothing more than standard procedure. It was only when the guard asked her to accompany him to another cordoned-off area that her suspicions were aroused.

"Is there a problem?" she inquired.

The guard said nothing, but merely beckoned for her to follow.

Her bodyguards stepped forward to her defence, but a man in a grey suit emerged. "Miss Likamolova?" he said. "Will you please follow me?"

"Do you mind telling me what this is?" she asked again.

"All will be answered shortly," he replied, then gestured to the bodyguards to remain where they were, assuring them that she would be in safe hands.

Tania wasn't so sure herself. She began to grow anxious. However, rather than protesting, she followed the man in the grey suit as he led her down a corridor like a prisoner, and escorted her to a waiting room.

She sat there for a few minutes in silence, with a uniformed officer keeping watch, while the grey-suited man left the room momentarily. Her growing concern was soon both alleviated and intensified when in walked Director Hassall, accompanied by the grey-suited man.

Tania sighed. "I should've expected to see you again."

"Going somewhere, were you?" he began flippantly.

As if he didn't know.

"Anywhere but here."

Hassall shook his head reprovingly. "I'm disappointed in you."

She frowned with disbelief. "What for? I never agreed to anything."

The nerve of the man.

"I don't think we made it clear enough," he said. "We need your help. We can't do this without you."

Tania exhaled a heavy sigh. Hadn't they gotten the message? They were going round and round in circles. "What if I don't want to help?"

"Well, it might interest you to know that because of your relationship with Volkov, you could be considered an accomplice and an associate of The Three Bears."

"But that's not fair," she protested. "I'd never even heard of any of them until Thursday. And I certainly didn't know anything about Piotr's true nature."

"Well unfortunately, the Director of International Intelligence won't view it quite so favourably," Hassall warned her ominously. "Think about it. It could spell the end of your tennis career. Is that something you want?"

Was that a threat?

Maybe he didn't realise what it meant to her. She laid it heavily on the line. "Listen, I've worked real hard to get where I am today. My family and I made a lot of sacrifices. It's not a dream I want to just throw away like that."

"Sometimes dreams have to be sacrificed for the greater good," he countered, seemingly unsympathetic to her plight.

"Then it has to be *my* sacrifice to make," she rose defiantly. "Something *I* choose to do. Not you nor anyone else. It's not something that you or anyone can take away just like that. You don't have that right. No-one does."

Hassall shook his head. "I know from the information we have on you that you and your parents are from a Russian Orthodox background, so maybe what I'm about to say next will mean something to you. What you call your own - all your tennis talent and skills, all you've worked hard for, and everything else you've achieved in your life - it's yours only in the sense that it's something that God has given you for your enjoyment, not something you can claim as your own outright. Don't get me wrong. I'm not saying you haven't earned it or that anyone in this world can forcibly take it away from you - but you're only a trustee of all your talents, so to speak, not the ultimate owner of them. So if you want to talk about rights, well owners have rights, trustees have responsibility. That's what you have here - a responsibility to use your talents and God-given abilities for a greater good - for the good of others, not just for yourself."

Tania sighed. "Don't get preachy with me. Doesn't God also give us the freedom to choose, even if it means we make the wrong choice? But if you're forced into something, then it's not really your own choice at all. It's not that I want to use everything for my own selfish gain. I understand that. But like I said before - that sacrifice has to be mine to make, and my choice alone."

"Be that as it may, the stakes here are too high to leave open the possibility of you running off. So let me outline to you exactly what your choices are, as I see it. If you do help us, we would be able to offer you immunity from prosecution once we've gained the information from

Volkov. But if you don't help us, then when we do bring Volkov in, you could be prosecuted along with him by virtue of his association with The Three Bears and the fact that you were in possession of sensitive information passed on to you by Natalya Shikolenko relating to that. Now, it's not something I want to do, but those are the facts. That would mean the end of your freedom and, therefore, your tennis career."

"Well let's suppose I played your game. Then even if I helped you, it could still mean the end of my tennis career anyway. With RISK or The Three Bears out there, how would I be able to go out in public anymore without being a permanent target? It's not like I could assume a new identity and go into some witness protection programme either. Someone's bound to recognise me."

"At least if you co-operated, you'd still have your life."

"Tennis *is* my life."

"But it's not the only part of your life. You need to decide, at the end of the day, what is truly important to you, and what isn't. So choose what is right."

Tania sat there pouting in stony silence as she reviewed the dilemma in her mind.

Help IRIS or lose my freedom? Help IRIS or lose my freedom? But if I do help IRIS I'll lose my freedom anyway. Goodbye tennis career. That sucks! But at least I'll still be free. Or will I? What good is it being technically 'free' if I'm unable to do the things I love most in this world? But then what good is it if I were to have the whole world at my fingertips but lose my life? That's no good either. Hmm. Maybe it won't be so bad if I can't play tennis anymore. After all, I'll have to retire someday anyway. I'd just be doing it sooner than later. Lots of tennis players disappear into obscurity. I could go to college, get a job. If anyone asks, I could just say I'm one of these celebrity look-alikes. Yeah right. Who would buy that? Help IRIS or lose my freedom? Oh, this is too difficult...

Under the circumstances, she decided on the lesser of two evils.

As if she had much of a choice.

"Okay," she said reluctantly. "You've got my help. What exactly do you want me to do?"

"For starters, you can board that plane to St Petersburg."

"What plane? I'm not booked on that flight."

"Don't worry. We've already arranged for your ticket to be transferred. Your flight is scheduled for 1 pm."

A wave of anger descended upon her, the frustration slowly simmering under the surface. Tania wasn't usually this way, considering herself fairly laid back and easy-going. But in the past few days, she had been pushed to her limit, and now she struggled to keep her feelings in check. She bit her tongue, merely choosing to ask for further information as a means of diffusing the negative emotions. "What am I supposed to do once I get there?"

"You'll meet your contact whom you'll be working with," he replied.

Tania shook her head. She still had her concerns about the whole mission. There were points that needed clarification. "So essentially, you want me to deceive Piotr?"

"You shouldn't worry about that. He had no qualms about doing the same to you."

Tania nodded, thinking back to all she had learnt in the file on her boyfriend. "I know. It's just that I'm not used to doing this sort of thing. Lying all the time, and pretending to do one thing while doing another."

"Sometimes using deceitful tactics can operate as a pre-emptive strike, preventing someone else from doing the same. If those covert and clandestine methods ultimately reveal The Three Bears' plan with minimal effort, then that's all the better for you, and for us too. You can finish with this more quickly and be on your way, and we will be able to use the information you gained to maximum effect. Everyone's happy in the end."

"Sure," she sighed in resignation. "Everyone's happy."

Hassall tried to reassure her, sensing her apprehension. "Don't worry. I think you'll find that it is far easier to adapt than you think. If you like fairy tales, you'll love the world of intelligence. We're in the business of make-believe. You'll be in and out of there before you know it. Just think of yourself as Goldilocks."

"Goldilocks?" Tania gave him a look of disbelief. "You seem to enjoy mining this particular metaphor."

"You can't have a Three Bears without a Goldilocks," he clarified. "As part of your assignment, you'd be acting in direct opposition to them. You'd be going into their cottage, so to speak, as an intruder upon their plans - to sleep in their beds, break their chairs and eat their porridge, all under the guise of a sweet and innocent girl."

Inside, the Russian shuddered with a distinct chill. This sweet and innocent girl had inadvertently found herself embroiled in something way over her head.

Chapter 11

Sunday afternoon.

After an interminable delay from the connecting flight via Moscow's Sheremetyevo Airport, Tatiana arrived at Pulkovo II International Airport, located south of the St Petersburg city centre. The building was relatively small and primitive, built in a Stalinist architectural style. Quite a contrast to JFK, or the other airports to which she was normally accustomed. This was the first time back here in Russia for a number of years, and immediately she began to compare it with other parts of the world she had visited.

Fortunately, she did not have to wait in the customs line for long. IRIS had told her that this would be a quick assignment and that she should keep her belongings to a minimum, unlike her usual kitchen sink. IRIS would provide everything for her, including accommodation, clothing and any other travel arrangements. Her usual bodyguards were also replaced with special IRIS agents who accompanied her, dressed in dark suits and glasses, their sombre dress matching their equally sombre demeanours.

Emerging from the terminal, there was a distinct chill in the air with the first signs of snowfall. Although early for this time of year in

September, it was not altogether unusual, as the weather could sometimes be unpredictable in St Petersburg. Tania pulled her outer coat around her to keep warm and placed her Siberian fox fur hat on her head. The hat was a little excessive perhaps, but when in Russia, do as the Russians do. Besides, having grown accustomed to playing tennis in warm climates most of the year round, now she noticed even the slightest drop in temperature. She sighed to herself. *To think I was in sunny New York less than twenty-four hours ago.*

Near the queue of yellow *Moskvich* taxis and mini vans parked outside, a prearranged limousine was waiting to pick her up. The two IRIS bodyguards helped her into the car, before speeding off to its destination. The city centre was eleven miles away and although the journey was meant to be only forty minutes long, the traffic was heavy. The drivers here could also be completely crazy, driving too fast and sometimes on the wrong side of the road, with lane discipline meaning nothing to them. Tania shook her head and took a deep breath as the car accelerated north towards the city.

Upon reaching the centre, the limo made its way through a radial system of streets, interwoven with a network of canals, rivers and bridges curving around them.

"Cool," she exclaimed, as she removed her fur hat then switched her American cell phone SIM card to a Russian one, so that she would only have to pay local rates for her phone calls.

The IRIS bodyguards did not engage her in conversation, but sat silently, their faces blank.

"I guess I'll just have to talk to the driver instead," she sighed, deciding they were no fun.

The entire city was built on water, and many had compared it to Amsterdam and Venice. Tania was unsure about that. Although she hadn't visited either of those two cities, she was fairly certain those comparisons did not do justice to the true character of St Petersburg.

The limousine driver, at the tennis star's request and the IRIS agents' approval, took a slightly more scenic route to the hotel, passing by a number of familiar sights. The young Russian was astounded by the elegant architecture adorning the city, much of which appeared to be in a European style dissimilar to the rest of Russia. The city was filled with ornate churches, palatial buildings and museums, and a mass of rectangular structures near the city's embankment.

The limo headed down *Nevsky Prospekt*, the busy boulevard boasting a wealth of impressive buildings and what many considered the life of St Petersburg. In the distance, she could see a glittering spire.

"What's that?" she asked the driver.

"The Admiralty," he replied. "The former headquarters of the Russian navy. You'll see it soon enough."

Once they reached the end of *Nevsky Prospekt*, Tania asked the driver to take a slight detour towards the corner of *Dvortsovaya Ploshchad* or Palace Square where stood the stately, neoclassical General Staff Building, once headquarters of the secret police and Russian Army. In the centre of the square, in front of the curved yellow structure, stood the Alexander Column, a towering monument made of red granite with a bronze angel crowning it. Further in the distance was the magnificent Winter Palace, a lavish façade of green, white and gold, once inhabited by Catherine the Great. This grandiose building formed part of the Hermitage, one of the most renowned museums in the world.

After this ensemble of breathtaking buildings, the car turned back on itself and headed past the gilded spire of the Admiralty which Tania had seen earlier. Adorning the building's golden façade were various sculptures of mythical figures celebrating the Russian's triumph over the sea, while framing the main entrance on either side were statues of elemental nymphs holding up huge globes of heaven and earth. Glancing over at it, Tania sighed. The irony was not lost on her. Right now, she felt like one of those very nymphs burdened with the weight of the world squarely upon her shoulders.

They turned down *Voznesenskiy Prospekt* where Tania was afforded a closer look at the impressive Saint Isaacs Cathedral. She gazed at its exterior, which was decorated with sculptures and massive red granite columns.

"You'll get a better view from your room," the driver informed her in Russian, as he pulled up alongside the Astoria opposite the Cathedral and helped her out. The seven-storey hotel was one of the city's most luxurious and centrally-located places of accommodation, with the entirety of its front offset by pilasters.

Tania was glad to be out of the car as she hurried to the door, keen to stretch her legs again, leaving the IRIS bodyguards to attend to her luggage. The hotel doorman welcomed her warmly, priding himself on the fact that the Russian star would add to the glittering list of distinguished guests ranging from the Bolsheviks to ballet stars who had resided there at some point or other.

Tania walked through the red-carpeted hallways to her suite, with the bodyguards following closely behind, having instructed a bellboy to bring her luggage to her room. The interior décor of the hotel was adorned with antiques from various museums as well as garlands and medallions.

The bellboy escorted her and the IRIS agents to one of the Deluxe Suites, then waited as one of the agents unlocked the door. The agent showed the bellboy where to leave Tania's luggage and then tipped him, after which he left promptly. Tania sauntered through the entrance hall into a two-room suite with a spacious lounge. Seated there, by a cocktail table, was the familiar face of Jonah Bull, while at a computer on a writing desk was Elvin Xiu, both of whom had arrived earlier.

"Hello," she said, waving at them. "What are you doing here?"

"We're here to brief you on your mission at the Catherine Palace tonight," Bull replied.

"I see," she said, nodding her head tentatively. "IRIS must've been rather short-staffed."

Her remark caused Bull to frown, but he said nothing.

"And these heavies who so kindly acted as my travelling buddies?" she continued, as she watched them leave. "What's up with them?"

"Well, as I'm sure you must've realised, they're here to give you some added protection before the mission tonight."

Tania giggled. "No, I meant, why are they so sombre and laconic? Are they usually such great company?"

"They were just doing their job," Bull replied simply.

"Which was?"

"Ensuring you didn't run off again."

"Oh great!" Tania sighed.

Bull dismissed the agents, feeling that he could handle things from here.

In the meantime, Tania kicked off her shoes and shed her outer garments, then began to traipse around the room, feeling the soft pile of the plush carpet beneath her bare feet. She walked over to the window and gazed out at the magnificent view. Opposite her room, dominating the St Petersburg skyline, was the glistening, gilded dome of St Isaac's Cathedral which she had seen earlier, basking in the faint hint of early afternoon sunshine that was breaking through the snow clouds. From up here, she could see there were four smaller bell towers and a number of statues on the roof.

Down below in St Isaac's Square, Tania spotted a number of visitors waiting to enter one of the cathedral's porticoes. Near to the cathedral were the Mariinsky Palace and the equestrian statue of Nicholas I in the centre of the Square.

"You know," Tania began, "the atmosphere here leaves me breathless. You should see this - it's really cool."

"I'm sure it's a great view," Bull spoke, deflating her glee.

"You're *sure*?" Tania replied, turning around in amazement at his lack of interest. "Have you even looked?"

"Don't need to. You've seen one city, you've seen them all."

She sighed wearily. "You must be a barrel of laughs on a date."

"Don't mind him," Elf said, as he disappeared into another room. "He works all the time. He doesn't go on any dates. And unfortunately, because of my meagre social skills, neither do I."

Tania shrugged her shoulders and let her gaze wander around the room, pausing as it caught sight of a few armchairs upon which lay cushions embroidered with the letter *A*. Next to these was a large coffee table upon which were copies of *Pravda* and *MosNews* as well a Russian edition of *Vogue* bearing her image on the cover.

"I ought to go check out this place," she announced.

"Disappointed you didn't get the Presidential Suite?" Bull suggested light-heartedly.

"Well, yeah, only the best will do," she joked, ignoring the implication. "No, really, I'm just curious as to what kind of room I've been assigned." She began walking around to explore the rest of the suite.

She peered inside the white, three-piece marble bathroom, noting the luxurious Italian toiletries and fluffy towelling robes, giving her a sudden thought. "Hey, I just got here after a sixteen-hour flight. Do you mind if I soak in the tub and freshen up first?"

"Well, if you don't mind me briefing you while you're in there," Bull replied. "We are kind of short on time."

"No thanks," Tania said, letting out a half-embarrassed laugh as she shook her head. "No chance of that."

Sensing that her comments so far were probably an attempt to make light of the situation, Bull gave her his full attention. "Listen, Miss Likamolova, I know you're probably feeling apprehensive about this, but if it helps…"

"You don't know the half of it, Mr Bull," Tania interrupted him.

"Jonah will do," he replied.

"Jonah?" Since they were dropping the formalities, she pointed to herself. "Call me Tania. That's *Tarnia*. Rhymes with…"

"Narnia? I know. I was there at your press conference."

She nodded, smiling. "I didn't notice."

"But if it helps at all, Tania-rhymes-with-Narnia, the first time most of us IRIS agents were…"

"I'm not an IRIS agent," she said, quick to clarify that. "I shouldn't even be here. But now that I'm in a hotel room across from some fantastic view, at least I could make the most of it. But no. I'm stuck here with a bunch of guys who've forgotten how to have fun."

"Like I said, we've got work to do. You weren't brought over here for a sightseeing tour." He walked over to a large coffee table which was draped in a white table cloth and then pulled out a chair for her. "Have a seat. I'll need to explain a few important things, so you'll probably want to sit down."

Tania sighed in resignation. She walked over and sat herself down. In front of her was a selection of Russian dishes on the table, including Beef Stroganov and, of course, Borsch soup. There were also various desserts such as ice cream and a range of cakes. She began eyeing them longingly, but then noticed that Elvin Xiu hadn't emerged. "Where's your little helper gone?" she inquired.

"My little helper?" Jonah sat puzzled, not making the connection.

"Elf," she clarified with a grin. "Where is he?"

"Never mind about him," he replied dismissively. "He has other errands to run."

Tania's mouth turned downwards for a moment in bewilderment, before shaking her head. It dawned on her that Elf had probably gone into the bedroom earlier. Was he taking a nap?

"Okay, here's the deal," Jonah began, sipping coffee out of a curious, chequered design of cup that matched the coffee pot. "You'll be attending the masked Imperial Ball at the Catherine Palace with your boyfriend, Piotr Volkov. Act completely normal. Make out that there is nothing bothering you at all. If you do let on at all, he will suspect you and it will blow the whole operation."

"I understand," she replied, slightly distracted by the food in front of her.

"Now he's going to have you picked up by limo at 7.00 pm. He won't be accompanying you himself but will meet you there at the Palace. However, one of those 'heavies', as you put it, will be accompanying you, posing as your bodyguard, but will leave you once you've arrived safely. It's about a fifty-minute drive, but allowing for traffic, you'll arrive at approximately 8.30 pm. The host there will be Oleg Korsakov, whom I'm sure you will meet. Now Volkov is to receive critical information at the Catherine Palace from Konstantin Chernovsky, whom we have briefed you about already. We need you to obtain this information."

"How am I supposed to do that? Like I keep saying. I'm not a spy."

"Well if you'll come with me this way," Jonah said, as he stood up. "I'll fill you in."

"Where are we going?"

He did not answer, but began to walk into the bedroom, beckoning with his finger.

Tania was filled with a sense of alarm. "Now wait a minute. When I accused you of not knowing how to have fun a moment ago, I didn't say to go to the opposite extreme. I'm not that kind of girl."

Jonah smirked at her insinuation. "It's all part of the briefing," he assured her.

"Oh I'll bet," Tania said, her eyes turning circles. "Is this what you really mean by sleeper agents?" She began to follow, more out of curiosity than anything else.

As she entered the room, she saw Elf was standing in there, but her attention was immediately focused on a king-sized bed with silken sheets. Laid out carefully, to her delight, was a shimmering ballgown the colour of primrose. Her eyes immediately shot out on stalks.

"Oh my gosh," she gasped speechlessly, overwhelmed with awe. "Is that for me?"

She did not wait for the answer, but, forgetting temporarily about the mission, immediately rushed over to examine it.

The Basque bodice was strapless and made of satin and tulle with sparkling sequins. It also had a flowing, bouffant skirt, matching elbow-length gloves and a masquerade mask.

"It's gorgeous," she exclaimed, giddy with excitement and beaming with a radiant smile that lit up her entire face.

"It's what you'll be wearing tonight," Jonah informed her simply.

"Oh, it's really lovely," she cried gushingly. "I was just thinking that I needed to find a ballgown for this evening, but this is perfect. Thank you." She scrunched up her nose and rolled her shoulders in girlish abashment.

Jonah hastened to direct the credit away from himself. "Don't thank me. Thank Elf, and thank IRIS - compliments of them."

Tania turned to Elf and thanked him. "Now who says Elves don't deliver the best presents?"

Bull smiled, then began to brief her on her mission. "RISK agents carry a lot of their current operational information on their smartphones. It's something they keep with them at all times. When Volkov and Chernovsky meet tonight, they will both use their phones to transfer the information we're after. Apart from finding out anything you can from talking to Volkov, you'll also need to get hold of his smartphone temporarily so we can clone it. Now it's vital that you acquire the phone only once Volkov has the information and not before. Is that understood?"

"Sure. It's perfectly straightforward," she replied, her voice tinged with a hint of sarcasm. "Hey, in case you didn't notice, I've never done this sort of thing before."

"We can work on the actual technique later," he assured her. "The larger problem we face is once we acquire it."

"Oh? In what way?"

Elf picked up one of the gloves and held it up towards Tania's hand. "Here. Try this on."

"That's okay," she said, still smiling, and thinking that he was simply eager to see her in her ballgown. "I'll try it on later once I've freshened up."

"Try it on now," he insisted. "It's all part of the briefing and answers your question."

Tania nodded her head, and took the glove from him. She slid it slowly over her slender fingers and up the lengths of her arms. "Hey, the insides feel a bit funny."

"That would be the vascular biometric scanner that I built specially into the inner-lining of each glove," Elf said.

"The *what* scanner?"

"Vascular biometric. It's designed to scan the palms of anyone you make contact with and record their unique vein patterns."

"Vein patterns? Why would I want to do that?"

Elf began a thorough explanation. "All RISK phones use Fujitsu palm-vein recognition technology in order to prevent unauthorised users from gaining access, so even once we've cloned Volkov's phone, we still need to bypass the security. Each person in the world has a unique set of vein patterns within them that act like a sophisticated fingerprint. These can be recorded digitally onto a phone as a security measure. Then, whenever a person wants to turn the phone on or access certain functions, it scans the user's palm and compares the scan with the stored pattern in order to authenticate the user's identity like a PIN number. Unlike say, fingerprint scanners, where one can simply lift and create a copy of any print left behind, the same cannot easily be done for veins. That's where the vascular scanner in your glove comes in. Now if you wouldn't mind holding Agent Bull's hand please."

Tania looked at Jonah for a second, unsure of what to do as he offered his hand. She took it and gripped it firmly.

"What the scanner does," Elf continued, "is disperse an invisible beam of light through a person's hand. That light is then absorbed by the blood flow in their hand, creating a map of their veins that can then be used to gain access to whatever they have biometrically encrypted. Now when you use it tonight on Volkov, you need to hold it in place for at least ten seconds in order to record an imprint, which will then be transmitted to a receiver which Bull will have."

"Okay, I think I've got it." She let go of Jonah and then slid off the glove. "You know, this all seems rather daunting. Am I supposed to do this all on my own?"

"I'll be with you at the Catherine Palace," Jonah reminded her. "I'll be providing you with backup should anything go wrong. But I'll have to remain in the background, since I can't get close to Volkov. Only you can do that. However, we'll be maintaining continuous radio contact with each other."

"How will we do that?"

Elf reached for a box lying on top of the bed. Tania's eyes widened as he flipped the lid. Inside was a pair of sparkling earrings.

"These are a couple of gizmos I've adapted that you will need, courtesy of *Swarovski*."

"*Swarovski*?" she joked. "Not Tiffany's?"

Taking the question more seriously, he explained, "Crystals are easier to modify than diamonds. And besides, they have a long history of providing earrings for celebrities." He brought it closer for her to examine. "Now, the earrings house miniature two-way stereo transceivers with noise-cancelling technology. They have speakers close enough to your ears that you'll be able to hear Agent Bull when he speaks, while the large crystals on the lower parts of the earrings contain devices that create a field around the speakers to cancel out his voice outside a radius of two centimetres from your ear. So someone standing next to you will not be able to hear him even if he shouts at you. There are also microphones that will pick up what you're saying, even in a crowded room. Got it?"

"Crystal clear," she grinned.

Elf held up a tiny glittering object between his thumb and forefinger. It looked virtually indistinguishable from the other sequins on Tania's ballgown. "It's a miniature bugging device," he said. "Again, the crystal sequins are courtesy of *Swarovski*. You can pop it out and put it into his pocket. It's only a temporary solution, so once he changes out of his tux, that will be the end of that. But we only need it for this evening anyway."

Tania's eyes squinted as she peered to take a closer look. "I can't even tell them apart."

"That's the general idea," he replied. "Make sure you place it on him as early as possible."

She nodded in understanding, albeit with some measure of scepticism.

"Now there's one last piece of equipment to show you. In fact, Agent Bull is holding it right now."

Tania saw that Jonah had the masquerade mask in front of his face, seemingly fascinated as he peered through it.

"This mask has a thermal imaging camera that can take pictures from a distance of thirty feet," Elf explained. "It transmits the information directly back to Bull. There's a button on the detachable stick you use to hold the mask. This operates the camera. It enables you to see through objects or clothing."

Tania gasped. Bull was holding it directly in front of her. She gave him a long and marvellously direct look as she attempted to break the spell, then quickly brushed his arm away.

"Well you did tell me before I should admire the view," he said with a twisted grin.

Tania did not reply, but simply rolled her eyes and sighed.

"Now, any questions so far?" Elf asked, ready to go over anything again if necessary.

"No, I'm good," she replied.

"Well, if that's all, then I'll be off now."

"What, already?" Tania asked, as she watched him leave. "Where are you going?"

"I'm still working on cracking the encryption on the file uploaded to your phone," he replied.

"Really? What's on it that's so important it's worth killing over?"

"I don't know. We'll find out soon enough. I'm nearly done, but there's still a few hours' work. Well, it's been fun, but I have to go before it gets too late. I'll see you both later."

As Elf left, Tania and Bull walked back out into the living room and sat down at the table once again.

"He came all this way to Russia just to show me that?"

"Oh don't worry. He's off to our Moscow branch now," Jonah replied. "But he wouldn't have missed working with you for the world. Apparently he's a big fan."

Tania was flattered. She focused her attention on Bull, teasing him gently. "And you're not?"

He took the question seriously. "To be honest, I'd never actually heard of you before this mission."

She was slightly disappointed. "No way!"

"Yes," he replied earnestly. "I don't watch tennis. Never have."

She shrugged. "Well, neither do a lot of the guys who come to watch me play. Many are there to do a spot of sightseeing because they heard there was a tourist attraction there."

Jonah shook his head. "Not me."

Tania gave a look of surprise. "Well, in a way, that's a refreshing change. Most people treat me like a celebrity these days. Underneath I'm just an ordinary girl."

"Well, you'll get no special treatment from me."

Tania laughed uneasily. "I'm not sure how to take that." She reached for one of the dessert bowls on the table, dipped her spoon into the ice-cream and began swirling it around unconsciously. Sticking it straight into her mouth, she caressed the spoon lovingly with her tongue, savouring every bite. She stopped, suddenly florid with self-consciousness. He was watching her, as if she was performing some bizarre ritual. Spoon still firmly in mouth, she tried to stifle a giggle, her face reddening even further. "Sorry. You must find this all very weird, watching me eat."

"Oh no," he replied, a hint of sarcasm in his voice. "It's fascinating."

She began to giggle in a most delightful manner, but then attempted to make conversation to avoid leaving him sitting there in silence while she ate. "So is that all I get?"

Jonah raised an eyebrow. "What, that selection isn't enough?"

Tania grinned. "No. I'm talking about the equipment. Just a few recording devices? No cool gadgets. No form of training? After all, if IRIS is sending me undercover..."

"Don't worry," he assured her. "You're only going in to recover information. It should be a breeze - no action or anything involved at all."

"So what do I do once I've obtained what I need from Piotr?"

"When the evening is over, there'll be a car waiting to take you to a private jet at Pulkovo airport to fly you to wherever you want to go next. It's not far from the Catherine Palace, so it should only be a short journey."

Tania was curious. "And what will you do?"

"I'll head over to the Moscow branch and get any data analysed. Are you okay with everything we've discussed?"

"Yeah, I guess." She sounded hesitant, as if there may have been other concerns, but she was unsure whether she should share them with him.

Picking up on this, he probed further. "You don't sound convinced. Let me guess, you're still uneasy about this whole situation?"

"That would be an understatement," Tania smiled thinly. She looked down pensively for a few seconds, saying nothing, as she played with the dessert spoon in front of her.

"Well, just think of yourself like Maria Konnenkova," Bull suggested.

"Maria Kournikova?" Tania exclaimed, rolling her eyes in disbelief as she let out a frustrated sigh. "Oh, not you as well! Will these comparisons with previous Russian tennis players never end? And now you roll them both into one? I'm not the next..."

"She's *not* a tennis player," Bull replied, quickly setting her straight. "Maria *Konnenkova* was a Russian spy who went to the US in 1924, and dated Albert Einstein in order to gather top secret information on the US nuclear weapons programme, codenamed 'the Manhattan Project' and feed it back to the Soviets without arousing any suspicion."

Tania shot him a look of incredulity. "You're making this up, right?"

Bull shook his head. "Hey Google her if you don't believe me."

"I'm sorry," Tania apologised. "I'm afraid I don't spend much time at the net."

"Well it's there if you want to look her up," Bull suggested. "Anyway, you could be just like her, except of course you won't be dating a nuclear scientist, just a RISK agent."

"Well I'm kind of uneasy about deceiving Piotr, lying to him and doing things behind his back."

"You already know he's bad and that he's done the same to you. You've seen his file."

She grimaced. "But people are more than just a file. You can't simply judge someone on what it says on a few pieces of paper or on a computer. A file doesn't say anything about what that person is like in real life. It's only a sketch, not the whole picture."

"Well, you might not really see what a person is really like until you've known them a few years. They could maintain an image whenever they're around you, but only show their true colours once you've grown used to seeing them through rose-tinted spectacles. There's a lot you could miss. I mean, you didn't know anything about his daughter."

She nodded her head dully in agreement. "Well, that's true."

"I mean, how long have you been dating him?"

"Oh, about five months," she replied. "But I've been pretty busy on the women's tour, so we don't always see each other all that often."

"Then how can you think you know him well?" Bull seemed determined not to let this go without making his point.

Tania shrugged her shoulders. "Some people you connect with more easily than others."

Bull nodded in acknowledgement. "True. But first impressions aren't everything."

"No, they aren't," she agreed.

"How do you know him anyway?"

Tania pursed her lips as she recalled the event. "We met at a post-Oscar bash earlier this year that I was invited to. I guess he swept me off my feet there and then, but because of our schedules, we didn't see each other for a couple of months or so, until out of the blue he turned up again. Then things just developed from there."

"And what won you over?" There was a definite ring of inquisitiveness in his voice which he did not attempt to disguise.

Tania studied him. Why was he so curious about her personal life? Was he genuinely interested or simply trying to manoeuvre her into relinquishing any lingering feeling she may still have for Piotr?

"Maybe his humour?" she offered tentatively, almost running each quality by him like a checklist. "And his acceptance? Oh, and his openness too? He seemed like he was one of these people where 'what you see is what you get.'"

"I can see that worked out well," he said sardonically.

She hung her head sadly. "Well I thought it at the time."

"Sometimes love brings two people so close together they can't see what's wrong with each other. Especially when they're that intimate."

Tania frowned, trying to gauge whether she had understood him correctly. "I haven't slept with him yet, if that's what you're suggesting. Like I said, I'm not that kind of girl. I prefer to wait. Make sure he's the right one and everything's perfect."

"Some might call that outdated or too idealistic."

"Or romantic."

He shook his head. "Personally, I think that romance is over-rated."

"Now that's a rather cynical statement if I ever heard one."

"Not cynical," he countered. "Just cautious. There's a difference."

"You could've fooled me. You almost sound as if you've given up on love, and I'm almost tempted to say on life in general as well."

Bull shifted the conversation back to the mission at hand, feeling that he might be prying too deeply. "Well, maybe he does have some redeeming qualities, but that doesn't change the facts about him, and that we need that information from him."

"Yeah," she nodded understandingly, if not entirely convinced. Tania had no urge to continue discussing this either, so she raised a different question instead. "What if I run into trouble? Say I have to fight someone off?"

"That shouldn't happen…"

"Humour me. Let's say it does."

"Well then your Systema training should come in handy."

Tania sighed anxiously. "So I've been told. But remember, I'm not a spy, I'm a tennis player, and the Systema was more to help me with that. I'm not sure how helpful my training will be, unless the baddies are planning to challenge me to a game of tennis." She mimicked a backhand motion with her dessert spoon as she spoke these things. To her surprise, the contents of it flew across the table, landing on Jonah's shirt. A big, sticky red stain that looked more like blood.

Bull glanced down at his shirt, then raised an eyebrow. "Hey that was an expensive shirt."

Tania gasped, clasping her hand over her mouth before bursting into a fit of shrill giggles, laughing with repeated intakes of breath. "I'm so sorry," she chirped, reaching for his shirt with a paper napkin as she dimpled with a mischievous grin suggesting she might secretly have found it too funny to truly be sorry after all. "Here, let me clean it up for you."

"It's okay," Bull assured her, lightly brushing her hand away from him. "You don't have to do that. I'll clean it up myself."

"No, I don't mind. I'd feel a lot better. I'll even buy you a new one."

At that moment Tania's phone beeped, causing her to glance down at it.

"Text message?" Jonah asked, as he wiped the stain off his shirt.

"Yeah," she muttered, still in a good mood as she read the message to herself. "Now who could be texting me here?"

"Something important?" Jonah inquired.

"Uh, it's my friend, Isabelle," Tania replied. "I'll have to make sure to call her later."

"Look, don't worry about the mess," he assured her, switching back to the matter before they were interrupted.

"Well I'd tell you to keep your shirt on," Tania said drolly, with her characteristic cheeky Cheshire Cat grin spreading across her face, "but I'm sure you'll be eager to go and change it now."

"Yes." Bull cleared his throat. "Now might be a good time for a break. You might as well get some rest. We have a mission to carry out tonight."

Rest? Tania glanced down at her watch. She had less than five hours to take a nap and then get ready. And with her stomach turning somersaults at the prospect of what lay ahead, could she hope to get any rest at all?

It was going to be a long evening.

Chapter 12

Sunday evening.

A sleek black stretch Limousine pulled into a dazzling white, snow-filled courtyard in the town of *Tsarkoye Selo*, the Tsar's village, that resembled a fairy-tale winter scene. The other guests were also arriving in style.

Within seconds, the chauffeur was no longer behind the wheel. He hurried around to the rear of the car to help the passengers out, secretly imagining himself as a faithful footman waiting on a golden carriage with Cinderella inside. He drew open the shiny black door and extended a gloved hand. The first thing he saw emerging was a pair of impossibly long, slender legs in open-toed stilettos. His eyes would've remained fixated there, ogling them, but as a professional driver trained to maintain the proper decorum, his face was like stone and he averted his gaze. The female to whom the legs belonged took his hand firmly and clambered out, gradually and gracefully.

With her golden hair swept up, and dressed up to the nines in the stunning ballgown under her mink fur coat, Tania looked more

Hollywood starlet than tennis star. Inside however, she felt like a Russian princess.

Tania's eyes bulged, her mouth wide open in child-like astonishment as she stood there, beholding her breathtaking surroundings.

So this is the Catherine Palace.

Before her was a magnificent, elaborately ornamental baroque structure that stretched out as far as she could see. The grandiose building was in fact three hundred and twenty five metres long, with the entire length of its vibrant azure façade punctuated by row after row of snow-white pilasters and balustrades with massive gold-leafed Atlas-shaped figures supporting the upper floors. At the northern end of the palace sat gold onion-shaped domes above the Palace Church. A tidal wave of celebrities, businessmen and dignitaries was still pouring in through the main entrances.

The Catherine Palace sat atop a small hill, surrounded by lush, geometrically-laid out gardens with elegant pavilions, classical statuary, decorous ponds and avenues, as well as a ceremonial courtyard. It was regarded by many as one of the masterpieces of world architecture and art. But to the wide-eyed Russian, it was more like an enchanting fairy-tale castle from the stories she had read as a child.

"Impressive, isn't it?" a familiar voice sounded from behind. It was Piotr.

"Wow," was all the awestruck tennis star could manage. She was in her element.

"It was built as the Summer Palace of the Russian Tsarina, Catherine the Great," Volkov informed her.

"It's so cool," she cooed. "I love the style."

"It's called rococo. It was designed by the Italian architect, Bartolomeo Rastrelli, the same person who designed the Winter Palace near the Hermitage. But Yekaterina disliked it. Apparently she thought it looked like whipped cream."

Tania stood there wistfully, taking a moment to soak in the magical atmosphere that appeared even more wondrous bathed in the silvery light of the full moon. The chatter of guests outside faded out of consciousness as she was momentarily caught up in her own reverie.

This place is so romantic. If only I had been coming here under better circumstances.

She paused to feel the chilly night air tingling on her skin. It made her feel alive with exhilaration, even though the light, wintry wind was nipping at her ears. She had left behind her Siberian hat, as there was simply no question of messing up her beautifully-styled hair that had taken hours to fix. She pulled the fur coat more tightly around her as her gaze wandered down towards the thick blanket of snow, still fresh on the ground like crisp powder beneath her feet.

"A little early for snow in St Petersburg?" Tania remarked as she turned to Piotr, seeing for the first time that he was clad in an elegant tuxedo.

"Perhaps," he agreed, whispering into her ear. "It should clear up by next week. But at least the guests can enjoy the troika rides now." He drew a circle with his open hand to point towards the courtyard.

Tania surveyed the area to see where he was pointing. Sure enough, there were a few colourfully-decorated troikas, currently stationary, each drawn by a team of three powerful and immaculately-groomed horses. Nearby, the horsemen stood next to them, marking their territory whilst taking pride in their animals. She noticed several elegantly-crafted carriages, some of which were painted with light blue or lilac flower motifs, with a removable canvas hood attached to the back. The harnesses were adorned with rosettes, leather tassels, and not least of all, duga bells. When the horses were on the move, these could be heard into the night for miles around. In the summer, the troikas were driven on wheels, but the far more popular option was with sleighs in winter. Naturally this evening, they were fitted with the latter, so that everyone could experience the thrill of gliding across the frosted landscape.

"Sleigh rides in September?" Her voice tinkled with a soft giggle. "This should be fun."

Somewhat bemused, Tania reached to take Piotr's arm, as they strolled together towards the palace entrance where the guests were still bustling. At the corner of her eye, she caught sight of several Ural motorcycles with side-cars, along with a number of black Volga Sedan FSB patrol cars parked outside. Dotting the perfect field of white, like craters in a piece of Swiss cheese, were tracks of boot and paw prints alongside each other. Taking a further look, Tania saw several dark green-uniformed FSB guards were patrolling the area. Some were wearing black, rabbit fur *Ushanka* hats with ear flaps, and had German Shepherd dogs with them. This was obviously a high security event if it merited such measures.

After a formal welcome inside the entrance, the tennis star left her outer coat and arrived at the bottom of the Grand Staircase at the centre of the palace. On the walls and ceiling around the staircase area were white plaster ornaments, a carved marble balustrade and stucco decorations moulded in various baroque sculptures and garlands. The white marble steps ascended from both sides to a central landing at the top of the staircase with three arched windows dressed with crimson draperies.

She reached the upper landing. The floor had a chequered pattern resembling a giant chessboard. The staircase led to the state rooms on the first floor. With some time to spare before the formal banquet and ballroom dancing, she and Piotr began to explore the area. They ambled to the north of the staircase on the courtyard side towards the State Dining Room, Crimson and Green Pilaster Rooms and the Portrait Room. Each proved to be a curious mix of eclectic styles. Piotr explained that this was in large part because Catherine II was not fond of the palace, despite its beautiful design. Consequently, she had had many parts of the interior design altered to suit her tastes.

Brushing past more guests along the way, also engaged in their own individual tours of the building, Tania eventually arrived at one of the most splendid areas in the entire palace - the famed Amber Room. Built from over six tons of amber and presented by the King of Prussia to the Russian Tsar, Peter the Great, its treasures had been looted by the Nazis. The original room had then literally disappeared at the end of World War II, with the location shrouded in mystery and numerous conspiracy theories. However, a new version of the room had recently been reconstructed from photos and inaugurated at the Catherine Palace in 2003. This boasted original carved reliefs and panels in Florentine mosaic.

Tania pulled away from Piotr to walk freely by herself, taking in the splendid baroque surroundings and pondering the fate of the fabled room and the air of intrigue surrounding it. *Hmm. How does one lose something like that?*

Suddenly, she heard a voice coming from her earring. Seeing Piotr still strolling through the room behind a number of guests, she moved further away towards the exit to gain some privacy, brushing a few strands of hair over her ear instinctively, even though this action was unnecessary and might have been seen as somewhat conspicuous.

"Tania," the voice said. "This is Jonah. Can you hear me?"

"Uh huh," she confirmed. "Where are you?"

"I'm here," he replied, touching her on her shoulder.

Tania spun around to see Bull dressed in a tuxedo, looking decidedly more elegant than she had been used to seeing him thus far. Bull had already made a quick but thorough reconnaissance of the immense complex, checking for emergency exits and potential pitfalls.

She took a moment to size him up. *Hmm, not bad.*

"What are you doing here?" she inquired. "I thought you wanted to keep a low profile tonight. Piotr might see you."

"Well it can't be helped. There was one piece of equipment that you forgot to take with you."

"Oh what's that?"

"The bug," he said, placing the device disguised as one of her dress sequins in the palm of her hand. "You left this behind."

"Oh whoops," Tania exclaimed, inwardly kicking herself for not remembering. "Well thanks."

"No problem. Just be more careful next time," he assured her. "Now I'll be wandering around in the background but I'll be tuned into you all evening and will be able to hear everything that's said."

"That's fine," she replied. But was it? Tania wasn't entirely sure she was comfortable with the idea of someone listening in on her every conversation, allowing her no personal space of her own. But she fully understood the need for such things.

"By the way, if I may say so, you're looking particularly lovely tonight. Very fetching."

"Why, thank you for the compliment," Tania beamed, blushing slightly. "I didn't think you had noticed."

"Don't you worry. I've got my eye on you. Professionally speaking that is."

"Oh. Standard IRIS policy to be checking me out then?" she quipped.

"Of course."

Tania laughed sweetly. "Well you look dashing too."

Their light-hearted little moment was interrupted as a voice called from behind. "Tatya. Who is this? I don't believe we've been introduced."

"Oh no, it's Piotr," Tania whispered. She whipped around and gave him a nervous, flashing smile. "Piotr, this is Mr...."

"Ivan Bulsky," Bull lied, adopting a fake Russian accent before Tania could give away his real name.

"Well Mr Bulsky, a pleasure to meet you. I'm Piotr Volkov. How do you know the lovely Tatiana?"

"I'm just after an autograph, that's all."

"Oh really?" Piotr remarked. "From the laughter there, it seemed as if you knew each other."

"I like to chat to my fans," Tania interjected.

"I see, Piotr nodded encouragingly. "So have you obliged the gentleman yet?"

"Hmm?"

"The gentleman wants an autograph doesn't he, Tatya?"

"Oh, of course," Tania said with a flustered smile, realising that Piotr may not be buying the story. She looked over at Bull. "Do you have something for me to sign?"

Bull pulled out a photograph of Tania from his pocket, the same one that Elf had given him days before. He handed it to the Russian tennis star.

"And what line of business are you in, if I may ask?" Piotr inquired, as Tania scribbled her name hurriedly over her image. He seemed rather inquisitive.

"I'm just an eye specialist," Bull said dryly.

"How interesting," Volkov exclaimed. "Well people always say that the eyes are the windows to the soul – a reflection of a person's heart inside. You can usually tell whether they're deceiving you or not, or they can reveal hidden truths about a man."

"Is that so?"

"Indeed. For instance, if I were to gaze through the looking glass into your eyes right now, I'm sure it could tell me many secrets."

Tania's heart started beating rapidly and for a moment she forgot to breathe. Was Piotr suspicious?

Taking the bait, Bull looked at Volkov unflinchingly. "And what secrets do my eyes tell you?"

"Hmm." Volkov's brow furrowed in concentration, studying Bull for a tense moment that seemed to last forever. "I spy with my little eye…"

Oh no. Tania bit her lip. *He does know something.*

Finally Volkov broke into a smile. "Your eyes are telling me that deep down, you're a very ardent admirer of Miss Likamolova here."

"Well naturally," Bull agreed, humouring him. "She is a very beautiful young woman."

Tania breathed a sigh of relief. This verbal swordplay was too much for her. "Come on, Piotr," she said. "I'm sure Mr Bull…"

"Mr Bulsky," Piotr corrected her.

"Mr Bulsky," she repeated, kicking herself inwardly for that little slip. "I knew it was something bovine-related. I'm sure Mr Bulsky doesn't like being put on the spot like this."

"Oh, I hope you'll forgive me," Piotr offered, extending a hand graciously towards Bull. "I didn't mean to do that at all."

"No problem at all," Bull assured him.

"Well nice to meet you, Mr Bulsky," Volkov said warmly. "And you take good care of your eyes, won't you?"

"Don't worry," Bull muttered, barely audible as the couple turned to leave. "I always have them open."

Tania followed Piotr back towards the Grand Staircase. She could hear the magnificent sound of music emanating from the Great Hall. They turned right and walked through the First and Second Exhibition Halls. Among the various items included here were a quaint, scale wooden model of the Catherine Palace, display cabinets with historical documents and photographs, and sketches, plans and materials relating to the restoration of the Palace after World War II.

She entered the Great Hall, which was buzzing with the low hum of chatter and activity beneath the orchestral music of Tchaikovsky. She stood speechless. The entire ballroom was also designed in a Russian baroque style of rich décor and ornamental splendour. The first thing that struck her were the hundreds of glittering, golden chandelier-mounted lights reflecting like stars in the elaborately-carved pier-glass mirrors and the polished dark and light oak parquet flooring. She looked more carefully and saw that these mirrors sat between two tiers of gilt-framed windows on each side of the hall, giving the impression of an enormous room filled with a sea of guests awash in colour. The men were dressed in elegant tuxedos, while the ladies wore beautiful ball gowns made of velvet or satin, in shades of crimson, damson or pearl. Yet, despite the abundance of high fashion, Tania still cut a glamorous figure, like the brightest jewel in a crown.

A number of immaculately-dressed waiters and waitresses sauntered around the room, balancing silver salvers laden with blini and black caviar, and of course, *Zolot* Vodka. Without a second thought, Piotr went over to intercept one and fetch her a drink, leaving her standing by herself.

She craned her neck upward. On the ceiling above was a huge painted mural entitled *The Triumph of Russia*, by Giuseppe Valeriani, depicting a colonnade reaching heavenward, with various figures floating on the backdrop of a blue sky, giving the illusion of even more space above.

This place looks amazing. Who'd have thought my first time coming here would be for some mission instead of a social event?

As the evening wore on, Tania enjoyed the company of the distinguished guests as she engaged in lively conversation and banter, trading back and forth anecdotes and new introductions, while the orchestra now played highlights from Tchaikovsky's *The Sleeping Beauty*. However, in the back of her mind, a sense of anxiety was building and overshadowed every exchange. She was eager for Piotr to make his move so that she could get down to business and be done with this whole affair.

Her chance came unexpectedly.

"Tatya", Volkov announced. "I need to speak to a colleague privately. Would you excuse me?"

"Oh sure," she replied, giving a gentle wave of her hand. She suddenly remembered that she needed to plant the bugging device on him that Jonah had given her, just as her phone began to ring.

Damn. Of all the worst possible moments.

Attempting both tasks together, she popped out one of her sequins and slipped the sparkling stone into Piotr's pocket just as he was pulling away, and at the same time pressed the answer button on her phone to take the call.

"Tania," a female voice spoke brightly. "It's Isabelle."

"Oh it's you," she blurted out surprisedly. She had not expected anyone to call her now, least of all her best friend.

"Of course," Isabelle chuckled. "Who else? You sound kind of shocked to hear me."

"No, it's just… I wasn't expecting anyone." Tania loved to speak to her friend under normal circumstances, but these were hardly normal. As if she needed the added distraction right now.

"You pretty much disappeared after the end of the US Open," Isabelle continued, accepting her friend's explanation. "You haven't been returning any of my calls."

"I'm sorry," Tania replied. "I didn't feel like seeing anyone. I was a bit upset."

"Sure," Isabelle sympathised. "I understand. Did you really have to get rid of your dress so soon though?"

"My dress?" Tania paused for a moment, trying to keep two trains of thought running in parallel. A trace of anguish became evident in her voice. "Well, I just thought it would be better to auction it off. Maybe my fans might like it. After all, it didn't bring me that much luck at the US Open this year, and it's for a good cause."

"Okay, well if that's how you feel I won't argue with you."

Tania's phone conversation was interrupted by Bull's voice coming from her earring. "Have you planted the bug on Volkov yet?"

"Oh hang on a sec," she told Isabelle, moving the phone away from her ear. She whispered to Bull. "Yes I did. Can you hear him?"

His reply was unexpected. "No, you still have it on you."

"What?" Tania's mouth fell open in horror. "But I just slipped it into his pocket." She began to double-check for herself, examining the sequins on her Basque bodice. Sure enough, to her dismay, it was still there. "Oh no, Jonah. I've planted the wrong one on him."

"How could you do that?" he groaned.

"I was a little distracted by the phone."

"Well you're on a mission, so hang up and go and put it on him now."

"I can't do that," she replied. "It's my friend, Isabelle."

"So where are you at the moment?" Isabelle inquired, overhearing her name and thinking it was her cue to resume the conversation again.

Tania placed the phone back to her ear. "Um...nowhere in particular." She pulled the sequin off, planning to wander over to Piotr with some excuse, and plant it for real this time.

"Nowhere in particular?" Isabelle exclaimed. "You must be somewhere. I hear music playing in the background. You sound like you're at a party. Did you go to St Petersburg after all?"

"Uh, yeah," Tania was forced to admit as she began walking towards Piotr before he got too far.

Isabelle was puzzled. "I thought you weren't going to go."

"I changed my mind at the last minute."

Suddenly, Tania was jostled by a passing guest who knocked the sequin out of her hand. She gasped, watching helplessly as it bounced and went sliding across the floor, while her boyfriend moved towards the Ballroom entrance area and began conversing with another man.

"So wait, let me get this straight," Isabelle said, summarising the situation from her perspective. "You didn't want to see anyone, including me, and yet you're socialising at a party?" There was a distinct ring of hurt in her voice.

"Umm..." Tania was cornered. Unable to think clearly. What excuse could she possibly give? And even if she could find one, she was a little distracted at the moment.

"What's the matter?" Bull pressed her.

Tania pulled the phone away from her ear. "Someone bumped me. I've lost the bug."

He was incredulous. "You were supposed to plant it on him earlier."

"Well I got mixed up."

"And we both know why."

"Well you did say they were virtually indistinguishable from each other. At least you can tell Elf he did a good job. I'll just have to find it on the floor." She began searching frantically for the sequin amidst the reflective parquet surface. It was impossible to see. A veritable needle in a haystack.

"You can't do that," Jonah said. "There are hundreds of people in there. It will look suspicious with a celebrity crawling around down on the floor."

"So I'll just tell them I lost an earring or something. People do that all the time, you know. Even on tennis courts."

"Tania are you still there?" came the voice on the end of her phone again. "I hope you're not avoiding me?"

Oh no. Isabelle. She had temporarily forgotten about her.

"No, I promise you I'm not," Tania assured her apologetically.

"Who's that you're talking to?" Isabelle quizzed her.

"No-one. Just a guest. I'm actually kind of in the middle of something right now though."

"Leave the bug," Bull said, coming through Tania's earring again. "Use the zoom on the camera in your mask to see what they're doing instead."

Tania ignored him, stubbornly intent on finding that blasted listening device. Where did it roll to?

Isabelle's voice softened. "Look, I'm not trying to put you on the spot or anything. Maybe that came out harsher than I meant. I just called to remind you that it'll be a black tie event."

"What will?" Tania was flustered, her concentration all over the place.

"My birthday party, silly. You haven't forgotten already have you?"

"No, of course not," Tania lied. The truth was, with all the mayhem that had transpired in the last few days, it had temporarily slipped her mind. But she had no intention of missing it.

"Good, well listen if you're busy right now I'll see you there on Tuesday."

"Okay, see ya."

Tania sighed in frustration as she disconnected the line. It was no use. She threw her hands up in despair. Time for Plan B.

"Okay, I'm using the thermal camera now," she whispered. She held up her mask on the stick and attempted to watch Volkov and his contact from a distance.

"Don't let them out of your sight," Bull cautioned her.

"I'm trying," she whispered, her lips barely moving. "But I can't get any closer without looking conspicuous."

As she stood there, a voice from behind her spoke. "I've caught you at last."

Caught?

She whipped around, startled. "I'm sorry?"

The man gave a proud, patrician smile, emphasising his avuncular appearance. "I'm Oleg Cyrilovich Korsakov, your host for this evening."

She returned the smile, breathing an inward sigh of relief. *That was close.* It wouldn't do to be caught so early on in this mission. But still, he was diverting her attention away from where she knew it should be focused. As if one distraction hadn't been enough.

"I was hoping to catch you before I left," he continued.

Lowering the mask so her face was revealed, she asked, "You're leaving already?"

He nodded. "Yes. In a few moments at least. I am afraid that this Ball is largely for my guests to enjoy. I must retire early for the evening. I have a business meeting early tomorrow morning. But enough about me. Although everyone knows you, we haven't been formally introduced."

Damn. There was no way she could divide her attention between Piotr and Korsakov now without it appearing rude. She would simply have to humour her host for a few minutes and pray that she could figure something out. Hopefully Jonah would understand her current predicament.

She extended a hand towards Korsakov and announced proudly, "Tatiana Ulyanovna Likamolova."

"Tatiana? It is a beautiful Russian name." He complimented her urbanely as he took her hand and pressed it to his lips, kissing it lightly. "Derived from the name Titania, I believe - a fairy queen from *A Midsummer Night's Dream*. Quite fitting for a tsarina like you at a summer palace fairy-tale ball, do you not think?"

She acknowledged him and smiled artificially. *That sounded like a line.*

If it did, the next one intrigued her.

"Do you know you have a heart of gold?" he continued benignly.

"*Prastiye?*" She gave a bemused look. "Pardon me?"

"Your name. Tatiana Ulyanovna. Ends in A. Begins in U. Au is the chemical symbol for gold."

She had to admit she never noticed that. Even so, it sounded like another line.

He's totally hitting on me, she told herself. However, with constant professions of undying love both on-court and off, she was used to it by now. Besides, she had work to do here.

"Speaking of gold," she said, steering the subject onto something else, "I hear you head up your own company, Red Gold."

"Yes," he replied, his ego having been stroked. "Have you tried *Zolot* Vodka yet?"

"No."

Korsakov grabbed a glass from a passing waitress and proffered it to her. "Here. Drink up."

"Thanks." Tania bravely took a sip and almost choked as a burning sensation rose up in her chest. "Strong stuff," she sputtered, clearing her throat.

"Nonsense," he replied, waving a dismissive hand. "You get used to it."

Well there was no time for such luxuries. Tania needed to have her wits perfectly about her tonight. She would simply hold the glass for the remainder of the conversation.

"So I remember you were in the Forbes 100 list," she said, scrambling around for something of interest to say which would keep Korsakov talking while she allowed her eyes to glance over at Piotr's location.

"You've obviously been paying attention, Tatiana Ulyanovna. But must we talk about business tonight?"

"I'm just interested, that's all," she lied. The Siberian beauty smiled demurely, turning her charm up several notches as she placed her hand on his arm.

"Really? Well if you're that interested, perhaps you might consider endorsing some of my products? We're having a shoot in Xi'an this Tuesday with a number of supermodels. Of course, with your catwalk looks, you would fit right in."

"I don't know about that. You know how it is playing tennis full time."

Another quick dart of her eyes in Piotr's direction.

"Well here's my business card if you ever change your mind." He placed it in Tania's hand. "But pardon me for saying so, you seem somewhat distracted."

"How do you mean?" Her eyes quickly refocused upon him. Was he growing suspicious? She had been careless.

"You keep peering over my shoulder." He turned around to see where Tania was looking. "Ah, your boyfriend Piotr Sergeyevich?"

"Yes. Just checking up, you know." She let out a fake laugh to confirm her excuse. No need to let him know that she was actually observing him for other reasons. "So how well do you know him?"

"He works for me. We know each other in a business capacity, that's all."

"And who's that he's talking to?"

"Why, that's Konstantin Chernovsky."

***

Volkov waited patiently as Chernovsky removed a smartphone from his pocket. Tapping a few buttons on a miniature keyboard, the man accessed the PDA function.

"You will forgive me for the delay, Comrade Volkov," he explained in Russian. "But I am sure you'll understand that I haven't been carrying the details with me until now."

"That is fine," Volkov assured him. "We must all take precautions. But please, none of this 'Comrade' business. We may both serve RISK, but this is modern Russia, not the Cold War Soviet Union. We don't want to be addressing each other socially in that way."

"I apologise, Comrade… er, Captain Volkov. You are young. For me, old habits die hard."

"Well get with it, as the Americans would say," Volkov replied, slightly irritated as he watched while the details were being transmitted to his phone.

When the transmission had ended, Chernovsky looked up. "Everything is in order here."

"*Kharashó*. Very good."

Just then, the strident sound of Chernovsky's phone began to ring, with the sound of Tchaikovsky's *Trepak Russian Dance* from *The Nutcracker*.

"Excuse me a moment," Chernovsky apologised as he looked down. "I must take this call. It's my wife. She has me on a tight leash. She's been bothering me all evening."

Volkov grinned, slightly amused. "Catchy ringtone you've got there. But with that tune, tonight it could almost blend in with the rest of the orchestra here."

Chernovsky laughed as he put the phone to his ear. "Not likely. I can hear this a mile off."

Volkov smiled. "Well I'll take your word for it. Anyway, I'll let you take your call. Good luck. *Udachi*."

***

Korsakov exchanged a few more words with Tania before thanking her for the conversation and leaving to mingle with other guests before he retired for the evening.

"I'm sorry about that," Tania said to Jonah, as she turned her back away from Piotr's direction.

"Your timing leaves a bit to be desired. You should've been concentrating on Volkov and Chernovsky at the time."

She sighed. "Well, it wasn't entirely up to me."

"You could've gotten rid of him."

"But that would be a bit rude."

"Never mind. Did you see whether they exchanged information?"

"I think they did," she replied. "But I can't be sure." She had to admit it was somewhat difficult to see with Korsakov breathing down her neck.

"You need to find out."

Suddenly, a voice spoke from behind her. "Are you okay?"

Tania spun around. It was Piotr.

"Sure," she replied, her eyes blinking rapidly as her cheeks turned a rosy red, and a guilty look stole across her face.

"I thought I heard you talking to someone."

"Oh that?" Tania began fumbling around for an excuse. "I… I sometimes like to go through my tennis routine by talking to myself. It's called visualisation."

"Here?"

"Why not?" Tania lied. "I need to keep up the practice, even when I'm not on court."

Piotr looked unconvinced. At least that's what her paranoia told her. His eyes seemed to be probing hers. "You're blushing. Is everything okay?" he inquired. "You seem a little tense. Not quite comfortable around me this evening."

Tania shrugged, forcing a smile. "No, I… I'm fine. I'm just tired from playing at the US Open, and I guess I'm still upset by my loss."

"It meant a lot to you, didn't it?"

"Yes. Of course." Her shallow breath grew fuller, as the pressure began to subside ever so slightly. Piotr seemed to buy it.

"I saw you talking to Korsakov. What were you talking about?"

"Nothing much. Just small talk." At least that was mostly true. She decided to direct the attention away from herself. "Who were *you* talking to?"

"Oh, a colleague," he prevaricated, giving away nothing.

"Uh huh," Tania nodded, pretending to believe him.

"Well, I'm glad you decided to come here tonight, take your mind off everything."

"Yeah, I guess you were right," Tania agreed, taking Piotr's hand in her own. "I'm having a great time." She held his hand for a few seconds as she gazed intently into his eyes and smiled. The vascular biometric circuitry in Tania's glove began to scan his palm, recording an imprint of his veins.

"That's great." Piotr replied, attempting to wrest his hand out of hers.

"Just a few seconds longer," Bull whispered in Tania's ear.

She clutched Piotr's hand more tightly in order to complete the scan, then made a suggestion. "We should dance."

"Scan received," Bull informed her. "You can let go now."

As she released her grip, Piotr looked at his watch. "Unfortunately Tania, as much as I'd love to, I'm going to have to leave early."

"What?" She was stunned. Hadn't expected this at all. "And may I ask why?"

"I have other pressing business to attend to."

Tania tried to think quickly. "Well, take me with you."

"No, no. You stay here and enjoy yourself. You came all this way for this and it will help you forget your loss."

"But... you can't go yet." She hadn't had the chance to get hold of Piotr's phone.

"Oh, I can't, can't I?" he teased her.

She composed herself. "I mean, when will I see you again?"

"Soon," came the vague answer. Before she could finish protesting, Piotr kissed her goodbye.

She did not enjoy it, now armed with the knowledge she possessed about him. She pulled away from him and tried to shift the attention away from the kiss. "At least tell me where you're going."

Volkov placed a finger over his lips. "A man's got to have some secrets." He winked at her and left.

Tania stood there, not knowing what to do, as she wiped away the lingering trace of him from her lips. With things the way they were between the two of them, it left a bitter taste in her mouth. "He's gone," she said frustratedly. "What do I do now?"

Bull let out a sigh of impatience through her ear-piece. "Why did you let him get away?"

"Well I couldn't exactly beg him to stay."

"Why not? You need to do what you have to do."

"He'll get suspicious," Tania replied. "Besides, it'll make me look desperate. And I'm definitely not that."

"So now this is about your image or reputation?" he snapped.

"I told you I wasn't cut out for this line of work." She began to walk slowly through the ballroom. "So what do I do now?"

"Okay, Plan B. Find Chernovsky," he huffed. "You'll have to get from the source instead. Use your mask. You should be able to get a thermal image of where he keeps his phone."

Tania positioned herself so that Chernovsky was in her line of sight. She held up her masquerade mask and gazed in his direction, studying him surreptitiously. The thermal image revealed it was located in his outside left side-pocket.

"You'll have to swipe it from him," Jonah told her.

"Swipe it?" Tania exclaimed. "How do I do that?"

"Use your imagination. And don't forget to scan his palm."

Tania sighed wearily. *Use your imagination?* What was she supposed to do?

Ditching the holding stick, she put on her mask and sauntered over to Chernovsky to the strains of the *Entrance of the Good Fairies* from the *Prologue* of *The Sleeping Beauty*. Could she pull this off, or would her nerves threaten to overwhelm her? On court, she was fearless when it came to playing the big points, even when the pressure was mounting. Now, however, her legs were weak with fear. She was out of her depth. Making this up as she went along. Yet there was precious little time to formulate another plan.

Chernovsky was engaged deep in conversation with a few of the other guests, although fortunately, it appeared light-hearted and therefore not something that he would be averse to having interrupted.

"Ask him to dance," Bull suggested.

"That's all very well," she replied, fiddling with the diamond bracelet around her wrist, "but I'm more used to dancing in a nightclub than a ballroom."

"Just ask him," he repeated, urging her on. "And make sure to let him lead."

Tania took a deep breath. Steeled herself for what she had to do. Then, assuming an air of confidence, she flicked back her hair and entered Chernovsky's circle, her head held high.

"*Privet*," she greeted him in Russian, offering her hand out towards him and lacing her voice with syrup, as she gave a salacious smile. "Would you like to dance with me?" Through the holes in her mask, her large emerald eyes were both aloof and inviting, her expression seductive and mesmerising.

Chernovsky looked up at this most enchanting Russian nymph standing before him, amazed at such a request. He was hesitant in taking her hand. It was unusual that one might be graced by her company so unexpectedly. "Me?" he asked cautiously.

"Sure," she confirmed, rolling her shoulders upwards in her typical demure manner, which was more indicative of her true self. "You know how it is being a celebrity? Everyone feels intimidated by you, so you can sometimes end up being alone at the party?"

There was a silent pause for a few seconds. Chernovsky appeared to be studying her carefully. She was fluctuating oddly between being both seductive and innocent, causing a contradiction in his mind. Would he accept her invitation? She waited to see how Chernovsky would respond for what seemed like an eternity. As she was about to try another strategy, hopefully something more diplomatic, he unexpectedly extended his hand towards her.

"Please, lead on," he said, escorting her across the ballroom floor as the orchestra segued flawlessly from one piece to the next.

Recognising the romantic music playing as the famous *Waltz* from *The Sleeping Beauty*, she was swept up in the moment as they began to move in unison. In her heels, the statuesque Siberian towered over her partner by at least a couple of inches.

With her hand held firmly in his, she began scanning his palm with the biometric scanner built into her glove. Her partner drew her towards him as they glided skilfully like two ice dancers across the floor, carefully avoiding any collision with the other couples. Strangely enough, despite the unusual situation, she found herself enjoying this interplay between music and movement. As the dance progressed, she suddenly felt an unwelcome hand wandering from her waist across her bare back.

She cringed inside. *Oh great. What's he up to?*

She would never normally allow that with someone she didn't know. But what choice did she have? Of course, if Chernovsky was going to let his hands deviate from its proper place, perhaps she could return the favour and swipe the phone from his pocket. He might not notice at all.

"What are you waiting for?" Bull urged her through her earring. "Grab it and get out of there."

Tania ignored him. She pulled her partner closer and tried to move her hand towards the area in question. She felt the rectangular bulge of the phone through the cloth. Just one quick sleight of hand and it would be hers for the taking.

As she began to reach in, suddenly, she felt Chernovsky pulling her arm upwards, firmly but gently. She gasped silently. Had she been found out?

"You're letting your elbows drop too low," he said, smiling. "You need to keep them up at a certain height during a waltz."

Tania pressed her lips together to return a nervous smile. "You know, I'm not that great with waltzes. Let's not make this dance overly formal.

Why don't you just hold me close and just move to the music without worrying too much about form?"

Chernovsky glanced briefly at his dance partner. "You're right." He let his arm drop and relaxed.

"That's better," she remarked.

"Quit the small talk and get his phone," came Bull's voice, whispering through Tania's ear-piece.

"Yes dad," she muttered, before realising that she had spoken this aloud. Chernovsky was eyeing her in a strange way, almost suspiciously.

"Did you just call me 'dad'," he inquired, his curiosity piqued.

The flustered tennis star scrambled through her mind to find an excuse. "Sorry, I was just thinking of him for some reason. Not that you look anything like him at all."

Chernovsky grinned, and let the comment go, chalking it up to youthful absent-mindedness.

She breathed a sigh of relief. *That was a close one.* He didn't seem to think anything of that little slip.

But now she had to focus her mind on the task at hand. At least with Chernovsky now making less of a deal about keeping her arms in a certain position to dance, this would make her task easier. Hopefully. As her partner pulled her closer, she reached in. Trapping the phone in her slender fingers, she turned up the electricity on her smile, compelling him to watch while she prised that precious object out of his pocket, gently and gingerly.

Got it.

But had he noticed? She looked at him to double-check. He was looking elsewhere, but instantly turned his head to face her as soon as she gazed into his eyes. He hadn't realised. Good. She continued to smile as she held the phone behind his back.

Almost fittingly, the waltz came to an end. There followed a brief period of inactivity, during which the orchestra took a temporary break, as various couples retired to their seats or towards the sides of the hall.

"Thank you for the dance," Tania said courteously.

"It was my pleasure," Chernovsky replied, tilting his head graciously, as if to take a bow.

Tania nodded her head and smiled politely. All she could think about during the dance was acquiring that phone, not co-ordinating her feet. The Russian beauty was barely able to breathe as she began to edge away. Now all she had to do was hand it over to Jonah for him to clone, before somehow slipping it back on Chernovsky. It seemed simple enough.

Perhaps.

"Hey, wait a minute," a voice called after her.

She froze in her tracks. *Oh my gosh! He's found out. Now what? Do I keep walking or try to bluff my way out of this?*

Before Tania could chose an option, Chernovsky caught up with her. She closed her eyes, waiting for him to confront her with the inevitable storm of accusations.

Instead, Chernovsky calmly extended an open palm in front of her. "You dropped this," he said.

She fluttered her eyes rapidly to take a peek. In his hand lay her diamond bracelet. She must have dropped it somehow.

"*Bal'shóye spasiba*," she exclaimed. "Oh, thank you very much." She struggled to maintain her composure. He probably had no idea why she was so grateful. *What a close call.* Exhaling quickly, she summoned up her most endearing smile. "Don't know what I would've done if I found out later it was missing."

"*Pazhálusta*," he replied, tilting his head again as he walked away. "You're welcome."

A rush of adrenaline shot through her as she drew in a deep, shuddering breath. Her nerves felt like they had been put through a shredder. The orchestra hadn't yet started up again, but Tania began moving away, eager to get out of there, as the beginnings of a faint smile flickered across her face.

I did it. He hasn't noticed anything is missing. That wasn't so hard. Her heart sang with excitement. She was exhilarated, her spirit soaring.

Suddenly, like an intruder alarm waiting to catch her red-handed, Chernovsky's phone began to ring.

Chapter 13

Like a cornered animal, Tania stood rooted to the spot paralysed by fear and indecision.

Chernovsky heard the ringer sounding. The shrill sound of Tchaikovsky's *Trepak Russian Dance* that pierced through the indistinguishable chatter of guests. Immediately, he recognised the ringtone as his own and began rummaging through his pockets frantically.

Tania closed her eyes and bit her bottom lip. The back of her neck prickled as a drop of sweat trickled slowly down her spine.

Caught. No excuses. No way out.

So much for thinking this might be easy.

"Forget about cloning the phone," Bull shouted in Tania's ear, his voice full of urgency. "Just take it and get out of there now."

Chernovsky looked up with a start. He pointed an accusing finger at Tania. "That's my phone!"

"What are you waiting for?" Bull repeated again.

Tania swallowed hard. A rising sense of trepidation threatened to overwhelm her, freeze her where she stood.

Oh crud. Too much at stake for that. She mustered up all her determination and bolted like a scared rabbit.

"Stop!" Chernovsky called after her.

Tania's heart was racing. Samba drums at a Brazil soccer match. Her legs were like overcooked spaghetti. Rubbery. About to disintegrate beneath her. Yet, fired on by a mixture of adrenaline and the fear of being caught, she forced her legs to move forward automatically on their own. She charged through the crowded ballroom as the orchestra started up again.

The superstar skidded towards a group of guests. Models? Diplomats? Who knew? It was all a blur. She attempted to brush past them.

"Hey, watch it," one of them shouted.

"Sorry," she replied apologetically.

The guests looked at her, bewildered by her action. What on earth? Who could be running away?

Tania was grateful that she was still wearing her ball mask. Apart from the fact that no-one could see her face, she felt a measure of safety behind it.

"Stop her," Chernovsky ordered his bodyguards, running after her himself, as the henchmen unsheathed a couple of Makarov PM auto-pistols from their holsters.

The ringtone on the cell was still playing. Whoever it was seemed determined not to cut off.

"Hey," Tania cried. "I should see who this is."

"No, don't answer it!" Bull urged her. "Turn the phone off."

Too late. She slid open the cover and answered. "Hello?" Her voice was breathless as she ran. "Konstantin Chernovsky's phone."

"Hello?" came the surprised female voice on the other end.

"Who's that?"

The voice sounded both suspicious and defensive. "His wife. Who's *that*?"

Chernovsky's bodyguards carved a swathe through the guests, shoving several people out of their way, and onto one of the dining tables. The guests fell back with a loud crash.

Tania whirled around the corner. Her eyes darted about, making a quick scan of the area for a means of escape. *There.* She hotfooted it through the First and Second Exhibition Halls towards the Grand Staircase like a hunted gazelle.

A frantic rush ensued as the two bodyguards hurried after their prey.

Suddenly, the phone began beeping. *Not Chernovsky's wife again, surely? No.* Tania looked down. A message began appearing on the screen in Cyrillic. "Hey," she exclaimed. "This phone's doing something really weird."

"Doing what?" Bull's voice showed a little irritation.

Tania translated it. "It says FILE DELETION COMMENCING"

"Turn it off!" he barked.

"Turn what?"

"The phone. Turn the damn thing off. *Now.*"

Tania located the off switch and clicked the button. The screen faded to black.

She began pushing her legs to the limit. She turned left out of the Exhibition Halls near the top of the Grand Staircase. Then suddenly, a loud crack! Beneath her. Tania lost balance. She was sent sprawling across the chessboard floor. She scrambled quickly to her feet. She checked the heel on her stiletto. It had broken off.

Damn. Ruined a perfectly good pair of shoes.

Tania could hear the footsteps gaining on her. She glanced behind to see the angry faces. Flamingo-like, she hobbled about on one leg as she yanked off her shoes. She couldn't run in these heels in the first place, let alone a half-broken pair.

The gracile Russian flexed her toes and then continued to run in her bare feet, carrying her stilettos in her hand.

"Where are you?" she demanded.

"Meet me out the front on the north side of the Palace," came Bull's reply.

Tania headed for the red-carpeted marble staircase. But wait. There were pursuers charging up the stairs, jostling various people along the way. FSB agents? They certainly looked like. They were there simply to preserve the peace and maintain some semblance of order, but were not operating strictly in conjunction with Chernovsky and his men.

Trapped.

That exit was ruled out for her. She had to find another way. But the FSB agents reached the top of the stairs. They were upon her. Coming at her from everywhere.

Tania kicked out her right leg. Her toes were pointed like a spear, but she struck the FSB agent in his abdomen with the ball of her foot. Losing his balance, he fell on top of a number of the officers behind him. Three of them tumbled down the marble stairs, domino-style, crashing to the bottom, while the others side-stepped out of the way.

Tania cupped her hand over her mouth. She hadn't meant to do that. But this was hardly the time to consider her actions. The others were coming for her.

She spun around again, then darted nimbly through the length of the corridors, traversing each room as she ran. The FSB, having regrouped, pounded furiously behind her. But she was too quick.

Suddenly, one of the FSB security guards appeared around a corner. Out of nowhere. He made a grab for her, startling the lithe tennis star, but only succeeding in pulling off her mask. Exposed. No hiding behind it any more. Before the guard could get a good look at her face, she swung a long and limber leg in his direction with a reverse roundhouse kick. Her foot struck him in the stomach, knocking him to the ground immediately. The other guards appeared in the distance, still in pursuit of her. No time to spare. With no other choice, she pressed on, leaving her mask behind.

"What's going on?" Bull pressed her.

"I lost my mask," she cried.

"How?" But on second thoughts, he didn't want to know. "Never mind. Why didn't you use the stairs?"

"They were blocked off," she informed him. "Where are you now?"

"Outside. You need to find a way out quickly."

Find a way out? Maybe he should try it.

Tania looked around. A plush, cushioned chair was sitting there. It looked expensive. She bit her lip, contemplating for a split second what she was about to do. What had she become? A vandal? No time to worry about that now. She picked it up and hurled it through the window, closing her eyes to shut out the damage. The glass shattered everywhere.

The FSB agents were coming.

She smashed out the remaining pieces of glass and climbed up onto the window sill. Peering down, she tossed her shoes out to test the height. Within a few seconds, they landed below. It had to be between twelve to fifteen feet. Not the sort of distance one would normally wish to leap. What on earth did she think she was doing? Was she crazy?

Her adrenaline might help her. Or it might simply dull her senses as to the ludicrousness of her potential actions.

The Russian took a deep breath as she poised herself on the balcony to jump. With her long legs, she would probably end up breaking them if she landed incorrectly. Maybe even break her neck the way things were going tonight. Her only consolation was the thick blanket of snow surrounding the palace that might cushion her fall. Still that was no guarantee she wouldn't be badly injured. But it was either that or be captured by the FSB.

Oh. The heck with it.

Tania leapt.

She sailed through the air and landed suddenly with a thud. A little bruised and battered, she immediately rolled over and toppled onto the snow. She checked herself immediately. *Nothing broken. Good. Thank God for the snow.*

But now her toes were turning blue, freezing themselves off beneath her. And where was Jonah?

Tania heard the distinct tinkle of bells and the beating of hooves on the ground, together with the metallic scraping of blades cutting through the snow. She looked up. One of the troikas was heading her way, drawn by three powerful white horses.

It was Jonah Bull, driving it like a Roman gladiator on a chariot. He pulled the reins tightly as the animals drew to a halt with a deafening shriek.

"Jump on," he urged her.

"What, are you crazy?" she began to protest.

"Hurry. There's no time to argue."

Tania stood there hesitantly. Surely they weren't going to escape in that?

"What are you waiting for?" he barked.

She glanced around. Chernovsky and his bodyguards were bursting through the entrance like an angry mob. A spread of dark green uniforms was also approaching outside in the courtyard. The message had obviously been relayed to the FSB. They were onto her.

Only seconds to spare. Tania tossed her shoes into the carriage. She swung her leg up and climbed on board, leaving the enraged voices behind her.

Bull snapped the reins in one sudden motion. The sleigh lurched forward abruptly under the power of the horses, as they galloped off into the night, their manes whipping about in the wind.

A coachman standing nearby yelled after them in Russian. "Stop! That's my troika."

Tania waved her hands outwards and shrugged her shoulders, apologising in the same native tongue. "Sorry, I was waiting for one of these rides all evening."

Chernovsky and his henchmen flagged down another troika that was pulling in, drawn by three ebony horses. They forced the coachman to surrender his vehicle. One of the FSB officers attempted to intervene. But a henchman fired a shot from his Makarov before robbing the uniformed guard of his Uzi sub-machine gun and mounting the carriage. Once on, the driver gave the whip an almighty crack. The horses brayed violently then launched headlong into a gallop like wild stallions.

The FSB officers found their own modes of transport in the nearby parked Volga patrol cars and Ural motorcycles with side-cars. The tyres squealed, labouring to overcome the snow, then skidded as they gave chase.

Nearby, a number of FSB agents unleashed their German Shepherd dogs. It was as if the smell of food filled their noses as they began tearing after the sleigh furiously, eager to devour their prey.

The sleigh ploughed from side to side along the icy track as Bull steered the horses in a circle around the grounds of the Catherine Palace. The middle horse moved in an extended straight-forward-trot motion, while the two side horses galloped smoothly, swinging as their bent heads pointed outwards. The ride in the carriage proved to be bumpy and uncomfortable, snaking about like a rollercoaster. Tania did her best to hold on.

A number of amazed onlookers stood outside in the courtyard, watching in disbelief as the troika headed their way. Bull tried to slow down, but it was too late. The horses ploughed a path through them, forcing the people to jump out of the way in every direction.

Behind them was the continual sound of engines revving and wheels struggling as the cars began to lose traction on the treacherous surface.

Tania could hear the incessant panting and barking of the dogs behind them. They were closing in. Relentless. Her nerves began to sing with fear. *Oh no.* What if they caught up and ripped her to shreds? However, the canine noises were quickly drowned out by the jangling of the bells rattling on the harness, and the wail of sirens from the pursuing Volgas.

The sound of the metal blades scraped on the ground beneath them from the troika skidding roughly over the snow-packed mounds. Blasts of powder sprayed everywhere as they began a hazardous journey through the surrounding gardens of the park. The horses brayed as Bull cracked the reins. He was forcing them to work harder and harder. Their heads were thrust high in the air, their eyes full of determination and passion.

Then came the furious snorting of nostrils, and a second set of hooves pounding away behind them, growing ever closer. Tania gasped. Chernovsky's troika was rapidly approaching, the driver whipping the animals with fierce intensity.

Suddenly the staccato of gunfire punctuated the air. A barrage of bullets whizzed past them from Chernovsky's henchman, sitting in the back of the troika, brandishing the Uzi sub-machine gun.

"Duck," Bull shouted. He shoved the startled tennis star downwards immediately.

The bullets disappeared into the wind, as Chernovsky's sleigh edged closer.

"Hey, they're shooting at us," she cried. Her heart was now thumping, echoing the beating of hooves around her.

"Well did you expect them to throw snowballs?"

A few more cracks of the whip, and the pursuing troika gained a few more inches on them. The hooves rumbling on the ground were like crashing waves threatening an imminent collision with a helpless ship. The horses galloped. Faster and faster. The duga bells were clanging everywhere as Chernovsky's sleigh bore in alongside them.

The henchman aimed his Uzi at them again, but Chernovsky placed a restraining hand in the way, ordering him instead to seize the girl, and consequently, his phone which was still in her possession. The troikas scraped alongside each other and Tania was sure they would be torn to pieces in the process, but Bull steered it away in the nick of time.

The other troika moved in again, and the henchman reached over. Tania saw him. She flung her leg out, intending to knock him away from her. Big mistake. The henchman seized her ankle and heaved her towards him. The hapless tennis star was snatched from her seat. Ripped right out of the sleigh. At the last moment, she managed to clasp hold of the edge of the carriage. And there she was, dangling between the two sledges, hanging on for dear life as Chernovsky's men sought to anchor her in.

She screamed, as her fingers began slipping from its grasp.

Bull looked back and tried to extend his hand towards her. She was being prised away ever so slowly. Either Chernovsky would seize her, or she would take a serious tumble from the vehicle, crushed underfoot by the surrounding horses. With one eye on the road, he made a valiant effort to save her.

Tania dared to peer upwards. She immediately turned white. She let out a speechless gasp before forcing a high-pitched shriek. "Look out."

Bull whipped around to see where she was pointing. His eyes bulged like saucers. One of the FSB Volgas was approaching in the opposite direction like an express train. He seized the reins desperately, steering the frightened horses out of its path. As he pulled away, Tania was yanked abruptly, still held by her ankles, into the hands of Chernovsky's henchman. The FSB passed between the two sleighs, causing them to diverge in different directions. The driver of Chernovsky's troika fired upon it. Three shots. The bullets tore through one of the windows, causing the driver to lose control. The Volga careered and skidded into one of the Ural motorcycles, instantaneously bursting into flames.

With those nuisances out of the way, Chernovsky placed a hand around his captive's waist and hauled her in. She struggled as she found herself in the same vehicle with the man she had danced with earlier, and now attempting to grab at the phone she had stolen.

In a flash, Tania instinctively sent a couple of punches his way. Chernovsky attempted to shield his face from her blows, but the henchman moved in to restrain her. Picking up the Uzi that was lying there, she swatted the henchman away with it, knocking him backwards, but sending the sub-machine gun tumbling out into the snow. With the henchman disorientated, she seized him by the scruff of his neck and slammed his face into the side of the carriage.

Bull navigated the horses towards Chernovsky's sleigh, determined not to let Tania slip away. But the gap between them was still wide. To make matters worse, the driver began plugging away with his Makarov again.

It was time to fight back. Bull unholstered his pistol. A Beretta PX4 Storm. He intended to use it, but the other troika moved out of position such that he would be in danger of hitting the beautiful blonde.

Tania shoved the henchman backwards into Chernovsky. Then brushed him away with a kick to the face. They turned a bumpy corner, and the Russian was thrown backwards. She recovered in time. But immediately the henchman was upon her again. He stood, ready to pounce upon her. As he lunged forward, skilfully she used his momentum to toss him out of the moving sledge. He went flying headlong, tumbling about in the snow like a mannequin before coming to a stop. His battered body was immediately savaged by the pack of dogs that had been chasing the sleighs, devouring him like a piece of meat.

Tania gasped. What a horrible fate to befall anyone. But horror quickly gave way to other concerns. Having managed to wrest herself free, she caught sight of Bull's troika passing alongside her sleigh, inching ever closer, as another fleet of Volgas and Urals skidded through the snow, renewing their onslaught. One of these was making a straight line for her carriage, about to plough into her.

"Jump," Bull shouted.

She hesitated, then looked at him confounded. "What? I can't do that." She shook her head determinedly.

"You can," he assured her. "You can make it."

The Volga was honking at Chernovsky's horses, ordering its driver to steer out of the way before the impending crash. The driver, however, was temporarily distracted in an attempt to shoot at Bull. He fired off another round, ricocheting off the side of the wooden harness that framed the horses. Bull flinched, then returned a shot. It tore through the driver's shoulder, causing him to lose control.

With the driver out of commission, Chernovsky's main concern was his own safety, and not the phone he sought to recover. He instantly forgot about his quarry, and tried to clamber towards the front of the sledge and into driver's seat before the head-on collision.

Bull seized this opportunity and attempted to spur the tennis star into action. "Jump," he urged her again.

"I can't," she wailed.

"Listen to me," Bull told her. "You have to or you'll be crushed."

Teeth clenched tightly. Poised on the edge of the carriage. Could she possibly manage such a dangerous leap? Tania's heart was pounding as she gazed anxiously at the troika before her. The gap between her sleigh and the adjacent one was constantly alternating between being a hair's breadth away, and edging just out of reach.

It was now or never.

Without thinking, she pushed off from the wooden frame with those long, willowy legs, and bounded towards the sleigh driven by Bull. What was she thinking? She slammed into the side, narrowly missing. But she managed to grab on to the edge in the nick of time.

Chernovsky was almost at the front of his carriage, but had still to shift the wounded driver out of the way. He peered over as he saw the daring Russian girl hanging on with all her might, perilously close to falling off in the same tragic way his own henchman had earlier. With that momentary lapse in concentration, he forgot about the oncoming FSB car.

Too late.

The Volga mowed straight into him, sweeping aside everything in its path, as debris and bodies flew everywhere. The car gave a loud screech in a desperate attempt to brake, but skidded. It clipped a nearby statue, and immediately overturned and exploded. The flames engulfed everything around, including Chernovsky, the driver and the horses.

Tania was slipping, struggling to stay on with every ounce of strength, her fingers weakening little by little, her arms growing tired and ready to let go. Then, like a lifeline, Bull offered his hand, ready to pull her in to safety. *Just in time.* Taking it gratefully, she managed to haul herself up and clambered into the waiting carriage.

"You okay?" Bull inquired, with surprising concern as he checked that she was definitely on board.

"Let's just say it's not my idea of dashing through the snow," she moaned, shaking as she breathed a deep sigh of relief. "Couldn't you have picked something else with wheels?"

"Sorry," Bull replied, in a dismissive tone, his voice once again aloof. "I didn't have time to choose."

Tania sighed. Her beautiful hair was a mess after all the rough and tumble she had endured. She pulled out the pins holding it in place, leaving those long tresses to flow loosely around her shoulders.

The sleigh skidded down through a wooded area of slender, silver-white birch trees that appeared almost eerie in the moonlight, with the two remaining Urals and a Volga following close behind, picking up speed on the downhill slope.

Bull whipped the reins harder and increased the pace of the horses. The sleigh zig-zagged through the wintry forest in an anguineous manner, dodging past a number of fallen birch trees and attempting to avoid a collision on this most dangerous of obstacle courses.

The rapid-fire of shots sounded out again. This time, she didn't need to be told twice. Tania ducked instinctively.

"Here," said Bull in an urgent tone of voice. He shoved the Beretta into her hands, as if it were any casual object, expecting her to use it without hesitation.

Tania glanced down at the weapon with both a mixture of disdain and alarm, still trembling from her ordeal. "What am I supposed to do with that?"

He grimaced, as if the question was completely ridiculous and his intention was entirely obvious. "Shoot."

"Them?" She wavered. "But the FSB aren't strictly after me."

"They're firing at us," he yelled. "Isn't that enough for you?"

She shrugged her shoulders. "Mind telling me how you got that weapon past security at the Palace?"

"Trade secret," he replied evasively. "Now pull the trigger and shoot."

"I can't do that," she protested. "I've never fired a gun before, and I'm not open to lessons."

Bull sighed. Some things he'd simply have to do himself. "Take the reins," he ordered.

Tania gave him a look of bewilderment.

He shook his head in frustration. "Well you can steer, can't you?"

Tania nodded. Handing the pistol back, she grabbed the reins and climbed into the front as Jonah Bull exchanged places with her. The horses were harder to control than she had imagined. They were like fierce racing steeds, unpredictable, with a mind of their own, and needing constant discipline to keep them in line.

Bull fired a round of shots at one of the tyres of the Volga. The bullet punctured the rubber, and immediately, the car wheeled around in a circle, spun out of control and collided with one of the Urals.

Tania heard the sound of metal crunching behind her and flinched, as a fireball lit up the night. The exploding wreckage soared upwards before landing back down in a heap.

"You said this would be a simple matter," she scolded him.

"Looks like RISK had other plans."

"Great," Tania mumbled. "First time back in my own country in years and already I'm a fugitive."

One more Ural left. The side-car passenger began firing at them, with a few shots soaring past their heads. Bull clicked the trigger on his Beretta. *Empty.* And the cyclist was gaining on them.

Bull looked around. Nothing to use as a weapon. He glanced at the removable canvas hood, giving him an idea. He flicked open his Emerson folding knife and began cutting away at the cords, keeping an eye on the oncoming Ural as the side-car passenger started firing again.

Tania whipped the horses harder as they pulled violently on their harnesses, dragging her forward. The troika began heading downhill, gathering both speed and momentum as the pace increased.

The Ural followed down the same path, with the FSB determined to catch these troublemakers. Suddenly, Bull released the canvas. It blew backwards in the wind towards the motorcycle, enveloping their heads and obscuring their vision. Riding blind, they spun out of control and snowballed down the hill before coming to a fiery end.

As the troika speared forward, the Russian's long blonde hair was swept up behind her, dancing about her face like licks of fire as she rode the wind. For a brief instant, it was as though she was one with the horses. She was overcome by a strange sense of both intoxication and exhilaration as the sleigh glided forward under the surging equine power with her firmly at the helm. She imagined herself as a mysterious Siberian princess of folklore, trekking either across a wintry Russian countryside or the harsh terrain of the frozen Russian tundra, centuries before, towards some remote and uncharted destination.

Then, without warning, the troika went over a bump and they seemed to take off. For a few short moments, it was like they were flying, sailing through the air, even though the horses were firmly on the ground, working furiously. The sleigh landed with a thud and nearly overturned, bringing Tania back to reality, and threatening to throw both her and Bull out of the carriage completely.

"Watch it," he shouted as he grabbed hold of the side to maintain his balance.

"Hey, it's not every day I play Santa Claus."

Tania saw that they were reaching the edge of the park. In the distance was a black Lada parked discreetly at the side of the road.

"Head towards that," he instructed her.

Tania cracked the reins as the steeds raced forward for one final dash. Upon reaching the car, she strained on the harness to bring the frightened horses to an abrupt halt. Bull ordered her off, and they both scrambled out to where their contact was waiting.

"That's our ride," he said. "Let's get out of here."

A Romani-looking man with a thick moustache and traditional dress opened the back of the Lada. They piled in quickly as the car sped off, leaving the trail of destruction behind them.

Chapter 14

"**T**hanks a lot," said Bull to the driver, as the Lada sped away from *Tsarkoye Selo* towards Pulkovo Airport. "You were just in time."

"Don't mention it," the man replied. "You are very fortunate. I wasn't sure you were going to make it."

"We almost didn't," Bull replied.

Tania saw that the man was staring at her through the mirror with increasing curiosity. She tried to look away, but his eyes seemed to be trained firmly upon her, unwilling to look away until that curiosity had been satisfied.

"You didn't tell me you'd be bringing her along," the man said. "What's she doing here?"

Tania gave a pout, her eyebrows constricting. Speaking about her in the third person, as if she wasn't even present, seemed rather rude. "Nice to meet you too," she commented, hoping he'd take the hint.

He did, and addressed her directly, his voice full of enthusiasm. "I am Yojo. You are very famous in Russia, and in Istanbul where I'm from, Tatiana Likamolova."

"For all the right reasons I hope," she grinned, her face softening.

"Yes," he replied. "When my children grow up, they want to be just like you."

Tania smiled as she gazed pensively out of the window. That was a real honour to hear that other youngsters considered her some kind of role model. The thought that she might inspire others to be like her, to take up a racquet and play. She was overwhelmed. But then, she might not be playing much longer if things kept up the way they had been in the past few days. She had found herself deep in situations which, up until now, would have seemed inconceivable. And more scraps in the last few days than she had in her entire life! Her expression darkened, as she let out a sigh of frustration.

Bull sensed an air of tension and probed her. "You seem upset. What's up?"

Tania gave him an amazed look. "What's up? I'm still astounded at what happened back there?"

"Couldn't be helped," he replied. "In a situation like this, it's either them or you. They would've exposed you and jeopardised the whole mission.

"I hate violence," she stated categorically.

Bull rolled his eyes. "This coming from a girl who just fought off a horde of FSB agents."

"There's a difference. I could never kill anyone."

"Sometimes you have no choice."

"No choice? Surely there had to be some other way? Otherwise what makes you any different from the bad guys you're after, or even someone like Piotr?"

"I'm nothing like them or Volkov," he retorted.

"Well, you haven't proven otherwise so far," she replied.

"Look, I don't think those guys were chasing after you so you could all sit down and discuss things rationally over Vodka. I'm not saying that I like what I have to do, or that I would simply advocate killing in cold blood. But when faced with a split-second decision, you have to do what you think is best in the situation."

Tania reflected on his words. There was some merit in what he said. And as far as jeopardising the whole mission, at least that much was probably true. Inside she agreed with the reasoning if not the methods used. But how could she condone his actions?

"Well at least we got his phone," she said, her voice rather unconvincing in hiding her true feelings.

"Yeah, well it might not be much good to us now," Bull replied. "Let me see it."

Tania looked at him for a minute, somewhat troubled at the brusque way Jonah had demanded it from her. She shook her head and then handed it to him.

Bull pressed the on button. The phone did not respond. Instead, it prompted him to place his palm on the screen. He shook his head.

"Aren't you supposed to use my gloves?" Tania inquired.

"It doesn't work like that. The scanner merely records an imprint of the user's veins, but that's simply used to create a mould for a synthetic glove that has to be manufactured in a lab. We won't be able to do that until I get your gloves to our Moscow headquarters."

"So you think you'll be able to use the information on there?"

"Well, even if we can access it, there's no telling whether there'll be anything still there."

Tania thought for a minute, and then remembered the message that had flashed across the screen before Jonah ordered her to turn the phone off. "What did it mean 'FILE DELETION COMMENCING'?"

"Chernovsky was probably using some kind of kill signal."

"A what?"

"Kill signal," he repeated. "It's like a remote transmission that the owner sends which acts like a digital neutron bomb. It can be used to erase sensitive information in the event of a major security breach, without destroying the phone itself."

"Does that mean that everything's deleted?"

"I don't know," Bull replied. "That's why I told you to turn off the phone immediately. On certain phones, the kill signal won't work if the device is switched off. Unfortunately, it might be too late since the deletion was already in progress."

"I'm sorry," she apologised.

"Well I did tell you to switch it off earlier."

"Well Chernovsky's wife was on the line."

"And what were you going to do? Take a message for him?" Bull said derisively.

"Well even if I had switched it off," Tania protested, "you still wouldn't be able to open it anyway since you said it's bio... what did you call it again?"

"Biometrically encrypted," Bull helped her out.

"Yes that. You still wouldn't be able to open it."

"But we might still have had the information on it," he snapped.

Tania was forced to admit to herself that he might be right.

Jonah Bull reached into his own pocket. Removing his phone from there, he dialled a number and then placed it to his ear. "Elf? Bull here. There's something I need you to analyse when I come in."

"You're coming into Moscow?" Elf inquired. The tone of his voice sounded as if he had reservations about that.

"Yeah," Bull replied. "Is there a problem?"

Elf sounded grave. "There's been a terrorist alert at Pulkovo. The whole airport has been shut down."

"Both airports?"

"Yes. As a security precaution."

"For how long?"

"No idea, but no planes are allowed to leave at the moment. It could be like that for the next few hours."

"So what does this mean? Are we stuck here?"

"Unless you can find alternative means of transportation, then yes."

Jonah breathed a heavy sigh. "I have Tania with me. She was meant to have a private jet meet her at Pulkovo to fly her to her next destination."

"No planes can leave from St Petersburg, including private jets. We can arrange for Tania to catch a private plane from Moscow, but you'll both have to find another way to get there first. I'll let Hassall know that you're going to be late."

"Okay, I understand," Bull replied. "Keep me informed if there are any developments." He hung up.

"What is it?" Tania inquired.

Bull did not answer her, but spoke to Yojo instead. "There's been a change of plans. We need to find alternative transportation."

"What?" Tania exclaimed. "What do you mean? I thought we were going to the airport."

"There's been a security alert," Bull said simply. "Both airports have been temporarily closed."

"So what does this mean now?"

"You'll have to accompany me back to Moscow instead of flying straight out from here. IRIS will be able to get a private jet there for you."

"I thought you said this was going to be a breeze?"

"Well sometimes unforeseen events happen that take the wind out of your sails."

Yojo spoke up. "It is no problem, as you Americans say. We can head back into St Petersburg, towards *Moskovsky Train Station* and take the Aurora Express instead."

"Are you sure?" Tania asked.

"Yes. As they say, all roads lead to Moscow." Yojo changed direction at the next exit and drove the car back towards the city centre, where Tania had been hours earlier.

The rest of the journey was travelled in silence, until they neared *Moskovsky Train Station* at *Ploschad Vosstania* on *Nevsky Prospekt*.

"You can get down shortly," Yojo announced. "You should be able to catch the train from here."

"But everyone's looking for me," Tania replied. "As far as the FSB are concerned now, their letters stand for Find Siberian Blonde. It's not like people won't know what I look like either."

"You need to disguise yourself," Yojo informed her. "I have some spare clothing in the trunk." He pulled over and hurried around to produce some traditional Romani costumes. "They belong to my daughter who is about your age and almost your height. I hope it fits."

"I thought you said earlier 'when my children grow up.' I was under the impression they were still small."

"I have many children - from many mistresses. You understand?"

Tania grinned. However, she was still sceptical. "But I look nothing like one of the Roma. I mean, I'm not dark enough for a start." She took a look at Jonah too, pointing to him with the flat of her hand while shaking her head to confirm it sounded too unbelievable. "And well - neither are you."

Yojo had the answer to that. "Here. One of these headscarves will help cover your golden hair." He glanced over at Bull. "I have some clothes for you too. Maybe not such a good fit, but they will do."

After a few minutes, Tania and Bull had changed clothing. The Russian, now wearing a floral scarf on her head, was clad in a shoulderless white top and a blue knee-length skirt. But most important of all, she had some flat shoes for her poor feet. Not a perfect fit - slightly on the small side - but better than nothing. Bull wore a waistcoat which belonged to Yojo himself, but was slightly too big. Nevertheless, they were both grateful.

Accompanied by Yojo, they headed into *Moskovsky Train Station*, where all major trains to Moscow left and arrived from here. The station was crowded, but no-one seemed to notice the tennis star. The disguise seemed to work. For the moment.

Once inside, Tania groaned when she saw the line for the ticket office stretching back indefinitely. "You mean we have to line up?" She did not welcome the idea of possibly queuing. "We're likely to have a couple of hours' wait here, plus eight hours overnight by rail."

"Five hours, if we take the express," Yojo informed her.

"Still, that's a long time. Sooner or later, someone's going to notice a well-known tennis star standing about, disguise or not. And don't we need to show our passports to travel on the train? Not that I have mine with me."

"That's why we're not lining up."

"What do you mean?"

"We're getting straight onto the train. If we buy the tickets unofficially from either the conductor or the restaurant manager, we can bypass the need for that."

"Are you sure?" Tania looked doubtful.

"Trust me." Yojo assured her. "I've done it before. There are usually police teams who come round to check the train at each stop, plus two conductors in each carriage, so we need to be discreet. I'll have to sneak you both on board"

Bull glanced at her. "Look on the bright side. With all this security, at least you'll be safe here."

"Great," Tania sighed, rolling her eyes. "You sound like you've really thought this out. I bet you just want to spend the night with me in a sleeping compartment."

"Actually," Yojo said, dashing her hopes. "You'd both be lucky if you even get third class."

***

Tania sat in silence as the Aurora Express train sped through the night. She was alone in Jonah's company, as their new-found ally, Yojo, had gone to sort out their tickets and arrange for some food.

Jonah turned away to gaze out through the windows into the darkness as the scenery whizzed by. Noticing he seemed oddly distracted, lost in his own world, Tania broke the silence. "What about my phone?"

He glanced back, surprised at the intrusion into his thoughts. "What about it?" His slightly abrupt reply surprised her.

Refusing to waver, she pressed on. "Why didn't The Three Bears simply use a kill signal to destroy the information Natalya uploaded onto my phone instead of sending someone after me, or Natalya for that matter?"

"Because that information was a file she created herself, and not merely the contents of a smartphone belonging to The Three Bears. Unless they had the technology, the kill signal would only work in relation to the original stolen phone itself and not on data copied from that phone onto another, or data created by someone else on an entirely separate phone altogether. But that's all beside the point anyway. It still doesn't change the fact that you should've switched off Chernovsky's phone when I told you to."

"I said I was sorry." She felt his gaze upon her, angry and tense, and it unsettled her.

"That's not the only mistake you made," he continued, refusing to let up on her. "You let Volkov get away without getting his phone. That was the whole point of this mission."

"Well we got Chernovsky's phone instead, didn't we?"

"No, that was something we had to improvise. But that wasn't part of the original plan."

"Well I've apologised profusely. What more do you want me to do? You do this every day. I don't. I can't change the fact that I'm not a spy."

Bull was quick to concur. "You'll get no argument from me there."

Tania shrank back in silence. *I'm not a spy or anything. So why is he expecting so much from me?* Dejected, she watched him, studying his body language. She bit her lip and tried to look away, not wanting to meet his eyes for fear he'd see her vulnerability.

She tried to change the topic of conversation to fill in the awkward silence. Putting on a brave face, she spoke. "Are you sure Piotr didn't suspect anything earlier when he spoke to you?"

"Maybe. But in his business he's probably suspicious of everybody. It comes with the territory."

"So how long have you known that Piotr worked for RISK?"

"Not long. A few months perhaps." His words were terse.

She pressed on. "But I know for a fact that he works for Red Gold. Why would he have gone to all that trouble to establish himself there?"

"Remember, with RISK agents, just like with the old KGB, it's common to have spies within all kinds of fields where you'd least suspect them, blending into society."

"Like tennis?"

"Yeah. Like tennis. Although I have to admit that apart from the espionage connection, I'm not much of a fan of the game."

"No? Well what do you like? Are you into any other sports? Basketball maybe?"

"A little, maybe. I don't have time for fun."

"Of course you do," she said playfully. "Where are you from?"

"Jefferson Park, Illinois."

"Where's that?"

"Just outside of Chicago. But what does that have to do with anything?"

"I'm just trying to find out a thing or two about you." She smiled warmly, trying to maintain a friendly atmosphere. "Chicago. Home of the Bears and the Bulls. Kind of ironic under the circumstances..."

He cut her off. "Has anyone told you that you talk too much?"

She giggled again, not taking offence. "No. Usually fans want to talk to me all the time."

"I'm not one of your fans," he reminded her, snubbing her attempts to keep things light-hearted between them. His voice was cold, and emphasised his apparent lack of affinity for her.

"So what you said back there to Piotr at the Catherine Palace..."

"That was just part of the act. You'll often say things you don't mean in this business."

"Woah, that's a bit of a dagger," she said flippantly, her voice masking her true feelings as she put her hand to her heart. She already knew Jonah's perspective on her before, but had hoped that he had somehow changed his mind. Coming from him at this particular moment, it filled her with a tinge of hurt. Although it was more likely a neutral statement, she couldn't help feeling it sounded like a rejection. It's not that she sought after fans, or at least that's what she told herself. But when she started to interact with someone on a personal level, she didn't like to hear that the person was, at best, indifferent towards her. Perhaps she did have a need for approval, a need to be liked after all.

"Look, Tania," he explained. "We're not here to be friends. We're simply here on a mission to get a job done. Nothing more."

"But that doesn't mean being unfriendly either. What is that, some sort of professional distance you're trying to maintain?"

"Something like that," he replied.

She huffed. "Well I sure am glad I'm not a spy. I'd hate to have to be like that."

That seemed to touch a nerve, as Jonah, who had so far been somewhat economical with his words, suddenly broke out into a barrage. "Fine, you want to know why I choose not to socialise with you? Becoming friends with someone means that you start to develop at least some kind of personal feelings towards that person."

"And that's a bad thing?"

"Well, it may lead you to make a judgment based more on emotion than on something rational, and can ultimately jeopardise the whole mission. If I were friends with you, I wouldn't be doing my job. As I said before, we're not here to have fun. I certainly don't have time for it."

"But everyone's into fun. Some people just don't know it. They think they can exist without it by simply working all the time, crowding it out so that it doesn't fit anywhere into their lives. But if you ask me, that's just an excuse to hide behind."

"And aren't you always working on your game, trying to be the best in the world?"

"Yeah, that's true. But tennis is also fun for me, even though it's work. If it wasn't, I certainly wouldn't be spending so many months training on the women's circuit."

"But you do. And you do that because you're constantly seeking something else instead of being satisfied with what you have. I saw your post-match interview, remember. You said so yourself. How was it you put it? You want everything in life to be 'just right'."

"And what's wrong with that?" Her voice hardened at his sardonic tone, becoming slightly defensive. "At least I'm alive and living out my dreams, if but for a few years. Isn't there anything you dream about?"

"Well, if by dreaming you mean wish fulfilment, then no. It doesn't seem very down to earth to me."

"There's nothing wrong with dreaming, you know. It depends how you dream. You IRIS agents are always saying 'Keep your eyes open.' Well I like to dream, and dream with my eyes open and try to make them come true."

"Well, dreaming might be fine for a while, but sooner or later you need to put away your childish things, grow up and take responsibility. But you live your life every day with all of it scheduled. Everything is a routine, and you have the world pretty much at your feet. All you need to do is go out there and play, and never worry about anything else while you remain oblivious to and ignorant of the real world that goes on around you."

"You mean your world? The darker world of espionage?"

"That, among other things."

The spotlight had been shining on Tania long enough during this conversation. It was time for a change. "Well, has anyone told you that, even with a name like yours, you're more like a sitting bull than a red bull?"

Jonah's eyebrows contracted. "What's that supposed to mean?"

"It means you're someone who never sees red. No passion at all. Nothing gets you excited enough to charge towards whatever the world might wave in your face. Instead you've become static and prefer to play things safe, to proceed cautiously through life. And ironically, because you prefer to play things safe, you'll never 'take the bull by the horns' and try something in a different way, because you're afraid of getting burnt."

"Excuse me, but you don't know anything about me to make that sort of judgment."

"No? I know what you've been telling me just now, and also your comments back in the hotel. I might be blissfully naïve and innocent to the ways of the world as you think, but I would rather live a fairy tale. I would rather see life in a positive way and dare to dream, than become cold, cynical and delusioned with everything and lose all joy for living. You've stopped believing in others and in the possibility of dreams. And now you hide behind the excuse of taking responsibility when the truth is probably something deeper which, for whatever reason, you prefer to keep to yourself."

"Well you're right about that. I do have my reasons, and I'd rather not discuss them with you. Like I said, we're not on this mission to become friends or anything. And from our discussion just now, I get the feeling we're too different from each other for such a possibility to occur, even if we were meeting under different circumstances."

"Fine. Whatever," she lied, trying to sound as though she was not bothered by his words. "Not that I'm asking for it, but it's your loss. But since we *are* currently working together, let's at least agree to be civil to one another. If that's not too much to ask?"

"That's fine by me."

Tania sighed as she folded her arms and slumped back in her seat, her heart suddenly feeling much smaller. It was futile at this point pressing the matter any further. If there was anything bothering Jonah, he seemed reluctant to talk about it.

Tania looked out the window, lost in her thoughts.

And people wonder where they get this cliché of the cold, hard spy who works better alone because he's afraid to let anyone get too close to him. Just my luck for being stuck with one.

At that moment, Yojo walked in, having managed to find a few scraps of food from the dining car. He was oblivious to the fact that they were in the middle of a tense moment. "Borsch anyone?"

***

The next few hours were spent in silence as the train hurtled through the night towards its destination.

Jonah broke the silence, his voice softening as he attempted to clear the air between them. "I must say, you handled yourself pretty well back there."

"If you're referring to our earlier disagreement, I'm used to dealing with the press," she replied. "They can be quite forceful at times. They keep me on my toes."

"No, I meant back at the Catherine Palace when you handled all those guards and Chernovsky. Seems you had things mostly under control."

She shook her head modestly. "Yes, well don't let that fool you. That was just fighting spirit to stay alive through sheer desperation. I do the same thing in tennis matches, you know - survive by the skin of my teeth."

"Oh, I don't know about that. You seemed to know what you were doing."

"Probably just the result of having done some kickboxing and Systema. Sometimes I'm forced to save myself when I have no other choice. Unfortunately that's starting to become quite a habit these days. But I'd be quite happy for others to play the hero."

"So let me get this straight," Jonah began. "You're telling me you're like the proverbial princess in the tower, waiting for her handsome prince to come and rescue her from the wicked witch. So he climbs up, mounting a daring rescue, but on the way there, he slips and falls, and breaks his leg. So, rather than waiting for him to recover or another prince to ride by, you decide that if you're ever going to escape, you'll have to fight the wicked witch yourself and climb down the tower on your own, because there's no-one else to help? But then, once you're out, it's back to being Miss damsel-in-distress again, until the next time when the situation requires you to take a stand once more?"

"Well, I don't know if I would've put it that way," Tania grinned. "But yes. That's probably me in a nutshell."

"Well, from the little I know of you, you don't come across as some tough-as-nails chick at all."

"I'm not," she confirmed. "Not in the least. Are you surprised?"

He nodded. "A little. Most women these days want to compete with men as equals. It's this modern attitude of 'act like a man, think like a woman'."

"Men are always so competitive," Tania mused. "At least we play by the rules."

"And that's why women will always be the fairer sex."

Tania raised an eyebrow in amusement. "I know some girls on the tennis circuit who 'look like a man, think they're a woman'. But like I said before, I have nothing to prove. Don't get me wrong. I'm very competitive once I'm on the court, but I'm quite happy being a girl with all that it entails."

"A girl who just happens to be able to hold her own against a bunch of RISK agents?"

A flicker of a smile broke across Tania's face. "I guess."

Jonah returned her smile as his eyes met hers. The tension had begun to ease. He grinned. "Come on. You should try to get some sleep before we get to Moscow."

Chapter 15

Monday, early morning.

Like a huge, rolling behemoth, the Aurora Express train pulled into Leningradsky station in Moscow. Tania was fast asleep and did not rouse, even when it lurched forward suddenly.

Jonah Bull had remained awake, deciding that someone needed to keep an eye out while the weary Russian took the opportunity to rest. In her slumbering state, she looked extremely vulnerable and innocent. No longer a glamorous tennis star but a young girl sleeping peacefully. Really quite adorable in fact. Although they had been at loggerheads with each other earlier, he couldn't help feeling a sense of protectiveness towards her. Then there were her words. Oh yes. No forgetting that. They would not wash away easily. There was some truth to the expression she used. He had been a sitting bull. Whether or not he could fully accept that, there was no denying that he had stopped dreaming in the last year or so. He had played things too safe.

By contrast, she took quite a different approach to everything. She had an openness, an honesty about her that was refreshing, even though he wouldn't admit it to her at this point. She was indeed following her dreams and attempting to make the most out of life, even if it meant not always finding the right balance.

Bull shook his head. Enough navel-gazing for one day. "Time to get up," he whispered, shaking her lightly.

"Where are we?" Tania mumbled drowsily as she pried open her eyelids one by one and let out a stiff yawn.

"Moscow. While you were asleep, I called and arranged transportation for us. There should be a car waiting to take us to IRIS headquarters here."

Tania and Bull emerged from the station, while Yojo bid them farewell as they continued the rest of the journey by themselves. Leningradsky station was an immense, green and white-bricked neoclassical edifice swarming with homeless drunks, beggars and weary passengers. It was dark outside, being early morning, but there were still a large number of coaches, taxis and gypsy cabs parked, ready to take potential customers to their destinations. They piled into a black Mercedes that was waiting, and headed towards IRIS headquarters.

The journey there was long and uncomfortable. Moscow was a city built in the formation of a series of concentric rings that radiated the centre. Passing through each ring could prove to be an effort, with traffic usually heavy and the roads scarred with potholes. To make matters worse, where were they actually headed? IRIS headquarters? Although it had been a number of years since Tania was last in Moscow, that wasn't something she remembered existed as an actual building. At least not a building that was publicly known. All she knew was that they were headed somewhere south-west. South west? Where would that lead? She couldn't quite remember her bearings correctly.

"Why didn't we take the metro?" Tania had asked him when they first boarded the car. "Wouldn't that be quicker?"

He quickly convinced her. "Do you really want to sit on another train with all these passengers again?"

Tania had to admit that she didn't. In the car, at least she had her own space.

They were soon heading towards the centre, avoiding the FSB headquarters in Lubyanka Ploshad, but passing by the Polytechnical Museum. Wherever they were going, the driver seemed to be taking the scenic route. Well, she might as well enjoy the ride. Tania's mouth fell open in amazement as they neared the vast expanse of Red Square and the glittering domes and towers of the Kremlin. They still impressed her, making her feel like a visitor to the city for the first time. As they passed by the festive-looking St Basil's Cathedral, Tania smiled to herself. With its candy-coloured onion domes sitting atop the red brick building, it looked to her more like a giant sweet factory. Okay, maybe that was the first impression she had when she was a child, but somehow it always stuck with her.

The Mercedes turned left onto the Kremlin embankment, the highway that ran alongside the length of the Moskva River. Soon they were passing the Cathedral of Christ the Saviour and the Ferris wheel of Gorky Park on their left. A while later they turned off right somewhere and headed down *Bolshaya Pirogovskaya Ulitsa*, with the house of Leo Tolstoy on their right. They seemed to be driving for hours and Tania was still no closer to finding out their destination. The only thing down this way that Tania could think of was the Novodevichy Convent. Surely they weren't headed there were they?

Apparently they were.

Tania saw the imposing blood and snow-coloured baroque-styled structures looming in the distance, surrounded by a high masonry fortress wall with twelve towers. The lofty, six-tiered Bell Tower and the Church of the Assumption, and the huge, five-domed Smolensky Cathedral were the first things that immediately caught her eye. She knew that the Convent's name often translated as the New Maiden's Monastery. At various times in history, it had served as a fortress, a military hospital for soldiers of the Russian army, and an orphanage for abandoned children. In 1994, nuns returned to the convent. It was now probably the best known cloister in Moscow.

What were they doing here?

The Mercedes stopped outside. Bull alerted someone that they had arrived, and then he led her through two entrance gates. They walked through a dark cemetery where lay buried writers such as Anton Chekhov and Vladimir Mayakovsky, and composers such as Skriabin, Prokofiev and Shostakovich. She was intruding on a part of history! She followed as Bull led her down the stairs of a secret crypt.

Was this really the headquarters of IRIS's Moscow branch?

"Isn't this a listed building?" Tania remarked. "How on earth did IRIS manage to set up their headquarters here?"

"It's the last place anyone would think to look," he replied. "Hide it out in the open where everyone thinks they know about this place. We have another one under Smolny Cathedral in St Petersburg."

The Russian had not seen the entrance to the New York headquarters of IRIS as she had been unconscious at the time. As she and Jonah entered the crypt, Tania took every opportunity to examine her surroundings. They walked down a long, stark-white corridor until they reached a checkpoint where a security guard waited at a desk. The two of them were x-ray scanned for any unauthorised weapons, and then allowed to pass into the next checkpoint area. Here, there appeared to be a biometric scanner which verified their identities before granting them access to the secured area of the compound. Jonah stood still about two feet away from the camera while a beam of red light was directed towards his eye, projecting an image of the world onto its surface.

"Retinal scanning?" Tania queried.

"Iris scanning actually," Jonah replied. "More reliable."

"Iris?" Tania rolled her eyes ceilingward. "Of course."

A couple of further security measures later, and having had her own iris scanned, they were inside. It was a similar set-up to the New York branch. Again, there were monitors everywhere lining the walls, while on the floor the same, now-familiar multi-coloured logo of IRIS was displayed.

They were greeted by Elvin Xiu, who had arrived there earlier after the briefing in St Petersburg. "Hassall's going to want to speak to you both via satellite feed," he informed them. "I worked with Chauncey remotely, and we managed to break the encryption on the information uploaded from Tania's phone. We've made a few discoveries, but I'll let the boss fill you in on that himself."

"Later," Bull said, handing Chernovsky's phone to him and Tania's gloves. "We need to get these analysed."

"Great," muttered Elf. "More phones to decrypt. Just when I thought I'd seen the last of them."

"So do I get to go now?" Tania asked.

"I think it would be better if you hung around for a while," Bull replied.

***

About an hour later, Elf came back with results of his analysis. "We've processed the biometric scans made from Miss Likamolova's gloves and were able to access Chernovsky's phone. Unfortunately, once we were in, we found that part of the information on there had already been deleted by the kill signal."

"How much?" Jonah asked.

"About forty percent."

Jonah sighed, shaking his head.

"We were able to piece together some of the details though," Elf continued, "but other parts are sketchy."

"What have you found?" Jonah asked. "Is there anything of use?"

"There appears to be some details of a meeting here in Xi'an this week, but we don't know the exact location."

"Xi'an?" Tania exclaimed. "Piotr told me he was going there for a commercial shoot this week."

"Did he say where?" Jonah inquired.

"The Museum of Qin Terra Cotta Warriors, I think. Apparently Red Gold wants to use it as a backdrop as part of its aggressive marketing campaign to promote *Zolot* Vodka in China. In fact, now that I think about it, Oleg Korsakov mentioned something about this. He gave me a business card. Said if I ever wanted to endorse his products…"

Jonah took the business card from her and examined it.

"Do you think maybe it's some sort of cover for this meeting?" Tania inquired.

"It's possible. Or it could be that it's simply killing two birds with one stone. I don't know why they'd pick the Museum of all places if it were merely a meeting. When exactly did you say Volkov is organising this photos session?"

"I think it might be Tuesday," Tania replied.

"I need to speak to Hassall back in New York."

Bull entered an empty conference room, followed by Tania and Elf. He walked over to a work station and contacted the Director via satellite. It was Genette Zetterling's austere image that first came up on the large screen monitor, peering over a pair of half-moon tortoise-shell spectacles.

"Mr Bull," she said, shaking her head like a stern headmistress. "You were meant to report in earlier."

"I know," he replied. "There were a few problems. We had to take a slight detour."

"That sounds very much like an excuse similar to 'your dog ate your homework'," she chided him. "If you want to be on time, you must leave well in advance. Don't leave things until the last minute."

"Thank you, Mrs Zetterling," Bull replied grudgingly. "Next time I'll just phone my mother. Now how about putting me through to the boss?"

She harrumphed, then patched him through. "Director Hassall will speak to you now."

The IRIS Director's image appeared shortly on the screen. Bull immediately filled him in on the situation regarding the potential sale in Xi'an.

"Good work," said Hassall. "I take it Mr Xiu has brought you up to date on other matters?"

"You mean the info downloaded from Tania's phone," Bull double-checked. "Not exactly. I was rather preoccupied with other things tonight."

"Sorry, sir," Elf apologised, knowing he had been negligent in that regard. "I was about to get to that eventually."

Hassall ignored Elf and proceeded to explain to Jonah Bull himself. "Mr Xiu retrieved some vital information on The Three Bears."

"What kind of information?" Tania asked, stepping forward.

"Perhaps Elf would be kind enough to show you," he replied.

Elf called up the details on one of the presentation screens and brought up a picture of a Russian man in his mid-forties.

Viewing the same information at his end, Hassall stated in a matter-of-fact tone of voice, "The man you are looking at is Boris Medvedev."

"The former Russian billionaire?" Tania exclaimed.

"Yes. According to Natalya Shikolenko, he is one of The Three Bears."

Tania screwed up her lips as she mused upon this. "Now what are the chances of that? Someone with a name like Medvedev becoming one of The Three Bears?"

"As you may be aware," Hassall continued, ignoring her comment, "Boris Medvedev was one of a number of Russian individuals who amassed a fortune worth billions during the early 1990's, after the fall of the Soviet Union and Communism. If you recall, during this period Russia tried desperately to become a capitalist society, almost at any cost. However, instead of becoming a democracy and stable market economy, it simply became a breeding ground for corruption. These Russian individuals took advantage of this situation, exploiting establishment connections, appropriating public resources and government funds, and finding any kind of loophole in the former Soviet economy. Soon, these billionaires - or 'oligarchs', as they became known - were running Russia's most powerful industries such as oil or the media, when all of these industries became privatised. The oligarchs prospered in what was essentially a bear market, while leaving the rest of the Russian economy in financial ruin."

"Okay, I get the picture," she replied, nodding her head in acknowledgement. "But you've only told me about one 'Bear'. Correct me if I'm wrong, but shouldn't there be two more? Unless it's all a metaphor?"

"Unfortunately, that's where the information ends, and Agent Dare-Brown hasn't been able to deduce anything further so far using ASAP."

"ASAP?" Tania interrupted. "I've heard you mention that several times now. What is that?"

"It's just IRIS's highly-sophisticated surveillance network for monitoring, tracking and examining world events, long-term trends and various data streams," Elf informed her. "Short for Asymmetric Strategy Analysis Program. Chauncey Dare-Brown, whom you've already met, developed this piece of computer software under the supervision of the Director of Science and Technology, Ezekiel Thyme. We use ASAP in conjunction with all of our human intelligence gathering to extrapolate data in order to anticipate any number of permutations and combinations of terrorist strategies and pre-empt potential asymmetric global security threats - as soon as possible."

"Thank you Mr Xiu," Hassall grumbled, irritated that not only had the over-eager IRIS techie revealed highly classified technology without thinking, but that he had nearly caused him to lose his own train of thought. "Now as I was about to say, we don't know who the other two 'Bears' are or their agenda. It's possible, like Boris Medvedev, they are all Russian, hence the obvious reference to 'bears'. But it's also conceivable that they might be a coalition of three different nations altogether. Alternatively, this alliance could simply be 'bears' in the Stock Market sense of the word, or more likely shorthand for the Three Billionaires, since we know that Medvedev wouldn't be able to finance his current operation on his own."

"What exactly are The Three Bears planning at the moment?" Tania inquired.

"Like I said before, we aren't sure at this point. We know it involves the oil spill bacteria that was stolen from the *Chang Yudong* research facility in the Xinjiang Autonomous Region in China. However, having access to one of the Bears' identities allows us to know at least one of their members' motivations, enabling us to make an educated guess as to their plans. When we've combined our most recent findings on Medvedev with previous intelligence we have on The Three Bears, we are fairly certain that, as part of their agenda, they are targeting Russia in some way."

Tania was puzzled. "Why on earth would they want to do that? Did someone eat their porridge?"

"In a manner of speaking, yes." Hassall began to pace around, forgetting that he was not in the same room as them and occasionally disappearing from their viewscreen. "At least as far as Boris Medvedev is concerned. You may remember that, for many of the Russian oligarchs, this wave of prosperity did not last."

"I have a vague idea, but I don't really keep abreast of Russian affairs," Tania said. "You'll have to explain it to me in more detail."

"Well, when Vladimir Putin was President of Russia, he sought to reassert the power of the state, by targeting various oligarchs, either imprisoning them or effectively leaving them as exiles from their own country. There was that whole *Yukos* affair, which sent out a warning to all the other oligarchs not to interfere in Russian politics. At the same time, he sought to restore confidence in the Russian economy by re-nationalising privatised industries such as oil. While many saw these actions as a threat to Russian democracy, a number of oligarchs still managed to avoid any form of prosecution on the basis that they were not seen as significant enough to warrant further measures. One of these was Medvedev."

"So what happened?"

"By the time President Dmitry Zolkin came to power, he took Putin's reforms to an extreme, pursuing a state-managed capitalism more akin to communism while attempting to get rid of the oligarchs completely, including Boris Medvedev. Medvedev believed Russia was becoming Communist again in all but name. Naturally he protested, but was a little too vocal, and soon found himself facing fraud and money laundering charges which may or may not have been justified. His own company *Zharkholneft* - short for *Zharka Kholadna Neft* - was seized when it was in the final stages of negotiations for a lucrative super pipeline deal between Siberia and China, commonly known as 'Project: Beanstalk.' Well, as you can gather, the Beanstalk was cut down, so to speak, and Medvedev ended up in Chita, one of the harshest and most remote prison camps in Siberia."

"Well that sucks. So you're thinking Medvedev wants some sort of revenge against Russia for his own financial ruin?" Tania asked.

"Yes, and for his imprisonment."

"But obviously, if he's now carrying out various operations, he's no longer there, right?"

"Correct. Our information doesn't completely cover this, but somehow he managed to secure an early release. He always protested his innocence and even suggested there was evidence to prove it, which would've implicated members of the *siloviki* - essentially the former military and security personnel employed within the Kremlin. But as far as we know, this evidence has never been brought forward. How he managed to get out after that is anyone's guess."

"Where is he now?"

"No one is sure. He virtually disappeared in the last few years, exiled from his homeland like many other former Russian oligarchs, with the possibility of being rearrested if he set foot on Russian soil again or attempted to conduct business there. Since then, he has carried out various covert operations to regain a foothold in Russia. We do know that one of these covert operations is this sale in Xi'an that's going down on Tuesday between the Three Bears and Volkov."

"Hmm," Bull mused. "What puzzles me is why Volkov would pick Xi'an, and more importantly, a museum of all places, to carry out business."

"Well, if there's a reason, you'll only be able to find out once you're there," Hassall replied. "I want you to head over to Xi'an and find out anything you can, while Elf, you need to head to IRIS headquarters in Beijing where I will meet all of you later."

"What about me?" Tania asked, hopeful she could finally go about her own way. "Can I leave now?"

"No. I think we're going to need your help again," Hassall informed her.

"What?" she exclaimed. "I thought my mission here was over."

"Unfortunately not. We'll also need you to fly to Xi'an and make contact with Volkov."

"But, you said that I could go after this. I did what you wanted me to do."

"Well, technically, we wanted you to gather information on Volkov. We haven't obtained everything we need so far, so your mission with regard to him is far from over."

"That's not fair," Tania moaned, going into a pout. "I knew it wasn't going to be as simple as you made out before. That's how it starts. You think it's going to be just one distraction here. And then it turns into another one, and another one. Then pretty soon it will completely interfere with my tennis schedule."

"That's not open for discussion. You know the deal. Or have you forgotten?"

"No," Tania replied grimly. He saw to it that she wouldn't.

"I assure you that you are vital to our plans," Hassall said. "We can't get to Xi'an to intercept the sale without looking suspicious unless someone goes there under a ruse. We need you to set up a photo shoot with Red Gold."

"But that's hardly going to look *not* suspicious," Tania replied. "Won't Piotr wonder what I'm doing there?"

"Well you said Oleg Korsakov wanted you to endorse some products for him?"

"Yes. But I said I wasn't sure about it."

"Well you'll just have to contact him and tell him that you've changed your mind."

"And if he talks, won't Piotr know that I set this up?"

"Then ask him not to say anything."

"I don't know about that. I've already told him as well that I wasn't ready to take on any further assignments right now. He'll think I'm messing him about."

"Can't be helped. He'll know that you're going to be in Beijing anyway, so it's not overly far for you to travel. As for Volkov, since you have a relationship with him, you can make out that you were partly motivated out of wanting to see him."

Tania thought for a moment. Did she, in fact, want to see him again at this point? If she did, she would probably have to make up some lie.

"Use your charm. Do what you have to, to get to Xi'an," Hassall said. "In the meantime, Wendell Krennick is flying out to join you. He'll meet you in Xi'an."

Bull raised an eyebrow. "May I ask what the Deputy Director for Operations needs to fly out all this way for, sir?"

"He feels that he can provide additional assistance in this situation, and, given the circumstances and everything else we've discovered about The Three Bears, I don't disagree with him. I myself will be travelling to Beijing where we will all rendezvous with each other at IRIS headquarters there. Good luck in Xi'an, and keep your eyes open." His image on the screen faded, leaving Tania alone with Bull.

"So much for the Beijing Open," the Russian sighed, almost having to laugh at the situation. "That went down the spout."

"Explain to me why it's so important that you go there," Bull asked. "Is it one of the top events or something?"

"Well come on. I mean – do I really have to explain all this?"

"Humour me."

"Well apart from the fact that China is a big market and that the 2008 Olympic Games were held there, I won the event last year. That's really the main reason. I'm going back there to defend my title and see my fans."

"Would it be so bad if you didn't defend?"

"Uh… yeah!" she exclaimed. "It's kinda complicated. You see, each round in a tournament is given a certain number of points – say ten for round one, twenty for round two, thirty for round three and so on, just to make it easy for you. For each subsequent round you reach, you're awarded that number of points which are then added to your overall personal point total for all the tournaments you've competed in over the past year, and that's used to calculate your computer world ranking. However, after a year these points are wiped clean, so to speak, and need to be replaced with new ones by playing the same tournament again, so you can maintain your cumulative total."

"So maintaining some kind of state of equilibrium – preserving the balance of power in a way?"

"You could say that. If you don't earn any new points, you lose the ones you gained for that event from the previous year. That gives your nearest-ranked opponents the chance to overtake you in the rankings if they gain points for themselves by doing better than you or just winning more tournaments. Since I already lost a lot of points at the US Open for not defending my title, it means that I might now slip down to Number Three or Four in the world if I didn't go to Beijing and play at all."

"And what's so bad about that?"

"Well, you know - I've been trying to get to Number One for a long time. I don't want to get this close and have it slip from my grasp, and not only that, but lose my Number Two ranking as well. If nothing else, I want to be able to do just well enough, at least, to keep the status quo."

"So it's all about points at the end of the day?"

"Yes. Well, I mean, no. Of course not. But ranking is almost as important to me as winning itself. Then there are also the fans and the sponsorship deals I have in Beijing this year. So I really need to be at the tournament, if for personal reasons alone. I don't want to let all these people down."

"Why do you need their approval?"

"Because… well it's something I don't think you'd understand. You're not a sports personality or celebrity."

"Well you're right about that. I'm not, nor do I have any desire to be. But don't worry, if you really must go there, there's still plenty of time for you to get to Beijing. It starts in a week, doesn't it?"

"Well yeah, but I was planning to be there before. I have a few endorsements and sponsorship deals before the tournament starts. I'm contracted to be there."

"There are more things at stake here than you playing tennis or your endorsements."

"There's also my friend Isabelle's birthday this week. I promised her I would be there. I already missed it last year you know?"

"You'll have to call her and tell her you can't make it. She'll understand if she's really your friend."

Isabelle was less than thrilled to hear the news.

"I'm really sorry to do this to you," Tania said, apologising profusely. "I'm going to have to miss your party."

"Oh, no," Isabelle shrieked. "Don't do this to me."

"I'm sorry," Tania murmured remorsefully.

"You know how much I was looking forward to this. I really wanted you to be there."

"I can't help it. Something's come up."

Isabelle was aghast. "*C'est toujours la même histoire,*" she exclaimed, slipping momentarily into her native French. "What can have come up that's so important that you can't even be there for me? It's just once a year and it's not something that will happen again."

"I can't explain now."

"No, you owe me an explanation. At least give me that. I know there's nothing on this week that you have to miss it. Is it Piotr?"

"No. I mean, not exactly."

"So it *is* something to do with him. Do you absolutely have to spend every moment with him that you can't be with someone else?"

"I don't. It's not how you think. I'm not socialising with him."

"Like you weren't socialising at that party?"

"No, you've got it wrong."

"*I've* got it wrong?" Isabelle's voice sounded like a wounded animal. "And here you're the one who's making all the apologies to me. Seems you haven't got everything right yourself. I've gone out of my way to look out for you and support you. Live in your shadow even. But now when it's something as simple as my birthday, I can't even rely on my best friend to be there."

Tania hung her head in shame. "I'm really sorry, but I can't talk right now."

"No," Isabelle protested. "Don't cut off. You always do that when you don't want to talk to someone."

"I really can't talk now. I'm sorry, Isabelle. I'll call you."

"Don't."

The phone went dead.

Well that went well.

She had let down her friend. Again!

However, such regrets would have to be put out of her mind as she had preparations to make. Next stop: China.

Chapter 16

Tuesday.

The Emperor Qin's Terra Cotta Warriors Museum in Xi'an and the Great Wall of China were two places Tania had always wanted to visit whenever she was in China. So far, she had never had the opportunity to explore either. Xi'an was 800 miles south of Beijing, and too far to simply hop onto a bus to make the journey. Certainly last year after she won the China Open, her hectic schedule took her straight on to her next destination. Or was it another endorsement? She could barely remember now. Everything happened so quickly. No time to think at all.

Well at least she could cross one of those historical sights off her checklist today. The Great Wall would have to wait for another time. Xi'an proved to be a city awash in green accents: lime-painted double-decker buses and taxis circling the arterial network of roadways laid out in a grid-like pattern; women garbed in jade-coloured traditional Chinese ceremonial robes twirling a flurry of emerald silk ribbons atop a crimson carpet as they welcomed visitors to the city. Tania found this kaleidoscope of colours fascinating to watch.

Surrounded by a verdant cluster of lush green trees and grass, the Terra Cotta Museum was twenty-two miles east of the city centre and incorporated a compound of three buildings, each spanning a vast pit of battle-themed statues. The museum had been hired out exclusively for the purpose of the *Zolot* Vodka photo shoot, since visitors to the museum were usually not permitted to take photographs. It certainly helped that Red Gold made a sizeable donation to the museum to overcome this hurdle. Free advertising for the Xi'an museum while serving as an exotic backdrop for the latest *Zolot* marketing campaign.

The pit where the photo shoot was taking place was a huge arch-domed steel structure that looked like a giant aircraft hangar, and was located at the centre of the museum, encompassing an area of 14,260 square metres. The pit itself was about twenty feet beneath ground level, with a bizarre array of warriors, horses and chariots placed in corridors that were divided by earth-rammed partition walls. On the eastern and western sides of the pit were five sloping roadways to allow access between the rows of warriors. The warriors were tightly arranged in a rectangular battle formation, making it difficult, but not impossible, to stand between them or weave one's way around the individual figures. Tania never imagined she would be seeing the 2000-year-old Terra Cotta Warriors in quite these circumstances. Still, it was a breathtaking sight to behold.

It was between and around the myriad of warriors that the elegantly-dressed supermodels were provocatively strewn. The Siberian beauty had a variety of outfits with her, including an aqua-hued tennis dress with an accompanying racquet for a set of sports-themed promotional photographs. Later, leaving the racquet to one side, she changed into a figure-hugging, blue floral cheongsam, or Chinese silk dress, with high-cut leg slits, a mandarin collar and matching open-toed stiletto sandals, in order to emphasise the oriental flavour.

"It is quite a surprise to see you here," Volkov admitted when he heard that Tania would be arriving. Fortunately he did not question her further.

Tania was grateful for that. She hated having to lie to him, whether she felt she could trust him or not. She was also thankful that, when she contacted Oleg Korsakov, he was more than enthusiastic about her suggestion.

"Tatiana Ulyanovna," Korsakov said. "It is good to hear from you. I heard there was some commotion at the Ball after I left."

"Oh, I think it was some party crasher," Tania had tried to explain it away. "I didn't see it myself. I was too busy trying to fend off all these guys chasing after me all night."

"But of course," he replied. "A beautiful young lady like you is bound to have many pursuers."

Tania's response was to laugh nervously at that suggestion. If he only knew how close to the truth that was.

"But I don't understand," Korsakov continued. "What made you change your mind? What happened to your 'no endorsements between tournaments' policy?"

It was true. She had been quite adamant before. How would she explain that?

"Okay, you might find this a dumb reason, but my boyfriend, Piotr, is going to be there organising the shoot. I kinda wanted to see him, especially since he left the Ball early."

"Oh. I see." Korsakov appeared to accept her reasoning. "It's this thing called 'love', huh?"

"Something like that. But please, when you're speaking to Piotr, please don't mention that I arranged this."

"There's no need to be concerned," he assured her. "I perfectly understand. And don't worry. Everything is set up."

Tania wrestled her thoughts away from the earlier conversation as she smiled at Piotr before her. He appeared to be acting completely normal towards her. *Well at least he seems to be out of the loop. Either that, or he's a very good actor.*

The morning passed by swiftly, with Tania entirely at home in front of the camera. Having posed for a growing number of modelling assignments, she was quickly becoming adept at giving the photographers exactly what he or she wanted. On demand, she could now produce looks ranging from sensuous or innocent, to sporty or playful, all of which perfectly encapsulated each facet of her personality without seeming incongruous. The photographers also knew how to bring out the best in her. It was true. If she ever decided to quit the tennis scene, she could easily fall back on a career as a supermodel. Not that she was planning for her tennis days to end any time soon, if she could help it.

"Let's take a break," Volkov suggested around lunchtime. "We can resume later." The photographers left their equipment for the afternoon as they dispersed in various directions to eat separately.

"Where are you going now?" Tania inquired innocently. As if she didn't know.

"I have some business to take care of," he replied. "I'll be back later. Don't you worry your pretty head. You just relax for the moment."

As Volkov left, Tania took out her cell phone and placed a call. "Jonah, Piotr is leaving."

"Keep your eyes on him," he advised her. "I'll meet you shortly."

Within a minute, Bull emerged, and the two of them crept stealthily behind Volkov as he walked hastily towards the pit.

"Looks like he's going to this meeting with his buyers," Bull said.

They followed him as he moved past a vast row of clay warriors and horses, and disappeared around a corner.

As they edged closer, a Chinese man in a lab coat emerged and shook Volkov's hand.

"Who's that?" Tania asked.

Jonah shrugged his shoulders. "No idea." Yet, with the Chinese man clearly in his line of vision, he seized the opportunity to snap a few photographs of him with his camera phone in order to send on to Elvin Xiu for identification.

Then, Volkov and the Chinese man began moving away, with the latter's head turned from the camera.

"Where are they off to now?" Tania inquired.

"Let's follow and find out."

The two of them hid out of sight, unable to see clearly everything that was before them. All they could hear was the faint murmur of voices, but as to the subject matter, that was anyone's guess.

Suddenly, the voices seemed to peter out, as if they were moving away from the area. Tania and Bull stole around the corner to check, but there was no-one there.

"They've gone," she exclaimed, a look of bewilderment darting across her face.

"They couldn't have just disappeared," he replied. "They must've moved to another area. Just stand still while I try to locate them."

Stand still? She sighed frustratedly. *Where does he expect me to go to?*

Bull scouted around for a few moments before beckoning the Russian over. "Volkov must've disappeared down there," he said, pointing to a pathway between a number of statues that led to a clearing. "Stay here while I follow him."

"What, I have to wait here by myself?" Tania exclaimed. "No thanks, I'm coming with you."

"Well make sure you stick close to me. Don't do anything unexpected."

The two of them proceeded cautiously, with Bull leading the way. He placed a phone call to Elvin Xiu, sending him the pictures he had taken. "See if you can find out who this is," he requested.

After a few moments, once the call was ended, they continued onwards, walking across some wooden boards that had been placed on the ground. Suddenly, Bull stopped and looked back at Tania, then down at her feet.

"What?" she asked. Why was he looking at her that way and shaking his head? What had she done now?

"You're making too much noise when you walk."

"It's the heels on these sandals," she replied.

He huffed impatiently. "Why didn't you wear some tennis shoes instead?"

"They'd clash with the cheongsam," came the answer. Wasn't it entirely obvious?

"Well take them off."

"Pfft!" She gave a dismissive wave of her hand. "And walk about in this place without any shoes?"

"Well either that, or you stay here by yourself."

Tania sighed, but decided to ignore him, pressing on while trying her best to walk as stealthily and quietly as possible.

They arrived at the clearing which led into another pit. This did not appear to be open to the public, and was still being heavily excavated. However, there seemed to be various pieces of equipment there, including a number of cylinders, vertically-mounted on the floor around a rotating central axis. Each cylinder comprised twelve barrels spaced equidistantly around the circumference of the cylinder, like a Gatling gun. Inside each of the barrels appeared to be vials of liquid loaded like bullets. Bull examined the cylinder, attempting to find a release mechanism which would eject the vials so that he could take a closer look.

"What is this place?" Tania inquired curiously. "What are they doing here?"

Bull contemplated for a moment. "It seems to be one of the previously undiscovered hidden chambers being used as some kind of secret makeshift lab."

"Who on earth would decide to conduct experiments down here? It's not exactly the best place to carry out research."

Jonah placed a finger over his lips, indicating that she should remain silent. "I hear voices coming this way." He motioned to her to hide behind some equipment.

They waited in hiding as two scientists emerged, carrying pads with which they made various calculations. One of the men walked towards one of the Gatling-gun-like cylinders and pressed a button. The cylinder rotated clockwise, releasing some kind of self-contained magazine with chambers into which each of the vials were slotted, while the vials themselves slid upwards out of the individual barrels. Bull watched carefully as the scientist took one of them out and began to inspect it.

Crouching down there, Tania felt a tingling sensation in her feet, like standing on a bed of tiny nails. Pins and needles. She shifted her weight slightly onto her left hip to alleviate the numbness, assuming a sitting position with one leg tucked under the other and her feet pointing off to the side.

As she continued to sit there, she heard a faint scratching noise next to her, like tiny feet scuttling along close by. She lowered her gaze to the ground. *Oh my gosh.* She had to cup her mouth to stifle what would otherwise have been a clearly audible gasp. Her eyes widened like a couple of fried eggs at the sight before her. Those unmistakable pincers. That distinct, whip-like jointed tail with a stinger on the end. That silky poison sac.

A scorpion!

It was heading her way.

Her heart began pounding intensely like a drum roll on a snare, which she was sure the scientists could hear. Perspiration began forming on her forehead, on the nape of her neck and down her spine, creating a pool in the small of her back and where the base of her spine met her buttocks. She wanted to scramble out of there as quickly as her legs would carry her. Or drop a large brick on it. Not that there was one to hand. However, not only would that blow her cover, but Jonah's as well. But what was she to do? She couldn't simply stay there either. The scorpion was scurrying along, having caught sight of all that lovely, golden flesh on her ankles and along that endless sea of legs. At any moment, it would dig its lobster-like claws into her skin and inject her with its venom, leaving her paralysed like a stiff on a morgue slab.

Oh please hurry up. What the heck were those scientists doing? Why were they taking so long?

The two men continued to discuss matters among themselves, taking their time as they went along, and then even seemed to be laughing about something they found amusing.

Oh come on. Now is not the time to make jokes. What can possibly be so funny? That's not work they're doing. They're just killing time.

She shifted her leg slightly as that blasted insect edged ever closer, about to move in for the kill. It was nearing the sole of her stiletto. She was grateful she hadn't listened to Jonah or else she'd have one foot in the grave by now, for want of a better expression. The thought of writhing about in agony before meeting a sticky end filled her with dread. Too unbearable. *Bite me.* She forced it out of her mind immediately.

Eventually, after what seemed like an eternity, the two scientists left the room, much to the Russian's relief. Without a second thought, she scampered away to safety like a frightened deer, leaving the scorpion to find other food elsewhere. Jonah, on the other hand, had been completely oblivious to her plight. Failing to notice her flustered demeanour, he went back over to the Gatling-gun-like cylinder to take a look at the vials of liquid for himself. However, his glance was caught by some documents lying around on the table next to them.

"What's that?" she inquired, exhaling a huge sigh as that drum roll within her chest faded into the background.

He studied the documents for a moment, leaving her hanging in suspense before finally answering. "They look like a set of blueprints for some sort of capsule, as well as schematics for something else of which I'm not entirely sure."

"I thought we were here to observe a sale going down?"

"Sure," he replied. "But we have to check out anything else unusual." He took out his cell phone, slid open the camera shutter and began photographing the documents.

Tania watched as Jonah clicked away. After a few minutes, her face prickled with concern. "Okay, you've had your look, now let's get out of here."

"Just a second." He walked back over to the Gatling-gun-like cylinder, located the release switch and picked up one of the vials of liquid.

"What are you going to do with that?" she asked.

"I'm taking a sample." He slipped it carefully into his shirt pocket for safe keeping.

"And I suppose, when the scientists find one of them is missing, they'll simply think they misplaced it?"

Before Bull could reply, his phone began vibrating in his pocket. It was probably Elf with the results.

"Hey Bull," Elf began. "I've run the pictures through our IRIS database. The man you photographed is a Dr Wei Sheng Wu. He's a microbiologist in bacterial research and its effects on oil at the Xi'an Shiyou University, formerly known up until May 2003 as the Xi'an Petroleum University."

Suddenly, they heard the sound of voices returning, and Jonah had to cut off abruptly. He motioned again for Tania to find a place to hide, as he restored the cylinder to its previous state and took cover himself.

Upon entering the lab, it was apparent the two voices belonged to Volkov and the man with whom he had been conversing with earlier, now revealed to be Dr Wei. The two continued in discussions for a further few minutes before heading back towards the area where the photo shoot had taken place earlier in the day.

"They're leaving," Tania whispered.

Jonah beckoned to her and then pointed in Volkov's direction. He and Tania began to follow, walking back the way they came. Within a few short minutes, they too were outside, within sight of the two men. As they lay in wait, Jonah filled her in on the brief snippet of information with which Elf had provided him.

"So that must be why they're meeting in Xi'an of all places," Tania concluded. "Although this Terra Cotta Museum is kind of way out from the city and the university. Not the sort of place you'd think to normally conduct business."

"No," Jonah agreed. "But perhaps that's precisely why."

"And what's this Dr Wei doing involved in all of this anyway?"

"I've no idea. I didn't have time to find out."

She nodded in understanding. "So what's happening now?"

"Looks like they're about to engage in the sale."

"With whom? The Three Bears?"

"Either them, or a representative. We'll have to wait and see."

Sure enough, within a few minutes, they heard the sound of another couple of voices arriving, both female.

Tania tried to position herself so that she could gain a better view, but her vision was partly obscured by some of the terra cotta statues. However, she could make out that the two females who had arrived on the scene were garbed in exotic Romani-style costumes, almost resembling lingerie, with fishnet stockings and high leather boots. One was clad in deep scarlet, the other in white, while both dresses were shoulderless with a laced-up décolletage.

"Well they don't look like any bears to me," Tania remarked. "In fact, they look like a couple of rejects from Victoria's Secret."

Bull put a finger to his lips. "Sshh. I'm trying to listen."

"Good day, Mr Volkov," one of the females spoke. She had a distinct accent that sounded Hispanic. "It's a pleasure to finally meet you."

"Believe me, ladies," Volkov assured them, "I have been eagerly waiting to meet one of The Three Bears. But I thought they'd be coming in person."

"Unfortunately, they had other business elsewhere, so they sent us instead. By the way, you don't mind that we brought along some of our own muscle, do you?"

Volkov looked up to see several extra henchmen standing by. "As long as they don't get in the way."

Bull turned to Tania and explained in a low whisper. "The two women are named Carolina Cabral and Valentina Rednikova, better known as Snow White and Rose Red respectively."

"Snow White and Rose Red?" She gave him a look of disbelief. "No prizes for guessing which one is which?"

"Right."

"And I suppose, like in the fairy tale story, they're both inseparable and have decided to make friends with a bear?"

"They're a couple of hired killers actually. Both use an exotic array of weapons and interesting methods to dispose of their victims."

"Well it's nice to know that there's no limit to the kind of bizarre individuals you'll meet in this business. What's with their outfits though?"

"They're both a couple of acrobats. One of them is Russian, the other Brazilian, but raised in the Romani tradition, in a circus of all places. I guess they never outgrew their humble beginnings."

Tania nodded. "Either that, or they like to play dress-up."

Volkov strode towards Snow White and Rose Red. "Let's get this over with."

"As you wish," Snow White replied.

"Do you have the list we agreed upon?"

"First, Dr Wei's research." Snow White extended an open hand as she glanced over at the bewildered Chinese scientist next to Tania's boyfriend.

"You can have Wei himself," Volkov announced unexpectedly. "He's far more valuable to you than his research alone."

"What is the meaning of this?" Wei demanded.

"Be quiet," Volkov barked. He shoved the hapless scientist towards Snow White.

"Escort Dr Wei to safety," Rose Red ordered one of her henchmen. "Make sure he's well looked after. We'll need him."

The henchmen escorted him away, leaving only Snow White and Rose Red.

"Now, how about the list of *siloviki* names," Volkov said. "That's what we agreed upon."

"So impatient," Snow White chided him. "What's the hurry? Are you going somewhere?"

"As a matter of fact, I do have other pressing business to attend to. So if you don't mind, the list please."

Tania watched in fascination as the negotiations proceeded. "What list are they talking about?" she asked, shuffling her feet backwards on the ground. As she did so, the heel of her stiletto stepped back onto a loose shard of terra cotta pottery, making a cracking sound, clearly audible for all to hear.

Volkov looked up in surprise, then ordered one of his men, "Go and see what that noise is."

Bull gave Tania a scolding look, then motioned to her to hide herself, as he retreated behind a collection of statues with her.

The henchman drew a Yarygin PYa automatic pistol - probably standard issue for RISK, as it seemed they all carried them. After searching around for a few moments, he eventually gave up, shaking his head at Volkov, as if to indicate that he could find nothing there.

Bull breathed a sigh of relief. They were safe for the moment. "I told you to take off your shoes," he whispered to the Russian.

But there was no answer. Only the distinct sound of a hammer being cocked somewhere behind them.

Bull turned around to see that someone was holding a Yarygin at her head, with the Russian beauty's hands raised high in the air. The henchman began moving his pistol in a threatening arc, motioning for them to move forward.

They had been caught.

Chapter 17

Tania lurched forward as the RISK agent confiscated Bull's Beretta, and escorted them both into the area where the sale was taking place, with various photography equipment still set up in an arrangement.

The beautiful red-haired assassin known as Rose Red looked up. "Well, well, what have we here?"

A surprised Volkov did a double-take. "Tatya, what are you doing here?"

"I caught them spying on you," the henchman informed them.

"Friends of yours?" Snow White asked Volkov.

"The girl is," he replied. "As for the man, we've met before. He calls himself Ivan Bulsky, if I'm not mistaken. Claims that he's merely a fan, although showing up in the same place here with Tatya thousands of miles from St Petersburg is taking fandom to an extreme."

"Well then introductions are in order," Snow White announced. She strutted over to Tania. "He called you Tatya?"

"Well he shouldn't," Tania retorted, staring at Piotr with a look of disgust. "That name's only reserved for someone close to me. And right now, I really don't trust you. I know about your association with RISK."

"You do, do you?" he replied in mock surprise. "Well congratulations. You should pat yourself on the back for that startling find. But you want to talk about trust? If so, then it appears that you haven't been entirely straight with me yourself. I thought I left you here for lunch and now I find that you've been checking up on me."

"Well that was a real betrayal, wasn't it?" Tania remarked.

Snow White interjected. The Brazilian's accent was soft and musical. "Much as I enjoy watching a good spat, we haven't been properly introduced. Although, I do actually know who you are my dear."

"I'm flattered," Tania replied, her voice laced with sarcasm.

"You should be. Your beauty and reputation precede you, Miss Tatiana Likamolova. Or should I call you Tania, or perhaps Tatya?"

"I'm sure you will anyway."

"Don't be so uncooperative. I'm Snow White, and my friend there goes by the name of Rose Red. I guess you could say we're freelancers for The Three Bears."

Tania rolled her eyes at the Brazilian in disdain. "No doubt they're your codenames?"

"Perhaps." Snow White smiled at her slyly. "Or perhaps we just have a penchant for kinkiness?"

As if to prove this, Snow White began circling the Russian beauty like a vulture, inspecting her closely, and showing just a little too much interest for her liking. Her large, feline, emerald eyes stared unflinchingly upon her prey, causing Tania to swallow in discomfort. Tania observed the vulnerable, come-hither look and bewitchingly sweet smile of her tormentor, as well as her flawless skin. Flawless, apart from the fact that her body was adorned with exotic snowflake tattoos. These having caught her attention, she saw that Rose Red also had a set of rose tattoos herself.

Snow White noticed her staring and smiled. "Like them do you?"

Tania secretly did. Had it been under different circumstances, maybe they could've been friends, as the Russian found herself strangely drawn to her, almost as if this enchantress were casting a spell. Finally, the gorgeous Brazilian assassin broke away, and Tania breathed a sigh of relief.

Snow White refocused her gaze upon Volkov, her mouth slightly parted as she licked her luscious, bee-stung, scarlet-hued lips. "So this is your girlfriend?"

"Not any longer," Tania hastened to point out. This was as good a time as any for them to part ways.

"Oh, don't break up on our behalf," Snow White said, feigning an attempt at sympathy.

"She's not," Bull spoke up. "She already knew about him before."

"And who's this with you?" asked Snow White, strutting towards him with piqued interest as she began examining him like a lab specimen. "Who are you? CIA?"

"If you say so."

"Well you won't mind if I double-check, will you?" She took out her cell phone and photographed him. Then, sending his image to another source, in the same way Bull had done for Wei, she waited for the results. Within a few minutes she had the relevant information she needed.

"Your name's Jonah Bull, former US Air Force Pilot and you now work for International Reconnaissance and Intelligence Service, also known as IRIS."

"So your name was in fact something bovine-related?" Volkov exclaimed. "That little slip by Tatya at the Catherine Palace. And you're neither Russian nor an eye specialist after all? So now we no longer see through a glass darkly. I knew there was more to you when I looked into your eyes before."

"Well it takes a spook to know one," Bull muttered under his breath.

Snow White continued to browse through her information. "Hmm. There's quite a bit on you here which I won't bother to read out. So, one has to ask: how ever did the lovely Tania here get herself mixed up with the likes of you? It's quite a jump from being a simple tennis player?"

"I wonder that myself," Tania muttered.

"I'm disappointed in you, Tatya," Volkov remarked.

"You're disappointed in *me*?" she was incredulous. "What about you? Why did you lie to me all this time? For instance, you never once told me you had a daughter."

Volkov went red with anger, as if she had touched a raw nerve. "She is none of your business."

"Let me guess," Snow White cut in with a mocking tone. "You never told her about your secret life?"

"There are some things that aren't meant to be shared between couples," Volkov replied.

The blonde assassin shook her head in concern. "She already knows more than enough. And I don't mean about your sordid past."

"Well, she won't be around much longer," he assured her.

"You're planning to get rid of us?" Tania asked.

Piotr's answer was abrupt and to the point. "What do you think?"

"Oh, I don't know that Tania has to be disposed of right away," Snow White suggested, as she began to invade the Russian's personal space once more. Playing with a lock of her golden hair and stroking her face like a kitten, she continued. "You know, I've always been a fan of yours. Such a combination of beauty, youth and sheer athleticism. I admire that in a woman. If it wasn't for my friend Rose Red here, I might've saved you for myself, but she might get jealous."

"Well we wouldn't want that would we?" Tania replied flippantly.

"I'm sure we could all smooth things out between us," Snow White suggested, pouting her lips provocatively at Tania. "I do enjoy a good game of tennis. Tonsil tennis, that is. What do you say? Are you game?"

"Look, you're very pretty," Tania responded, feeling a knot in her throat as her cheeks began to flame red. "But don't you already have a girlfriend?"

The Brazilian gave her a sly wink with those bedroom eyes. "Well, perhaps we'll have to play best of three. Don't you think so, Rose Red?"

"Most definitely," the red-head replied. "I never could resist a girl in a tennis dress."

"Leave her alone," Bull spoke firmly.

"Hey, you'll get your turn," Snow White hissed. "We'll make sure you aren't left out."

"That's all very well what you want to do on your own time," Volkov interrupted, growing restless at the fact that the deal had not been completed and at the two assassins' puerile behaviour. "But I've already delivered my end of the bargain. Now RISK Directorate want the information on the *siloviki*."

"I'm afraid there's been a slight change of plans," Rose Red informed him.

"I don't have time to play these games," Volkov replied. "My patience is running out."

"And so is your time," Bull cut in.

Piotr was intrigued by this daring statement, considering that both the Russian and the IRIS agent were currently at the mercy of his men. "What do you mean by that?"

"Think about it, Volkov," Bull continued, pressing his advantage. "Why do you suppose this sale is taking so long? Do you think Snow White and Rose Red are trying to print out a receipt for you? These two ladies here probably have no intention of delivering. In all likelihood they're planning to kill you off in the same way they disposed of Natalya."

"You killed her?" Volkov exclaimed, his gaze turning towards the two assassins as if someone had stoked a fire.

Rose Red looked over at him, with an expression of mock timidity stealing across her face. "Afraid so. Guilty as charged."

"*Suka!*" Volkov swore angrily in Russian, confronted by a full-blown confession, even though he already suspected it was the case.

"Oh don't act surprised," Snow White chided him. "I'm sure you must've realised that already. You mentioned you don't have time for these games, but you were playing one yourself with The Three Bears. You attempted to extort a higher price and that *siloviki* list from them by threatening to expose one of their identities. The evidence you had was something that only Shikolenko possessed, and she was unable to get that information to you. Nevertheless, you still tried to proceed with your original extortion plan, attempting to bluff your way through this sale on the basis that she might still have somehow given it to you anyway. What you didn't know is that the Bears already caught onto your extortion plan a while ago, and asked us to get rid of her before she could do any damage with it."

"What, you think we didn't know?" Rose Red added. "As they say, the game is up."

Volkov remained silent. There were no words to respond in his defence. Eventually, he spoke up. "So where is the information now?"

"That's what we would like to know," Snow White remarked. "When we killed Natalya, she had already transferred it to someone else, presumably for safekeeping, hoping that it would find its way into your hands. I'm willing to bet that she gave it to your girlfriend, 'Goldilocks' over here."

"Where is it?" Volkov demanded, shooting Tania a stern look which she had never seen before.

"I don't know what you're talking about," she lied.

"Of course she does," Snow White said. "She's probably handed it to IRIS by now. They'll want that back, by the way."

Tania ignored her, and allowed her gaze to probe Piotr. "Why the concern over Natalya?" His reaction seemed a little too strong. "I understand she was your partner in RISK, but..."

"My dear," Rose Red interrupted, deciding to enlighten her. "Indeed they were partners. But you might be interested to know that they were more than that. Much more."

Tania looked stunned. "What do you mean?"

"Just ask your boyfriend. Who's been sleeping in his bed?"

Tania looked at him, her eyes searching his face for any hint of an answer.

"Oh you didn't know?" the red-head said, cupping her mouth mockingly and making matters worse.

"What do you expect me to say?" Piotr muttered, seeing that it was useless to deny it any longer. "It's true."

Tania's jaw dropped as her heart ascended into her throat. She squinted, attempting to stifle a tear. Not that he was worth crying over. *Definitely not.* But this man whom she had been seeing for the past few months had not only been completely dishonest with her, but he was a bit of a womaniser as well. And like a naïve schoolgirl, she actually fell for his charms. How could she have been so stupid? "I can't believe I ever liked you," she said, her voice laced with hurt. Yet she was angrier at herself than at him.

"I was wondering what you saw in him myself," Rose Red continued, showing a distinct lack of sensitivity to the delicate situation. "But don't worry, we'll get rid of him shortly for you."

"Is that so?" Volkov replied.

"Yes," Snow White confirmed. "Obviously the sale is off, not only because The Three Bears don't respond well to threats, but also because they no longer have any need for you. RISK have already been more than helpful in locating Dr Wei, so you've outlived your usefulness, I'm afraid."

"I see," Volkov muttered disdainfully. "I expected something like this might happen, so I took a little precaution of my own."

"Precaution?"

Piotr gave a signal, and a small army of RISK agents emerged, with AK-47 assault rifles, Uzi sub-machine guns and a range of other artillery including, of all things, a shoulder-held RPG-29 rocket-propelled grenade launcher.

Tania watched as each of these were trained upon the exotic assassins. Talk about using a sledgehammer to crack two nuts.

"You see?" Volkov gloated. "Do you think I was so stupid as to come unprepared? As you may notice, there are other RISK agents here besides the few here you've seen with me."

"So there are," Snow White said. "A bit excessive, isn't it?"

"I call it taking no chances. Now, if you recall, your other operatives have already left with Dr Wei. That means that there's only the two of you, and as I see it, you're heavily outnumbered by at least twenty to two. Pretty slim odds, as those in the west would say. So if either of you want to walk out of here alive, I suggest you hand over the list now and leave while you still can. You can tell your employer you have what you need."

"You'd better do as he says, Snow," Rose Red conceded, her voice full of mock-resignation.

"Fine," the Brazilian blonde answered. "No point in fighting a losing battle." Snow White slipped her hand into a utility pack, seemingly to retrieve the list. However, instead she pulled out an incendiary device. Before anyone could react, she tossed it into the air, causing all present to run for cover. It exploded with a tremendous burst as the pit was shaken like an earthquake.

With everyone dispersed and distracted, a massive shootout ensued. Snow White and Rose Red leapt out of the way while the RISK agents opened fire, spraying the area with a fusillade of bullets.

Bull automatically slammed Tania to the ground, as the rounds from the AK-47s and Uzi machine guns rained in from every direction, tearing into bodies and tossing them about violently. The bullets that went astray shattered a number of Terra Cotta Warriors with little regard for their value, and smashed the expensive camera equipment in the process.

With a relentless torrent of gunfire overhead, Bull motioned to Tania to crawl away to safety along the ground, following closely behind her as he retrieved his Beretta from the now-dead RISK agent. They edged their way across, inch by inch, keeping low to avoid being caught in the crossfire. The silk blue cheongsam that Tania was wearing was filthy by now. Oh well. At least it was paid for, courtesy of Oleg Korsakov.

They passed by some of the photographic props and the tennis equipment that had been left there earlier before she changed outfits. Tania stretched out her hand. Maybe she should grab the racquet for safe keeping.

"Hey, leave that," Bull ordered her.

"No way," she replied, ignoring his pleas. "These things don't come cheap."

Like pulling rabbits out of a hat, Snow White and Rose Red produced an odd assortment of weapons, including their own firearms, as they fought back valiantly against the RISK agents. Although heavily outnumbered, they more than held their own as they picked off the agents one by one.

The Brazilian blonde pulled out her deadly fan with blades and arrowheads on the tips. The same weapon she had previously used against Natalya Shikolenko, except that now, this one was repaired. With one sudden flick of the wrist, it flew out of her hand and straight into a RISK agent's head. He howled in pain as he fell down in a bloody heap.

Rose Red, meanwhile, placed her hand into the cloth sling on her shoulder, and out came the diabolo again, her deadly juggling prop.

From behind a statue, Tania watched in fascination as the red-head began to twirl it around on the string between her diabolo sticks. The

Russian had never seen one of these devices before. The sheer skill and dexterity that Rose Red displayed left her speechless in amazement. She was like a rhythmic gymnast performing her floor routine. It flew straight in the air, shattering another RISK agent's skull like an eggshell.

Suddenly, one of the men lurched forward to the left of Tania. She froze as he prepared to open fire, but Bull whipped around and shot him first before he could discharge his weapon. Another man appeared, this time tossing a hand grenade in their direction.

The projectile came flying towards them like a tennis ball, but with far deadlier consequence.

Bull's jaw dropped open before he swore. "Quick, get out of here."

Tania gasped but then, miraculously standing her ground, swung the racquet she was holding in a double-handed backhand whipping motion. The grenade was sent soaring back the way it came, towards an oncoming troop of agents.

The man shrieked but it was too late. The grenade exploded before he or the others had time to escape, obliterating them on the spot immediately.

Tania pumped the air with her fist instinctively, before the impact of what she had done hit her. *Oh no. What was I thinking?*

Bull breathed a huge sigh of relief. "They won't be returning that one any time soon."

Tania let out a nervous laugh and nodded. That was all she could do to drown out the thought that she had just used her tennis skills to blow up a group of Russian spies. She looked down at the racquet and sighed. The strings were broken after having pounded the grenade so hard. So much for that. But at least her quick thinking had saved them.

"Come on, we've got to hide amongst the statues," Bull advised her.

"Sure, just a second," she replied, yanking off her shoes and tossing them to one side. "I can't run in these."

He shook his head in despair. "Now you decide to ditch them."

She abandoned the stilettos and the tennis racquet as they began heading deeper into the pit to escape the continuing onslaught.

The RISK agents were swarming everywhere, pressing Snow White and Rose Red back. With little choice, they were also forced to retreat amongst the Terra Cotta Warriors where Tania and Bull were hiding. Determined to get rid of anyone around them, the two assassins began a deadly cat-and-mouse chase of their own, pursuing the Russian and the IRIS agent through the labyrinth of terra cotta statues.

At the clearing where the shootout had occurred, the RISK agents, now diminished in number, paused tentatively at the edge of the pit.

"Get after them," Volkov yelled in Russian. "Don't let them get away."

A number of RISK officers rushed forward into the terra cotta battlefield to give chase to the escapees.

"I'll smoke them out," a brash, cocky officer bragged, recklessly grabbing one of the RPG rocket launchers, and shoving a PG-7VR high-explosive anti-tank grenade down the launch tube. Still standing outside the maze of warriors, he aimed it in their direction, holding it steadily on his shoulder as he took a cursory glance through the optical targeting system. Target located. Crosshairs aligned. He squeezed the trigger, igniting a powder charge. A rumbling followed by a whooshing sound was heard as the grenade blasted out of the tube with deadly force.

Tania's jaw dropped open as she saw the rocket coursing through the air trailed by a cloud of light greyish-blue smoke. It headed towards them, with the arming device on the warhead swiftly kicking in.

Bull yanked at her arm urgently. "Run. Get out of here." He grabbed her hand as they turned abruptly, hurtling down the narrow path between the terra cotta statues with the two assassins close on their heels.

The missile accelerated, and a terrible, ear-splitting explosion filled the air behind them. The terra cotta shards came showering down like confetti as the rocket ploughed through the statues with breakneck speed. Obliterated. Completely. Tania and Bull, as well as the two assassins, were thrown forward by the concussive force, narrowly avoiding being engulfed by the resultant fireball, while the ground shook beneath them. However, some RISK agents who were accidentally caught in the full brunt of the blast were not so lucky, and were ripped to shreds in a hundred fiery fragments.

Although the terra cotta warriors on the front line were utterly destroyed, the impact of the explosion unsettled the inner ones, causing them to begin to topple over, straight onto the statues directly behind. This produced a massive chain reaction. A domino effect. Each statue began cascading rapidly, threatening to crush everything in its path.

"Let's get out of here," Bull cried, shoving Tania forward as they sprinted as fast as they could, trying to stay ahead and outrun the devastation.

The face of the RISK agent who had fired the rocket flared up in delight, thinking he'd stumbled onto an excellent strategy. Within mere seconds, he packed another grenade down the muzzle and fired again. But this time the stabilising fins failed to deploy properly. A few metres through its trajectory, it changed course and double-backed on him and the other RISK agents in the clearing, including Volkov, sending them all running for cover.

Another explosion followed, with bodies sent flying everywhere.

"You stupid idiot!" Volkov shouted furiously at the soldier, as he picked himself up off the floor. "You'll kill us all."

"You said not to let them get away," he retorted in his defence.

"We still need them alive." He drew his Yarygin and, in order to teach him a lesson, shot the incompetent fool straight between the eyes.

In the meantime, the domino rally was in full force as the warriors in the pit came toppling down, one by one. An unstoppable army. They began gathering momentum as the wave of destruction threatened to overtake and overwhelm the escapees completely.

Tania glanced back momentarily behind her to see the collapsing battlefield disintegrate before her eyes. She heard several cries of agony as some of the RISK officers were enveloped by the cascade and crushed like fleeing ants.

"Don't look back," Bull urged her.

Too late. In her distraction, she stumbled over a loose stone on the ground and fell, face forward, onto her hands and knees. She barely managed to cushion her landing, gaining a few scrapes and grazes in the process.

The tumbling warriors were almost upon them.

Through sheer desperation, Bull dragged her to her feet and managed to pull her into a clearing to the side, out of the immediate path of the impending collision. They were just in time to see the toppling statues bulldoze past them, missing them by a hair's breadth. A narrow escape if ever there was one.

Snow White and Rose Red weren't so lucky however. "*Puta que pariu!*" the Brazilian blonde screamed as she disappeared behind a cloud of dust and debris, followed shortly by her red-haired partner, as a swirling mass of terra cotta crashed down on top of them.

Rising slowly to her feet, Tania breathed a huge sigh of relief. "That was insane," she exclaimed, staring in disbelief at the widespread devastation as the dust settled. "Like a bull in a china shop."

Bull cleared his throat as he shot her a bemused look. "Very funny."

"Sorry," she grinned, dusting off the soles of her feet. "I couldn't resist."

"We've got to get out of here," he informed her. "There are RISK agents still out there."

"We'll never get out of here alive," she wailed. "There are too many of them."

As Bull examined their options, he was startled to hear a familiar voice coming through a megaphone.

"Agent Bull," the voice boomed. "If you're still alive, you can come out now. We've got you covered."

"That's Krennick," Bull whispered to Tania. "He must've arrived with some backup. It should be safe."

As Tania followed Bull towards the entrance of the Museum, she saw a mass of bodies strewn among the carnage and debris. Bewildered at what had taken place, she looked up to see Wendell Krennick with additional IRIS agents rounding up the few remaining RISK officers. Among them was Piotr.

"Are you okay?" Krennick inquired, noticing the mass of bodies lying on the ground.

"What took you so long?" Bull replied. "We could've used your help here earlier."

"We couldn't get here sooner, but it looks like we came at just the right time. Most of the RISK agents were blown up by their own rocket launcher. We cornered the few remnants and were met with limited resistance, before they gave themselves up. I guess they didn't want to die fighting."

Tania looked over at Volkov as he was being led away. Despite her anger, her heart still went out to him. "What's going to happen to Piotr?"

"We'll take him back with us," Krennick assured her. "But we need to get you to safety. We don't want to be around here either with all these priceless treasures completely destroyed. We should be able to take it from here now, and sort out any damage control. I suggest though, we all go back to Beijing as soon as possible."

Tania was unable to think right now, so she agreed to accompany them.

As they walked away, beneath the rubble came the first signs of movement. A bloodied female hand emerged and began to ease the debris away, heaving a statue off her. It was Rose Red, still alive, but in poor shape. She crawled out from under it and dragged herself up, before locating Snow White and digging her out.

Snow White's body lay limp and lifeless, her skin deathly pale.

Rose Red held her closely to her breast, cradling her in her arms and sobbing as she whispered Snow White's real name, Carolina, over and over again. She swore she would get revenge on those responsible for her death.

Chapter 18

Tatiana accompanied Jonah Bull back to the IRIS headquarters in Beijing, while Volkov was taken into IRIS custody by Wendell Krennick. Both Elvin Xiu and Director Hassall had flown to China to meet them.

"Elf," Bull said, upon arriving there. "I want you to look into something for me. Snow White and Rose Red were able to access some kind of database to find out my identity and other information on IRIS. Since our own databases aren't publicly available, they must've hacked into our computers somehow."

"I don't know how," he replied. "They'd need special access codes or something. But I won't be able to do that myself, since I'll be busy analysing other new data. I'll have to forward that task onto Chauncey Dare-Brown back in New York. He'll be able to find out for us."

"Thanks."

After a few hours of tests and analysis, Hassall called everyone into a meeting. "First of all, Miss Likamolova," he began, "I realise this is a difficult time for you, I want to thank you for your assistance so far in helping us to bring in Volkov. I also want to thank you for returning here to Beijing with Agent Bull."

Tania said nothing. He was speaking as if she had done him a favour. What choice did she have?

Bull spoke up. "We didn't manage to stop the sale of the bacteria, sir. I'm sorry we failed."

Hassall responded to him. "While that may be the case, all is not lost. Mr Xiu examined the bacterial sample you retrieved, as well as Volkov's smartphone, which could still help us in determining The Three Bears' plans. We've also gathered further information on this Dr Wei in the intervening time since you sent the photos."

"What have you found," Jonah asked.

"Perhaps you'd like to share your findings, Elvin," Hassall said. "We already know that the bacteria was originally stolen from the *Chang Yudong* research facility in Xinjiang. So if you would be so kind as to continue from there..."

Elf nodded, and then brought up a series of slides on the screen that he had prepared earlier. He produced a pointer to call attention to a particular area of the schematics that appeared on the screen. "The way this particular bacteria is normally distributed in an oil-polluted ocean is through a device which explodes special capsules built somewhat like a medicine time-release tablet. Each capsule has an external shell containing thousands of microscopic bacterial spores which can neutralise the polluting properties of oil and make it easier for a clean-up operation. Now, it appears Dr Wei was developing a second generation version of the bacteria as part of his research at the Xi'an Shiyou University. He has worked on it extensively and knows precisely how it behaves. Agent Bull, that sample you took from the lab in Xi'an is of the bacteria which has been modified to make a more powerful strain."

"Modified?" Bull grimaced. "What for?"

"At the moment, the bacteria can be used in a positive way to treat oil spills on a moderately small scale. However, by modifying its properties and dispersing it on a larger scale, it could be used to contaminate an entire oil supply."

"So you're thinking that The Three Bears are intending to do something like this to Russia's oil supply?"

"That's right," Elf confirmed.

"Why?" Tania asked. "Don't tell me - their... what was it? 'Anti-Goldilocks' agenda?"

"Yes," Hassall replied. "Russia is currently the second largest oil producer in the world, with the world's largest consumers - the US, China, and India - reliant on every barrel Russia can produce. With President Zolkin currently in talks for an OPEC-like energy cartel in the

Central Asian territory of the former Soviet states and Xinjiang, that dependence could be made even more acute. Currently, the price of oil is already over $120 a barrel, which is having the same kind of impact as the price shocks in the 1970's. A further spike in the Russian oil supply could send prices sky-rocketing into the stratosphere to almost twice that, while creating a huge windfall for other oil producing nations. That would have a massive impact on the rest of the world."

"What kind of impact?"

"If you recall the world financial crisis in 1998 when the rouble was devalued - this occurred in part because of the crash of the Russian economy. Contaminating the Russian oil supply is likely to severely cripple the Russian economy, leaving it in a similar state to the post-Soviet Russia of the 1990's. This would almost certainly result in another global financial crisis, except that its effect could be catastrophic this time. With oil supplies tight enough with the Middle East's grip on production, everyone will be scrambling for control of the unaffected oil reserves throughout the world. Nations could go to war in a rerun of the Great Game - the nineteenth century struggle for control of the Central Asian region of the Xinjiang Autonomous Region and the former Soviet States such as Azerbaijan, Kazakhstan and Tajikistan - but on an unprecedented scale, this time with everything to play for. The Three Bears would have effectively created a situation where the world economy is vastly overheated or freezing cold. An anti-Goldilocks economy in the form of a global bear market, ironically brought about using black gold or oil itself."

"So Medvedev is doing this all for revenge against Russia for his financial ruin and imprisonment?"

"Partly. Revenge can be a strong, all-consuming poison. But using ASAP, we've ascertained that it's probably also an opportunity to regain prosperity under his own terms. What he wants is to strike at the heart of what he considers a neo-Communist Russia and return to that very type of economy of the early post-Communist 1990's and the power associated with it, which he feels has been stolen from him."

Krennick interrupted. "It seems that Boris Medvedev isn't the only one who shares this anti-Communist sentiment. We think that the list that Volkov was trying to obtain from the Bears contained the names of certain Kremlin members - the *'siloviki'* - who may have shared similar views of total democracy to Medvedev but who also conspired in his arrest because of their own personal agenda."

"But what would Piotr want with such a list?" Tania inquired.

"We're not sure. Volkov may have been hoping to use this for extortion purposes, yet again - this time, against members of the *siloviki*, since their anti-authoritarian views would inevitably have landed them on the wrong side of President Zolkin. Now, unfortunately, the Bears have both the list and the means to destroy Russia."

Tania sighed. She didn't want to know any more about Piotr's sordid past. She changed the subject slightly. "Forgive me for asking, but what's wrong with wanting a democratic and capitalist society? Isn't Communism a step backwards to the old Soviet times?"

"For many Russians it's something that has worked for decades," Krennick answered. "It provides structure and order to an otherwise chaotic society. Many Russians regarded capitalism as something to be hated. You should at least know that."

"Maybe I do. But I guess I've had it too good growing up mostly in the States," Tania replied.

"Although Communism might've provided structure," Hassall said, "ideally, you want a balance between the severe Communist regime and the so-called fully 'democratic', but anarchical free market economy that was seen during the term of President Yeltsin. Medvedev may have partly the right idea with democracy and capitalism, but his views are too extreme, and too unworkable for Russia, and certainly his methods are amiss."

"So Medvedev thinks that, by contaminating the Russian oil supply, his own goals will be achieved?"

"It would appear so."

"But that seems a rather ambitious task," Tania remarked. "Sure, we know The Three Bears might be using oil spill bacteria, but it doesn't seem practical. How would anyone be able to disperse it on a large enough scale to create that sort of damage? Are they simply planning for someone to stand over an oil well and drop a vial into it?"

"No," Elf replied. "If you recall, we mentioned those capsules earlier. They were created to house the oil spill bacteria and to be dispersed in water, which is less viscous than the crude oil inside a well. The lower viscosity means that it also requires a lower explosive yield to fragment those capsules. Now, when it comes to dispersing the spheres through crude oil, the explosive yield would have to be increased. That's where the blueprints Agent Bull photographed at the lab in Xi'an come in. These contain designs for a special industrial oil perforating gun which was also developed at the *Chang Yudong* petroleum research facility."

"Sorry for my ignorance," Tania said. "But the only guns I know about are water pistols. What's a perforating gun?"

"They're special hollow cylindrical devices used in oil extraction, ranging from a few feet to several hundred feet in length." Elf called up an image onto the screen for all to see. It looked like a concert flute, but with none of the holes covered. "Normally, these guns are suspended on a length of tubing or a drill pipe, and lowered into an oil well, but these ones developed at the *Chang Yudong* facility are huge, heavy-duty devices, inserted into the well on giant drill rigs. The perforating guns are then fired to create penetrating holes in the area of the well known as the pay zone, where hydrocarbons - the building blocks for petroleum, if you like - are contained, in order for the oil to enter the well and make extraction easier."

Tania tried to clarify matters. "So these perforating guns are fired, you say? Like a pistol?"

"No. Forget about pistols. Wrong imagery." He brought up another slide of a conical-shaped component. "Although older oil perforators use special 'bullets' to make the holes - hence the term 'gun' - most of the devices these days are fitted with shaped charges of high explosives made of triaminotrinitrobenzene or TATB, which fire a unidirectional blast to punch the hole in the well in a controlled manner. The shaped charges on these particular perforating guns are triggered using a remote laser-initiated ordinance."

"A what? In English or Russian please."

"A laser detonator. It's similar to normal detonators that use electrical voltage to ignite the explosive charges, but this is far superior. Think of it like the laser on a CD player. When you press the remote control, it sends a signal to the player that activates the 'stylus'. In the case of the detonator, when it is remotely triggered, the laser built into the perforating gun focuses a beam of light through miniature lenses to cause a rapid rise in temperature. When the temperature reaches a certain level, it ignites the shaped charges and blows out holes in the hydrocarbon area of the well. The internal components of a perforating gun are somewhat disposable. They can simply be drilled out once the holes have been made in the well, and extraction can begin."

Tania frowned. "I'm not sure I follow. How does this fit in with the capsules?"

"They would be inserted into the perforating gun," Elf replied.

"So you're saying the capsules aren't a standard part of the guns?"

"No," Elf replied. "You wouldn't normally find them there. The blueprints Bull recovered are for non-standard perforating guns that have been specially modified in order to contain these capsules. They're essentially combining two different technologies into one device - oil spill treatment and oil extraction. When the shaped charges in these guns are detonated, instead of merely blasting holes into the well, the capsules would be ejected into the oil supply. Once the spores are released from the capsule, they would be able to contaminate the oil supply by altering some of its basic properties so that it can no longer be processed by normal extraction methods."

"But wouldn't the explosion simply destroy the capsules or even the rest of the gun before that happens?" Tania inquired.

"Not necessarily. The capsules appear to have a hard and resilient, insulating shell that shields the spores from the initial blast, and also protects the bacteria from the heat generated by the explosion. Apart from that, it partly depends on the number of charges detonated."

"How do you mean?"

"Each charge has an exact blast potential, and generates a specific amount of heat," Elf explained. "If too many charges are set off simultaneously, either one of two things may happen: the blast may damage or fracture the outer shell of the capsules, or the heat generated may melt the shell or casing. In both cases, the bacteria would be destroyed before they could be released into their optimum environment. What The Three Bears must calculate, therefore, is the charge coefficient – the maximum number of charges that may be detonated without cracking or incinerating the shell."

"And how would The Three Bears know this information?" Tania asked, looking increasingly baffled. "It seems a rather hit and miss affair."

"They wouldn't," Elf replied. "They would need someone who actually worked on the capsule or perforating gun in order to do the requisite calculations precisely."

"Like Dr Wei, for instance?"

"Well, he would know about the design specifics of the capsules, but that's only one side of the problem. They also need someone like an engineer or the designer of this particular perforating gun to work in conjunction with him."

"And who would that be?"

"From the analysis of the data uploaded by Natalya Shikolenko onto your phone, and the data found on Volkov's phone, we've learned that those two RISK agents were communicating with a Dr Yan Mai Pian, a top engineer at the Tsinghua University in Beijing. Dr Yan developed the perforating gun and would know how to calculate the charge coefficient precisely. Once that's done, the heat from the explosion, rather than destroying the bacteria, could actually assist in warming up the environment so that the bacteria can reproduce at their optimum temperature. When the correct temperature is reached, the capsules would disintegrate, releasing the spores into the body of the crude oil beneath the Earth's surface, and starting the contamination process. Does everything I've said so far make sense?"

"I'm thinking about it," Tania replied.

"Perhaps you could try to explain the oil contamination by way of a simple analogy we can all understand, Elf?" Hassall suggested.

"Er... okay, sir," he agreed. "Let's see. Okay, imagine a man and a woman doing the deed..."

"Modifying these components?" Tania asked without blinking.

"Er... no. Making '*lurve*'. Now the man is like the perforating gun with his...er... his thingamajig, while the woman is like the oil well with her...er...er..." Growing increasingly flustered, he turned to Hassall embarrassedly and whispered, "How shall I refer to it, sir, especially with a girl in the room?"

"I'm sure we all get the picture," Hassall pressed him irritably.

"I'm sorry sir," Elf apologised. "I usually find I'm at a loss for words around people of the opposite sex."

"Okay," Hassall acknowledged. "Well why don't you just explain further?"

"Well I've often tried to explain that one myself, sir," Elf continued, "and I think it stems back to my childhood when..."

"Not that Mr Xiu," Hassall growled irascibly. "Explain the spores."

"Okay, very well sir," he said, breathing a sigh of relief. "Well, those bacterial spores are like Woody Allen in '*Everything You Always Wanted To Know About Sex, But Were Afraid To Ask*', waiting for that inevitable explosive climax - in this case, the detonation of the shaped charges. When things finally go out with a bang, Woody Allen and millions of his buddies are sent swimming, once more into the breach, with any luck, setting the woman on course for her membership in the... uh... pudding club."

"He means getting them pregnant," Krennick clarified.

"Er, yes," Elf confirmed. "Pardon all the euphemisms. This sort of intercourse... I mean... er... discussion makes me rather nervous. It goes without saying however, that rather than doing any impregnating, the spores would contaminate the oil well instead. But it's the same sort of principle."

Tania grinned. "Okay, I understand that now. I think."

Bull raised his hand. "I have a different sort of question. Have these perforating guns already been modified, or are the blueprints I photographed in the lab merely for planned modifications?"

"I think it's the former," Elf replied.

"But then, when exactly would that have happened? How would The Three Bears have gained entry to any Russian oil well in order to install them there? Surely there would've been some security measures?"

"That's a good question," Hassall acknowledged. "And I think I can answer it. At the time, we thought that the break-in at the *Chang Yudong* research facility, now four weeks ago, was simply to steal the oil spill bacteria. Unfortunately, this information wasn't entirely accurate since ASAP only had an incomplete picture at the time. In the light of new evidence, we believe that the break-in was a diversion to conceal another purpose."

"What purpose?"

"We believe that the perforating guns kept there at the facility were tampered with. Those investigating the theft would've been concentrating on the missing bacteria since that was what the intruders wanted the investigators to see, but would've overlooked the fact that certain components of the perforating guns had been exchanged for modified parts."

"So RISK would've already been working in conjunction with The Three Bears prior to the sale of the bacteria?" he asked.

Hassall nodded. "Yes."

"But wait a minute," Tania interrupted. "What was the purpose of the sale in Xi'an then?"

"To sell the Bears the bacteria, remember?"

"So if it was the first time the Bears received the modified bacteria, are you saying these bacterial capsules haven't been inserted into the perforating guns yet? They aren't already installed in an oil well somewhere in Russia right now?"

"Not yet," Hassall replied. "According to our sources, we've learned that Russian oil engineers are planning to do just that within the next few days, and will then be testing the gun shortly afterwards. Sometime between now and then, The Three Bears will want Dr Wei, whom they've kidnapped, to produce as much of that bacteria as possible, and then have those capsules containing the bacteria loaded into the guns before installation. They'll also want Dr Yan to calculate the maximum number of charges to be detonated. Ideally, we want to stop them before the installation, and before they get to Yan."

"Do we know specifically which areas of Russia Medvedev has targeted?" Bull asked. "After all, Russia's a big place."

"Unfortunately, that information is currently unknown," Krennick said, having not spoken for a while. "But again, it's something that Dr Yan would probably know."

"Is there any way to contact him?"

"Our best bet would be to ask Volkov himself," Hassall suggested.

"Well, we may have some trouble with him," Krennick remarked. "When I brought him in, he wasn't the most co-operative."

Hassall nodded. "Do whatever you have to. Agent Bull, you accompany Deputy Director Krennick in the interrogation room."

***

Piotr Volkov was brought into a cell-like interrogation room with a two-way mirror and hidden microphones, while Tania remained outside behind the glass in an observation room with Hassall and Elf, able to hear every word that was said. Hassall stood by in a supervisory capacity, PDA in hand, in order to communicate with either Bull or Krennick and transmit any written instructions to their PDA's if necessary.

"Okay," Krennick began, sitting down at the table opposite Volkov. "I'll get straight to the point. We want any information you have on The Three Bears' plans."

"That's a rather general request," Volkov replied, being deliberately obstructive. "Can you be a bit more specific?"

"Fine. We know about their plans to contaminate the Russian oil supply. You're going to tell us which areas the Bears have specifically targeted."

"I'm afraid I can't help you with that," Volkov said with a sense of finality. "I am not privy to that sort of information."

"You're saying you don't know?" Bull was almost dumbfounded. "I find that hard to believe. You were selling the parts to them."

"That is correct, Mr Bull. A very elementary observation. That is precisely what I was doing. Nothing more, nothing less."

"So who would know such information?"

"Is there a reason you believe that I should be helping you? What sort of incentive is there in it for me?"

"Listen carefully," Bull said. "You're not here to strike some sort of deal. If you think that's going to be the case, you're seriously mistaken.

You're in our custody now and you're required to give your full co-operation."

"Am I supposed to feel threatened by that, Agent Bull?" Volkov taunted him. "Some sense of fear that I am now a prisoner of IRIS? If that's the best you can do, then perhaps you need to go back to school and learn some basic interrogation techniques."

"Well how about this?" Krennick suggested. "We know about your daughter, Sasha at the RISK safe house."

"Now you leave her out of this," Volkov replied, his calm demeanour becoming unsettled.

"Touched a nerve have I?" Krennick got up from his chair and began circling Volkov, walking behind him so that he would be out of his immediate line of vision. His wealth of experience from having served in the elite German counter-terrorist group known as GSG9 now stood him in good stead for unsettling uncooperative detainees. "I'm not saying *we* will do anything personally to her. That's not how IRIS operates. But we can notify the Russian government that we have you in custody. What happens when, as a result, word gets out to your superiors at RISK Directorate that you've been colluding with The Three Bears rather than investigating them as you were originally ordered to?"

Volkov glanced at him through the corner of his eye, trying to maintain his cool. "My 'collusion' with The Three Bears was ultimately to extort information from them."

"But that's not how RISK Directorate are going to see it." Krennick bent down, peering over Volkov's shoulder and whispering close to his ear. There was more than a hint of arrogance in his voice. "Do you think they'll congratulate you for showing some initiative and acting outside the scope of your original orders? I somehow doubt that. Even if they did, once they learn that you're being interrogated here by us, prudence would require them to assume that you've been broken."

"Not if I don't say anything. They know they have my loyalty, even if it is simply out of fear for Sasha's safety."

"But they aren't going to take that chance, are they? Maybe if you were a regular family man, they might view things differently. But since you are a RISK agent, they'll more easily believe that you'd sooner save your own skin, even if that isn't true. And then what do you think RISK might do to your daughter? Or her mother?"

Volkov appeared to be considering the implications for a few moments.

"Think about it," Krennick continued, sounding very self-assured of his own position. "Your daughter is currently in that safe house for protection. But now, she'd be right at the mercy of those who are meant to be protecting her. At the moment, RISK Directorate don't know we have you, but that can all change. All it takes is a simple phone call. Is that something you want?"

"You're bluffing," he countered. "And you're right about RISK agents. I would sooner save my own skin than others'."

"Now you're the one who's bluffing."

"Am I?"

"Your words a few moments ago indicated you were loyal to RISK simply out of fear for your daughter's safety."

"That was simply a manner of speaking."

"Well, we'll soon see." Krennick took out his cell phone and began keying in some numbers.

"Stop," Volkov barked, conceding on the matter. "Okay, you've made your point. You'll have my full co-operation. But I need your assurance you won't inform RISK."

"You have our word," Krennick replied, putting the cell phone away.

"Okay. Fire away. What do you want to know?"

"First off, the location of the targets," Bull pressed him.

"Haven't we been over this already?" Volkov protested. "It doesn't matter how much you threaten me. I cannot tell you what I don't know."

"Who would know?"

"Well I'm sure Dr Yan Mai Pian - the petroleum engineer who developed the technology - would have knowledge of such things."

Krennick took over again. "You've set up a meeting with Dr Yan before. I want you to contact him and ensure he provides us with the relevant information and anything else we might need to know."

"Ah, that I can't help you with."

"You said you were going to co-operate," Bull reminded him.

"And make no mistake, I shall. But unfortunately, even I can't do the impossible."

"What do you mean? You've met him before."

"Met him, yes. Set up the meeting, no."

Bull's eyebrows furrowed. "Now you're getting into semantics."

"No semantics. You said you wanted me to set up a meeting. It's simply the case that the late Natalya Shikolenko was in fact the one who made contact with him, while I was the one who met him in person. An unusual arrangement we had worked out, I know, but that's the way it happened. I suppose it's unfortunate and ironic that the person you need to complete the triangle is now dead."

"Well you're going to help us. You'll have to contact him somehow."

"As I told you before, I don't know the contact protocol. But Natalya does, or rather she did. I'm sure she probably kept a copy of it somewhere - perhaps on her smartphone. You figure it out, then get someone posing as Natalya to contact him, and I'll gladly go to meet Dr Yan for you."

"What? You don't seriously think we'd actually let you go anywhere?"

"I'm completely serious," Volkov replied, remaining calm. "Without me you won't be able to have a meeting in the first place. Dr Yan is very secretive of his work and distrustful of others, so he won't simply agree to meet anyone. Oh don't worry, if you're concerned I might escape, I'm sure you can take all the necessary precautions and that you'll be listening in on the whole conversation anyway."

Bull assumed a less aggressive position, indicating he was open to hearing him out.

"That's better," Volkov said. "There is one other catch, however."

"What now?"

"I need Tania to accompany me."

"What? Now listen," Bull said, pointing a finger at Volkov and giving him a stern, steely look. "What do you need her for? You've already had more than enough dealings with her so far. Her work is done as far as we're concerned. We're not here to play games."

"Not to contradict you, Mr Bull," Volkov replied, "but I think you might find that such an assessment is somewhat premature. We would be there precisely to play a little game, and Tania would be vital to the meeting's success."

"In what way?"

"Although I don't know the precise contact protocol, I do know that Natalya only communicates with Dr Yan at certain allotted times of each month. This is not one of them. The prior arrangement Yan insists upon is that, if ever she should break with protocol, he meets her face to face to ensure the authenticity.

Bull was puzzled. "So what does Tania have to do with this? She's clearly not Natalya."

"Well, I should clarify that Yan doesn't know the specific identity of the person he has been communicating with all this time. Natalya always used a codename in all their correspondence, and he's never actually met her face to face."

"If that's so, then how exactly does Tania coming along help you?" Bull asked. "She could be anyone, in which case you could use someone else to stand in."

"Under normal circumstances, I might agree. But one piece of information that Yan does know about his contact is that she is a known Russian tennis player - just not which one exactly."

"What?" Bull exclaimed. "Why would he know that?"

"Because she told him herself, for whatever reasons she had," Volkov replied. "But it's not really your concern how or why he has that knowledge. All that's important is that he does. Tania would simply be going in Natalya's shoes - one tennis player in place of another."

Hassall appeared to be considering Volkov's proposition carefully from behind the two-way mirror. He handwrote a message on his PDA's touch screen. "Tell Volkov that we agree and tell him to set up the meeting."

Krennick's face became tense when he saw the message appear on his PDA. He wrote a message back. "You're not seriously thinking of going along with his plan?"

Bull continued the interrogation. "And how does simply turning up in person authenticate Natalya's identity?"

Volkov explained calmly. "Tania would, of course, need to be briefed on what to say, to reveal knowledge only Natalya would know. But she should be more than capable. I was under the impression that IRIS was already making use of her many talents."

"Only to get close to you," Bull snapped. "She doesn't need to be involved in this any longer than necessary."

"Oh?" Volkov taunted him. "Am I to understand from your comment that perhaps she's grown on you? That perhaps you care about her well-being? Perhaps I was right after all when I suggested that you were an avid fan at the Catherine Palace, even though I was just humouring you at the time. She's quite delightful, I can tell you from experience. All that innocent charm and girlish beauty."

"I'm merely concerned not to involve a civilian where unnecessary."

"All this time and you still think she's just a civilian? An ordinary tennis player? You're obviously a fool. She's hardly someone as simple as that. She's barely realised her potential, and far more qualified to assist me in the operation than you might give her credit for. She's in the same mould as Natalya."

"Now what are you talking about?" Bull demanded.

That was the same question that was on Tania's mind as she stood outside listening to the conversation.

"Have you never wondered why I began a relationship with her?" Volkov continued.

"The thought had crossed my mind," Bull replied. "But seeing as Tania has many more contacts than you, it seems pretty obvious."

"Contacts?" Volkov replied. "You think that's the only reason? No. Don't get me wrong. She has been helpful. But the real reason... well, maybe she'd like to hear it herself in person. I'm sure she's probably listening in anyway."

That was indeed true. Tania had heard everything, and she was stunned. Surely it couldn't be true what her erstwhile boyfriend had suggested. But then, she had heard so many new revelations in the past few days, any of which would have been hard to believe, and this was just one more. She had to know for herself.

"I'm going in there," she announced.

"Wait a second, you can't," Hassall said, making an attempt to stop her.

"Out of my way," she snapped, pushing him forcefully to one side.

The guard at the door stood in her way, blocking her entry. "Sorry, I can't let you go in there." He seized her by her left shoulder, attempting to move her aside.

"Let go of me," she cried. Immediately without thinking, she responded by bringing her free right arm upwards to elbow him in the neck. Then another sudden movement, and her hand swept outwards in a circle to scoop his head to the side and shove him out of the way.

"Stop her," Hassall ordered, stepping over the fallen guard who was coughing on the floor clasping his throat. But it was too late.

She had already gone in.

Chapter 19

Tania stormed into the interrogation room, her face like thunder.

"Well, here she is herself," Volkov gloated. "I take it you've obviously heard everything so far."

"Shut up," Tania barked. "I don't know why I ever liked you or what I saw in you. But I need to know. Why me? What have I ever done?"

"I'm sorry, sir," the guard outside interrupted, while the door was still wide open. "I tried to stop her. He attempted to restrain Tania again.

Hassall, who had followed her into the room, motioned silently for the guard to stay his hand.

Volkov answered Tania's question. "I'd like to say it was purely for your beauty and fame, but I'd be lying. I needed you to find out about your coach and to ensure you fulfilled your true status."

"What are you talking about? What status? And what does my coach have to do with all this?"

"If you really want to know the truth, why don't you ask him? I'm sure he can fill you in on some answers."

"Don't listen to him," Bull replied. "He's just trying to play you."

"Am I?" Volkov taunted her. "Why don't you find out for yourself? Ask your coach, Igor Rokovsky, if that is even his real name. Ask him how he used to be part of RISK and how he was grooming you as a trainee spy."

"You're lying," Tania exclaimed.

"Well if you don't believe me, why don't you think about it carefully? Look how easily and instinctively you disposed of that guard out there. Hasn't it ever crossed your mind why you know a fighting art like Systema?"

"It's all just part of my overall tennis training for better fitness and breathing control." Tania's voice was quivering.

"Is that what your coach told you?" Volkov said, sowing further seeds of doubt. "I can understand with kick boxing, but I think you'll find, if you do the research, that Systema is an improvised, realistic style of hand-to-hand combat for street fighting reserved more specifically for the *Spetsnaz*. Not exactly a typical sports-style fighting art, or something you'd expect from a regular tennis player."

"What do you mean?"

"If Igor merely wanted to improve your fitness or prepare you physically, there are plenty of other martial arts around. No. It's quite specific training as part of the RISK programme to develop tennis prodigies into spies. It was taught to you so that you would be capable of handling yourself in combat situations. I'm sure there are plenty of other things your coach could answer. Or if you don't want to ask him, why not ask your director here?"

Tania looked over at Hassall. "What is he talking about?"

Hassall did not answer. Yet by his silence, he was allowing various inferences to be drawn.

The Russian became alarmed, her voice quickening. "You know something about this, don't you?"

"Is that true?" Bull asked, looking over at his boss.

The IRIS Director remained silent. By his expression, he appeared to indicate that it just might be.

"It is true, isn't it?" Tania gasped in disbelief. "That's what you meant before by 'that's the official line'."

"Now is not the time to discuss this," Hassall said.

"Oh, I think it's well past the time," Tania replied. "If you even want any further help from me, you and I are going to talk about this right now."

"Okay, let's take this outside in private."

Tania followed Hassall back into the observation room, accompanied by Bull, while Krennick and the guards remained with Volkov.

"You need to calm down," Hassall said sternly.

Calm down? Tania's eyes widened with incredulity. He had to be joking.

"No. I will not," she retorted defiantly. "Not until you tell me everything I need to know."

"Fine." He began to offer an answer. "I know you'll find this hard to believe..."

"Hey, we're way past *'hard to believe'*," Tania hissed. "Everything I've been told today has been Planet Weird. If you've got something to tell me, then don't spare me. Just say it."

Hassall pursed his lips, pausing to speak. It was as if he wasn't quite sure how to break the next part of his news to her. "It's true. You are also one of those sleeper agents like Natalya."

"What?" Tania shrieked. She looked mortified. "An agent?"

"I'm afraid it's true."

"But I've known him for years as my coach. He trained me in tennis. How can you now tell me that we're both a part of this spy world?"

"There are parts of his life you know little about."

Tania let out a heavy sigh. "I think that's obvious."

Hassall began to explain in some detail. "Apart from being trained in tennis, your coach served with the Russian *Spetsnaz* - the Russian Special Forces - for a number of years. After leaving them, he became a member of the prestigious *Spartak Tennis Club* in Moscow, coaching young hopefuls in the skills of the game. However, RISK approached him to work as one of those tennis coaches I spoke of before, who trained cosmonauts, spies and diplomats, but eventually ended up coaching tennis players to be spies, instructing them in various espionage techniques and methods of combat, such as Systema."

"And exactly what kind of skills am I supposed to possess apart from combat ones? I don't see anything particularly special about myself."

"Increased spatial awareness, lateral thinking, an ability to solve problems and puzzles quickly and think on your feet. Even your ability to master languages. These are all skills which, while they integrate into your everyday life, have been specially honed as part of the programme. Of course, your training was incomplete, so you're still a relative novice."

"But... why me?" Tania's voice was full of emotion.

"RISK saw your potential at an early age and wanted another agent within the tennis world. It was almost a certainty that you would become a huge celebrity due to your talent, personality and beauty. You fit their profile perfectly. With your eventual connections and status, you'd be able to move around with the greatest of ease while no-one would ever suspect that their darling of the tennis world was really a Russian spy. A sleeper or agent of influence right under their very noses."

"And apparently under my nose too. Wouldn't I at least have known about this?"

Hassall shook his head. "No. Not if the RISK method of recruitment was effective."

"So wait. You're saying they programmed me as a spy without my knowledge?"

"No. As far as any psychological conditioning and programming is concerned, most definitely not. Neither you nor Natalya would have needed that, since everything was done so subtly. With both of you, you were simply recruited at a young age without your knowledge, trained on the side, and allowed to establish yourselves around the world before being approached by RISK and placed on active status when old enough."

"And what about me? When is my inevitable recruitment?"

"You're not being recruited by RISK. Not if we can help it. Your coach no longer works for them. We approached him a while ago, offered him a way out, and persuaded him to defect. He now works for us on a non-active basis, only when necessary."

"You knew all along? Why haven't you said anything all this time?" She turned to Bull, her eyes flashing angrily. "Did you know about this?"

"I had no idea, I swear," he assured her. "This is news to me too." His clueless expression suggested he was innocent in this matter.

"Your coach didn't want me to say anything," Hassall said. "He wanted to be the one to tell you eventually, when the time was right."

"And when was that supposed to be?"

"That was entirely up to him. If you want further answers, you'll have to speak to him. But while I respect his decision, I'm of the opinion that he should've told you earlier."

"For once, we agree on something," she replied.

Her whole world was falling apart. Everything she believed was true had been suddenly distorted into a shadowy, twisted version of reality in a few mere moments.

This was too much. She needed to retreat to another place where she could digest this unpalatable revelation. "I have to go," she said.

"Now wait a minute," Hassall started. "I understand you're upset about this, but we still need you."

"What for?" Tania asked.

"Don't tell me you're actually considering Volkov's suggestion?" Bull interjected.

"We may not have much choice in the circumstances, as time is of the essence," Hassall replied. "Remember, The Three Bears will be loading the bacterial capsules in the perforating gun within the next few days. We need to get to them before that."

"No," Tania hissed, shaking her head firmly. "I've already done more than enough for you so far."

"Need I remind you that you are still under an obligation to help us," Hassall said.

"No," Tania replied. "You told me before that you needed me specifically to gather information on Piotr because I could get close to him and that if I refused I could be charged as an accomplice to The Three Bears. Well, I fulfilled my end of the bargain. And in case you haven't noticed, you now have him in custody, so the initial reason you presented me with no longer stands. My involvement with IRIS is over."

"You still have a responsibility to help us. There's a lot at stake here. A lot more than just your tennis."

"I've told you before, tennis is everything to me. I've worked too hard to accomplish all I've achieved. I'd be throwing away a part of me I'm not sure I could get back again."

"But you're seeking an elusive ideal. You seem to live in this naïve fairy-tale world - the land of greener pastures of Flushing Meadows or Wimbledon, shut away from real life like a princess in an ivory tower. But the world isn't like that."

Tania breathed a sigh of growing frustration. "There you go again about this fairy-tale world I live in, which isn't true anyway. Do you have issues with that or something? Did your mother forget to read you bedtime stories when you were little?"

"All I'm saying is that for now you're the sport's golden girl, until the next one comes along to take your place. But how many will there be? How many have there been? How long can you be at the top? Five, maybe ten years if you're lucky before you can no longer keep up with the new and up-and-coming players? You'll always be striving for something that doesn't last."

"Well a spy doesn't exactly have a long life-expectancy either," she retorted.

"Neither does anything else in life. You could have the whole world at your feet today, but die suddenly tomorrow. No point in going out of your way to invest in transient riches for yourself here in this life which you could lose at a moment's notice, especially if you can't take them with you anyway. But you might be able to make a difference to others in the short time you have."

"A difference? What kind of difference can I really make? I may have been groomed as some kind of sleeper agent, but there's no way I'm a fully-trained spy. I'm nowhere near ready to make that sort of difference."

Hassall looked her in the eye. "'*Those who watch the wind do not sow, and those who observe the clouds do not harvest.*'"

She looked at him blankly. "I'm sorry?"

"It's from the Old Testament book of Ecclesiastes, he informed her.

"I'm not sure I know what you're getting at."

"You're like a farmer, waiting for the right time to go out into the field. If you wait for the perfect weather conditions you won't ever plant your seeds out of fear that they'll be blown away. And you won't harvest your crops out of fear that the rain might come. But you can't control either the wind or the rain, and you can't let them control you. Sometimes you've just got to venture out and get your feet wet even if it means dealing with the cold and the hot, or the possibility of failing, because standing still and doing nothing is failing as well. You've got to take a risk."

"Even if that risk means losing everything I've ever worked for?"

"Sometimes we're required to sacrifice that which means the most to us. However, once we've accepted the price we must pay, it can sometimes work out that we may not have to sacrifice what was so important to us after all. All that was required was a willingness to give it up and perhaps a re-evaluation of what is really important. Sometimes to catch something, you first have to let it go."

Tania thought for a moment, carefully weighing every word that had been spoken. There was some truth in what he said, but how could she, even for a moment, admit it? If she did, she might talk herself into a corner and find that she was forced to accept Hassall's request to continue assisting them.

She had to find another way around this.

"I can't do this. I won't. As I keep saying, that sacrifice has to be mine to make. I don't like being forced into doing things I don't want, or given choices that are no choice at all. You said that if I didn't help you, I'd be charged along with Piotr as an accomplice of The Three Bears, knowing full well that if I did help you, it could be the end of my tennis career anyway. But the way I see it, the dilemma you placed me in no longer stands."

"What gives you that idea?"

"Having worked with you for a bit now, I've seen the way IRIS operates, and I've also had time to think about the dilemma more carefully. You *won't* prosecute me, because it wouldn't be to your advantage. You've made it perfectly clear that you need me. If you did prosecute, not only would it mean that you'd be forced to call various agents to testify against me, whose identities IRIS would prefer to remain secret, but more importantly, it would almost inevitably attract a lot of publicity, since I'm a well-known celebrity. My association with you would be made public, which would defeat the very purpose for which you want to use me, and you'd be back to square one. All this unwanted attention therefore, would not only jeopardise this mission, but your entire operation. Is that something either you or IRIS really want?"

Hassall remained silent, his face not betraying any hint of emotion. Had he been outmanoeuvred by her clever counter-dilemma?

After a few minutes he spoke again. "Okay Tania, you've made your point. I don't agree with you, but I'm also a man of my word. You're free to go, and I'll have Agent Bull drive you back to your place, but I do think you're making a mistake.

"Well if I am, I'll live and learn. At least if I stick to tennis, I can go to sleep at night and dream, safe in the knowledge that I can still wake up the next morning and dream again, knowing that no-one is trying to kill me just because I defeated them in a tennis match the day before."

"Well I should warn you not to sleep too soundly at night. The Three Bears never do. Remember they're still out there. They might seem to be hibernating, but they can wake up at any moment."

"I'll take my chances," Tania replied evenly. "I know that Snow White and Rose Red are dead, so the pressure should be off."

"Before you get too comfortable, you might want to remember this warning from the former British Prime Minister, Harold MacMillan: *'Once the bear's hug has got you, it's apt to be for keeps.'*"

Chapter 20

Tuesday night.

Bull drove Tania back to her hotel where her coach was staying in Beijing in preparation for the China Open. The night air was cool outside, and a sombre hush seemed to descend on the usually frantic city centre. The journey was travelled in silence, but the anguish of broken dreams tainted every moment. They did not utter a word until he pulled up slowly outside her hotel.

"I'm sorry things turned out the way they did," he said, trying to offer some kind of consolation.

"If you don't mind, I'd rather not talk about it right now," she replied.

She looked devastated. Like someone had ripped this innocent girl's heart out and put it through a blender. Yet in her vulnerability, there was a sensitive spirit about her that seemed to surface, making her even more lovely than usual, and driving someone like Bull to want to hold her forever. Tell her everything would be okay.

"I can understand you feel betrayed," he said, weighing each word carefully.

The reply was like a Siberian winter. Gone was that usual warmth in her voice. "I don't think you understand at all. You've not suddenly gone from believing you were one thing all your life to finding out you were meant for something completely different. I just want to go back to leading a normal life, free from the pressure of having to be some kind of hero."

Jonah gave her a mock-bewildered look, trying to lighten the mood. "You're a celebrity supermodel-tennis player. Exactly which part of your life is normal?"

"Well it's the life I've chosen."

Summarising her feelings on the matter, he asked, "So your perfect world is shattered?"

"Yet again. Yes." The fairy tale had slipped away, only to be replaced by a dark, haunting world shrouded in secrets and lies. She wanted out. By any means necessary.

He looked at her squarely, trying hard to understand her point of view. "Why does everything have to be perfect for you?"

Why indeed?

And he wasn't going to let her off the hook that easily. His eyes were searching hers, trying to comprehend what drove her to such lengths, why she needed this 'Goldilocks' state in her life and was willing to do almost anything to achieve it.

Her heart was torn between wanting to end this uncomfortable conversation which probed too deeply, and a compulsion to finally reveal the secrets on her heart. After a few long wavering moments, she finally gave in to the latter.

"My dad is, and always has been, a perfectionist," she began. "He had considerable tennis talent himself, but never pursued it because his parents – my grandparents – liked to play things safe and thought that he would be better off doing something that was more guaranteed to succeed rather than setting himself up for disappointment. Of course, having adopted that mentality, he didn't try at all and just buried those dreams along with his talent. It became something he regretted his whole life."

"I see," Bull nodded.

"You have to understand that he came from a very poor and humble background with very few privileges. He continually tried to escape it, but never quite felt that he had - even after marrying my mom, who was from a slightly more well-off family, and always accepted him for who he was. He never fully accepted himself, feeling unworthy of her love, despite my mom's repeated assurances to the contrary. I think he reasoned that he needed to be someone in his own right, to have his own identity before she could truly love him, and before he could receive that love without question."

She paused for a moment, as her normally limpid eyes became bleary, recalling her past. "Even when we emigrated from *Nikolayevsk* to the States so I could develop my tennis, he still lived in the shadow of his origins and the regret of not having pursued his own dream. He believed that not only he, but his daughter had to be better than everyone else, in order to be accepted as an equal. He was constantly pushing for me to do better as a child, and I guess I had a strong desire to please him. In a way, he's been living his life vicariously through me, dreaming his dreams through me. The successes I've achieved are the very things he himself could never do, but in some sense it finally allows him to feel some measure of vindication."

"But you can't be living for someone else in that way," Jonah interrupted her, before biting his tongue and allowing her to continue.

Tania finally admitted, "You know, it's not that I didn't come from a loving home or that I didn't have my parents' full support in everything I did. Far from it. They made huge sacrifices on my behalf for me to get where I am today, sometimes even to their own detriment. I'm truly grateful and love them for that. But perhaps, in some strange way, my dad unwittingly placed an enormous burden on me to succeed, and passed down his own legacy and driving ambition to have everything in life just right. Yes, I wanted to be the best, and I even made a vow to myself and to others that I would do just that. I would show everyone, but most of all, my father, that I could be someone to be proud of. But the thing is, striving to be the best in all I do has become such a way of life for me, that I don't know how to do otherwise. I've driven myself to the forefront of the tennis world, but the truth is, if I'm not competing with others - if I'm not at the top of my game - I can feel inferior. I wonder if people would really accept me for who I am."

"And why do you care?" he asked, trying to assuage her anguish. "Why do you need that acceptance from others so much?"

"I don't know." She had to admit that she could not fully answer that question.

She turned those soulful green eyes away to avert his gaze, blinking them rapidly to avoid shedding any tears in front of him. He wasn't going to see her like this.

"I always dreamed of being a tennis player," she continued. "*Always*. Even before I could ride a bike. I was under the impression that it was because of some latent talent that I possessed that I was groomed into this tennis champion, not because I was some kind of guinea pig with tennis being merely a by-product. How would that make you feel? And how would I ever explain that to my dad?"

"Well, he doesn't necessarily need to know the truth."

"But Jonah, *I* know the truth. And that's what ultimately matters. I was being trained to be a spy by RISK. Yet we both know how ruthless and unethical they can be. So even if my training hasn't fully come to fruition, what it boils down to in the end is that I was being groomed to be something I never wanted to be. How can I live with that?"

Jonah thought carefully for a few moments, sympathising with her turmoil. "So you were originally trained to be a spy. But you already have the whole world at your feet. Why does it matter that things weren't the way you originally believed them to be? Isn't it the person you've become now that matters?"

"Please," she insisted. "Let me be. Don't try to say anything now. It won't change the situation. I still have to speak to Igor. I need to know the truth for myself."

***

Elvin Xiu stood nervously in front of Hassall in his temporary office at the IRIS Beijing headquarters, where the Director was discussing alternative options with his second-in-command, Wendell Krennick.

"Elvin," Hassall said, glancing up from his desk as he noticed him with the corner of his eye. "What is it?"

His voice was tentative, as if not wishing to incur the Director's wrath. "Sir, if I may speak freely?"

"Go ahead."

"What are we going to do about Tania?" he asked.

There's not much we can do right now," Hassall replied. "We'll have to do without her. She's made her decision. We need to come up with an alternative plan."

"Sir, perhaps if you'd been honest with her from the start about her coach, she might've had time for it to sink in and she might even have agreed."

"Please, Mr Xiu," Hassall said. "Don't tell me how to do my job. What I did or didn't do, I felt it was the right thing at the time. What I want you to think about right now however, is contacting Dr Yan. Volkov said that he didn't know the contact protocol but that Natalya was the one who set up the meetings."

"Do you think the data I gathered from Tania's phone - the information which Natalya uploaded - might have something of use in connection with this?"

"It's certainly worth a shot."

Elf nodded in understanding. "I'll get on it right away."

"He's right," said Krennick, standing in the doorway of Hassall's office as Elf walked away. "You should have been honest with her."

"It wasn't entirely my decision to make," Hassall replied. "It was partly up to her coach, who wanted it that way."

"Well, what Igor Rokovsky wanted is irrelevant at this point," Krennick stated. "She knows now, so it's too late for any recriminations or regrets. In any event, I'm still of the opinion that we should never have used her in the first place, but since we are friends, I'll support you fully in your decision, even if you don't completely agree. Things like this are bound to happen, especially if we use someone who isn't strictly one of our own agents."

"Well, maybe it's better this way," Hassall concluded. "She was bound to find out inevitably. She needs to know."

***

"I expected this day would eventually come," Igor sighed wearily.

"Well then, tell me," Tania urged him, her voice filled with trepidation. "Has it all been one big misunderstanding, or was everything Director Hassall told me true? Are you a RISK agent, and am I really some kind of trainee spy?"

"I no longer work for RISK," he explained. "IRIS approached me a while ago, offered me a way out, and persuaded me to defect. I work for them now, or at least I used to. I'm currently retired, but I help them whenever I can. Once I joined IRIS, I discontinued your training shortly after. Still, I have no regrets how everything turned out. I consider your training in Systema to be an invaluable skill which can help you survive both on and off the court. I had hoped to keep you out of the whole spy game, but taking all things into consideration with the developments over the last few days, and your relationship with Volkov, IRIS are keen to use you now as an agent."

Tania was incredulous. She felt like a broken Russian *Matryoshka* who had suddenly found other nesting dolls inside her – other aspects to her life that she never knew existed. But now she couldn't put the original outer shell back on again because it had been shattered. Her whole body was wracked with a mixture of anguish and betrayal at the words of someone she trusted implicitly. How could he have lied to her all this time? Kept something as important, as life-changing as this hidden?

Fighting back tears, Tania looked her coach in the eye. The voice of the confident superstar was now that of a little girl. "You knew all this time? Even after you spoke to me in the locker room after my defeat? And yet you said nothing? Why didn't you ever tell me?"

"I was not allowed to disclose such matters until now," he said flatly.

And what was there to say to that?

"What I find hardest to accept is that everything I thought was true, everything I thought was reality - all that was nothing more than a fantasy."

"Don't speak like that," Igor cautioned her. "You have to understand that I was simply following orders to train you as part of RISK. But I have always felt it a privilege to coach you, especially when I see how passionate you are for the sport, and that has never been a fantasy. I am not proud that I have kept the truth from you nor that I originally had other plans for you. But seeing your true passion on the court, I wanted to help you become the very best."

"The best at tennis? Or the best at spying?"

"Tennis, of course. I always wanted you to be a great player."

"A player?" Tania exclaimed. "You want to know what the true fairy tale was? That I was foolish enough to think that I was playing on an equal footing with everyone else. But it was all some kind of game. And the sad thing is that I didn't even know I was part of it. I never was a player. I was always the game." She sounded impetuous. Like a child, all of a sudden.

"Maybe I wasn't clear enough with you before," said Igor. "You remember when I said to you in the locker room that you need to play your own game and not someone else's? Well, there are at least three types of games. Those with rules that are clear and tightly defined and not subject to interpretation, such as tennis and other sports. Those with flexible rules that are within certain boundaries and subject to interpretation, such as you get in a court of law. And those with virtually no formal rules that are boundary-less and subject to change by any player, such as the world of international espionage. Since there are no rules, there is no such thing as 'cheating', because anything goes."

"I'm not sure I follow you here," Tania said weakly.

Well, despite the fact you're virtually at the top of your game in tennis - a player on the world stage - all this time you've been caught up in this business, you have unwittingly been trying to play another game - the spy game - without knowing the rules, and as such, that's why you've become the game. But, like I said before, if you're forced to play this game, you must learn the rules in order to change the game to your advantage. You must become a player first in your own life"

"As I've said before, I don't want to play this game."

"Then the other players will continue to play *you* until you change it."

"Right now, all I want is for things to be just right again."

Igor placed a hand gently on her shoulder. "Tania, I've known you for a few years now, and I think it's fair to say that I understand you well. I know you want everything to be just right, and if things aren't, you'll either always be searching for something more, or attempting to restore the status quo. But things can't always be that way. Sometimes you have to learn to stomach the hot and cold dishes that life serves you. Sun Tzu once wrote: 'Nature is the changes of night and day, the coldness of winter and the heat of summer, the order of the seasons… going with it, going against it… those who can master these things will win.' You have to be flexible and work with the natural laws that bind both polar opposites together, not fight them. That's the only way you'll achieve this ideal balance you seek. If you want things to be just right again but you don't choose the right thing, then you're still not being a player in the game at all and you can't win. Being a player means being responsible for your actions."

As tears streamed down her face there was a brittle silence interrupted only by the occasional sound of her sniffing.

Tania finally composed herself, her voice now flat and lifeless. "Well, if I'm going to be a player, then my first action as one is that I don't want you to be my coach any more."

"What are you saying?" he gasped. "You need me."

"No, I don't," she replied, even though her heart was screaming otherwise. "Many players get on perfectly fine without a coach, and even if I didn't, there are plenty of other coaches out there who don't have some hidden motive for helping me."

"You're not thinking clearly."

"No," she said solemnly. "I'm thinking clearly for the first time in my life. I don't want to do this, but under the circumstances, I think you can understand and respect me."

She paused for a moment, tears welling in her eyes. She knew it would hurt him, probably leave him feeling like a stake had been driven through his heart. But that was the decision she had come to in the end.

She wet her lips, and then spoke, barely a whisper, but the words were an icicle. Cold and to the point. "I don't want to speak to you ever again."

Chapter 21

A few days later.

Since its inaugural opening in 2004, the China Open in Beijing had been growing steadily in status.

In the early years, it had been viewed simply as another Tier II event which many top players tended to avoid, perhaps partly because it took place so soon after the US Open, and players by that stage felt like deflated balloons having already expended the magnitude of their breath during the US tour season in August. However, since the city had hosted the glittering tennis events for the 2008 Olympic Games, that, together with the dramatic increase in prize money, had given the China Open the much needed boost to push it over its tipping point and gain the full support of its star players, making it a highly prestigious tournament in which to compete. The organisers were certainly keen now to promote it as that, if not quite another Grand Slam.

Tania needed no such convincing. She enjoyed it simply because of its friendly atmosphere. Her adoring fans always made their appreciation known and were sure to give her a warm welcome, not least because she was the current defending champion. For Tania, she could just as easily have been turning up for another Grand Slam with the frenzied reception she received upon her arrival by car. Here, perhaps more than anywhere else, her legions of fans tended to view her more as a pop star or Hollywood starlet than a tennis player. There were huge billboards with her image emblazoned on the side of buildings. Some, she could've sworn, looked like they had nothing to do with tennis whatsoever.

There was a distinct spring in her step as she walked through the grounds of the Tennis Center and past the dozens of canvas screens erected around the site. She had a pre-match interview scheduled for later that day. From the previous year, she recalled that it would usually focus on her private life, her likes and dislikes, her favourite food and music, and then by the end of the interview, a bit of tennis was thrown in for good measure when the hosts finally remembered the real purpose of her visit. Still, even though interviews in general were becoming a real drag, compared to the events of the last few days, she would gladly take a whole day's worth of them. Anything to resume some semblance of a normal life.

The next few days before the start of the tournament were spent occupied with rather mundane activities. Well, mundane for a Russian superstar like Tania. Practising tennis for six hours at a stretch, signing autographs, posing for pictures or attending glamorous receptions wasn't the way any ordinary girl usually spent their time. But it was good enough for her.

The Siberian blonde also had a bye in the first round - one of the perks of being one of the top players in the world. That meant that her first match wasn't scheduled until late Tuesday next week. Even though she was here in Beijing several days before she was due to compete, she was grateful to be present. To soak in the atmosphere. To do something she truly loved.

During one spare moment, Tania took the opportunity to log onto her own official website simply out of curiosity. She barely had time to check it recently, both with everything that had occurred in addition to all the tournaments she had also played.

After a few mouse clicks she arrived at the page where her US Open dress was up for auction. She blinked at the screen in surprise.

Well, whaddaya know? Someone's actually paid two-thousand dollars for it.

Elsewhere around Beijing, preparations were being made for the Mid-Autumn or Moon Cake Festival which was to take place on Sunday. Typically, this traditional holiday to celebrate the abundance of the summer's harvest always fell around the same time as the China Open, so the players had some idea of what to expect from the previous year. Being a public holiday, everyone would be out in full force. Some were sure to turn up to watch the men's finals, the men's own event taking place the week before the women's. Then, there would be the inevitable firecrackers outside the stadium erupting in an explosion of colour. Elsewhere around the city, Chinese friends and families would soon gather together to admire the moon at its fullest while feasting, naturally, upon moon cakes. Children would be found carrying brightly lit lanterns to ring in the celebrations, or going to watch the magnificent must-see fire dragon dances.

Just think. All this splendour Tania could be missing if she were still involved with IRIS. *Can you believe it?* They actually wanted her to go along with that harebrained scheme of Piotr's to meet this Dr Yan in Natalya's place. *Yeah right.* That was definitely not happening now. What would they do as an alternative plan? Perhaps they might arrange the meeting anyway and improvise without her?

Forget that. Why was she even thinking about this? She was a tennis player, not a spy, and she had left that murky, Byzantine world behind. This wasn't her concern any more.

***

Friday.

On Friday morning, Tania threw on a blue, floral-print dress and flat, leather-thong Helene sandals with laces that criss-crossed around her ankles, while pinning those golden tresses in a couple of pretty hair clips. She strolled through the lush banquet room of the Shangri-La, the tournament's sponsor hotel, where the players' pre-tournament reception was being held, happy to be mixing with her own crowd of like-minded people - the other tennis players. Or so she thought. As it turned out, perhaps her remembrance of the reality had dimmed since being away from it all in the last week. Finding significant conversations to talk about with them today was like pulling teeth.

There was only one person with whom she could really talk: Isabelle. Sweet, wonderful Isabelle. Or at least that used to be the case. Who knew where their friendship stood now?

Strangely enough, since she arrived, Tania hadn't seen her lovely friend anywhere. Not a peep. She certainly didn't appear to be here at the reception today. Maybe Isabelle was still angry and avoiding her? Well, if that was the case, Tania would make it a point to go and seek her out and apologise. Things would be different from now on. Most definitely.

She wouldn't let her down again.

As she moved towards the banquet table to survey the abundant range of delicacies, Tania heard a familiar voice peal out behind her. Her very friend of whom she had been thinking.

She whipped round, greeting her with a welcoming smile. But when she saw that the gesture wasn't returned, the smile faded.

The moment was tense, both of them treading on eggshells around each other, each one trying to find their feet again. Guilt spilt over her like a bucket of freezing water. She ought to be the first one to break the ice! And yet, while the sentiments came easily, the words didn't. Fearing rejection, she bit her lip nervously before finally speaking her mind. "I'm really sorry I missed your birthday. I know it's no excuse, but I couldn't help it. There was something really important I had to do."

Hope welled up inside her. Would her show of remorse be well received?

It wasn't.

Isabelle sighed wearily. "That seems to be your line these days. There's always something else you have to do. I hate to say it, but it's as if you don't really know how to be happy."

Tania, who normally towered over her friend by a couple of inches, suddenly felt as small as a matchstick that had been snuffed out. "I *can* be happy."

Isabelle shook her head sadly in disagreement. "Sure you're all smiles and sunny personality all the time, and you bounce back from disappointments easily. That's part of what I like about you. But are you really happy in yourself, and living in the moment? Or does your happiness depend on other things and other people? It's as if you aren't sure what you really want. You're always searching for something intangible that will satisfy you completely, and you won't stop until you find it, even if it means not being content with what you have and those around you. Or if it means doing the wrong thing and hurting others in the process."

"That's not true," Tania protested, trying to steady herself. But perhaps there was something in Isabelle's words.

Maybe she couldn't enjoy living in the moment wholeheartedly - tasting the thing that was right there before her - because she always had one eye on the vain hope that the next person, the next thrill, the next win might be the thing that would make her feel ultimately fulfilled. And inevitably, it always failed, never measuring up to her expectations. Either that, or the sudden come down from that temporary high was in such marked contrast to her previous state of bliss that she would sink into a deep funk. Then the cycle would begin again, making that search even more desperate and intense. Anything to avoid that deflated, post-win syndrome.

The truth cut deeply. She sighed in frustration. "Isabelle, I can't always find the right balance, I admit, but I won't hurt others intentionally."

"But you do. And ironically, you end up in a state of imbalance because your life is crowded with too much and you're never quite at peace with yourself. What do you want, Tania? To do what's right or to have everything just right? Because sometimes to have one means you can't have the other."

"Look, I know I haven't been the best friend to you, but it's all different now. I lost my way for a while. I got distracted. But that's changed now."

Isabelle was sceptical. "*Voir, c'est croire,*" she muttered in French. "I'll believe that when I see it."

"Listen," Tania said, touching her friend's arm gently in an attempt to mollify the situation. "Maybe you don't feel you can accept this from me right now, but I've brought you a little present. It's not the proper gift as I haven't had time to look for it, but it's a little something for the moment." She handed her friend a small wrapped package.

Isabelle took it from her reluctantly, but did not open it.

"It's a book of Russian sayings," Tania added, smiling gently to lighten the mood. "I thought it might remind you of me."

She waited for a response. Anything. Perhaps being reminded of her right now was the last thing her friend wanted?

She never got to find out. Her conversation was interrupted by another familiar voice that sent an acute feeling of dread through her body.

Oh no. Tania's publicity agent, Samuel Kurtzberg.

"So you finally decided to show your face," he said disparagingly.

She forced a smile. "Oh, hello."

"Don't 'oh hello' me," he countered, probably sensing that she wasn't entirely pleased to see him. "Where have you been the last few days? You've been completely incommunicado."

"I'm really sorry," she said, offering no explanation.

"You are impossible, do you know that? What kind of image will this give? Huge billboards all over the place advertising a celebrity who remains largely invisible."

"You're right," she interjected, her voice almost a whisper. If things were going to be different, then she would have to change her attitude towards him too.

He failed to hear that, fixed on his own thoughts. "You're not advertising '*Vanish*'," he deadpanned. Then he paused as it suddenly registered. "What did you say?"

"I said you're right. I don't have any excuses. I should've told you. But I'm here now for keeps. I promise I won't be going anywhere. I've just said the same thing to my friend Isabelle."

She turned around, but Isabelle was no longer there.

Now where has she disappeared to? Tania looked perplexed, and her heart sank even further. Why wasn't she able to finish her conversation on a more positive note? Her friend probably thought she was ignoring her again and left. *Damn.*

"You'd better not go anywhere," Kurtzberg replied, moving towards the banquet table and loading his plate up with extra helpings of Peking Duck. "Don't forget - you have a live interview on national television this Sunday at 11.00 am. They're expecting you there as their star guest. Then, there are lots of kids wanting to meet you at the tennis clinic later today. Although you might want to visit a clinic yourself and get your head checked."

"Hey, my days of running off are over," she assured him. "I'm all theirs, and I'm really looking forward to that." She definitely was. Her face lit up with excitement at the mere mention of it.

"Well, we'll see about that." Kurtzberg sounded doubtful, as he continued to stock up excessively on further courses of exotic food. He stopped at one of the bowls in front of him and glanced down suspiciously. "Excuse me, but what is this?"

"Bird's Nest Soup," one of the nearby caterers informed him plainly.

"What?" he exclaimed, making a face of outward disgust. "Bird's Nest? What the heck's in that?"

"It is delicacy of swiftlets' saliva," the caterer stated in broken English.

He grimaced again. "Ugh. That's even worse than I thought. You're joking, right? I hope these swiftlets didn't have the bird flu. I'd hate to think they coughed up some phlegm while spitting this out for the chefs."

"Sshh," Tania whispered, placing a finger in front of her lips. "You'll offend them."

He waved a hand dismissively. "Hey, do you see any birds at the moment? They won't be offended by what they can't hear."

"I meant the caterers," Tania replied. "And it's apparently very popular here as an aphrodisiac."

Kurtzberg shook his head. "No thanks. The Chinese can stick to their lovebirds. I think I'll stick to my Viagra."

Tania let out a giggle in amusement. She then turned to face him. "Look, I meant what I said before about my days of running off being over."

Kurtzberg stopped what he was doing and took a moment to behold her. Her expression was sincere and relaxed, suggesting that she seemed less unsettled than when he had last spoken to her in Flushing Meadows. "Hey, you sound like you really mean it. And from looking at you today, I'm almost inclined to say it like you've suddenly grown up since I last saw you."

"I don't know about that," Tania laughed.

Kurtzberg shrugged. "Maybe there's hope for you yet."

Later that day, Tania enjoyed her time immensely at the tennis clinic, coaching the aspiring young hopefuls. The kids were in awe of her, but still eagerly participated, all wanting to please their role model. She demonstrated various techniques and helped them to stretch and warm up.

Following this, she gave them a good pep talk about dedication and sacrifice, and the value of working hard at their game. There were plenty of laughs too, topped off with congratulatory high-fives every time they did something well and performed beyond her expectations. She made sure to capture it all on both her palm-corder and digital camera, brought along to keep a record of the memories. She couldn't remember when she had had so much fun.

This was her calling. Being a tennis player. Not playing spy.

***

There were few things or people that unsettled Valentina Rednikova, also known as Rose Red. Unfortunately, Boris Medvedev, one of The Three Bears, was one of them. Her words had that distinct nervous edge to them as she treaded the phone lines of their conversation with extreme caution. His cold, stern voice - like a frosty breath in the dead of winter - always sent a chill down her spine, even though she herself was an assassin whose heart was made of ice.

"I realise I have failed you," she apologised. "But give me another chance, at least to avenge Snow White."

"I don't pay you handsomely just so you can carry out your own personal vendetta, Miss Rednikova," Medvedev replied. "There is a far bigger picture here than your own agenda."

"So what do you want me to do?" She attempted to appease him by showing some measure of enthusiasm.

"Nothing, for the moment," he replied dispassionately. "We must lay low and strike when the time is right."

"What about IRIS? Or Tatiana Likamolova?"

"Where is Likamolova at the moment?"

Valentina was quick to respond. "She's in Beijing, training for her tournament there."

Medvedev thought for a moment, weighing the advantages and disadvantages of utilising this erstwhile street urchin-turned-circus-act-turned-hired-killer. "I'll have someone take care of her. But if you are seen anywhere near the within the tennis centre grounds, you'll end up jeopardising everything. I have someone else on the inside who will deal with the matter."

***

Saturday morning.

The eve of the Moon Cake Festival arrived, and not a moment too soon. Tania was eager to be back competing at tournament level again, but first, she had to get through this weekend. The days before the first match seemed to pass far too slowly.

With a few hours to spare, Tania began to work on her game on a practice court. She certainly needed the training. The last time she played competitively, she was handed her racquet and given a good, albeit unwanted, lesson by a far stronger opponent.

During this session, she decided to use the tennis ball machine. She had seen them around the courts, and although they couldn't compare with playing against a live hitting partner, they would still give her a good workout.

Unfortunately, the ball machine could sometimes prove difficult to operate without having read the instruction manual properly. A thorough read through should have been simple enough, except that the manual was in Chinese, and she had neither the time nor the inclination to try to figure it out all on her own. At least not if there was someone else at hand to help.

While she limbered up with her usual stretching exercises and eye-hand-ball co-ordination routines, she asked one of the assistants to programme the machine for her. They were used to doing that for the tennis players anyway. Why make life any harder than it had to be?

The ball machine had a capacity of three hundred balls in total. She asked the assistant to programme it to fire thirty balls in succession for one drill and then pause automatically for a five minute delay to allow her to catch her breath.

With Tania's back turned and completely focused on her exercises, the assistant began loading up the balls and programming the control pad. He removed a few balls from a tennis ball tin and laid them carefully on the ground. These balls looked identical to the others, except that they had been primed with explosive charges designed to detonate on impact like a mortar once the ball machine had launched it.

The assistant placed them into the ball bin and then loaded the rest of the balls in, mixing them up so that no-one could tell where they were, or when exactly they would be launched. Since the drills were usually performed quickly, this did not matter. Sooner or later the explosive tennis balls would destroy their target.

Tania's cell phone rang before she had even begun. It was her father, Ulya Alexandrovich Likamolov.

"Papa," she said, surprised to hear him. "Where are you?"

Her father's voice sounded sombre, tinged with a hint of irritation. He addressed her frankly in Russian. "Your mother and I had hoped you would show up in *Nikolayevsk*."

"I was busy," she replied, also in the same tongue. "Something unexpected came up in the last week. I tried to get out of it but I couldn't." That was the truth. At least, in its most distilled form, although it didn't account for the fact that she was reluctant in the first place to travel out to that small town near Sakhalin Island. How could she tell him that she had, in fact, been drawn into a world of mayhem and deceit which prevented her from even concentrating on her beloved sport? She had let the people around her down in the last week, and she knew it. She tried to apologise, hoping he would understand.

"Busy?" her father exclaimed. "Sometimes you have your fingers in too many pies."

"Oh not you as well," she groaned. Warning bells went off that her father was going to launch into another one of his monologues for the umpteenth time, reminding her of her tendency to try too many different things until she had found the perfect balance. But perhaps he was right. Her failure to manage herself adequately simply seemed to confirm the things he had been saying. She was being drawn, like metal filings to a magnet, into another one of their tension-filled conversations, all the while wishing there were some way she could extricate herself before things got too heated.

It was time to nip this conversation in the bud.

"Do we have to fight all the time, Papa?" she said with a tinge of regret in her voice. "We seem to do that a lot these days. It wasn't always like this. Sometimes I want things to go back to the way they were before. Just you and me, and our team, and not the whole media constantly glaring in, watching our every move."

"You know we can't," her father replied simply. "That's the cost of becoming a champion and a celebrity. Sometimes living a fairy tale comes with a heavy price tag."

***

Elf was on the phone in his workshop, where a bizarre array of equipment was stored. "Okay, thanks Chauncey," he said, before hanging up.

"Any progress?" Bull asked, popping his head in.

"Well if I compared myself to a snail, would that answer your question?" Elf had been sitting at his computer console, attempting to analyse the contents of the file that Natalya had uploaded to Tania's phone, so far, to no avail. "I just spoke with Chauncey though. He's looking into that thing you asked me before, regarding Snow White and Rose Red hacking into IRIS personnel files."

"Good. Well let me know about that," Bull replied, as he began browsing through the various pieces of equipment stored there. A number of items looked like everyday objects which probably housed some hidden gadgets within them. Everything from toiletries to accessories to various items of clothing. "You've got some rather unusual toys here," he commented.

"Don't mind those," Elf replied modestly. "They're just a few nick-nacks." He continued on the previous subject. "While I did manage to crack the encryption before, to reveal Medvedev's name, there appear to be various levels of encryption for different sections of the file. Since I didn't even know we were looking for something specific before, I hadn't worked on this part."

"Well let us know when you're done."

"Actually, we do have something. It's not much, but it is something."

"What is it?"

"It looks like Natalya and this Dr Yan made contact via some kind of instant messaging service. His codename was THE_ENGINEER478'. Hers was VASILISSA."

"Well that's a start, isn't it?"

"Yes, but there's a codeword response which needs to be entered before either of them can progress."

"Do you know it?" Bull asked.

"Uh... no," Elf replied. "There's only a password prompt to which you're supposed to reply."

"What is it?" Bull asked.

"It's all rather cryptic. It says: IN RUSSIA, A BULL'S HEART MAKES NO SOUND"

Bull gave a blank stare. "What's that supposed to mean?"

***

Tania ended the phone conversation with her father feeling like a damp squib. However, she refused to let the fire within her be quenched. After all, she was back where she wanted to be, practising on a tennis court. Igniting her own enthusiasm, she called out from across the court. "All done?"

"Yes, just finishing up," the ball assistant replied. He walked over to her and placed a small pad in her hand. "You can control the speed and oscillation with this remote control."

"Thanks a lot," Tania said.

"Have fun. You'll get a real kick out of this."

Tania hit the remote control and the balls began exiting through the large opening in the front of the machine, firing in various directions of the court. The ball machine allowed her to adjust the ball speed, feed frequency, power, trajectory and the variety of the shots.

Tania began to perform one shot after another, her heart rate rapidly rising as she gave herself a thorough workout.

Thirty balls later, the ball machine stopped. She wiped the perspiration from her forehead with her towel as she took a breather. This was more strenuous than she imagined. Then, at the corner of her eye, she saw her coach, Igor, entering the tennis court. What was he doing here? Hadn't he gotten the message before? Had he come to appeal to her again? Less than pleased to see him, she turned her face away to avoid his gaze.

"Tania," he said, in a conciliatory tone.

"I said I don't want to speak to you," she muttered, determined to maintain her resolve. She bit her tongue. It hurt her to say this, but he had betrayed her, and she wasn't ready to deal with him right now. "Please, leave me alone."

Tania pressed the remote control and the drill started again. The ball machine began its next round of thirty balls. Although her eyes never wavered away from each ball as she struck it, her mind was still overwhelmed with the knowledge that she had been deceived by her coach. And now, here he was, asking forgiveness. She hit the balls on pure instinct, her mind almost detached from her movements like an automaton.

"You can't keep avoiding me," Igor said.

She spoke through clenched teeth. "I think I'll do fine without your help. Not everyone has a coach anyway."

"But you still need one."

She huffed. "Then I'll find another. Anyone other than you. At least someone whose only agenda is tennis, not something more."

He was distracting her with his talk. She began to miss a few balls, as her focus shifted onto whether there was any way she could overlook what he had done. Could she simply go on as before? No. Things were too different. He had betrayed her.

"I'm trying to practise here," she said, pounding the balls even harder, as though she were trying to crack a stubborn walnut, in order to vent her frustration. A string on her racquet broke, and she threw her hands up in the air in frustration. "Now look what you've made me do."

She ran quickly to the side of the court to change her racquet as the ball machine continued shooting.

Suddenly, there was a fizzing sound coming from the machine like an effervescent vitamin tablet dissolving in water. The next ball that launched seemed to crackle with sparks as it coursed through the air towards her.

Igor recognised it instantly. "Get out of the way," he ordered Tania as she jogged back to her position.

She was completely mystified by his command. "What?"

There was no time to explain. He pushed her to one side, as the ball exploded where they were standing with a deafening blast. The force of it knocked Tania to the ground as a cloud of smoke filled the air.

Chapter 22

Elvin Xiu stared pensively at the encrypted file's password hint for a few moments. IN RUSSIA, A BULL'S HEART MAKES NO SOUND.

"Anything else we know about this?" Bull asked him, peering over his shoulder.

Elf shook his head. "All I've worked out is that the answer seems to be a minimum of six letters."

"So now we have to play a guessing game?"

"I don't know." He shrugged. "It sounds like a cryptic clue to me. How difficult can it be?"

"Well you're the expert around here, so you should be able to crack this," Bull assured him. "I'm sure you're more than up to the task."

"Thanks for the vote of confidence." Elf began to think about the various possibilities. "Maybe the 'IN RUSSIA' means something. Perhaps it refers to MOSCOW. Yeah, that could be it. That's at least six letters."

"Why MOSCOW?" Jonah couldn't see the connection.

Like a game of six degrees of separation, Elf made the link. "Russia. Bull. Bulls are like cows. Hence MOS*COW*."

Bull grinned at his colleague's inconsequence. "You're crazy. What kind of logic is that?"

Elf shrugged. "Sometimes you have to think in a roundabout way to crack a code. At least that's what I learnt from the guys I hung out with at MIT."

"But MOSCOW wouldn't account for the rest of the clue," Bull pointed out.

"Well I can only try," he replied. He keyed in the word.

ACCESS DENIED.

"Okay, that didn't work," he muttered. "What else? Maybe it's a reference to you."

"Why would she pick me as her password hint?" Jonah replied, doubtful of the suggestion. "It's not like we knew each other at all. And besides, there are not enough letters."

"I meant what if it's a reference to other words for bull or like a bull?" Elf clarified. "Quick, what synonyms are there?"

Bull put on his thinking cap and began to brainstorm. "Bullock, Bovine, Taurine, Bulsky..."

Elf typed those entries in, hopeful that one would hit the target.

ACCESS DENIED.

"No such luck," Bull sighed.

Elf's face lit up with enlightenment. "I've got it, I think. What if it's TAURUS?"

"TAURUS?" Bull was unable to follow. "Why that rather than the others?"

"Well apart from the fact that the other ones didn't work, I was thinking along the same lines as MOSCOW. TAURUS would also be bull, and it contains RUS, which is the abbreviation for Russia."

"Genius," Bull replied, as he watched his colleague type it in.

ACCESS DENIED.

Elf sighed. "Or not."

***

A team of doctors burst through the doors of the emergency room of Beijing's Friendship Hospital, wheeling Tania's coach, Igor Rokovsky inside.

"That's as far as you can go," the nurse said, as Tania watched helplessly, her access blocked by the doors to the theatre.

Tania placed her hand on the window as a tear rolled down her cheek.

"There's nothing you can do at the moment," the nurse informed her. She escorted the tennis star to the hospital waiting room. "You'll be alright here. You're very lucky to escape with only a few bruises. You're just suffering from shock, but the doctor wants to keep you under observation for a few hours."

"Will my coach be okay?" Tania asked, more concerned about Igor than herself.

"We don't know yet," the nurse replied. "The doctor will be with you shortly and he'll answer your questions."

Tania slumped into a chair as she wiped away a tear. The television screen was on in the room, playing in the background, and briefly grabbing her attention. The programme appeared to be a documentary on tsunamis and tectonic plates.

The narrator spoke. *"A tsunami can be generated by any disturbance that causes the sea floor to deform abruptly and rapidly displace a large mass of overlying water. Such large vertical movements of the earth's crust can occur at the boundaries of the tectonic plates."*

Tania began to tune out, oblivious to the images that flickered across the screen.

The doctor came in to speak to Tania. His expression looked foreboding, as if he were about to deliver her a heart-wrenching message. Inside her chest, it felt as if someone had turned up the speed on a metronome to its highest setting.

"How is he?" she asked.

The message was not what she expected, but nevertheless still grave. "His condition is stable, but he's slipped into a coma. There's no telling how long he will be in that condition."

"Thank you," she replied, the metronome beginning to slow down to a gentler tempo. She was obviously shocked but at the same time relieved it was not worse. "Please keep me posted if there's any change."

Tania sank back into the chair in despair. *That should've been me there instead of him. Igor's got to be okay. He just has to be. It was because of me that the tennis machine was rigged with explosives. IRIS warned me that The Three Bears were still out there. But then, what does that mean? Will I never be able to go out on a tennis court again without being afraid that someone's going to try to kill those closest to me?*

Her thoughts were interrupted by a familiar female voice. It was Isabelle.

"Hey, Tania," she said.

She looked up and smiled weakly. "Isabelle. I thought you weren't talking to me. I'm so sorry for missing your birthday…"

Isabelle sighed. As if that was important right now. Taking a seat next to her friend and placing a reassuring arm around her shoulder, she said, "Don't be silly. Of course I forgive you. Sure I was angry at the time, but that's only because you mean a lot to me and I wanted you to be there. If you weren't, I wouldn't have batted an eyelid. But let's not talk about that now. I can't possibly stay angry with someone as sweet as you, especially after the lovely present you gave me. By the way, I haven't had the chance to thank you for it."

Tania mustered a half smile. "That's okay. You're welcome."

Isabelle pulled Tania in close to hug her, and immediately the Russian buried her head on the French girl's shoulder, absorbing the warmth of her friend's body, drawing strength from her.

When they broke away, Isabelle looked Tania squarely in the eye. "I don't understand. What on earth happened today?"

"I'm not completely sure myself," Tania lied. She knew full well what had probably occurred. But how could she share that knowledge with her friend? That could jeopardise her safety. And there had already been quite enough of danger to others close to her. Nevertheless, she offered a partial answer. "There was some kind of explosion on court."

Isabelle gasped. "What? Are you okay?"

"Yes. I'm fine." But the truth was that inside, she was overwhelmed by pangs of guilt. "Igor pushed me out of the way. He was caught in the blast."

"Oh my goodness. You're probably worried sick about your coach."

Tania hung her head sadly. "Yes."

"How is he?"

"He's in a coma at the moment." The mere mention of those words primed the water pump in her eyes.

"Oh, Tania. I'm really sorry about that." Isabelle stretched out her arms, wrapping her in an embrace which lasted for a few moments.

The Russian's voice was a mere whisper when she eventually pulled away. "Yeah. I know."

"Well at least he knows he has you by his side."

Tania shook her head. "I'm not so sure about that."

Isabelle was puzzled. "Of course he does. What are you talking about?"

"I can't really go into it right now. But I told him that I didn't want him to be my coach any longer."

"Well… that shouldn't be too much of a problem. If you needed a new coach, he won't hold that against you."

"You don't understand. I told him I never wanted to see him again."

"What?" Isabelle was unsure she heard her correctly. "Tania, what on earth?"

"I know," she nodded. "I feel stupid right now for saying such a thing. If he doesn't pull through, he won't know…"

Isabelle placed her hand on Tania's knee. "Sometimes we say things in anger to those closest to us, and often it's the last thing they'll hear. But if they're truly understanding, they'll look at it within the whole context of the relationship and not that one isolated incident."

"Well, I blame myself that he's lying in that coma. It should've been me."

Isabelle grimaced, trying to comprehend her friend's reasoning. "What are you saying Tania? How on earth can it possibly be your fault? You wouldn't have known what was going to happen."

"No, but I could've anticipated."

Isabelle gave her a blank look. "You've totally lost me there. In fact, I've stopped trying to figure you out these days. There seems so much stuff in your life."

"Well I'm trying to sort some of it out. I'm just torn between different things at the moment. I don't know who I am anymore or what I'm supposed to be doing, or whether I'm even doing the right thing."

"Hey," Isabelle said, reaching inside her *Givenchy* handbag. "I want to show you a few things I've been reading that you might find relevant. It's that book of Russian sayings you bought me."

Isabelle thumbed through several pages. "Here. Listen to this: Ever heard this one? '*One who sits between two chairs may easily fall down?*'"

"I'm sure I've probably come across it a long time ago. I haven't thought about these sayings for ages."

"I think it just means that you can't be in two minds about everything, trying to wait for the thing that is just right, even if it means that you make a mistake in the process. When it's your ass on the line, you need to decide what you want to do, or it will be your ass that ends up on the floor if you don't."

"Hmm, that's funny," Tania remarked, with a faint semblance of a smile on her face.

"Yep," Isabelle nodded. "But you want to know what's really funny? The way these are grouped together."

Tania looked up briefly. "What do you mean?"

"Oh, it's almost as if the editor had the story of Goldilocks and the Three Bears in mind. There are a couple more here in the same vein: '*As you cooked the porridge, so must you eat it.*' And '*As you make your bed, so will you sleep.*' But you must excuse me. I'm babbling here now. I'm sure it's been ages since you thought about that fairy tale. You've probably got more important things on your mind."

She was wrong. It hit home far more than she had ever imagined.

I've definitely made my bed and now I have to sleep in it, I've cooked my own porridge, and now I must eat it. I chose this path and now I'm reaping the consequences. By pursuing my own dreams and running away from my responsibilities - even those I didn't want which were thrust upon me - other people have gotten hurt. The Three Bears wouldn't have targeted me in my practice session if I hadn't been there in the first place. I just wanted that World Number One position more than anything and I knew that all it would take would be winning a few matches and gaining a few points to get me there. I wanted everything to be 'just right'. But all that means nothing now if Igor were to die.

As Tania thought upon these things, Hassall's earlier words also came flooding back like a tidal wave:

"You're only a trustee of all your talents, so to speak, not the ultimate owner of them. While owners have rights, trustees have responsibility. That's what you have here - a responsibility to use your talents and God-given abilities for a greater good - for the good of others, not just for yourself."

Perhaps he was right. And perhaps it took something like this to finally make her see that. She was always seeking that 'just right' elusive ideal. She couldn't deny it. On top of Hassall's words, her coach had also told her that he wanted her to be a player. But maybe being a player meant growing up and being responsible for her actions, using her talents for a greater good where possible. However, if her desire for things to be 'just right' also meant not choosing the right thing, then she was still not a player at all. In fact, all this time she thought she was in the game, she had unwittingly become the game herself.

It was time for her to start playing her own.

Tania turned to her friend, her bleary eyes suddenly transparent and full of resolution. "Listen, Isabelle. I have to go."

"Where are you going?" she inquired.

"I can't explain right now. But there's something I have to do. I may not be back for a few hours, but will you stay with Igor while I'm gone?"

"But what are you doing?"

"There's no time to explain." She took hold of her friend's hand and squeezed it tightly for a moment, gazing earnestly into her eyes. "Will you call me if he wakes up?"

Chapter 23

After a few phone calls were placed, Tania arrived back at the IRIS headquarters in Beijing. Passing through the various security checkpoints, she was led into a room where Abraham Hassall had convened an impromptu meeting in the knowledge that she would be returning. Jonah Bull, Wendell Krennick and Elvin Xiu were also present.

"Welcome back Miss Likamolova," Hassall said. "It's good to see you again. I'm sorry about your coach."

The Russian tennis star was in no mood for formalities. "Let's save the friendly chit-chat for later. You've got me here now. I'm all yours. What do you want me to do?"

"Okay," Hassall replied, granting her request. "We've been considering the viability of other options, but now you're back, that's all changed. As soon as we're ready to go, we proceed with the plan that Volkov initially proposed."

"You mean, me go in Natalya's place?"

"That's right."

"What do you mean by 'as soon as you're ready to go'?"

Hassall quickly explained the current position and how Elf was attempting to crack the encryption in order to set up a contact with Dr Yan.

"So let me get this straight," she said. "You've no idea when or where the meeting is going to take place? What am I supposed to do in the meantime?"

"It shouldn't take too much longer to crack," Elf assured her. "I've eliminated a number of possibilities already."

Sensing her ambivalence, Krennick spoke up. "I have to ask, Miss Likamolova. Why the sudden change of heart? You seemed quite adamant before that, under no circumstances, were you going to offer us your help."

Tania sighed. She didn't really feel like having a long discussion on the subject. "Let's just say I wanted to start being a player in the game."

"Well, I'm glad you've come to that decision," Hassall said. "I think it's the right one."

"But please understand," Tania quickly clarified. "I'm only doing this on this one occasion because I want The Three Bears as much as you do for what they've done to me and my coach. After this little mission, I'm done with them and with IRIS, and I *am* continuing my career as a tennis player. No spy or anything like that."

"Very well. But we're glad you're on board for this. It looks like you have a heart of gold after all."

Tania grinned, then let out a faint laugh in irony.

"What's so funny?" Bull asked.

"Nothing," Tania said. "It's just the last time I heard that, this Oleg Korsakov was feeding me a line. Some tenuous link between the letters of my name and how I have a heart of gold."

"That's it," Elf exclaimed, in a eureka-like tone of voice that suggested he had just had an epiphany.

He rushed back into his workshop, brimming with excitement, with the others following closely behind.

"What is it?" Krennick inquired, trying to contain Elf's enthusiasm.

Elf sat down at the computer. "I'm thinking, what if TAURUS *was* the word we were after?"

"We already tried that, remember?" Bull reminded him. "It didn't work."

"Just bear with me. What if the 'heart' in the clue refers to something in the word that we're supposed to type in?"

"Like what?"

"Like GOLD. I'm going by what Tania said back there about having a heart of gold. The letters between her first name and her patronymic, Tania Ulyanovna - are AU, the chemical symbol for gold. AU is also in Taurus."

"AU," Bull muttered. "That's not quite the 'heart' of Taurus. That would be UR."

"Well AU isn't quite in the 'heart' of my name either," Tania teased, "but evidently some people seem to think it works."

"Okay. I guess there's nothing to lose." Elf breathed a sigh of trepidation. Could it be right? "But AU would just give us GOLD. The password must be at least six letters. Maybe it's GOLDEN instead?"

He typed that in, his heart rising in hope that this would be the correct answer.

ACCESS DENIED.

Elf sat back, a look of defeat on his face. "I was sure I had solved it."

"Oh well, good idea," Hassall said, patting him on the back.

"Wait," Elf interjected, piping up again. "Maybe we're thinking about this the wrong way. Perhaps GOLDEN is just the first part of the clue, and when we've solved one word, it's meant to be a prompt for us to fill in the next part."

Bull was puzzled. "What have we been missing?"

"Okay, think about this. IN RUSSIA, A BULL'S HEART MAKES NO SOUND. So far, GOLDEN is the closest we've come to fulfilling all the parts of the clue."

"But we just tried GOLDEN" Hassall said. "It didn't work."

"Yes, but AU was in TAURUS, which also contains the letters RUS, the shorthand for Russia. AU is also gold. And what if 'makes no sound' is another way of saying 'silence'? When you put it together, you've got that saying 'silence is golden'. So maybe we're required to complete that sentence."

"Well in Russia," Tania began, "the saying is this: 'The word is silver, the silence is gold'."

"SILVER?" Elf exclaimed, open to any suggestion. "Could it be?"

Tania's phone produced a beep. She looked down to read a new text message in her inbox in Russian. "Excuse me while I reply to this," she said, turning away to key in a message on her bilingual keypad.

Elf typed in the word suggested by Tania.

ACCESS DENIED.

"Damn. That still isn't right."

"Well it's a start," Bull encouraged him. "It's further than we've gotten so far. But I was thinking - would it be simply a word? Wouldn't that be too easy?"

"Are you saying this was a piece of cake all this time?" Elf retorted.

"No. But lots of passwords will only let you enter a numerical code. Maybe the letters in the word corresponds to the numerical values of the alphabet."

"You could be right." Elf typed that in. 19-9-12-22-5-18

ACCESS DENIED.

"Hey," said Elf, glancing over at Tania who was still responding to her text message. "Maybe it's the letters on a phone keypad. After all, the information was originally stored on Natalya's phone. So the letters ABC would correspond to the number 2, while DEF would correspond to 3 and so on."

Bull pulled out his own cell phone. "That would mean that SILVER, if that's the correct word, would be 7-4-5-8-3-7."

Elf typed that in.

ACCESS DENIED.

"What?" he gasped. "How can that be? We're running out of options here."

"What's up?" Tania asked, when she had finished with her message. "I thought you were in already."

"So did we," Bull informed her. "But it didn't quite work. Then we figured it might be a numeric code. We tried the phone keypad numbers for SILVER, but 7-4-5-8-3-7 didn't work."

Tania looked down at her own keypad. Suddenly she had a flash of inspiration. "What's the clue again?"

"IN RUSSIA, A BULL'S HEART MAKES NO SOUND." Elf replied.

"What if 'IN RUSSIA' is meant to tell us it's something in Russian?" she speculated. "After all, Natalya was Russian herself."

"What are you suggesting?"

"What if it's SILVER in Cyrillic?" She scribbled something down on a piece of paper. The word read 'серебро́.' "Serebro. That's the word for silver in Russian. So on a Cyrillic keypad, of course, the letters would be in slightly different places to a western keypad. Fortunately, mine has both, so 'серебро́' would be 6-3-6-3-2-6-5."

Bull nodded. "Okay, it's worth a shot."

Elf keyed in the numbers, his hands trembling slightly as this was their last ditch attempt to crack the code.

ACCESS CONFIRMED.

"I don't believe it," he exclaimed. "You did it. We're in."

"Cool," Tania beamed with delight, scrunching her nose up. "Did you hear that? I solved it."

Bull smiled at her. "You may yet make a spy."

She screwed up her face in mock contempt, looking at him with the corner of her eye. "Let's not get carried away here."

"Good work," Hassall said. "Make the contact and set up the meeting."

Tania raised her hand. "Hey, do you think I could go back to my hotel and get a change of clothes?"

Hassall shook his head. "That probably wouldn't be wise. The Three Bears have already made an attempt on your life once today. It's far too risky to allow you back out there again for the moment. You'll simply have to stay here until other arrangements can be made. If you need other clothes, I'm sure we can find you some to wear."

Tania looked around her at the other female agents walking past. "Not to be difficult, but I don't think anyone here would be quite the right size. Especially not my shoes. Mine were partly damaged from the blast."

"Then you'll just have to make do with what you're wearing," Hassall dismissed her impatiently, unconcerned about the finer points of her wardrobe.

"Just leave your shoes with me," Elf suggested. "I'll fix them when I'm done here."

Tania gave him a bewildered look. "You?"

"Hey, they don't call me the Shoemaker for nothing."

Taking up his offer, Tania followed Bull and Krennick out of Elf's workshop, as they left him with Hassall to make preparations to meet Dr Yan.

"Can I get you a drink?" Bull asked Tania.

"Just some water, please."

She followed him to the water dispenser in the kitchen area.

"By the way, I think we should be able to find you some clothes to wear at least, if not some shoes," Bull assured her.

"Thanks."

A few awkward moments of silence passed by before Bull spoke up again.

"You still look tense," he said, noticing the Russian's body language. Her back was turned towards him with her arms crossed, and her hands tightly gripping onto the upper part of her arms.

"I'm worried about my coach," she whispered.

"That's understandable. You were close to him."

"*Were*, being the operative word." She breathed a sigh of anguish. "He was trying to tell me something about not playing other people's games but playing my own. I never quite understood. Maybe I simply wasn't listening. I thought he was merely referring to tennis but he was meaning something deeper. And there I went, simply being the game once again. And this time, someone ended up paying for that."

"Look, if it's any consolation, I know what it's like to lose someone close, so I wouldn't wish that on anyone else, least of all you. I hope he recovers soon."

"Thanks," she replied, nodding her head up and down. There was not much anyone could say that would alleviate the anguish she felt. That being the case, she would stop looking inward to herself and out to others instead. She slowly uncrossed her arms and turned to face him. "So what happened?"

"What happened about what?"

"You said you know what it's like to lose someone close. I was asking you what happened."

Jonah took a deep breath, swallowing hard as if there was a kink in his throat. It appeared that he was poised on the threshold of holding back and ridding himself, once and for all, of the inner demons that had plagued him. Yet it was almost as if he didn't know where to begin.

Tania sensed his hesitation and apprehension. She brushed her hand gently on his to give him courage. "Look, if you don't want to talk about it, that's fine."

Encouraged by her touch, the floodgates opened.

"About a year and a half ago, I was in a relationship with a wonderful girl named Felissia Mazetti. She was a beautiful Italian woman with a zest for life like you, eager to live every moment to the fullest."

He gave a rueful smile as if he were recalling her with bittersweet memories.

He continued, his countenance noticeably darkening. "At the time I was also working undercover on a case for IRIS in Colombia, tracking Miguel Acosta, the leader of a right wing paramilitary guerrilla movement, and ensuring the protection of a number of Colombian trade unionists who had been blacklisted. I was assigned to deliver supplies by plane twice a week to a village Acosta was using as his base of operations, while secretly monitoring the situation there and collecting any information gathered by a man we had on the inside there posing as one of Acosta's troops. Felissia was in the dark as to what I was really doing there, as she had no idea that I actually worked for IRIS. That put a strain on our relationship. I barely had enough time to see her, let alone spend any quality time with her. As the weeks went by, I decided that I seriously needed to reassess my priorities. That opportunity came sooner than expected."

"What happened?"

"One day, after Felissia had arrived in Colombia to surprise me, I chose to take some free time off and charter a plane to go flying with her. Of course, she was up for it, since she knew I was an experienced pilot, and she was confident in my abilities. I didn't want us to be interrupted, so I decided to switch my radio off so IRIS would leave us alone for a few hours and we could actually have some fun. Well we had lots of fun that day alright. I showed off my flying skills trying to impress her, and doing loops and dives over some cornfield out in the middle of nowhere. Felissia thought it was hilarious when this crazy farmer decided to take a few shots at us with his rifle, because he thought I was being a pest and just wanted to get me away from his land as quickly as possible. Well fortunately, the bullets missed us and no damage was done, and we just quickly flew somewhere else for a picnic, with Felissia laughing all the way, telling me I should see the funny side of it."

"She sounds cute," Tania noted.

"Yeah, she was. Anyway, I was out of radio contact for the whole day, unaware that an emergency had unexpectedly cropped up. We were flying on our way back home when I finally decided to check in. That's when I heard the terrible news. Acosta was storming the village, killing trade unionists who were being held hostage there and civilians. He had discovered our inside man. I was urgently required to fly to Acosta's village and mount some kind of rescue mission along with some of the other IRIS agents, since our inside man needed extraction. On top of that, we needed to get those trade unionists and civilians out of there."

Jonah paused for a moment, knowing the next part of the memory was the most painful and that he was bracing himself for it.

"IRIS had planes, but were short on pilots and they really did require my help. With no time to land, I took a decision at that point to fly straight there without stopping to drop Felissia off. Of course, that would take a lot of explaining to her as to what on earth I was doing taking a detour to this remote village, but that couldn't be helped. I told her what I really did, and while she was angry as hell that I had lied to her, she said I needed to do what I needed to do. Of course, she was naturally concerned about suddenly getting involved in this, but I assured her that everything would be okay. About half way there, we discovered that the fuel gauge had actually taken a hit from that crazy farmer, and fuel was leaking out of the tank. We were forced to make an unexpected landing in the mountains. At least, that was the plan. However, there was no suitable place to land, and we eventually crash-landed in a forest nearby. The plane collided with a tree and Felissia was killed instantly, while I wasn't so lucky."

Tania gasped. "I'm so sorry…"

Jonah acknowledged her sympathy, but pressed on. "In the end, Acosta and his men stormed the village and massacred thirty-two innocent civilians and trade unionists - those who didn't have the benefit of a rescue plane. I was responsible both for not being there for them, and for getting Felissia killed because I was off that day doing my own thing instead of doing what I was supposed to be doing. Things could've been a lot different had I made another choice. Acosta wouldn't still be at large. We wouldn't have gone flying, and I would've been there for those civilians. And Felissia might still be alive."

Tania looked at him with teary eyes, visibly moved. "I'm sorry for your loss," she said softly, her voice resonating with compassion. "Really I am."

He nodded. "Thanks. But you were right before."

She gave him a look of puzzlement. "Right about what?"

"Me being a sitting bull. I was a bit reckless before, but since that time, I've probably gone to the opposite extreme. I've come to a standstill in my life, unable to move past that incident. I transferred to the New York headquarters of IRIS and requested a desk job where I could do the least damage, only taking on minor assignments in the field with minimal risk until I felt ready to go back out, or start living again."

"Don't pay attention to what I said before," she told him, giving a gentle, dismissing wave of her hand. "Considering what you've been through, it's a wonder you've come out as well as you have. I don't know what would happen if I were to lose someone. I probably didn't know what I was saying at the time. I was just frustrated, that's all. Maybe there is no way to avoid growing cynical with the world, especially when others around you get hurt."

"I don't know about that. I don't want you to end up like me, especially if your coach doesn't pull through. You remember I said before that I didn't want to go on this mission with you…"

"You don't need to explain." Her words radiated warmth and assurance like a fireplace in winter. "You said it's because you don't want to get too attached to people and let that sort of thing get in the way of the mission. I understand. It's the same with tennis. You can't always be friends with the other girls on the tour because it makes it harder to play against them and be ruthless on court later on. And maybe it's not good having others close to you either as a celebrity. If other people target you, your loved ones could get hurt."

"No, wait. You don't understand. What I'm trying to tell you is that the reason I..."

However, Jonah was unable to finish his sentence as he was inopportunely interrupted by Wendell Krennick, who entered the room like an unwanted intruder on their conversation. "Hassall wants to see you both in the briefing room. He has some news."

Tania and Bull followed him into the conference room where Hassall stood waiting for them. Elf was seated around a table.

"Here are your tennis shoes, by the way," Elf said, handing them back to her. "All patched up. Good as new."

"Elf, you're a star," she exclaimed, giving him a light peck on the cheek. She took them gratefully and slipped them back on her feet.

"I see I've been displaced in the pecking order of your affections," Bull quipped.

Tania laughed, but resisted the urge to respond.

"We've managed to arrange a meeting," Hassall informed them.

"Oh? What happened?" Krennick asked, surprised that they had produced such rapid results.

Elf explained. "I communicated with Dr Yan via this instant messaging service using Natalya's ID. Of course, he assumed that I was her. He's agreed to an emergency meeting tomorrow morning."

"Well that's great," Bull replied.

"He says he prefers to meet in a public place," Hassall said. "According to him, he would feel safer, especially since it's the Moon Cake Festival and there will be plenty of people around."

"When and where exactly?" Tania asked.

"Tiananmen Square at 11.00 am by the Monument to the People's Heroes."

Hassall looked over at Bull, giving him a set of instructions. "Get Volkov and everyone prepared for this meeting. You and Elf are to accompany Tania. I want Elf monitoring. Keep your eyes open. Make sure Tania is fully up to speed on what she needs to do."

Krennick spoke up. "I think I should go along for this one. We'll need all the backup we can get. I've spoken to Volkov and know how to deal with him. I can keep him in line. Make sure nothing goes wrong."

"Good idea," Hassall replied. "Now time is running out. Dismissed."

Chapter 24

Sunday morning.

Tania gazed out of the window intently as she sat in the back of an IRIS surveillance van that was weaving its way steadily through the lanes of traffic along the *Chang'an Jie*, the Street of Eternal Peace. This busy, 125-foot-wide road intersected the immense plaza known as Tiananmen Square at the heart of Beijing. At the wheel of the van was one of the IRIS agents from the Beijing branch, while in the back with her were Jonah Bull, Wendell Krennick, Elvin Xiu and Tania's erstwhile boyfriend, Piotr Volkov. Each one sat in silence except for Elf, who took it upon himself to act as a tour guide and point out key places of interest, much to the irritation of the others.

Tania did not mind the running commentary herself. On previous trips to Beijing, she had not been afforded the opportunity for much sightseeing. So now, although she was visiting under circumstances less than ideal, she marvelled at the massive open space before her - a vast expanse of paving slabs, each individually numbered for troops to stand upon during a parade.

Built in 1417, and adjacent to the Forbidden City, Elf remarked that Tiananmen was the largest square in the world, measuring 880 metres north to south and 500 metres east to west. That was the equivalent area of 1,687 tennis courts put together, Elf explained - a fact that was certainly not lost on Tania.

Wow. I've been on lots of tennis courts in my time, but imagine them all being stuck together in that way and put in one place.

This morning, with the Square filled with thousands of people out for the Moon Festival celebrations, the crowds were interspersed with a spread of dark green uniforms as the soldiers stood, like imperial guards, keeping watch for any sign of trouble. Elf pointed out that apart from the uniformed and plain-clothes policemen patrolling the Square, the huge lampposts were fitted with security cameras.

Around the edges of the Square, to the east and west were a number of monumental, austere-looking public buildings built in an almost Soviet style. One of these was the Great Hall of the People where the Chinese parliament, the National People's Assembly usually met. Opposite this, on the east side, lay the National Museum of Chinese History and the Museum of the Chinese Revolution.

On Tania's left, to the northern side of the Square, stretched the imposing red structure known as the Gate of Heavenly Peace. On top of this classic piece of Chinese architecture sat a double-tiered, yellow-tiled roof, while along the top of the wall, red flags swayed gently in the breeze. Adorning the wall itself was a giant portrait of Mao, with two signs on either side in Chinese characters. The Gate, previously reserved for the emperor alone to pass through, served as the entranceway to the Forbidden City, the largest ancient palace in the world surrounded by a wide moat and set on 200 acres. Elf compared the Forbidden City to a bunch of connected indoor stadiums without a roof. Having known the immensity of the National Tennis Center in Flushing Meadows, Tania was awestruck by its size.

At the centre of the Square, towering over the masses, was a huge obelisk known as the Monument to the People's Heroes, which Elf informed them was dedicated to those soldiers who fell during the Cultural Revolution. That was the place where they were meant to be meeting this Dr Yan, with Tania pretending to be the person Yan had been in contact with all this time.

Tania exhaled a heavy sigh. Would Yan buy it? Or would her lack of Natalya's inside knowledge give the game away? To calm her nerves, she smoothed the pair of figure-hugging, black sweat pants she was wearing and fiddled repeatedly with the zipper of her white training top. IRIS had donated both of these items to her from their store of spare clothing. Fortunately, they were an almost perfect fit, but the tennis shoes which Elf had repaired had to suffice, as there were none in her size.

Not that she liked the idea of stepping into another person's shoes anyway.

As the van snaked its way through the *Chang'an Jie*, Tania noticed a fleet of rickshaws and bicycles making their way alongside the traffic. On both the north and south sides of the Square, crowds of people in brightly-coloured attire were swarming, some gathering for a dragon dance procession. Others were holding elegant umbrellas to shade themselves from the already-fierce sunshine, even though it was not yet 11.00 am. Above them, flitting colourfully through the air in the forms of exotic birds, insects or beasts, were a number of stunt kites in various shapes, designs and sizes, remote controlled by celebrators dressed as traditional Chinese animals.

She smiled to herself. *How pretty. Especially that red and yellow one over there in the distance that looks like a dragon.*

"Now you're clear what to do?" Krennick checked, interrupting her thoughts.

She turned to face him wearily and shrugged. "I guess so." Her head bobbed up and down hesitantly. She probably didn't sound very convincing. She added, "And even if I weren't, that's never stopped any of you before from using me."

"We need to know you've understood everything you have to do," he pressed her.

"Don't worry," she assured him nonchalantly. "I'll be fine."

Bull spoke up, hoping to put her mind at ease. "We'll maintain radio contact at all times. If there are any problems, you know the abort code, right?"

Tania nodded, adjusting the Alice band on her head housing a two-way radio. "Sure."

Krennick glared over at Volkov, his expression full of hostility. "As for you, if you try to escape or if there are any false moves on your part, just remember, we'll be watching you at all times."

"Don't worry," Volkov replied. "I'm sure you'll be fully in control of the matter."

Tania sat there, looking down at the floor. Suddenly, her phone rang, causing her to jump out of her seat. She spoke cautiously. "Hello?"

"Tania, where are you?" the voice on the other end demanded.

"My agent," she whispered, holding the phone away from her mouth.

"Get rid of him quickly," Krennick snapped, giving her a reproving stare.

"What's going on?" Kurtzberg inquired. "I heard about the explosion on the practice court yesterday."

"I'm fine," she replied.

"You're fine? Good. Then get your ass back here. You're meant to be doing a live interview on TV this morning at 11.00. It's 10.45 right now, and you're nowhere to be seen."

Tania gasped. She was meant to be seen as the face of Beijing at this year's tournament. She had completely forgotten about her appointment.

"I can't," she said weakly.

"You can't what? Don't tell me you're going AWOL on us again?"

"No, I can explain," she pleaded.

"Save your lame-ass excuses. Do you realise you're costing us and your sponsors millions of dollars? I knew that nothing had changed with you. Still as unreliable as ever."

"I'm sorry," Tania apologised. "I really can't do anything about this. It's an emergency."

"If you don't get over here right now, I'll be forced to withdraw as your agent. You'll be on your own."

Tania sighed in frustration. On top of the pressure of this mission, that was the last thing she needed to hear right now. "I really can't help it," she insisted. "I'd still like to work with you but you'll have to do what you think best."

"Get rid of him," Krennick badgered her again. He was unwilling to tolerate this nonsense any further.

"I will," Tania replied, feeling ambivalent about the whole situation. Should she try to resolve things before the last nail in the coffin was hammered in, or should she simply hide her head in the sand and hope everything would be okay?

"Now who's that you're talking to?" Kurtzberg demanded, sounding suspicious. "You're obviously off having fun somewhere else…"

"I can't deal with this phone call right now," she said, somewhat flustered. "I'll have to call you back later."

The phone went dead, and Tania's heart sank. Inside, however, she knew it had to be done.

Bull looked up, his eyes studying hers, as if to ask what that was all about.

She let out a deep sigh, shaking her head sadly. "Well I think that's just about taken care of my endorsement contracts for the foreseeable future."

"There'll be others," Krennick assured her unsympathetically. "Make sure you don't answer any calls other than ours."

The van pulled to a stop, and all except Elf and the driver disembarked. The IRIS techie remained there to monitor the proceedings from inside.

In the centre of the Square were two teams of dancers carrying images of colourful Chinese dragons made of fabric and bamboo, while performing the traditional dragon dance to celebrate the festival. Each train of people was about thirty feet long, with the dancers moving like snakes in an undulating manner, intertwining with each other. The dragon heads swept up, lifting, darting and thrusting while smoke occasionally bellowed out of the mouths. Having rarely seen anything so spectacular, Tania marvelled silently to herself. But now was not the time to lose focus.

Tania and Volkov walked towards the designated meeting place while Bull and Krennick assumed their positions, ensuring that they remained as inconspicuous as possible. A man fitting the description of Dr Yan was waiting at the Monument to the People's Heroes. He appeared nervous, glancing down at his watch intermittently, as if waiting for someone to arrive.

Volkov spoke through his two-way radio transmitter, disguised as a button on his shirt. "I've located him."

"Good," Krennick replied. "Now approach him carefully, but remember, don't try any tricks. We have you fully covered."

"You needn't remind me twice," he answered, as he edged towards the man, with Tania following cautiously behind.

The man looked up. "Ah, Mr Volkov. How pleasant to see you again."

Volkov shook his hand. "Dr Yan. A pleasure to see you too. I've brought someone for you to meet today."

Yan studied Tania carefully, his eyes probing her face like a searchlight for any sign of hesitation. "So this is the young lady I've been communicating with all this time?"

Tania nodded. "Yeah. That's me." Would her eyes betray her? She wasn't used to lying on a regular basis.

"Strange," Yan remarked. "I never expected it would be you of all people."

"Oh?" she asked, trying to steel her nerves and appear confident. "Disappointed with what you see?"

"Not at all. It's simply that I always pictured you to be older. How old are you, by the way?"

"Get him past the small talk," Bull whispered in Volkov's ear.

"I don't think we have time to get acquainted," Volkov said. "What matters is that we have certain things to discuss."

Yan nodded. "I see you are strictly business."

"As always," Volkov confirmed.

"Okay, what is it you want to know?"

He began to explain. "As I'm sure you're aware, the Russian government has been funding your research in Xinjiang on the oil perforating gun."

"That is correct," Yan replied. "Have some problems arisen?"

"You could say that."

Yan looked at them, puzzled. "What sort of problems?"

"That's not important. We need to know the exact locations where the perforating guns are due to be installed."

"You know that information is classified," Yan countered. "I can't give that sort of thing out casually."

"I don't know if you realise," Tania began, summoning up her most confident voice, "but your research is being used in a way that you probably never intended."

Yan frowned. "What do you mean?"

"Tell him about The Three Bears," Bull whispered in her ear.

Tania followed his lead. "Have you heard of The Three Bears?" She waited for his response, catching a glimpse of the large red dragon-shaped kite at the corner of her eye."

Yan shook his head. "I thought they are merely a fairy tale - an urban myth, so to speak."

"I'm afraid you have been misinformed," Volkov broke in.

"There's no time to explain," Tania continued, her voice carrying a sense of urgency. "They're after your research. They want to use it to release some bacteria that your friend Dr Wei developed so they can contaminate the Russian oil supply."

"What?" Yan looked over at Volkov in order for him to verify the story. "That sounds ridiculous."

"It's true," Volkov confirmed.

"But I don't see how they would acquire it unless..."

"They already have it," Tania stated.

Dr Yan's mouth dropped wide open in shock. "What? How?"

"The break-in at Xinjiang," Volkov said. "Surely you remember that."

"Yes of course," Yan replied. "But aren't the Chinese government currently investigating that in relation to the stolen oil spill bacteria? But what does that have to do with the perforating guns?"

"Parts of them were replaced with modified components," Tania clarified.

"I'm sure in time they will catch whoever is responsible," Volkov said coolly, looking the engineer straight in the eye, but knowing full well he was behind it. "In the meantime, it is imperative you reveal to us where they have been installed."

Tania glanced over at Volkov. He seemed to be extremely skilled at keeping a poker face while lying through his teeth. Is this what he did with her all the time? She shook her head in resignation. What she would give to be like one of those kites right now - perhaps that red dragon one - and flap her wings and fly away from here. But no. She had a mission to complete. She wanted The Three Bears to pay for what they had done to Igor. Stop them before they could hurt any more innocent people.

Volkov spoke. "Dr Yan, whatever feelings of doubt you might be having right now, I urge you to get over them. We need that information urgently. I'm sure you never intended for your research to be used in such a way, so you would do well to tell us the information while you still can."

Yan nodded, took out a PDA and punched in a few keys, calling up a world map onto the view screen. "The perforating guns have been installed around Sakhalin Island."

"Why there in particular?" Tania asked.

"Sakhalin Island is strategically one of the most important locations for the world oil markets, with the US on one side and China and Japan on the other," Yan explained. "New oil and gas reserves have recently been found there within the existing fields, and mining operations have already been set up. It's been estimated that the total recoverable oil reserves on Sakhalin Island are over 307 million tons of oil while total LNG reserves are at around 485 billion cubic metres..."

"LNG?" Tania interrupted him.

"Liquified Natural Gas," he clarified. "It's simply natural gas that has been processed, then condensed into..."

"Yes, yes," Volkov said with a look of boredom on his face, waving his hand in a circular motion to hurry the engineer along. "Please, spare us all the technical details."

"Sorry," Yan apologised. "Well, to cut a long story short, that's a lot of oil and gas at the Russians' fingertips. Suffice to say, Sakhalin Island is very important as one of the world's largest untapped gas and oil provinces."

"Okay," Tania nodded, starting to feel equally bored herself, but remaining inquisitive. "So why are the Chinese involved?"

"In this case, our interests are mutually compatible. As one of the largest consumers of oil in the world, we have vested interests in any major reservoir. Meanwhile, the Russians want the oil extracted quickly, while we have the technology to do that, hence our joint venture. With that in mind, where better to test these new prototype perforating guns than right where all the riches lie, so to speak?"

"Did you get that, Elf?" Bull whispered.

"Yes," Elf replied. "I'm looking into it right now and running it through ASAP."

"Okay, keep him talking," Bull said to Tania.

"You said Sakhalin Island," Tania continued, showing some concern in her voice, as she remembered the documentary she had glimpsed briefly in the hospital waiting room. "If you don't mind me asking again, these perforating guns use explosive charges, right? Isn't that potentially dangerous? Couldn't it cause a disturbance to the sea bed?"

"What are you doing?" Bull asked. "You're not supposed to go into that."

"No wait," Elf said. "If she's even somehow vaguely thinking what I'm thinking, then this could be serious."

"What?"

"Think about it," Elf said. "Sakhalin Island. Undersea detonations. Depending on the number of shaped charges The Three Bears decide to set off, ASAP predicts that it could be powerful enough to trigger a shockwave that could dislodge the tectonic plates and cause an earthquake."

Bull thought for a second before the realisation came crashing in. "Elf, you could be right."

"Furthermore, that sort of disruption could result in a tsunami," Elf added. "If something like that occurs, it could devastate Sakhalin Island and all the nearby areas in the immediate vicinity of the *Okhotskoe Sea* and spreading towards Japan."

Tania had heard everything over her communications. Her face became white as a sheet. Her parents were in *Nikolayevsk*, which was right along the coastline of *Okhotskoe,* and not far at all from the ecologically fragile waters of Sakhalin Island. If what Elf said was true, they would be wiped out instantly, along with her family there, and millions of other people.

"You've got to get in touch with Hassall," Bull advised Elf. "In the meantime, we need to bring Dr Yan in. As long as The Three Bears don't have him, we can prevent them from taking any of these measures."

"I'll get on it right away," Elf replied, as his cell phone suddenly began to ring.

"Oh no, no," he muttered. "Go away."

The caller would not take the hint.

"Leave me alone," he shouted at it again. "I've no time for you."

But the phone would not ring off. Frustrated, Elf picked it up. "Hello?"

"Elf," came the voice on the other end.

"Chauncey," he groaned. "I'm in the middle of an assignment with Tania."

"Out in the field, huh?"

"Yes. With Krennick and Bull. And Tania too."

"Tania? Ah, you sly devil, you," Chauncey chortled. "Managed to get in on the action, eh?"

"What's the reason for this call?" Elf interrupted him. "If this is merely a social chat, it's hardly the time."

Chauncey persisted, unfazed by his rebuffed attempts to speak. "Aww. No time for your old mate 'Chaunce'? Even after all the times I let you call me up in the middle of the night just to listen your problems…?"

"Chauncey!"

"But I digress." His voice took on a more serious tone. "I do 'ave a good reason for calling actually. But first, are you all connected to your two-way radios?"

"Yes. Why?"

"Trust me," he said. "You'll bloody well want to take the call on this cell phone privately."

Elf muted the other IRIS agents out temporarily and then gave his attention to his colleague. "Okay, what is it?"

"I just thought you might like to know the results of my research," Chauncey began. "I was checking through some of the transmission logs 'ere at IRIS. Snow White and Rose Red didn't quite 'ack into our databases as we thought to find out Bull's identity and all the other IRIS stuff. They simply sent the photo as an encrypted file to one of our agents. And you'll never guess who? It was Krennick. 'e was the one who provided them with the info."

"What?" Elf gasped, pricking up his ears as his jaw went slack. "Are you sure?"

"Yeah," Chauncey replied, with a mouthful of jelly beans. "Positive. 'e thought 'e'd fooled me, the little bugger, but listen to this…"

"Can't speak," he replied. "Thanks for the info, Chaunce. I've got to go." He cut off, and then, knowing that Krennick would be listening on their radio communications channel, speed-dialled Bull's cell phone instead. "Come on, pick up," he muttered.

There was no answer. It went straight to voice mail.

"You're correct about the explosive charges," Dr Yan confirmed, looking Tania straight in the eye. "But don't worry. They are carefully-controlled blasts. *Rosneft* holds the licence for geological exploration there and is currently running seismic operations together with *Sinopec*. In fact, there's also a satellite in space placed there by our joint governments and *Sakhalin Energy*, the consortium operating the *Sakhalin 2* oil and LNG project there. This satellite currently monitors seismic activity and can feed the signal for the laser detonator that will set off the perforating gun's explosive charges, all of which would be done by computer. As long as that is adhered to, the detonations via the perforating guns should be perfectly safe. Besides, there are still a number of checks to be carried out before we even detonate the first batch of charges."

Tania was not convinced. "But couldn't someone potentially detonate more charges than are safe?"

"Since I'm the one who built it," Yan assured her, "I don't see how. I'm the only one who knows how to modify it."

"Still, I think you should come with us. We can protect you," she said.

"Protect me from what?"

Before Tania could answer, she heard a noise from above, humming like a dragonfly. She looked up to see the source of the distraction, only to find that out of nowhere, the red and yellow dragon kite that had been flying around began heading straight towards them at frightening speed.

What the heck?

Suddenly, it swooped in, about to crash into them like a kamikaze pilot.

She gasped. "Look out."

Just in time, they dived out of the way as the kite changed direction, ascending again and quickly picking up speed before opening fire with a fusillade of bullets.

"Get out of there now," Bull ordered Tania as he rushed towards their location. "And get Dr Yan to safety."

But there was no time for Tania to think about the engineer. Once again, the kite sprayed its bullets everywhere, forcing her to dive for cover. The crowds of visitors and celebrators were now screaming, fleeing in terror for their lives.

In the meantime, Elf had been persevering with his attempts to contact Bull. Hearing the gunfire from outside like a snare drum, he began to panic, before calming himself down to think. He spoke through the two-way radio. "Bull, can you hear me?"

"Elf," Bull replied, his voice coming through in short breaths as he was running. "Can't speak now. They're under attack. Find the source of that radio control frequency and jam it now."

"I'll get on it. But you've got to pick up your cell phone," he urged him.

"I can't right now."

"But it's an emergency," he insisted.

No use. Bull had already tuned out to speak to Krennick instead.

"What was that about?" Krennick asked him suspiciously.

"No idea, sir," Bull replied. "But I could really do with some backup right now."

"I'm right on it," he assured him. "I'll get Tania and Dr Yan to safety. You go after the flyer."

"Will do, sir." Bull began scanning the area for anything unusual. From a distance, he saw a female dressed up as one of the Chinese animals littered around the Square. She appeared to be in control of the dragon kite. Hidden in plain sight.

Meanwhile, Volkov, thinking purely of his own survival, abandoned both Tania and Dr Yan and headed in his own direction. Shoving several women and children out of the way, Volkov was suddenly tossed about like a scarecrow. A round of shots tore into him. He let out a wounded cry before crumbling to the ground, crawling slowly as he attempted to save himself.

Tania was sprinting through the Square, pushed on by sheer desperation and athletic ability. The kite began to climb again and rained down another deluge of bullets. *What happened to Piotr? I lost both him and Dr Yan.*

She headed past the dragon dancers who were trying to scramble to safety but were trapped under their huge bamboo and fabric costume, struggling to break free themselves.

"Elf," Bull shouted, suddenly coming through on the two-way transmitter again. "What's happening with that frequency?"

"It keeps rotating," he replied, as he fiddled about frantically with various items of equipment in front of him to find the source. "But you've got to pick up your phone."

"There's no time."

"Just find the frequency, and jam it. I'll talk to you later."

Elf would not take no for an answer. Usually a mild-mannered man, his voice became more assertive. "Damn it, Bull. I said this is an emergency."

He had Jonah's attention, as the IRIS agent answered his cell phone immediately.

"Where's Krennick?" Elf inquired.

"He's seeing to Tania and the engineer."

"What?" Elf gasped. That was the worst possible scenario. "You've got to stop him."

"What? What are you talking about?"

But before he could explain, the kite soared down towards where Bull was currently crouching, forcing him to abandon the call and run for cover himself.

"Hello?" Elf said, hearing the line was dead. He looked at his equipment and then back at his phone. What was he to do? Try to find Krennick himself, or continue working on jamming the frequency? He shouted to the driver, speaking in Chinese. "You there, do you know much about electronics?"

The driver stuttered. "I... I started a degree in it, but transferred to a different subject in my third year because…"

"Close enough," Elf replied. "I need you to keep working on scrambling the frequency here."

"But…" the driver protested.

Elf did not wait around to argue. He burst out of the van and began running into the Square, knowing that he was placing his own life in danger. But he had to find Tania and the engineer somehow before Krennick did.

The sounds of terror and mass hysteria continued to escalate. People were stampeding in every direction like frightened horses, fending only for themselves. A young mother was screaming desperately in Mandarin for her child, whom she had lost in the mayhem, attracting the blonde tennis star's attention immediately. Heart going out to her, Tania allowed her eyes to dart around, scanning the area like a hawk until they settled upon a young girl of about two or three, sitting on the ground crying. She was about to be trampled underfoot by the oncoming rush of people, unable to get out of the way in time. Tania gasped with alarm. She ran towards the child, unconcerned for her own safety and scooped her up in her arms.

"Here you go," she said, as she carried the little girl safely back to her mother, who was now streaming tears of gratitude. "You've got to get out of here." Seeing the woman did not understand, she attempted a few words of Mandarin and repeated herself. *"Ni bi xu jin kuai li kai."* Do you understand? *Ni ming bai ma?"*

Did that make sense? Her tonal pronunciations were probably off, and Mandarin wasn't one of the languages in which she was fully fluent anyway. Fortunately, the mother nodded silently, and took off without a second glance.

Tania smiled inwardly. Her heart swelled in size after that selfless act of hers. However, her reflection was interrupted as the kite soared once again, punctuating the air with more bullets.

As she started to run, she heard a voice nearby calling out her name through the chaos. She turned to see Krennick heading towards her with the engineer.

"Miss Likamolova," he shouted. "Come this way."

"Am I glad to see you," she cried. "Where's Jonah."

"No idea. We've got to get to the van as quickly as possible."

"But…" Tania was hesitant to leave without him. Suddenly, in the distance, she saw Elf running towards her.

"Get out of there," he cried, waving his hands wildly like a madman.

She could not understand him. "What?"

"Get out of there," he repeated. "You can't trust Krennick." But his voice was drowned out under all the screaming and gunfire.

However, Krennick had figured it out. Caught. His duplicity discovered. But since the Russian couldn't hear, she might not catch on yet.

They hurried back towards the van where the driver pulled open the door and asked anxiously, "Where are the others?"

"Never mind about them," Krennick barked. "Just drive."

"Hold on a second," Tania exclaimed, turning to gaze out of the window. "We can't just leave them…"

Before she could protest any further, he slapped his hand against her neck, immediately knocking her unconscious. Moving his hand away as she slumped in her seat, he rotated a dial on his ring to withdraw the drawing-pin-like, hypodermic needle which contained some kind of tranquilliser.

"Hey, what's going on?" the driver demanded, while the engineer gave Krennick a look of trepidation.

Krennick pointed his pistol at him. "Shut up and drive."

The driver nodded reluctantly, and floored the pedal, speeding out of there with tyres squealing amidst the hordes of screaming people.

Bull was running towards the kite flyer when he saw the IRIS van headed the same way. *Good.* Krennick or someone must have gotten Tania to safety and the van was now in hot pursuit of the assassin.

But wait. Instead of the van ploughing into the exotically clad figure, its doors were opening. And the assassin seemed to be running towards it. *What the hell?*

No time to figure it out. Bull speared after her as the kite flyer dove into the back. He had to stop her, and whoever had hijacked their vehicle. But before he could get any farther, the female assassin turned around and began firing at him with an AK-47. He was forced to leap for cover while the van high-tailed it out of there.

With the abrupt cease-fire, a surreal calm descended suddenly upon the Square, as if it were a ghost town, the silence broken only by the familiar voice of Elvin Xiu as he ran towards his colleague.

"Where's Krennick?" Bull asked, as the IRIS techie caught up with him.

"He's gone," he replied. "Krennick's dirty."

Bull's jaw dropped like a stone. "What?"

"I tried to tell you."

He shook his head in frustration, inwardly chiding himself. Why didn't he listen? "Never mind about that now. What about Tania?"

"Krennick has her. He's got Dr Yan with him as well."

Bull swore. "Damn. The kite was a distraction to seize the engineer. It was all a diversion. And now, not only have we lost our only way to stop The Three Bears, but Tania is gone too."

Chapter 25

"What happened out there?" Hassall demanded as Jonah Bull arrived back at the Beijing IRIS headquarters with Elf.

"It was Krennick," Bull replied. "He betrayed us."

Hassall's mouth went slack. "What?"

There was no time for a full explanation. Bull quickly summarised the events and brought him up to speed. "He took Tania and Dr Yan while we were busy with the dragon kite, courtesy of The Three Bears."

"Wendell?" Hassall sat down to absorb the news. "Why would he do that suddenly? And what about Volkov?"

"I think he was shot. But he was nowhere to be found when we left there."

Elf brought further news to the table. "Actually, Chauncey contacted me today. Krennick was looking into an apparent breach of security for our confidential databases which Snow White and Rose Red used to discover Bull's identity. He managed to follow the trail back to Krennick."

"He must've been a mole for the Bears," Hassall concluded. "Why didn't you bring this to me earlier?"

Before Elf could respond in his defence, Bull cut in. "This is hardly the time for discussing what should've been done. The more important question is how we're going to get both Tania and Dr Yan back."

"Excuse me, Mr Bull," Hassall interrupted. "The last time I recall, I gave the orders around here."

"It's okay," Elf assured Jonah. "One of Tania's tennis shoes has a GPS tracking beacon implanted inside it. I took the liberty of embedding it when she asked me to fix them."

Hassall gave him a bemused look.

"Well I did say before, they don't call me the Shoemaker for nothing," Elf added. "We can locate her wherever The Three Bears take her, as long as her shoes don't get damaged or she doesn't suddenly decide to ditch them for whatever reason. But hey, what's she going to do between now and then?"

Bull had no time for such ruminations. Eager to cut to the chase, he said, "We need to hurry after them."

Elf's response was somewhat casual. "Hey, don't worry. We want to see where the signal will lead us."

"Well why aren't we tracking it more closely? If we wait until they reach their destination, we could be several hours behind."

***

Like a cattle prod searing into her brain, the dull pain of a splitting headache ripped her from semi-consciousness. She groaned wearily. This was the second time in the last week that Tania had awoken in an unfamiliar place. On this occasion, however, she was more prepared for the event, but that still did not help her in establishing her bearings or knowing the reason for her current predicament.

Where am I?

Around her were the roar of engines and the distinct feel of turbulence rocking her environment. She opened her eyes to slits, to see she was lying on a suite of cream-coloured leather upholstery. She had to be in some kind of private Learjet.

The back of her neck stung, as if she had been bitten by a mosquito. Still groggy, she tried to sit up. It was no use. She shook her head. Perhaps she could move her arms and legs? No. They seemed to be restrained. *Ropes!* She was bound. Captive. Unable to free herself.

Great.

As she examined the ropes again, suddenly she did a double-take.

Her clothes!

Instead of the black and white tracksuit she had previously been wearing, she was now dressed in her cream and white tennis dress with gold accents that she had worn at the US Open.

What the hell?

She turned her head to look up, but quickly wished she hadn't. There looming before her like a giant cannon was the cold, black barrel of a gun, and a familiar face holding her gaze.

It was Krennick.

"You," Tania gasped in surprise, her eyes large as tennis balls. Now she understood what had happened.

"Yes."

She frowned, trying to see where she had missed a step. "But aren't you supposed to be part of IRIS?"

"That's correct," he confirmed, bending over and helping her to sit up. "Unfortunately, however, my loyalties now lie elsewhere."

"The Three Bears?"

He nodded. "Correct again."

"But why?" Tania was puzzled. Wasn't he supposed to be on their side, helping them against that mysterious organisation? Since when did the premise change? "Why would you betray your own people?"

"Betray?" Krennick appeared to take offence at the use of that word. "I think you're being somewhat judgmental of me and what I've done when you don't know the full story. I've given everything of myself - over twenty-five years in intelligence. I've worked both in counter-terrorism and for the International Police. But no. That wasn't good enough for IRIS. Instead, the Director of International Intelligence had to appoint as Director some sanctimonious four-star US Army General with no international experience like Abraham Hassall."

"I thought the two of you were friends."

"Sometimes those we're closest to let us down the most."

"So you're merely trying to get back at him by defecting?"

Krennick shook his head. "No. For once, I can actually identify with the enemy we are meant to be opposing. The Three Bears know exactly what it is like to have power taken away and given to someone else. At least Medvedev does."

"So you would join in with them now in destroying innocent lives simply because you subscribe to their agenda?"

"They aren't as corrupt as everyone thinks," Krennick replied. "There is a lot of merit to their actions when you think about it. While I don't condone everything they are doing, sometimes things have to be done in an unorthodox way."

As if she could accept that after what they had done to her coach. "You're saying the ends justify the means?"

"No. Don't try to boil it down to something as simplistic as that," Krennick retorted. "This is about things which go far beyond your level of understanding. When you have lived as long as I have, then you might appreciate what I'm saying. In the meantime, to put it simply, I took advantage of certain opportunities when they presented themselves."

"So let me get this straight: you merely sold out to them?"

"Don't tell me a multi-million-dollar-earning girl like you doesn't understand the lure of that?"

She gave her head a definite shake. "Not if it means losing my soul."

"Idealistic talk for someone as young as you. Give it a few years, and time for your celebrity star to burn out, and I'm sure you'll change your view."

"Well, I'm guessing you don't intend for me to live that long anyway."

"Oh, it's not up to me," Krennick informed her. "It's up to The Three Bears. I'm sure you'll have the pleasure of meeting them soon."

"I can't wait," Tania said glibly. With her luck, they'd probably have her for breakfast.

"But you might as well relax, Tania. We still have a couple of hours to go before we arrive."

"Where are we going?" She looked over to the window, but the shutter had been pulled down.

"Lake Baikal," he replied. "I think you'll like it there."

"Great," she sighed. "I always wanted to take a trip there. By the way, do you mind telling me what I'm doing wearing this?"

"Oh that's not my doing," Krennick replied. "There's someone else here who'd like to get reacquainted."

"Who?" Tania searched her brain for possibilities.

A figure stepped out from behind one of the other seats.

"Hello darling. We never did finish up what we started in Xi'an."

It was Rose Red.

***

Elf sat at the computer tracking the dot of light that was blinking across the large screen displayed with an electronic world map and various grid lines intersecting it.

"Where are they heading?" Bull inquired.

"They seem to be going north of Beijing towards Siberia."

"Do we know where specifically?"

"I can track the signal and find out if there are any private planes currently in that region and try to determine their flight plan." Elf began typing a few keystrokes on the computer as various flight trajectory lines appeared across the screen. After a few minutes, he spoke. "I think I've narrowed her down to a specific plane travelling over that area."

"Good work," Bull replied. "Now all we have to do is call the company that chartered it to The Three Bears and find out its destination."

***

"I told you I never could resist girls in tennis dresses," Rose Red reminded Tania. "I hope you don't mind. I took the liberty of playing dress up with you while you were asleep. I think you look so cute in it."

"Again, I'm flattered," Tania replied, fed up of this nonsense. "But how did you get hold of this dress?"

"Why, I bought it of course. Especially for you."

Tania gasped. "So it was you who won that auction from my site?"

"Yes. I couldn't let it go to waste. At least the proceeds went to charity."

Rose Red smiled as she began stroking Tania's golden hair affectionately, feeling the silkiness of it through her fingers, and causing the blonde ace to realise that her Alice band housing the two-way radio was gone. Then, when it seemed as though the assassin was about to relent, she gave a wicked smile and proceeded to remove the tennis star's shoes and socks, much to her dismay, and toss them onto the floor to the side.

Oh no, what's she up to now? Tania could only watch helplessly, fearing the worst.

"Such pretty feet," the red-head complimented her. "Love the sock tan too." Her pupils seemed to dilate as she peered down to admire those toenails flashing back at her which were currently painted a cool coral pink shade. She began cradling the tennis star's left foot in her hand and running the tips of her fingers gently across its contours like a black widow scuttling on soft, tender skin.

"Oh God!" Tania yelped, flinching spasmodically as the sensation sent a shiver up and down her entire body, causing her toes to curl. She let out an involuntary kick in the process. Why did she have to be so ticklish?

And those ropes! They burned like hot wires as she strained against them as a natural reaction to those soft, sensuous caresses.

"*Pazhalsta bol'she nyet*," she gasped. "Please no more! "

She glanced at Rose Red uncomfortably through the corner of her eye, a lump ascending into her throat as her chest rose and fell sharply with each shallow breath.

"Was that good for you?" her tormentor asked, with the corners of her mouth turned up in a lecherous grin.

She could feel the heat, the smouldering intensity of the flame-haired assassin's gaze, every bit as magnetic as the red-head's late Brazilian partner, almost stripping away Tania's resistance little by little. It was as if this animal was ready to devour her. "Why don't you go find yourself another play-thing?" she gasped.

"Don't look so worried," Rose Red assured her, seeing Tania's frightened face and the unmistakable look of alarm in her eyes. "I won't do anything. At least for now. But I do have a bone to pick with you, as they say in the West. You're partly responsible for killing my very good friend, Snow White."

With that, she contradicted her previous words, and allowed her wandering fingers to flitter across her blonde captive's sensitive soles again, causing the poor girl to writhe and squirm about uncontrollably.

"I thought you were *both* dead," Tania managed breathlessly, when she finally composed herself after a few minutes.

Rose Red shook her head in disgust. "Now what kind of sympathy is that?"

"What do you want me to do? Send flowers?"

Affronted, the red-head slapped Tania hard across the cheek with the tennis shoe lying on the floor. "Friends like her don't come along so often," she reprimanded her. "She was a rare find."

Still smarting from the blow, Tania retorted, "Well blame the trigger-happy RISK agent who fired off without warning. Besides, you were both trying to kill us."

"Well next time I won't simply try," she promised, holding onto the shoe and fiddling about with it. "I'll make sure I'm more successful - *after* I've had my fun with you. By the way, I hope there are no hard feelings between us for me killing your boyfriend, Piotr Volkov."

What? Tania was stunned. Sure, Tiananmen Square had been the scene of a virtual massacre earlier with that killer dragon kite, but she had hoped that Piotr had somehow survived. She caught Krennick's gaze. His expression seemed to verify that it was true.

"I'll try not to weep," she countered, biting her lip to maintain her resolve as her eyes began to well up. She blinked them rapidly to hold any potential tears at bay. Hopefully it didn't show. She wasn't about to cry over someone like him. Or anyone for that matter. *No way.* However, the truth was his death did affect her more profoundly than she would care to admit. She wouldn't wish such a fate on him or anyone else. But there were other things of more immediate concern right now.

"Good," Rose Red added, observing that the news had unsettled her prey. "Because I wouldn't want you to be crying that pretty face of yours just yet. Best to save your tears for later on when you're begging me for your life."

***

Having managed to discover the relevant flight information, Elf pointed to the map on the view screen. "According to our information, the plane appears to be heading towards the region of Lake Baikal."

"Lake Baikal?" Bull asked. "Are you sure?"

"Yes. I can double-check for you, but I'm pretty sure."

"It's okay," he said, waving a hand and indicating not to bother. "I trust your abilities."

"Thanks."

"How far is it from Beijing?"

"About twelve to thirteen hundred miles. That must be about a two-and-a-half to three-hour flight."

"Yeah. I hope Tania's at least comfortable whatever she's doing at the moment."

***

Rose Red softened her gaze towards the Russian tennis star and moved to stroke her face where she had struck her earlier. "I am sorry I hit you," she apologised, with a sincerity in her voice that sounded almost genuine. "Really I am. We obviously seem to have gotten off on the wrong foot."

Tania rolled her eyes. "You'll pardon me if I don't take your words at face value."

"Your loss," the red-headed assassin replied. She gazed down at Tania's tennis shoes and moved it to the side. "By the way, you won't be needing these during this flight." She gave her a knowing wink, but then suddenly, her expression turned to surprise. Something that had been embedded in the shoe fell off, having been loosened after slapping the

Russian in the face. Picking it up between her thumb and forefinger, she examined it. It was small and circular, and appeared to have some loose microscopic circuitry protruding from it. "What's this?"

"It's a GPS tracking device," Krennick exclaimed, recognising Elvin Xiu's work immediately.

Rose Red's face wrenched tight, as if to suggest she had somehow been betrayed. She placed the device under her boot and began to crush it with her heel. "Not any more."

***

The blinking light faded from the screen. It was as if the last traces of a heartbeat had suddenly flat-lined. "We've lost the signal," Elf announced with understandable concern.

"Damn," Bull swore, shaking his head in frustration. "Is there any way to use ASAP to extrapolate the co-ordinates of the destination to find out specifically where they're headed? After all, Baikal is a big place. They could be anywhere."

"I'll try." Elf began to tap a few keys on the keyboard and brought up the relevant information. "I think it's the town of Baikalsk, on the south eastern shore of the Lake."

"What's there?" Jonah asked.

A few keystrokes later, and Elf had produced further results. "The only thing that seems feasible is the abandoned Baikalsk Pulp and Paper Mill near the Lake."

"I've heard about that," Hassall said.

Elf nodded. "According to our information, it was originally built in the 1960's as a military factory to manufacture high-quality cellulose for military aircraft tyres, until it was converted to make low-quality paper instead. It became a source of constant protests among Baikalsk residents over the pollution it was causing to the lake, ultimately attracting massive lobbying by environmental groups such as Greenpeace. Production eventually ceased a few years ago, and it was finally shut down when the plant was purchased by a little-known company, paying off the 3,000-plus employees who would be out of a job. And get this: the company that bought the plant appears to be a subsidiary for a company with which Boris Medvedev has connections. More than coincidence, wouldn't you say?"

"Could the mill be a front for The Three Bears?" Jonah inquired. "Is it possible they are now using it as a base of operations?"

"That would be a strategic location," Hassall agreed. "With the mill closed down, it would simply remain a historical landmark where no-one would think to look for them. They could carry out their plans with little or no interruption from anyone else."

***

With that red-headed assassin's attention off her for the moment, Tania attempted to put the pieces of the puzzle together as the long journey to Lake Baikal progressed. "So the dragon kite was a diversion, albeit a deadly one, to get Dr Yan?"

Krennick nodded. "You could say that."

She frowned. "And what am I doing here? Why have you taken me as well?"

"You were in the wrong place at the wrong time," he replied. "You must realise I did have your best interests at heart."

"How so?"

"I tried to convince Hassall not to allow you on this mission."

"That's so considerate of you," Tania said shallowly. "Remind me to send you a thank-you note."

"Unfortunately, you simply got in the way in the end. Once the plan was in motion, it was difficult to change it without raising any suspicions. For the moment, however, you're simply serving as valuable insurance."

***

Jonah Bull was growing increasingly restless and agitated by the second. It was as if someone had attached electrodes to him and was feeding a charge through his nervous system. "If Tania's being taken to Lake Baikal, let me go out there," he offered.

"It's not the easiest of places to get to," Elf said, stroking his chin.

"Well how am I going to get there? They've already gotten a head start, and while I can make it part of the way, apart from by hydrofoil, there's no other way across the lake. And that would take far too much time."

"Hold on," Hassall cautioned him. "Let's not rush into things. No-one's heading out anywhere just yet."

"What?"

"You heard correctly. We need to try this another way first."

Bull frowned. "What other way?"

"We can contact the Kremlin and inform the Russian President, Dmitry Zolkin. He's likely to hold considerable influence here and can take emergency measures to have the perforating guns uninstalled, at least temporarily, until they can be checked and any rogue parts replaced."

"I don't think he'll respond well to that," Bull replied. "First off, he's going to want to know how we've learnt of the locations and how we've pieced together all this information. We can't exactly tell him we used ASAP. Then, who are you even going to say you are? IRIS is largely unknown to the general public."

"We'll deal with each of these one at a time, if they even come up."

"Maybe so, but by the time we go through all the proper channels and red tape, it would be far too late. The Three Bears have already kidnapped the engineer and Tania. You don't seem overly concerned about that."

"What's this about?" Hassall asked. "Tania, or stopping The Three Bears?"

"What's that supposed to mean?"

"Meaning that if you're going to charge out there on account of her, then you're not thinking with your head. I realise she's a beautiful and charming girl, but that doesn't mean all reasoning goes out the window. We need to do things in the proper way and using the means at our disposal. That is a far more efficient means of stopping the Bears before they can even take action. If we go rushing into battle before the time is right…"

Bull challenged him. "Now who's going too much by the book? Didn't you talk not so long ago about 'those who watch the wind do not sow, those who observe the clouds do not harvest'? That we can't go through life being overly cautious, waiting for exactly the right time, but that we need to learn to take risks?"

"Yes, I did say that. But there are times when the risk outweighs the return. This is one of those times."

"I disagree. If we wait around too long, the risk could be far greater. If you can't convince President Zolkin to look into this, then you would be allowing The Three Bears to carry out their plans and we'd be too late to stop them."

"Well you're entitled to voice your opinions, but I'm afraid the matter is decided."

"What, are you going to present me with one of your dilemmas like you did with Tania in order to force the issue? Unlike her, I'm not going to play your games."

"I don't like what you're insinuating. Yes, I presented her with a dilemma, but you know as well as I do that I had no choice. I don't like what I have to do sometimes, but that's part of what comes with this job. Sometimes you have to send people - even civilians - into a situation that you'd never dream of doing under normal circumstances. It does mean that I'm not always able to sleep at night, but I'd be able to sleep even less if I stood by and did nothing, knowing that the only reason I didn't act is because I allowed my own personal feelings to get in the way."

"Well you don't seem to have a problem holding back right now."

"I've given you my reasons. Reasons which are perfectly valid. We have to think of everyone as a whole, not just one or two people."

"I think you're wrong here, sir."

"And I'm ordering you not to get involved. You're already in danger of insubordination. We wait until the time is right."

"Sorry sir, but as you said, I've been living my life for the past year-and-a-half being held back by fear and always playing things by the book. I think it's time I did things differently."

"Okay, that's enough," Hassall said with finality. "I've given you the chance. But now I'm ordering you to stand down. Is that understood?"

The air crackled with tension as the other IRIS operatives standing around waited to see how Bull would respond.

He remained silent for a few seconds, leaving Hassall hanging.

When he finally and grudgingly spoke, he only uttered one word. "Perfectly."

Chapter 26

"**Y**ou must realise that IRIS will probably send someone after me," Tania said with a glimmer of hope in her voice.

"My dear, what do you think?" Rose Red taunted her. "You'll just click your heels and wake up back in Kansas? Well I've already destroyed the GPS tracking device, so there's no using your magic shoes now."

Tania had previously been unaware of the GPS transmitter in her shoe, but now, even with it destroyed, it stood to reason that IRIS must have been tracking the signal before. Wouldn't her captors have known that at least? They couldn't possibly think they could get away so easily, could they? Well, whether they did or not, she was the one who needed the most convincing.

Krennick didn't help matters. He scoffed at her suggestion. "Do you really imagine Jonah Bull or someone will come to rescue you like a knight in shining armour?"

"Hope never did anyone harm," she replied casually.

"No, but it does lead one to wishful thinking if one is not careful."

She shook her head. "I don't think it's wishful thinking on my part that someone will come after me."

Krennick spoke with greater force. "Tania, if you haven't realised it by now, despite his name, Mr Bull is not the kind of person to simply charge into a situation without careful deliberation and planning. As his mentor at IRIS, I've known him for a while and I know it's one of his weaknesses. He has a tendency to think too much without acting, often paralysed by indecision. We'll be a few thousand miles away by then. By the time Bull decides to come after you, it will be too late."

"We'll see about that." She had to admit however, that from what she knew of Jonah, Krennick might be right.

***

An hour passed by, but for Jonah Bull, who was feeling completely powerless, it seemed far longer. Dressed in a pair of black combat pants and T-Shirt, he sat, lacing up his military-style, steel-reinforced boots. The clock was ticking away, each second drumming in time with the rhythm of his own heart. He had to do something. But what? Hassall had strictly forbidden him to take any form of action. Now he was a 'sitting bull' whether he liked it or not.

He passed by Elvin Xiu's temporary workshop, hoping he could garner some ideas from the IRIS techie. Elf was, as per usual, completely engrossed in his gadgets, tinkering away and tweaking the equipment so that it would operate at its optimum performance. Bull smiled to himself. If the brilliant science whiz wasn't working for IRIS, he'd probably fit right in at a toy factory.

The techie barely looked up as Jonah crept in and cleared his throat in order to make his presence known. "Elf," he began tentatively. "I need your help here."

Elf spun around immediately, knowing precisely what was being asked of him. "No. You know I can't help you. I'll get in trouble."

"But you know as well as I do that we can't wait around. Don't you agree? You said so yourself."

"Well yeah. I mean no, but..." He was hesitant, not wishing to get involved.

"Now Elf, come on. Are you willing to stand by and do nothing even when you know you could, just because you want to follow orders?"

"I've always followed orders. That's what I'm good at. I just get on with the job I'm given. But I'd get in trouble if I'm even seen to be doing anything to assist you."

"Well Hassall doesn't need to know, does he?"

Elf shook his head in futility. "No. It would never work. There's not much that gets past the security systems around here."

"But you could fix that, couldn't you?"

He frowned. "What do you mean?"

"Come on, Elf. You're able to bypass that with the greatest of ease, aren't you? You can cover our tracks."

"I don't know…"

Sensing Elf's reluctance, Bull tried appealing to a different side of him. "Correct me if I'm wrong, but doesn't 'Xiu' in Chinese also mean 'leopard' or 'brave' or 'courageous?'"

Elf shook his head firmly. "No that's a different character. It just sounds the same."

"Well then become a different character. Become a hero."

"I'm no hero," Elf said ruefully. "I'm not brave nor courageous. That's why I fix things, like my name suggests, instead of working in the field. 'Xiu' can also mean timid and shy, and even that's more descriptive of me."

"You're just accustomed to living up to your name. But you can have a new name and you can change."

Elf looked doubtful. "Can a leopard change its spots?"

"You risked your life back in Tiananmen Square to try to save Tania. That was pretty brave of you. It seems to me you already have without realising."

"I wasn't thinking. I just had to act because I had no other choice."

"Sometimes we can't think too much. We just have to act."

Elf looked at Bull, as if he were contemplating all the possibilities in his mind: the person he currently was and the person he could become. "What's gotten into you?" he asked. "I don't know you all that well as I only arrived after Hassall, but in the time I have been at IRIS, I do know you've gained a reputation for doing everything by the book. That's certainly changed in the last few days. At least since Tania has been around."

"Yeah, well I can't stay stuck in the same place all my life, and neither can you. And besides, she seems to have had that effect on us."

"I can't argue with you there."

"Just think about it," Jonah continued, sensing that Elf's resolve was quickening. "You said yourself that you were a big fan of Tania Likamolova. Do you really want to leave her all on her own at the mercy of the Three Bears with who knows what is happening to her, never to grace a tennis court ever again?"

"Well, no…"

"Exactly. Here's your chance to be a hero."

Bull could almost see the cogs turning as Elf appeared to be calculating how he could pull this off without getting caught.

"Look, if you're worried about getting involved," Bull said, with a final assurance, "I'll take full responsibility for it. You can tell Hassall that I forced you to cooperate. That you had no choice but to go along. No reason for both our careers to go down the drain."

Elf sighed as he relented. He probably knew better, but couldn't resist the urge to help the Russian ace. "Okay, well when you put it like that, I guess there's no talking you out of this. I can't support you fully, but I can try to make sure that you come back alive."

"Now you're talking. I need security clearance and access to some kind of air vehicle."

"Well, as it happens, the Beijing branch of IRIS have been developing a little surprise."

"What kind of surprise?"

Bull was led outside towards a large storage area which looked like a hangar. Inside was a small white aircraft of some sort. If you could call it that. It looked like a cross between a small aeroplane and a helicopter. He couldn't decide. Too many conflicting features. There was a gyroplane rotor mounted on the top, but short, fixed wings like a conventional aeroplane, an aft ramjet unit and a pusher propeller at its rear for main auxiliary flight.

"What is this thing?" he inquired, his interest rising steadily.

"It's a cross between an autogyro and an aeroplane," Elf replied. "It's based on the Carter Copter, originally created by *Carter Aviation Technologies*."

"I vaguely seem to recall reading about one of these. But I thought it was mostly an experimental sort of aircraft still under development and that it wasn't yet widely distributed or produced."

"Fortunately, *Carter Aviation*, with the additional funding from the IRIS Defence Budget, have built a souped up version for us," Elf beamed triumphantly. "They've managed to overcome some of the difficulties previously encountered and have given it extra mobility and increased speed."

"So what is it normally used for?"

"It's mainly a surveillance aircraft for long-range aerial reconnaissance missions, including monitoring enemy activity, mapping, and gathering photographs and information using its advanced avionics and tracking systems. However, we've equipped it with reinforced armour plating, two air-to-air missiles, wing-mounted machine guns, and an aft-projecting flare dispenser. It's still in the experimental stage, so we may upgrade the weaponry later on."

Bull nodded. "Well that's good to know. By the way, you mentioned earlier that you had increased the speed. If memory serves, the Carter Copter could theoretically manage 500 mph at a stretch. So how fast does this thing actually go?"

"Under normal auxiliary power, it can reach 500 mph easily," Elf replied. "But using the ramjets, it has a top speed of about 800 mph,"

"Wow," Bull marvelled. "Over Mach 1? That's over three times faster than any conventional helicopter."

"Yeah. That should cut down on the time it takes for you to reach Lake Baikal."

"Cool. And what does this switch do here?" Bull asked, pointing to a button on the side of the joystick.

"That engages the ramjet booster, allowing you to accelerate from about 200 mph to Mach 1 in two seconds," Elf replied. "But you don't want to do that unless you're in an emergency, since you'd experience a G-force of about 13g. You could blackout and lose control."

"Okay, thanks for the heads up," Bull said.

"Don't mention it. Now, you might want to note that although you can do a standard runway take-off, the rotors are designed for vertical take-off and landing like a helicopter, while the small wings help you achieve the high speed flight. I read in your files that you're an experienced pilot."

Experienced? The last time he flew he crashed and ended up killing someone he loved. *Yeah. Experienced all right. Experienced in killing fellow passengers.* Nevertheless, his reply was curt, revealing none of his reservations about being airborne again. "That's right."

"Think you can handle this thing?"

"It's been over a year since I last flew, but I'm sure I still have it in me." The truth was he had no choice. "I just need you to show me the main controls."

"There's an operations manual here for you to read, since it requires its own unique piloting procedures. I should mention that even if you're used to flying, it handles differently from helicopters and planes, so you really need to familiarise yourself beforehand."

"There's no time to practise," Bull replied. "I'll just have to pick it up as I go along. What happens if I don't bring this back all in one piece?"

"Exactly how many pieces are you thinking of?"

Bull shrugged his shoulders. "I'm just saying. Just in case."

"Just get Tania back safely," Elf assured him.

"You'll handle the security, right?"

"I can disable it for a short period. I can make the surveillance footage play in a continuous loop and disable the signal for the hangar being in use. You have a five-minute window in which to take off before the system automatically resets to prevent this sort of override, and someone detects activity here. Think you can manage it?"

"I'm always up for a challenge, but I guess there's only one way to find out," Bull replied as he climbed into the vehicle. "By the way, does this bird have a name?"

"This version is officially known as the I-Copter. But I prefer to call it 'Hawk Eye'."

***

"Where is Jonah Bull right now?" Abraham Hassall demanded, as he stood in the IRIS Strategic Command Centre planning how next to proceed. He glanced around the monitor-lined room for an answer while a number of operators and technicians were furiously studying all the data and charts, or listening on headphones.

One of the technicians looked up from his console. "I've no idea sir."

"Well someone find him and ask him to report here immediately," Hassall barked.

***

Within a few minutes, Elf took the security systems off-line from his computer console in the control room inside the hangar.

Clad in his leather aviator's jacket, Bull sat in the cockpit of Hawk Eye, staring at the instruments and dials before him. They looked unfamiliar, but he quickly acquainted himself.

He started the engine, leaving the throttle idle for the moment. That seemed simple enough. "Ready when you are," he said, motioning with his hand as he kept the collective on the minimum setting.

The hangar roof glided open slowly, revealing the afternoon sky above, as he began to engage the pre-rotator. As there was no runway here, he was planning a vertical zero roll or jump take-off. Elf kept a close eye on the clock, ensuring that everything took place within the allotted time schedule.

Bull began to apply the throttle to the full. The rotor started to spin slowly, the revolutions per minute gradually increasing and creating a circular current of wind.

"Your five minutes are almost up," Elf warned him.

Within moments, the rotors had reached the requisite 425 rpm and Bull released the pre-rotator. He began to pull steadily on the collective pitch stick, which controlled the angle of all the blades simultaneously, and enabled the aircraft to rise vertically. With his other hand, he shifted the cyclic stick forward. This controlled the angle of each blade individually, moving the rotorcraft's nose upward or downward, or to the side. Hawk Eye hovered for a moment above the ground, but it couldn't seem to get further. *Damn.* He wasn't doing this correctly. And it wasn't meant to hover anyway. This was going to take a bit of practice.

"Hurry up," Elf urged him. "You only have a few seconds left."

"I am hurrying," Bull replied, the frustration slowly building as, this time, the nose went up at a steep angle, only to crash back down. "I'm still trying to get the hang of this."

Too late. One of the IRIS technicians named Perrault, who was sitting at his console in the Strategic Command Centre, noticed that a security light had gone on. The security cameras came back on line. Bull's image was unmistakable.

"Sir, there's someone in the hangar," he informed Hassall. "It's the I-Copter. Someone's trying to take off."

Hassall had been directing his attention towards contacting the Kremlin when he heard the news. "It's Bull. It has to be." He turned to a number of IRIS operatives standing nearby. "Get over there quickly and stop him."

The men hurried down to the hangar while Bull fiddled frantically with the controls to get the bird started. For someone who was meant to be an experienced pilot, he shouldn't be having this much trouble. It should've been a piece of cake. Of course, it could have had something to do with the fact that he was more used to flying a conventional aircraft than a helicopter, and here it required the skills to fly both to pilot a VTOL – a Vertical Take-Off and Landing craft.

"Someone seems to have locked us out," Perrault informed Hassall as the men reached the sealed entrance to the hangar area.

"Where's Elvin Xiu?" Hassall growled. "We need him here."

"Sorry sir," Perrault apologised. "But Mr Xiu is nowhere to be found either."

"Well page him or get him on his cell phone."

"He's not answering either."

"Damn," Hassall swore. "He must be in on this too. That idiot. Can you bypass the security systems and allow those men access to the hangar?"

"I'm trying sir," Perrault replied. "It will take time. Someone obviously knows what they're doing."

"Put me through directly to the control room," Hassall suggested. "Elf will have to listen through the intercom."

The Director's voice came through angrily as Elf attempted to delay the operatives outside the hangar for a few moments longer. That was all that was needed.

"Mr Xiu," Hassall roared. "Open the doors at once."

"I can't hear you sir," Elf replied, making a hissing noise into the microphone. "You're breaking up."

Hassall was incensed, his face turning bright red. "Mr Xiu. That is *not* static on the line. You don't even do a very good impression."

But the communications went silent, as Elf tuned his superior out.

"Patch me through directly to the I-Copter," Hassall growled. Perrault did so and the Director spoke with added force. "Agent Bull. What do you think you're doing? Stand down immediately. I'm giving you an order."

Bull ignored him and switched off his radio receiver. He had to concentrate. No time for other distractions. He'd deal with the Director later when he got back. That is, if he ever got off the ground.

"Damn," Hassall cursed again. He turned to Perrault. "Can you seal the hangar roof? At least prevent Bull from taking off? If we can't talk him out of this, we can at least ground him."

"Sir, I think that can only currently be done within the control room. But I've managed to bypass the sealed doors. Our agents are in."

The IRIS operatives stormed into the hangar, swarming everywhere, and bursting into the control room where Elf was sitting. They overpowered him easily as the hapless techie attempted to struggle. But it was no use. They were too many and too strong.

"We've managed to secure the area," one of the operatives informed Hassall as he pressed a button to reseal the hangar roof. Elf watched helplessly. It was all out his hands now and entirely down to Jonah Bull.

The roof began closing up again, with the sky above rapidly disappearing from view. Soon there would be nowhere to go. It was now or never.

Jonah pulled up on the collective again. *Come on.* He shifted the cyclic control stick forward, this time just the right amount, sending the copter leaping upwards suddenly towards the gap in the hangar roof which was decreasing in size by the minute.

Hassall shook his head in both frustration and disbelief. "What does he think he's doing?"

Hawk Eye soared perilously close to the closing roof, the rotor whirring furiously. He had heard how difficult it was for camels to pass through the eye of a needle. This could be a close second. He had to position this just right with the craft's nose passing through first and blades spinning in a vertical axis like a windmill, as the rotor span was far too long to allow a straight-forward vertical ascent through the diminishing gap. There would be a terrible crash, and the whole thing would explode into a ball of fire if the rotor was even a few degrees out. *Blast.* No margin for error.

"He's going to get himself killed," Hassall muttered. "It will serve him right if he does."

At the last possible moment before the gap had become inescapably tight, Hawk Eye shot upwards, slipping out like a rat through a crack in the wall, rising steadily into the Beijing sky before hurtling away out of sight.

"I don't believe it," Hassall exclaimed in astonishment. "He got away. He actually pulled it off." He was full of grudging respect for the pilot's skill and audacity, yet furious that he had taken things into his own hands.

Jonah Bull was miles away by now, but even if he could hear Hassall's angry cries, he would barely have heard the next few words as the Director's expression softened, his voice lowering to an almost inaudible whisper. "Good luck, Agent Bull. And Godspeed on your journey. Come back safely."

Chapter 27

Sunday afternoon.

Jonah Bull piloted Hawk Eye through the clear, early-afternoon China skies, north of Beijing towards Siberia. He slipped on his pair of mirrored aviator sunglasses to shield his eyes from the glare.

Not having flown for a while, it took some time for the rust on his skills to wear away. At first, he proceeded cautiously, occasionally allowing the rotor speed to drop too low while his forward airspeed was travelling considerably faster. This had the unfortunate effect of nearly causing him to roll about in the sky or the rotor to start flapping wildly like a bird. He soon remedied that, balancing the lift on the blades so that they were equal.

The learning curve was steep, but he progressed rapidly as his confidence grew with each passing moment. He adjusted the angle of the blades and switched on the engine's turbo-chargers to push himself beyond the *Mu-1* barrier - the point where the forward speed of the aircraft was faster than the rotational tip speed of the blades. Here, the tip of the retreating blade remained motionless in relation to the wind, so that no lift was produced while the rest of the blade was moving backwards through the air. The result was to create a reverse airflow over the entire length of the copter, providing less air resistance, and enabling Hawk Eye to accelerate to a forward speed of over 500 mph. It appeared that Carter Aviation had fixed the problems previously experienced by pilots of the Carter Copter - the original vehicle on which this was based - for whom the top speed had always been considerably lower. Within moments, he was climbing steadily towards 600 mph and increasing, before going into overdrive and breaking the sound barrier as he finally hit 800 mph.

The air seemed to be exploding around him with the sound of thunder, ripping reality in half from the ensuing sonic boom. Massive shockwaves of over 200 decibels swept over Hawk Eye, engulfing it completely, while the boom appeared to be swept backwards, as if he were passing through a swirling, circular cloud or rift in the sky, almost wormhole-like in appearance, as Bull hurtled forward at supersonic speed.

"Woohoo." Bull gave a cry of abandonment, as he was overcome by a feeling of pure exhilaration, amazed at what this bird could do. The power of the aircraft at his fingertips. The rush of wind around him. The freedom of soaring through the clouds. It was intoxicating. Invigorating. He had given all this up because of an accident for which he held himself solely responsible. But now, back here in the cockpit of this strange hybrid plane-copter, he couldn't deny that it made him feel more alive than he had been in a long time.

It was going to be a tense but thrilling flight ahead.

***

Elvin Xiu was in trouble and he knew it. He had directly disobeyed orders by helping Jonah Bull, and now found himself explaining his actions before Abraham Hassall. But at least he had helped Bull to escape to Siberia, and at the moment, that was all that mattered.

"What the hell did you think you were doing?" Hassall demanded. "When I give someone an order, I expect them to follow it, even if they don't fully agree."

"I'm sorry, sir," Elf apologised, hanging his head in shame. "I'd be lying if I said that Bull coerced me into it. The truth is that I felt I should help him of my own accord. I hold myself entirely responsible. You can discipline me as you wish." That was mostly the truth, although he did have some gentle persuasion from the now-rogue IRIS agent. But why bother telling Hassall that? Jonah had suggested that he himself would take full responsibility, but when it came down to it, Elf couldn't allow him. That wouldn't be right.

Hassall sighed, his expression softening. "Look, Elf," he began, taking a less threatening stance as he sat at the edge of his desk. "I realise this is still a difficult time for everyone involved. You, Bull, the others at IRIS. It's still somewhat of a transitional period as you get used to doing things in a different way to when Director Southey was in charge eighteen months ago. But while we all need to be more co-operative with each other, I'm the head now and I don't tolerate disobedience of orders."

"I understand, sir," Elf assured him. "It won't happen again and I'll take whatever discipline you see fit."

"At ease, Mr Xiu," Hassall commanded him.

Elf relaxed his stance but maintained a formal posture.

"You think I was wrong in trying to stop Jonah Bull?" Hassall asked him.

"It's not really my place to say, sir."

"I'm asking you your opinion, Mr Xiu," Hassall encouraged him. "In other words, I'm giving you the permission to speak freely."

"Well sir, I do believe that we can't just rely on the Kremlin, not when we can do something about it. I'm fairly new to IRIS myself, so I don't really know what it was like before, but I do know that we should do whatever we can if we have the power, otherwise we might regret it."

"I see," Hassall mumbled.

"But of course, it's your decision sir and I can't convince you otherwise if your mind's already made up, especially if I'm suspended in some way."

"That's not going to happen, Elf," Hassall assured him. "It's true your actions were inexcusable, but I still need you here. You're the best techie wizard I have and I can't afford to lose you right now in the middle of all this. So if you don't mind, I'll ask you to get back to work."

"Thank you, sir."

***

An exhausted Tania arrived at the Baikalsk Pulp and Paper Mill with her feet feeling rather vulnerable, having used up most of her energy during the plane journey trying to keep that voracious red-haired gadfly at bay. Furthermore, unable to look out of the window, she lacked both the opportunity to behold the spectacular, breathtaking sight of Lake Baikal, and to gain any hint as to her journey's end. Having lost track of time, with one moment seeping into the next, when the end did finally come, she was grateful to be out of those ropes, have her shoes back, and stretch those long legs again.

Shortly after landing, Tania was led towards what appeared to her to look like an abandoned powerplant or factory. Around the property was an intact wire fence with 'No Trespassing' signs affixed.

"What is this place?" she inquired, not being familiar with Baikalsk.

"An old pulp and paper mill," Krennick answered her.

Pulp and paper mill? She had heard of this place before. Wasn't it at the centre of much controversy in the past? And then all fell silent for a while when it was apparently bought out. *Is this what it is being used for now?*

The Baikalsk Pulp and Paper Mill consisted of several interconnected buildings, with huge smokestacks protruding from one of them. Once, plumes of grey smoke billowed out of these, but now they merely lay dormant.

Although it was still some distance away, affixed to another part of the building on a latticework transmission tower was what looked like a satellite array. This consisted of interlocking multi-layered cylindrical units, with a series of flat vane-like panels emanating from the centre. Each panel had a complex, open framework and appeared to be acting as an aerial. The base of the transmission tower itself seemed to disappear within one of the buildings, as if it started inside but then continued on the outside.

Tania had no idea what this was for. However, since no-one was going to tell her any time soon, she merely concentrated on making her way cautiously over the rocky terrain, which proved somewhat tricky to cross. Eventually, she arrived at the entrance to the mill complex which contained troughs dug into the floor going throughout the building.

Once inside, Tania was confronted by a strange mixture of old and new. While the interior had been vastly modified from its previous function of pulp and paper processing, there were parts of it which still retained its original setting. Much of the equipment from when the mill was active did not appear to be altered. The remains of the old mill could clearly be seen.

The guards, accompanied by Krennick and Rose Red, escorted Tania and Dr Yan through a series of buildings which, after a while, all seemed to blend into one another. In one building, Tania saw a network of overhead pipes which once delivered steam to various engines in the building. Some of the items of electrical equipment were on elevated, grated platforms and scaffolding-like walkways that resembled catwalks.

Well, everyone is always saying I look like I belong on a catwalk. Now here's my chance. Although this isn't the sort of catwalk I would've imagined. Not exactly New York or Paris.

On the end of each of these walkways were staircases and safety railings going all the way down. She peered over - there was a deep plunge into a large pit in which a number of barrels and other equipment were stored.

In an industrial room, Tania saw further catwalks and grid-like structures. In fact, if she wasn't mistaken, it looked like one of those metal latticework structures was the base of the transmission tower she had seen outside previously. That probably led up to the outside where the satellite array was affixed.

In the same room were horizontal tanks and cylinders as well as several steel paper-machine rollers. Nearby were giant paper rolls weighing twenty tons and spanning ten metres, standing vertically and stacked on top of each other on a turntable. The turntables were placed on another track, shaped like a figure-of-eight, along which, it looked like the rolls could move if the power were turned on.

Off to the side, almost beneath the paper rolls were large, trough-like conveyor belts, at the end of which were pulp processing machines with sharp steel teeth. These looked ready to devour anything that was inserted there.

Similar giant paper rolls were found again several rooms later. This time, however they were stacked horizontally on their curved sides, placed, one on top of the other, on a large metal ramp. They appeared to be held stationary by some huge electromagnet that magnetically clamped the steel core at the centre of each roll to keep them from rolling, and could only be released from the ramp if the electric power was cut off and the electromagnet deactivated.

Tania had never seen so much paper before. Everywhere! *They look like giant toilet rolls. Either someone has a bad case of the runs, or they didn't have time to get rid of these when the factory was cleared out.*

In another room she came to, there were several more stacked in series on top of a sliding metal trolley. It looked as if they were there ready to be chopped into rolls of smaller sizes, but had long since been abandoned.

In what appeared to be a boiler room were several large boilers fired by natural gas through a superheater. On another level, the Russian tennis star saw an induced draft blower which sucked the combustion gases out of the boiler and blew them up into the smokestack.

Moving on further, she arrived in an area which looked like it was being used for some kind of laboratory. She noticed a large sign marked

DANGER: HIGHLY EXPLOSIVE, under which were stored shaped metal objects surrounded by other steel components. She stopped to take a closer examination.

Wait a minute.

It was something she recognised from before. She had seen it on a screen back at the Beijing headquarters of IRIS. They were those shaped charges to be loaded into the oil perforating gun. What were they doing here? Probably the scientists at this facility who had previously modified the guns had either left them here for storage or testing. At least that was the only plausible explanation she could see.

Tania noticed there was also another piece of machinery nearby, with mounted fibre optic cables protruding. At the end of the cables were attached small lenses. But she had no idea what these were for.

One of the guards shoved her forwards, clutching her arm tightly. "Get a move on. There's nothing for you to see here."

"Hey watch it," she yelped. "I have enough injuries on the tennis court without the likes of you adding to them."

"Where you're going, you won't be playing tennis," the guard replied coldly.

"And where is that?"

"You'll find out soon enough."

She was led on, coming to a room with a large, circular platform on the floor with a strange pattern on it. It bore an uncanny resemblance to the steel interlocking leaf plates of a diaphragm shutter found on a camera, as if there was the possibility that it could open and close from the centre outwards to reveal an aperture below.

"Come on, get rid of those wood chips," ordered one of the guards to a number of his subordinates, seeing a stack of timber stored nearby. "There's still plenty to clear away."

Tania watched as one of the guards there pressed a switch that caused the interlocking steel plates to slide open. Inside appeared to be some kind of well housing a huge vat-like cylinder between fifteen to twenty foot deep into which was fed unprocessed loads of wood chips for grinding into pulp. This cylinder, called a digester, would have been regularly used for this purpose when the mill was still active. However, when the mill ceased operations a few years ago, there was no time to dispose of all the spare timber, so now The Three Bears' employees had the unfortunate task of clearing away any spare scraps of wood still lying around.

Near the digester were canisters labelled sodium hydroxide and sodium sulphide, with metal tubes connecting the canisters to an opening at the side of the well. These caustic chemical solutions were normally mixed in with the wood while the grinding process took place to separate the chemical compound lignin that held the cellulose fibres of the wood together.

One of the guards activated another switch and the lignin-treating chemicals were pumped through the metal tubes into the digester, while he manually dropped a batch of the wood fibres down there. She heard an awful whirring noise, followed by the sound of wood being crushed inside.

Tania and her captors followed a spiral staircase up to the top, leading to a further catwalk. At the end of this walkway was a large hexagonal area which was once the plant's control room. There were monitors everywhere with indicators and knobs lining the metal interior. Now, it had been vastly modified for some other purpose. Manning the line of computer terminals were over a dozen scientists and technicians, busy in a flurry of activity, none of whom seemed to notice the tennis star enter at all.

In another nearby section, partitioned off by a glass pane, were further scientists, one of whom she recognised as Dr Wei who had been kidnapped earlier.

In the far corner of the room, a man stood with his back to her. At the sound of her entrance, he turned towards her, his face still in shadow, until he strode forward. When he spoke, his voice was calm, almost unnaturally serene, like the frozen surface of Lake Baikal in winter. Yet from the tone there was the faint trace of bitterness, as if someone had finally polluted that crystal sea with raw sewage waste.

"So I finally have the privilege of meeting the beautiful Tatiana Likamolova."

Chapter 28

The one-and-a-half hours or so it took Jonah Bull to fly from Beijing to Siberia passed by more quickly than expected, bridging the distance in less than half the time it would have otherwise taken. He certainly needed that if he was to catch up with Tania.

He was grateful for the short journey as he stretched his legs uncomfortably in his seat. What possessed him to wear those heavy, military-style, steel-reinforced boots?

He found himself high over the rugged snow-capped mountains and lush woods of Siberia. The mid-afternoon sun was now streaking through the trees, bathing the crimson and gold forest in a warm September light.

He adjusted the collective and eased off the throttle, decreasing both the forward and rotational speeds, and slowing the Copter down so that he was merely gliding gently at a reduced pace. He came to a clearing - a glittering expanse of crystal blue tucked away amid the growth, like a majestic, mystical ocean within an enchanted forest. A sacred sea set within a pristine wilderness. Lake Baikal. The Pearl of Siberia.

The Pearl of Siberia? Jonah thought about that accolade for a moment. Surely it belonged more appropriately to the beautiful Russian to whose rescue he was racing?

Nevertheless, he was mesmerised by the sea of splendour below him. The vast, glass-smooth crescent-shaped body of water was the world's oldest and purest lake, measuring 1,620 metres at its deepest, and covering an area of 31,500 square kilometres. He had read that, as one of the largest lakes in the world, many Russians regarded Lake Baikal as an ocean by any other name. It certainly stretched further than he could see, with a seemingly never-ending horizon. The slightly alkaline and transparent water had an unsettling tranquillity and a sense of deathly silence and isolation. This was no lake he was used to seeing.

He remembered that the lake was considered to possess a healing, spiritual quality about it, and seeing it for the first time, he could understand why. The lake was reputed to have a complex system of self-purification. The cold blue water had an unusual clarity allowing a strange visibility to see more than a hundred feet below the surface. The lake also contained one-fifth of the world's fresh water, with over 1,500 endemic species, including some fifty species of fish.

Although the lake was relatively pure, the threat of pollution from various sources had lingered, in particular from multiple industrial projects of the former Soviet-era. One of these was the giant pulp and paper mill at the lake's southern tip, where sewage waste was carried from Mongolia by the Selenga River.

The Baikalsk Pulp and Paper Mill had been approved during the Cold War era in the belief that heating Baikal's mineral-free waters and then spraying them over the pulp of Siberian pines would produce a super cellulose that could be used to make durable jet tyres for Soviet Air Force planes.

On the lake, he noticed a lone hydrofoil traversing. It would be a ten hour journey by such craft, but it was usually the only way to cross as there were no connecting roads. Imagine if he had used that mode of transport! He patted Hawk Eye's dashboard gently, thankful that it was ready and available when he needed it.

Jonah knew he would reach his destination soon. But what had happened to Tania? Would she even still be alive? And how would she deal with The Three Bears?

***

Tania blinked at the person before her. He was a deathly spectre of a man: gaunt and dour in appearance, with piercing, sunken eyes. He intimidated her with his austere presence, yet she tried to remain calm and unperturbed.

"I suppose you want an autograph?" she began.

He ignored what must have seemed like a feeble attempt at humour and spoke again. "I must apologise for the rough treatment you suffered at their hands. Allow me to introduce myself. I'm Boris Medvedev."

So this was finally him? The man she had heard so much about in the last week.

"Oh please," Tania interjected. "We both know I'm not here for a Lake Baikal TV special with The Three Bears."

"Hmm. Such feistiness in a girl so young," Medvedev remarked. "Now, I have to ask. How on earth did one such as you come to be mixed up in this business?"

"You're not the first person to ask," Tania replied. "I'm still trying to figure that out myself."

Seeing the others who had accompanied the tennis star standing there in the background, Medvedev turned to Krennick who was listening to the exchange. "I must congratulate you, Mr Krennick on bringing Dr Yan to me."

"It was easy once IRIS located him," he replied. "They did all the work."

"And you double-crossed them," Tania snapped.

"Be quiet," Krennick advised her. "Each person must follow their own path."

"And you obviously picked the wrong one," Tania retorted.

"I don't think so…"

"Mr Krennick," Medvedev cut in. "Try not to let this spirited girl goad you into a fight. We have no time for this kind of juvenile tit-for-tat. Is that understood?"

The former IRIS operative nodded.

Medvedev looked at the engineer. "Dr Yan, your research has proved most useful so far, but I'm afraid I'm going to need your assistance once again. I'll have my guards escort you to the appropriate workstation where you can begin work immediately."

Dr Yan began to struggle as the guards led him away to one of the consoles and sat him down.

Medvedev, in the meantime, re-focused his attention on the Russian tennis star, eyeing her statuesque figure with sudden interest, as if he were a collector examining a priceless piece of art.

With the silence deafening, Tania spoke up. "Is it all really worth it just for revenge?"

"I suggest you tame your tongue before making a judgment. You don't know what you're talking about. My company was negotiating for a super pipeline between Siberia and China named "Beanstalk". However, these plans were ruined when I was arrested and my company brought to financial ruin. *Zharkholneft* lost the pipeline deal, which was redirected between Sakhalin Island and Japan instead."

"In other words, you got a little burnt and now you want revenge on Russia, by contaminating their oil supply, which you hope will bring *them* into financial ruin. That's what I already said."

"First of all, you know nothing about my motivations and my own goals for this project, so who are you to judge me?"

"Why don't you enlighten me?"

"Enlighten you? You want enlightenment? How about this?" Medvedev walked up to Tania and grabbed her face, clasping her jaw between his fingers. "Look at yourself. Exquisitely beautiful by even the most attractive standards. Now look at my face. Take a good look."

Tania looked closely to see the disfigurement on Medvedev's face.

"Do you know why I look like this?"

"I don't know? Maybe it's all in the genes?"

The acid that spewed forth in his reply was as if he had spat out a mouthful of venom. "You mock me, but you wouldn't if you knew what happened. When I was thrown into prison, certain members of the *siloviki* decided that I knew too much about them. I could be dangerous to their plans, so they needed me out of the way. They tried to kill me with a slow-acting dioxin manufactured from what was formerly known as the KGB's poison factory. It would have been far better had the poison done its job properly. Instead, it wreaked havoc on my body and ultimately left me disfigured. As someone whose beauty is world renowned, you know nothing about the effect it has on a person."

"Looks, or rather, the lack of them aren't a reason to condone the sorts of actions you're taking."

"It's not as simple as that," Medvedev replied. "You make it sound simply like it's revenge."

"Isn't it?"

He shook his head resolutely, convinced of his own position. "Not at all. I'm telling you about the dioxin because I want you to know the sorts of people I'm up against."

"You mean you want my pity? Or sympathy at least?"

"Pity? No. Sympathy? Only in the sense that you understand what I'm doing and that these people are not mere innocents as you seem to think."

"Then surely there must be some other way?"

"For revenge, perhaps," he retorted. "They say that 'revenge is a dish best served cold', but like you, Miss Goldilocks, personally I like my dishes served at just the right temperature. I merely want justice against those who wronged me, to restore the status quo and to regain what is rightfully mine."

"Your place in Russia as one of the top billionaires?"

"No. The opportunity to conduct business without the constant threat of interference. And to that end, there is no sense in contaminating the oil supply simply as an end in itself. What benefit would that be either to me or The Three Bears as a whole? After all, we are still business men and need to use the world's resources."

"So, what is it then?"

"If you really must know then I'll let you in on part of the plan. After all, you're helpless to do anything about it. When I was still in the petroleum business, my engineers had developed an alternative means of processing oil. It was undeveloped at the time, but would've been used in Project: Beanstalk. The bacteria that is being introduced into the Russian oil reserves will alter the properties of the crude oil, making it unusable and unprocessable by existing refining methods. Naturally, this will have a catastrophic effect on the Russian oil supply since The Three Bears will be the only ones able with the means to process it, and the financial benefit of over $40 billion that the State would receive would be lost. Instead of President Zolkin controlling the Russian oil industry, that control will effectively fall to me."

"And what makes you think it will be any better in your hands?"

He paused, as if about to deliver a profound truth. "Have you never heard the saying 'There is precious treasure and oil in the dwelling of the wise, but a foolish man swallows it up'?"

"And I suppose the Russians are foolish in your opinion?"

"That's right," Medvedev replied. "The Russians have a valuable commodity, but what do they do? They misuse it instead to create an autonomy that merely serves their own personal agenda, and not the people."

"And how are you any different by what you're doing?" she challenged him.

"Oh, I'm nothing like them at all," he answered sharply, the abruptness in his voice cutting through the air like a scalpel through flesh.

"Okay, whatever," Tania replied indifferently. "But what about the other two Bears? Who are they, and what reason do they have for being involved? Why would they want to take part in your scheme? All I've heard about is how you were wronged. Not anyone else."

"You think that my imprisonment simply affected me? There was far more at stake there than my liberty or the loss of my company. Other countries and powerful individuals heavily invested in both the Beanstalk pipeline and my company, the identities of which you don't need to know. Suffice to say, these investors faced enormous losses. Now, two of them have joined forces with me into a powerful alliance to put right those wrongs perpetrated against us. It's called writing your own destiny rather than leaving it in the arbitrary hands of others who will pull the plug on you on a whim because they feel politically threatened.

"And do you mind telling me how exactly you plan to carry all of this out?"

Medvedev paused momentarily, examining her face to see if she were for real. Then, perhaps because of his ego, he gave in. "You are a brave young woman getting involved like this, and for your courage, I'll grant you the satisfaction of knowing. I take it you noticed the satellite array when you came in?"

"Yes."

"The entire oil-mining operation of the Chinese and the Russians in Sakhalin Island is computer co-ordinated. They have a surveillance satellite in space that monitors seismic activity and transmits the signal that activates the detonator for the shaped charges in the perforating gun. Although they aren't planning a detonation for a few weeks because of all the security checks required for the device or the precautions taken for seismic activity, my engineers in the Operations Room here are able to jam that satellite signal and transmit their own. This will relay information from our computers to detonate the explosive charges ahead of time, and will infuse the oil wells with the contaminating bacteria."

"But those explosions would probably also cause a huge tidal wave that will engulf the Island and the surrounding towns in Siberia as well as Japan. My family are in *Nikolayevsk* which isn't far from there at all. They, along with thousands of innocent people will be killed. Or hadn't you thought about that?"

"Of course I have," Medvedev replied. "And I'm sorry for your family. Truly I am."

"Yeah, sure you are," Tania sighed frustratedly. "You'll excuse me if I don't put much stock in your sympathy."

"Well if it's any consolation, Dr Yan is here, not only to assist us in determining the maximum number of shaped charges that can be safely fired into the oil well without destroying the bacterial capsules, but also, to advise us on the optimum time for detonation within our own schedule, so as to avoid catastrophic disruption to the tectonic plates."

"But that's still a risk. You don't know for certain whether he's calculated everything correctly."

"Well, it's a risk that I, and the other Bears, am willing to take."

She disagreed, not seeing his point of view at all. "And if Sakhalin Island should be destroyed, just how will that serve your plans, other than simply getting revenge?"

"As I said, I'm not the only one involved. If I were alone, I might have second thoughts about such extreme actions. But my partners had heavily invested in the Beanstalk pipeline and have the expertise in setting up oil rigs. *If* - and that's a big if - the tsunamis were to destroy the existing rigs at Sakhalin Island, it would mean that it would multiply a hundred fold the number of contracts to build these rigs as a result, so we would still profit from the disaster. But all these plans are only scratching the tip of the iceberg. This is only the start."

"You *are* insane," she concluded. "I don't care how you attempt to justify everything, bringing about a global bear market just so you can prosper yourself."

"Well, think whatever you want to think," he countered, dismissing her abruptly. "I didn't envisage you would be swayed around to my way of thinking, but…"

"But you wanted me to say that, considering what you've been through, I understand if not condone your actions?"

"Ultimately it doesn't matter," he stated, seeing that it was futile to try to convince her any further. "As I said, you're powerless to do anything about it now. In a short while, the perforating guns will be fired and everything will be set in motion."

Just at that moment, one of Medvedev's technicians interrupted the conversation with an urgent message. "Sir, we've picked up some kind of aircraft on the radar heading this way."

Medvedev looked startled for a moment. "Who knows we're here?"

"Bull," Krennick announced in disgust. "I bet that's him. Who else would fly here? He's probably come after Tania Likamolova. He's an IRIS agent. His name's Jonah Bull."

Inside, Tania's heart leapt. Jonah had come looking for her after all.

"I thought you had taken care of everything with IRIS," Medvedev grumbled. He turned to the operators around him. "Well don't just stand there. Get rid of him."

An operator spoke through the intercom on his communications console, patching through a command to another part of the mill.

Tania's heart shrivelled as rapidly as it had swelled. What were they planning to do?

***

From the air, Bull searched around for the Baikalsk Pulp and Paper Mill using Hawk Eye's sophisticated onboard computer and tracking sensors, determined to make this as quick a rescue mission as possible. He magnified the image, zooming in to get a close-up view of the huge industrial complex. With full concentration on the matter at hand, he was initially oblivious to the distinct sound of another set of helicopter blades rotating until a blip appeared on his screen. By the time the sound registered, it was too late.

Bull looked up and gasped.

Emerging seemingly out of nowhere, was a dark black mechanical monster approaching, ready to blast him out of the skies.

Chapter 29

Codenamed '*Hokum A*' by NATO, with its double-set of rotor blades mounted one on top of the other with the same rotational axis, Bull recognised the forty-four foot aircraft before him immediately: a Kamov Ka-50 Black Shark Russian single-seat attack helicopter. Appropriately enough, it was shaped just like the man-eating fish from which it took its name, with a black, streamlined body and a large, dorsal fin-like tail, but without the usual torque-countering rotor assembly there. Indeed, the twin set of contra-rotating, co-axial blades on top of the copter had entirely eliminated the need for a tail rotor.

Designed as gunships by the *Kamov Company*, Black Sharks were armed to the teeth with an impressive array of weapons under its stub wings and wing tips, such as the twelve laser-guided *Vikhr* anti-tank missiles, the unguided aerial rockets, the quick-firing 30 mm *Shipunov 2A42* automatic cannon with both armour-piercing rounds and high-fragmentation explosive rounds and a variety of other bombs and armaments. These helicopters – or helos for short - were used by the Russian military in the mid-1990's, but only a small number were produced, owing to the reduced military spending following the collapse of the Soviet Union.

Where the hell did The Three Bears get that from?

Before Bull could ponder that question any longer, the Black Shark's 30 mm cannon began to open fire.

Bull swore. He was in for one hell of a dogfight.

The burst of cannon fire continued. Bull about-turned and surged back across the lake, dodging the rounds of bullets that were raining everywhere. He cursed his luck. Elf had told him that Hawk Eye was only fitted with a limited number of light weapons. Whose clever idea was that? Two air-to-air missiles, wing-mounted machine guns and a flare dispenser? *Pathetic.* What good would a spy copter do against this flying fortress with its superior firepower?

Bull turned Hawk Eye around 180 degrees and released one of his missiles. A vain hope. But maybe that would do the trick. Perhaps he could shoot down that gunship before it got to him and finished him off.

No such luck. The absence of the Black Shark's tail rotor meant that it had super mobility, enabling it to perform a flat turn easily, thereby entirely avoiding Bull's poor excuse for a weapon.

What a waste.

Okay, Bull told himself. That didn't work. What about the machine guns?

Bull opened fire. The Black Shark merely hovered there, almost as if it were laughing at his puny attempts to keep it at bay. The Russian helo was installed with extensive, all-round armour to protect its pilot from 12.7 mm armour piercing bullets. The rounds from Hawk Eye merely bounced off it like little sparks of fire.

Maybe he could take out its twin rotors. Yeah, that was an idea. If he could disable it that way, then maybe he had a chance.

Bull squeezed the trigger again. But the Black Shark's rotor blades were also designed to withstand automatic weapons fire.

So much for that idea.

The Black Shark pilot had had enough and launched one of its laser-guided anti-tank missiles, designed for a lightning-fast air strike with pinpoint accuracy.

Bull saw the rocket heading straight for him and swore again. Without a moment to lose, he yanked the control stick desperately to the left, forcing Hawk Eye to go into a barrel roll, narrowly averting the oncoming missile. For a few seconds, Hawk Eye was flying inverted, spiralling along the axis of its flight path.

Dizzy from the constant rotation and the sudden increase in G-force, Bull breathed a sigh of relief as he came out of the roll and his stomach, which had felt like it had sunk down to his legs, returned to normal.

However, that was the least of his problems. He had merely bought himself some extra time. The anti-tank missile, which had skimmed past him during the barrel roll, was now doubling back on itself in a hairpin turn. It locked in on Bull's heat signature once again and would continue to track him mercilessly until its target had been destroyed.

Bull accelerated and began heading away from the lake, well clear of the Paper Mill. He would need to keep the missile locked on him for the time being until he could find a way to shake that infernal rocket. Although his orders were probably just to take out Bull, this trigger-happy Russian pilot on his tail appeared to be a little reckless. Probably not thinking straight. No wonder he used that heat-seeking missile here in this populated area. *That idiot. The Paper Mill was probably producing heat of its own. He could destroy them all, including Medvedev and Tania.*

***

Medvedev turned back towards Tania, whom he had temporarily forgotten about for a few moments. "I would ask you to stay around and watch, but I'm afraid you're going to be in the way. We'll have to take you somewhere where we can keep an eye on you for the time being. Make sure you won't get up to any trouble. So I'll leave you in the more than capable hands of my employees."

"Let me guess - more fun and games with Rose Red?" Tania said impertinently.

"Well, I presume you're acquainted with my employee, Asteria?"

The muscular, six-foot-ten-inch figure of the amazonian tennis player, who had beaten the Russian blonde so resoundingly in the US Open semi-finals, emerged from the shadows dressed in a black leather catsuit.

"You?" Tania gasped, her jaw dropping wide open.

"Surprised?" the giantess replied, giving her another one of her haughty looks.

"Just how many tennis players *are* real tennis players?"

Tania was led away from the Operations Room to a holding cell where she would remain until Medvedev decided exactly what he would do with her.

***

With the missile still pursuing him, Bull headed for the lush Siberian forests he had seen earlier near those snow-capped mountains. Perhaps he could lose the Black Shark and the guided missile in there. Bull poured on the acceleration, dodging and weaving in and out of the tall birch trees that were obstructing his path, taking care not to allow the rotor blades to catch.

Flying so perilously close to those trees up ahead reminded him of how he had been forced to make that emergency landing back in Colombia with his late girlfriend, Felissia. Instead he had ended up crashing through a dense forest. For months after, he wished that he had died together with her instead of going on by himself.

How ironic. Maybe he was about to be granted his wish and meet the same fate, dying in a similar, tragic way. Perhaps it was only fitting. After all, how long could he outrun those rockets?

But no. This was no time to give up. No time to think such thoughts of self-defeat. Tania might need him. And he had already decided that he was no longer going to be a sitting bull. Of course, with that missile on his tail, about to catch up at any moment, he was more likely a sitting duck.

He had to do something. But what?

Bull remembered the aft flare dispenser that Elf had described. He had only glanced over it briefly in the manual back in the hangar when he was still figuring out how to fly the damn thing. Searching around frantically for the dispenser, he saw a little red switch. *Voilà.* All he needed to do was press that.

Bull checked in his rear-view monitor to see the heat-seeking missile gaining upon him. He flicked the switch and ignited the flare dispenser. An incandescent fireball surged out of the back of Hawk Eye as he pulled upwards and out of the woods, as the rocket latched onto the flare's heat signature and exploded amongst the trees.

With smoke wafting up from the forest behind him, Bull exhaled deeply, attempting to clear his head after that near brush with death.

That was close.

But it was immediately out of the frying pan and into the fire. As Bull emerged into the skies above the Siberian forest, coming again out of nowhere was a second Black Shark attack helicopter.

As if one wasn't bad enough.

How did the second Black Shark know where to find him? Bull scrambled around for a second. *Damn.* These Russian helicopters could share target information between each other, allowing one to be able to easily engage a target that had been spotted by another. *Great.* So in other words, they had him cornered wherever he moved.

The second Black Shark began performing one of its characteristic 'funnel' manoeuvres, made possible by its increased aerobatic qualities.

This manoeuvre, also known as circlestrafing, involved moving around the target in a circle while facing it, allowing it to fire continuously while evading its opponent's sights. By circling him like a shark in this way, it prevented Bull from being able to launch an effective counterattack since he would be unable to keep track of the moving target.

Instinctively, Bull fired another air-to-air missile without thinking, in a desperate attempt to mitigate the Russian helo's weapons fire, but the second Black Shark easily avoided it as the first had done.

Damn. All out of ammo now. All he had left were those pitiful little machine guns. And with the near-invincibility of the Russian copters before him, that would be like firing a peashooter at a tank.

Bull was hopelessly outnumbered and outgunned.

Now what?

He turned to flee, before the second Black Shark's bullets connected. *But wait.* He remembered reading that the maximum speed of those Russian attack helicopters was about 220 mph. No match for Hawk Eye's top speed of 800 mph. So far he had kept his own speed down as he figured it could be dangerous to travel at such velocity in this area. But perhaps he had no choice.

His only hope against two gunships was to outrun them. After all, he was much faster.

Faster? Wait a minute.

He suddenly recalled the words that his former mentor, Wendell Krennick, had drummed into him countless times in the past concerning conflict situations:

"Surprise is an important strategy: an action must be so indiscernible that it cannot be anticipated, so swift that it cannot be outmanoeuvred, and so overwhelming that it cannot be repelled. Surprise can be far more effective than a full-frontal assault, and far more deadly. And by using what is unexpected in the mind of your opponent, you can manoeuvre them into weakness."

Krennick may have turned rogue, but there was still value in his expertise and special forces experience.

Bull had an idea.

The Black Shark helicopter pilots were probably unaware that Hawk Eye could achieve supersonic flight. For all intents and purposes, they most likely thought it was simply a light-weight surveillance aircraft with the speed of a normal helicopter. Maybe he could use that to his advantage, if he could provoke the two Russian gunships to follow him back to the lake and use the one ace he had up his sleeve.

Time to trouble the water to catch the fish. He would force them to play his game.

Seeing as they were determined to have the satisfaction of obliterating him no matter what, maybe it wouldn't be that difficult. As long as he managed to avoid their weapons in the process.

Great. Now he was acting as shark bait.

Hawk Eye raced through the forest again, narrowly avoiding the trees and another round of cannon fire as the Black Sharks attempted to smoke him out with their high-fragmentation, explosive rounds. With the Russian helos' high mobility, they appeared to have no difficulty slaloming in and out of the forest, leaving little hope that the Black Sharks' rotors might accidentally catch amidst the trees and dispose of them in that way.

Within a few minutes, Bull emerged through a clearing, as the mystical, crescent-shaped body of water came into view again. The majestic Pearl of Siberia had once more become the scene of a deadly showdown, with the two pursuing choppers ready to sink their pearly whites into him.

Hawk Eye traversed the entire stretch of Lake Baikal at around 200 mph, skimming the surface of the pure, clear alkaline waters below with the two Black Sharks hot on his tail. It was as if they were gliding balletically like ice dancers across a shimmering sheet of glass.

The Russian attack copters continued to fire upon him. Bull performed a series of complex aerial manoeuvres to avert the danger. Hopefully they would wise up this time and not employ those laser-guided missiles against him out here again, especially since he was heading back in the direction of the Paper Mill.

He peered in his rear-view monitor. The two Black Sharks were nearly upon him. With him out in the open and vulnerable like this, he was practically dead in the water.

"Come on. Closer," he whispered, as he seemed to be almost floating on the surface of the water like a speed boat. "Come closer."

At the last moment, with the Black Sharks coming in for the kill, Bull pulled up and applied full throttle. He flicked the ramjet booster switch that allowed him to jump from 200 mph to Mach-1 in two seconds. Like a streak of lightning, Hawk Eye surged forward at supersonic speed. Magically teleported from one location to another.

The sudden massive shockwave from the resulting sonic boom, coupled with the giant wave of water that was created from flying so close to the surface of the lake, swept backwards and upwards like a huge, swirling mushroom cloud, straight into the flight paths of the two Black Shark helicopters pilots, engulfing them completely.

Disorientated in their surprise at such a manoeuvre, the two pilots were now flying blind, as they attempted to avert both the back draft of the surging shockwave and the oncoming tidal wave that was about to envelope them. Distracted, one Black Shark helicopter spun out of control, and straight into the path of the second one. The two Russian attack copters exploded instantly, with the flaming fragments plummeting downwards into the cold blue waters below.

Bull yelled out loud as he experienced the sudden crushing sensation brought on by the awesome pressure of the G-force mounting against him. His face was screwed up in agony. His head felt like it suddenly weighed over ninety pounds. His legs and stomach were like lead. His vision began blurring, tunnelling, making him barely able to see that the G-meter registered around 13. The interior of the cockpit started to lose all colour.

Was he beginning to black out?

No. He couldn't. *Not now.*

Pulling himself together, he eased off the throttle, disengaged the booster and brought Hawk Eye back down to a normal cruising speed. His body screamed in relief. His stomach settled as his vision cleared, and he wiped the beads of sweat that had broken out over his brow.

That was a tricky manoeuvre, but it had paid off.

Round one was over.

With that diversion out of the way, he could get back to business: finding Tania.

***

"Well that should have taken care of him," one of the technicians informed Medvedev back in the Operations Room, having heard the explosion outside. "There's no way he could have survived an encounter with those attack helicopters."

The technician was unaware that the deafening sound he had heard was actually the shockwave from the sonic boom of over 200 decibels that had, for the most part, masked the destruction of the Black Shark helicopters.

"Let's hope so," Medvedev muttered to himself, somewhat cynically. "Let's hope so." He pressed a button on an intercom at one of the consoles. "Miss Hunter?"

The amazonian tennis player answered from elsewhere within the complex. "Asteria here."

"Please make sure we don't have any unexpected visitors dropping in."

***

With a bump, Jonah Bull landed Hawk Eye in a clearing by the lake. He descended vertically, lowering the engine and easing off the collective to slow his speed, while keeping the rotor spinning as quickly as possible. It wasn't the most comfortable of touchdowns, but the landing gear was designed for crash landing and that compensated for the rough manner in which he brought the copter to the ground in his haste. At least he had arrived safely, especially after that little skirmish he had just experienced. Now the next task was locating the beautiful Russian and then seeing what he could do to prevent The Three Bears from executing their plans.

He began to make his way towards the abandoned building, pushing past the 'No Trespassing' sign, and tracing the same path that Tania had previously followed when she was brought here hours earlier.

Bull crept stealthily through the maze of scaffolding and catwalks, making sure to avoid any of the guards who were on patrol, as he passed by the giant paper rolls and the various pieces of machinery. If Tania had come this way, it would be a near-impossible task finding her. The complex was enormous. Which way should he turn?

As he entered a boiler room he heard a few voices ahead of him. He hid behind some large vats to avoid detection. There were more guards stationed here than he imagined. Whatever kind of operation Medvedev was running here, he had taken great pains and spared no expense to turn this place into an unusual and personal setting for his headquarters.

As he watched the guards pass from a distance, a huge shadow appeared behind him. He spun around to face his would-be assailant. A fierce-looking amazonian female stood there, crowned with a Mohawk. Before he had time to react, she slugged him hard across the face. Her fist was like steel and packed the punch of a heavy-weight boxer. Before he even knew what hit him, the room started spinning.

His last thoughts before losing consciousness were upon the irony of his situation. He had survived a brutal air duel with two Black Shark helicopters and had narrowly averted blacking out from the G-force during that sonic boom manoeuvre, only to be felled now so easily.

Then all went dark.

Chapter 30

The darkness subsided like a thick fog slowly dispersing as Bull pried his eyes open. His vision still blurry, he saw a small light coming from about twenty feet above him that enabled him to make out the vague form of his surroundings. He appeared to be in some kind of holding cell, the walls of which were made of metal with hexagonal rivets dotting the surface, almost as if he were within a large drum or barrel. There was also an odd, distinctive pattern on the ceiling, but from this distance, it was too far and too dark to see clearly.

As he lay there, bruised and battered, trying to take stock of his situation, the faint but familiar hint of perfume above him filled his nostrils. A gentle hand brushed his hair as it positioned his head carefully on some kind of cushion.

"Are you okay?" a soft, silky, feminine voice inquired.

His eyelids suddenly blinked wide open to see the beautiful Russian hovering over him with a look of concern. "Tania" he whispered. He sat up with a start, pausing to check the floor beneath him where his head previously lay. There was no cushion there at all. Only her lap.

"Yeah," she replied gently. "The one and only. Am I glad to see you."

Jonah checked the floor beneath him and noticed there was a similar pattern to the one on the ceiling, except now he could make it out more distinctly. Steel interlocking leaf plates like a camera's diaphragm shutter.

"What are you doing here?" she inquired. "Not that I'm complaining."

"Long story," he said, his head still pounding. "I'll explain later. I came after you to rescue you."

"Oh that's so sweet," she cooed playfully, but with a sincerity in her voice. "I'm touched. Really I am. But from where I'm sitting it looks like we're both trapped in here and you don't look to be doing so well yourself. Unless that's all part of the plan."

"Well, you know the old saying: sometimes you get the bear, sometimes the bear gets you."

She smiled. "Hmm. Well whoever said that probably wasn't dealing with quite as many bears."

"No," Jonah agreed sadly. He stood up, removed his aviator's jacket and began to walk about, examining their prison. The diameter of the cylinder was about seven feet.

Tania looked at Bull in his black T-shirt and noticed his powerful chest and arms. "I see you work out."

He turned back towards her briefly. "Just a little. By the way, I could've sworn you were wearing something different the last time I saw you. How did you end up in that little number?"

"Long story," she chuckled, imitating his earlier response.

Bull raised an eyebrow, as if to acknowledge that he was getting a taste of his own medicine. He nodded, making a deliberate down-turned mouth expression before allowing it to retreat into a faint smile. "So how long was I out?"

"Fifteen minutes, maybe. Twenty at most. I suppose you've met Asteria, huh?"

"Who? The big lady? Is that her name?"

Tania nodded in confirmation. "Uh huh."

Bull's eyebrows knit together in bewilderment. "She's a tennis player, right?"

"I've often wondered about that myself. I thought you knew about all the spies in the tennis world?"

"Not all. They're very well hidden. But she's the one who, what was it... gave you the golden doughnut in your semi-final match, right?"

Tania laughed. "I believe the correct term is 'double-bagel'. And yes. You're right about that unfortunately."

"I assume you've beaten her before?"

She shook her head resolutely. "Never. She's got a killer backhand. But then I'm sure you know that now from personal experience."

"Well, this is a different game to tennis. Different rules."

"Then I'm glad to see you've already done so well against her. Faced her backhand head on."

"Hey, she caught me by surprise."

Tania smiled. "So I've gathered. I thought you're trained for this sort of thing. You seem to have a nasty bruise on your head."

"Yes, well there was a small hitch."

"Or a very big one, actually."

Jonah grinned. "It's nice to see you can keep up your spirits at a time like this."

"Oh, I've learned to from so many matches. If you can't ultimately laugh at your situation, then the pressure will get to you. Although I sometimes have a hard time following that philosophy myself."

"Well what's happening with Medvedev?" he continued, deciding to change the subject slightly. "I assume you've met him?"

"Yep. Given me the grand tour in fact. He plans to trigger those perforating guns remotely via the satellite array and detonate the explosive charges to release the bacteria into the oil supply."

"That's not good," Jonah replied. "We've got to stop him somehow."

"No kidding. Any ideas?"

"None that come to mind. We have to get to the controls and jam the signal, since we can't destroy the perforating guns remotely as that would be tantamount to releasing the bacteria ourselves. But I have to ask - you seemed as if you realised the implications of the explosive charges at Sakhalin Island when Dr Yan first mentioned it."

"Well it crossed my mind, but only because of something I saw before."

"What made you think of that?"

"I caught a glimpse of a documentary on tsunamis while I was at the hospital," she replied. "Anyway, Medvedev said that he and the other Bears would gain hundreds of contracts because of their expertise in building rigs if a tsunami occurred. I have family around there. My dad and mom are visiting my grandmother in *Nikolayevsk*, a small town off the East coast of Siberia. That's near to Sakhalin Island. They would be completely wiped out if The Three Bears were to succeed with their plan."

"Then we have to find a way out of here and stop them."

"No kidding. But how? This place is heavily guarded and last time I checked, we're stuck in this drum."

***

Boris Medvedev stood in the Operations Room next to Wendell Krennick, staring at the screens on the banks of computers like an investor watching his stocks. His concentration was interrupted as the towering figure of Asteria walked in.

"I see you've returned," he said.

"Yes. I was taking care of an unexpected visitor," she replied.

"I see," Medvedev nodded understandably. "Good work. But where is Miss Rednikova?"

"Rose Red?" Asteria referred to Rednikova by the more familiar name by which she knew her. "She was attending to our guests."

"I thought *you* were dealing with them."

"I was. But she wanted to make sure they were comfortable."

Dr Yan was seated at a console, closely guarded by a number of security personnel, when Medvedev strode over to him.

"Who are you?" Dr Yan demanded.

"That's not your concern at the moment," Medvedev replied. "I am more interested in who *you* are and what you can do for me. I know you've been heavily involved in the development of the oil perforating guns that are currently installed at Sakhalin Island."

"Yes," he stammered. "What about it?"

"We've already made a number of our own modifications before you joined us, but there are a few final details that we need you to check over."

"No," Dr Yan replied. "I won't cooperate."

Medvedev gave him an icy cold stare and spoke frankly. "Dr Yan, I understand you have a wife and three children. I can imagine they wouldn't want to be deprived of a father."

"They would be sad, but I am not indispensable. They will learn to live without me."

"But can you live without them?" Medvedev retorted. "You saw how easily we tracked you down. We can get to them without any difficulty. Is that what you would want? To see your family suffer?"

Yan shook his head, but said nothing.

"Perhaps a demonstration is in order?" He nodded in Asteria's direction as she picked up a tennis racquet which she had stored in a corner of the room, and removed a couple of metal spheres the size of tennis balls.

"I understand you like tennis, Dr Yan," she said. "Now you're about to get a court-side seat."

"What are you going to do?" Yan asked her, trembling.

Medvedev answered instead. "Watch carefully. Perhaps Mr Krennick here might like to serve as Asteria's hitting partner?"

"What?" Krennick exclaimed. "But I don't play tennis."

"I never said anything about you returning the ball," Asteria replied.

She positioned herself, as if she was about to serve. Krennick, realising that he was probably her target, made a frantic attempt to escape.

"Hold him," Medvedev ordered two of his guards.

"Wait," Krennick protested, as the guards restrained his arms. "I can be useful to you."

"You have already outlived your usefulness. You didn't think you were truly going to figure into my plans, did you? Besides, you let this Jonah Bull, or whoever he is, follow you here."

"How did I do that?" Krennick said, still struggling. "It wasn't my fault. And anyway, your attack helicopter should've destroyed him."

But it was no use. Asteria tossed the metal ball up, swinging her special reinforced racquet high in the air. In a sudden whipping motion, she pounded the ball with all her might. It went flying across the room towards a struggling Wendell Krennick, striking him firmly on the head. He gave an anguished cry, and then fell down dead.

"Why did you do that?" Yan exclaimed. It seemed a completely arbitrary and cold-blooded murder.

"As you will soon learn," Medvedev replied, lowering his voice to a hushed but urgent tone. "No-one here is indispensable. "The same thing could happen to your family. Is that what you want?"

Yan, now suitably terrorised, immediately became compliant. "What is it you want me to do?"

"Good. Now you're talking sensibly. I'll have someone show you."

***

While Tania sat on the floor, Bull continued to examine their holding cell. He noted that the hexagonal rivets protruding about an inch from the wall were roughly two and a half inches in diameter, vaguely resembling the foot and hand holds of a climbing wall. "From the looks of it," he said, "we're in some kind of huge barrel or drum."

"Really? I hadn't noticed," she replied grinning.

"Hmm. Seeing as this is a pulp and paper mill, my guess is that it's some kind of container used for grinding wood and processing pulp. A digester, if I'm not mistaken. Fortunately, it's only being used as a holding cell for the moment, or else we could be in deep trouble."

Tania shuddered to think about that. She had seen some guards disposing of wood chips earlier and knew what the machine could do. Changing the subject to something more positive, she asked, "So, is Hassall sending in some reinforcements after you?"

"Well," he began tentatively, "he hasn't actually authorised me."

"What?" she exclaimed. Her surprise was apparent on her face.

"He ordered me off the mission. Wanted me to wait until we had further information."

Tania frowned. "Then how come you're here?"

"I came on my own."

"Really?" She looked at him, positively doe-eyed. "Oh that's so sweet. Again I'm touched. Why did you come for me?"

Bull sat down beside her and spoke earnestly. "Because I thought it was wrong to just leave you on your own. And even though I knew it could land me in trouble - and it has - it still seemed like the right thing to do."

"So you went against Hassall's orders?" she gasped.

"Yes."

"Wow," she exclaimed. "That's rather unlike you. I guess no more Mr Sitting Bull huh?"

"Maybe. I can't keep watching the wind and looking at the clouds, waiting for the right time to go back out in the field."

"Hey, Hassall said that to me, you know."

"I know, but it hit home with me as well."

"Then maybe we're not so different from each other after all."

He gave her a quizzical look. "What do you mean?"

"I might take risks, but ultimately I have to admit that I do prefer a perfect situation above everything else."

"Hey, you're not the only one," he assured her. "I guess we all have a little bit of Goldilocks in us to some extent."

"Some more than others," she replied. "Maybe I am too naïve and innocent."

"Perhaps it's not such a bad thing after all. Perhaps that's why I like you."

"Oh, so you like me now?" she said in jest, playfully giving him a wide-eyed kittenish look. "I always thought you didn't."

"Now you know that's not true," he replied. "I wouldn't have come for you if..."

"I know. I'm just joking," she giggled.

"Well, seriously, what's not to like?"

"Are you always this understated with every girl you come across?" she asked playfully, before laughing it off.

He took the question more seriously. "Okay, well maybe I am, and that's something I need to work on. The truth is though - and I'm sure you hear this all the time – that I think you're…"

"I'm what?" she whispered, batting her eyelids furiously and trying to tease the answer from him.

His reply was unexpected. "You're a complete contradiction."

Tania looked surprised for a moment, then burst into a fit of laughter, almost sucking in air as was typically characteristic of her when she found something really amusing. "Actually no-one's said that to me before. What do you mean by that?"

"You sometimes seem so tough and yet so fragile in the same moment. Rather enigmatic. It's like someone could be completely disarmed by your looks and then you're in there for the kill."

She giggled shrilly. "*Okay.* Well you won't see me killing, but I understand the sentiment. So… thanks I guess."

"But that's not all," he continued, flashing an inscrutable grin.

"No?" She smiled sweetly, giving him a wonderfully coquettish look. "Now what other strange observations do you have in store?"

"Well, I should've said that I think your beauty comes from within because you have a beautiful heart, and that shows on your face. What I was trying to tell you back at IRIS in Beijing was that the reason I initially didn't want this assignment is because it was painful to be around you. In a way, you reminded me of Felissia, and also of the way I used to be when I was with her. She was like you - optimistic about life, full of passion and in search of her dreams, and she encouraged me to follow mine too. And I did that, going through life without being constantly over-burdened with responsibility. You were right before. I had lost that. That optimism died with her. But if there's one thing I've realised from being around you on this assignment, is that vibrant people like you or Felissia are what bring colour to this world – particularly this world of grey that I live in. If you were to lose that child-like quality and openness about you now, that would be a very sad loss. The world would be a much darker place." He reached out, gently touching her face with his hand, which she seemed to allow. "So if you are a little like Goldilocks, then hold onto it. Because without that, we could all end up Bulls or Bears. And that can't be a good thing."

"Aww. Well thank you," she said, shyness creeping into her voice. Jonah's words and his touch were reassuring. She blushed, lowering her head modestly. Perhaps, for the first time, he understood where she was coming from every time she had shared her thoughts before. He could finally identify with her. She beamed warmly, her smile lighting up her countenance.

She was about to pull away when she noticed his hand was still lingering on her face, and that those magnetic, blue-grey eyes of his were fixed intently upon her, searing into her soul. She tried to shift hers away, but found that he held her gaze hypnotically in a sudden moment of strange attraction. As he moved in towards her, she swallowed hard, trying to tell him that she wasn't ready for this, but her throat had become cardboard dry, and the words seemed to choke in her mouth.

She began to feel flush with desire, the maddening red rising across her cheeks again, while her skin bristled with goose pimples.

Her breathing grew heavy, at the same time feeling his warm breath so close to her she could virtually taste it. Her heart began pounding with increasing rapidity like a tennis ball bouncing on the baseline, booming with that same thundering resonance. Everything seemed to be moving in slow motion, almost frozen in time, as if she had entered the zone again - that trance-like state of heightened senses and increased awareness she would occasionally experience during a tennis match. Yet this was a completely different sort of game in which she was a relative novice. She ceased to breathe for a few seconds.

Was this really happening, or was she second-guessing him? And if so, what if she was wrong? Maybe he was really seeing who could stare the longest, and she had totally misread him. Did he want the same? What could he possibly be thinking?

Jonah had absolutely no idea. His mind was on autopilot. Any thoughts he might have had were completely blanked out as he drew her towards him, tentatively but involuntarily. He placed a hand firmly behind her head, feeling her silky golden hair flowing tenderly and gracefully down the nape of her neck and caressing it slightly.

As they sat mere inches from each other, he was driven by his senses alone. The flowery scent of her perfume filled his nostrils, drowning him in a kind of stupor, beckoning him nearer, as she gave him an intense stare with those oh-so-alluring emerald green eyes of hers. So full of fire at the moment. It seemed to emanate from within her soul. He watched her eyelids flutter gently as she closed them, as if that was the sign of permission for him to move in closer. He heard her gasp almost inaudibly as he cupped her chin in his hand and began tracing those exquisite Slavic features of hers with his fingers and thumb, those soft, sensual lips which were slightly parted and seemed to be inviting him to kiss them. His heart was thumping louder and louder like a Geiger counter gone off the scale, his emotions ceasing to be in control. He wavered slightly as he moved his lips to merge with hers.

The point of no return.

That fateful moment of sweet exchange, that could transform them both forever.

Tania felt a shudder. First, like a tiny spasm. Then a tremor of seismic activity. Then, a massive shockwave that enveloped her, oozing upwards and coursing through her body, filling the whole room from top to bottom. She paused for a second, her mouth mere centimetres away from his. Could he really have that effect on her before their lips even made contact?

"Did the earth just move?" she whispered, flicking her eyes open and breaking the spell. "Or was that somewhat premature?"

Another shudder.

Unmistakable this time. It appeared to be coming from a source other than the chemistry between them.

"No," he replied, withdrawing slightly from her presence. "There's something wrong." The connection between them lost, Jonah's body stiffened with alarm as he whipped his head around and began a quick scan of the cell.

The vibrations began resonating with increasing force and frequency, emanating from beneath them. It sounded as if something was rotating, gathering up speed slowly.

"What's happening?" Tania gasped.

"The digester must've been turned on."

"What?"

"It's started up," he said, pulling away from her completely as he began to examine the floor of their holding cell.

"Oh my goodness," Tania exclaimed. "We've got to get out of here."

***

In the Operations Room, while engineers oversaw the last few modifications made by Dr Yan, Boris Medvedev was growing increasingly restless by the minute.

"Is it nearly done yet?" he asked, pressing the petroleum engineering expert.

"Just a little while longer," Yan replied.

"Well, hurry up," Medvedev ordered him, bristling with impatience. "You understand the importance of completing this on time. For your sake as well as ours."

Medvedev was interrupted as a beeping noise was heard coming through one of the communication channels.

"Sir," one of the technicians informed him, "there's an incoming call."

"Put it on speaker," he replied.

A couple of electronically disguised voices filled the room, and immediately, everyone else there knew who they were. Medvedev's mysterious and unseen partners, the other two Bears, identifying themselves as Blue Bear and Green Bear. The voices instilled fear in nearly all present, including the giant Asteria.

They spoke, one by one, the impatience in their voices still detectable despite having been digitally altered.

"What is the present situation, Red Bear?" Blue Bear inquired.

"Everything is proceeding according to plan," Medvedev replied.

"And Dr Yan? Has he finished yet?" Green Bear spoke.

"He assures me he is nearly done."

"Good," Blue Bear said, taking over again. "What about the other two problems you experienced?"

Before Medvedev could answer, Rose Red walked in. "Have you seen to our guests, Miss Rednikova?" he inquired.

"Everything is taken care of," she replied. "Both Likamolova and Bull are safely stored away where they can't cause any trouble."

"What have you done with them?"

"I've arranged a little surprise for them," she smirked. "Let's just say they'll have their noses to the grindstone dealing with this."

"I thought you were going to save the girl for yourself," Asteria remarked.

"I was," replied Rose Red. "But evidently Tania Likamolova has decided she isn't game."

***

The vibrations and the whirring sounds grew louder, shaking the entire cylinder. Suddenly, the floor started to move, as if it was shifting outwards.

Tania glanced down immediately. To her horror, the steel interleaving plates were sliding away towards the circumference of the digester's walls. She saw the beginnings of a small star-shaped aperture in the centre of the diaphragm that gradually increased in size as the floor retracted beneath them.

"Jonah," she shrieked in panic, as she saw him drawing farther away from her as he stood on one of the opposite leaves, and the surface area on which she was able to stand began to decrease rapidly.

"Grab onto a rivet on the wall," he shouted above the noise.

Tania turned around and put her toes onto a rivet to get a foothold and grabbed onto another with all her might, hauling herself upwards, as the floor gave way completely. That was close, thank God. But was Jonah okay?

Fortunately he had done the same.

"We've got to climb," he yelled. "Quickly."

They tried to pull themselves up, but the rivets were too far apart and required a great deal of upper body strength. Holding onto one, and then stretching for another was almost impossible.

Suddenly, as if things weren't bad enough, something large and metallic arose from the depths of the hole beneath them. Blades. Deadly, and rotating furiously. Like those found at the bottom of a blender. It spun round propeller-like, making a terrible noise, as Bull watched his aviator's jacket that he had removed earlier cut into ribbons.

They were about to be ripped to shreds.

Chapter 31

Tania gasped in disbelief. Almost paralysed with fear, she drove herself on to reach for the next rivet.

"We have to climb quicker," Bull hollered.

"They're too far apart," came the reply. Not only that, but her arms were getting tired, and her fingers, aching from clasping the hexagonal shapes so tightly, were beginning to lose their grip.

"Lean backwards," he said, with urgency in his voice.

"What?"

"Just do it," he replied.

"But I'll fall," she screamed. "Are you crazy? What are you thinking?"

"Just lean backwards onto me on the count of three. Don't be afraid. I won't let you drop."

Tania was sceptical. But if they were going to die anyway, there was nothing to lose. After a rapid count to three, and with a step of faith, she let herself go into the unknown.

She fell onto Jonah's back, while he had simultaneously allowed himself to fall into that position as well. Tania and Bull's combined heights of six foot and six-foot-four respectively, stretched across the digester's seven foot diameter, but just barely, as they lost some range from being in a semi-seated position. Fortunately, the resistance of the two pushing against each other in opposite directions, with their feet against the opposite sides of the wall, allowed them to wedge each other in, preventing them from plunging downwards to their deaths.

"Put each of your arms around my mine," he said, as the spinning blades beneath them edged closer. Without question, she did so, their elbows interlocking, becoming one. "Now together, we've got to use our legs to push, and walk up the wall. Think you can manage that with those endless legs of yours?"

"This is no time to be making comments about them right now," she replied, as they began their arduous ascent to the top, back to back, scaling the length of the walls one foot at a time.

The whirring of the blades below was deafening, and Tania could feel the rush of wind as it began to rotate faster.

***

"What's that doing on?" one of the guards asked from outside.

"I don't know," another one replied. "Someone must have left the digester on to dispose of these wood chips still lying around."

"Well let's give them a hand." The guard pressed a switch on the outside. "Here, grab some of these chips and throw it into the cylinder."

***

"What happens when we get to the top?" Tania asked, looking up at the diaphragm above them. "It's closed up there."

"We'll worry about that when we get to it," he replied. The truth was, he didn't have a clue.

As if miraculously, the metal leaves at the top began to open. Tania's heart skipped a beat for a moment, rejoicing at this glimmer of hope. But no. It wasn't to their advantage. The interlocking steel plates of the digester's lid retracted to allow a batch of wood chips to drop down, narrowly missing the two of them.

Tania shuddered as she heard the ear-splitting sound of wood being torn to shreds down below them. But her surprise quickly turned to shock. A white-coloured liquid was being pumped in unexpectedly through an opening in the side of the cylinder. She gasped. The fluid slid down the side of the digester where Tania's feet were planted, making the wall slippery, as if she were gliding on oil.

"Oh no," she cried. "I'm starting to slip."

"Keep going," Bull urged her, his own side of the digester wall unaffected by the liquid. "Quickly. We've got to reach the top before it gets impossible to climb."

As if it wasn't already. Tania found her feet could barely get a grip. She started to lose her footing. She gasped as they slid downwards a few inches towards the blades. In her panic, she began to struggle, her feet shuffling against the surface of the cylinder wall, desperate to stay propped up. And it was in that struggle that she instinctively let her elbows unlock from Jonah's, trying to use her arms to steady herself.

Big mistake.

Her back slipped off his towards its right, causing him involuntarily to do the same. She screamed as she began to fall backwards. Her body began to rotate ninety degrees anti-clockwise to her left, about to lose that resistance between them that kept them propped up all this time. Arms flailing about wildly as she continued to rotate, she caught onto the right side of Jonah's waist in desperation with her left hand. In turn, he stretched out his left arm backwards behind him and clasped her tightly around her waist to steady her. Both of them grabbed onto a nearby rivet on the wall with their free right hands while simultaneously jamming their feet against the sides to stop the turning momentum. She was now lying perpendicularly on top of him in an awkward position, with her left rib cage pressing into his chest, but at least they had averted disaster. For the moment.

"You've got to turn," Jonah said, feeling the weight of her bearing down upon him. "I can't support you for much longer like this."

Nerves shredded with fear, but with no other choice before her, Tania let go of the rivet tentatively with her right hand while inching her left hand slowly over from the right side of Jonah's waist to his left. She rotated carefully a further ninety degrees counter-clockwise, twisting her supple body right around so that she was now facing horizontally downwards, her chest perfectly parallel to his with her breasts pressing into his abdomen. Both were now intertwined in a most intimate of positions, with his head practically in her crotch and hers... well, she didn't even want to imagine where. She allowed her right hand to join her other one already clasped around his waist, as he placed both his hands tightly around hers so that they were both embracing each other in a bear hug. Lying flatter than before, now with an extended reach, they were able to use their feet to climb with greater leverage as they began their slow ascent to the top.

Tania breathed a sigh of momentary relief, taking care to keep her feet on the part of the cylinder wall that was still dry. Thinking about it, that stuff seeping down the wall where her feet had been was probably the same liquid used to separate the cellulose fibres from the wood that she had seen earlier that had been pumped from those metal canisters. Now what were they labelled again? Oh yes. Sodium hydroxide and sodium sulphide. Or something like that. She wasn't that good on chemical names.

It suddenly struck her, as they pushed their legs hard against the wall, that they had never been this close before. In the circumstances, a little too close for comfort. She felt the warmth of his athletic body, like a blast-furnace, effusing through hers, and the strength of his muscles cradling her in a distinctly sensual manner as he struggled to maintain their balance. What's more, she could feel his racing heart pulsating, knocking like a diesel engine beneath her in the pit of her stomach. Every breath of his grew heavier and shallower with the strain of her weight and the strenuousness of their climb, producing a somewhat inappropriately exhilarating sensation in her and a hot tingling in her chest. She just had to hope that there weren't any similar thoughts going through his mind as well. But what was the likelihood of that?

No time for such thoughts right now. Concentrate. We're about to be turned into mincemeat. Ushering that out of her head, she edged up further, leadened limbs wracked with agony and exhaustion as the two of them neared the apex of the cylinder.

"Oh no," Tania screamed suddenly. "I think my shoes are dissolving." Having come in contact with the white liquid earlier, the caustic solution was beginning to eat away at her soles.

"We're nearly there," Bull assured her, seeing the top was almost within reach. "Hold on. Don't panic."

Her heart was pounding furiously to the point where she could barely tell it apart from the hum of the spinning blades beneath her. Almost against her will, she pressed on with grim determination, knowing the end was in sight. Then a shocking thought knifed through her. Even if they reached the top, how could they possibly release their arms from one another and grab hold of anything?

What's more, it was beginning to smell like rotten eggs in here. It had to be the chemical solution. She began to cough and splutter. Her throat was on fire.

"Damn," Bull swore, suddenly injected with an added sense of urgency. "We've got to move."

"What's happening?" she squealed, unable to see anything from her position. His sense of alarm shot through her as well.

"The steel plates are beginning to close in," he answered her, the dismay clearly evident in his voice.

Tania gasped silently to herself. Their last hope - gone. And those whirring metal blades below were rotating furiously now, about to tear them to pieces the moment they lost their grip. She had her whole life ahead of her. So many things she still wanted to do. So much she still wanted to be. How could it possibly end like this?

"We've got to jam it somehow," he cried.

"With what?"

Good question. Thinking quickly, if not quite on his feet, Bull lifted his leg and stuck his foot between the plates, jamming the boot of his left leg between two of the metal leaves, acting as a temporary doorstop, with his other leg still planted on the wall. He grimaced as the interlocking segments pushed against him, trying to cut into the reinforced steel of his boots like a nutcracker on a macadamia nut, but wedging him in tightly. He was grateful that he had worn these boots after all. The steel boot was buying them some precious time. Hopefully enough to get out of there.

"You need to let go," he whispered, her weight becoming almost unbearable now as the digester's spinning blades seemed to loom closer, almost beckoning them to their deaths. "Hook one of your feet onto the edges of the top while I hold this in place."

"But what about you?" she cried, concerned for his safety. She hesitated. For a start, she couldn't even see where the edge was.

"Just do it," he insisted.

Reluctantly, she felt around, then hooked the front of her right foot onto the rim of the steel plates for safety. Letting go of his waist slowly with her right hand, she placed it on the rim, on the same side as her right leg. Fortunately, she was extremely flexible from her hours of yoga training, her legs powerful and athletic from being a tennis player. Now hanging off the rim with her right leg and right arm, she let go of Bull's waist completely and intended to pull him upwards so that he was at least able to place his left hand on the edge of the rim as well, leaving him hanging in an almost hammock-like position.

Suddenly, his arm slipped from the Russian's hand above him.

Tania gasped.

Jonah lost balance and swung backwards, now dangling precariously by one leg. *Phew.* Saved only by the fact that his boot was firmly wedged in place between the interleaving steel plates.

With no time to lose, Tania wriggled her right leg about so that more of it was outside the rim. Then once at least the calf of her leg was clear, she clasped hold of the rim with her left hand. Now with one leg over and both hands on the rim, she hauled herself upwards and outwards to safety.

Without a moment's delay, Tania ran around quickly to the other side to hit the digester's emergency stop button and hauled Bull up with all her might until he was firmly out.

Both of them safe and having escaped a near-death, they crashed on the floor exhausted and gasping for air from the toxic fumes. They had made it. What a close shave.

"I guess it's true what they say about people named Jonah," Bull remarked as he breathed a heavy sigh of relief.

"What's that?" Tania gasped, equally glad to be free.

"You can't keep a good man down."

***

Abraham Hassall paced about restlessly at the IRIS headquarters in Beijing. "Do we have the President on the line yet?"

"No sir," Elf replied. "They've put us on hold."

"Well keep trying." Hassall refused to be put off by these obstacles. Inside, however, he was beginning to think that perhaps Jonah Bull might've been right. Trying to get through to the Russian President might take far too long, by which time things could be too late.

He watched helplessly, as Elvin Xiu continued to wait on the line, with the Kremlin putting him on hold indefinitely. Could there have been some other way? Well, if either Bull or, dare he say, Tania Likamolova found a way to stop The Three Bears, he would gladly and fully endorse that. But they had a very slim chance of stopping the Bears at the source. Who knew what kind of situation either of them could be in right now?

***

Heart rate returning to normal, Tania took a moment to survey her surroundings. They appeared to be in one of the plant processing rooms, with a large array of equipment around them next to the remaining stacks of wood chips. Nearby were several canisters of the same chemical fluid that had been pumped down the tube of the holding cell they had just been climbing up.

Turning her attention away from it momentarily, she examined the bottom of her tennis shoes which had been partly eaten away on the surface.

"I think they'll be okay," Bull assured her, looking at his own boots that had been mangled by the steel plates. "Mine aren't exactly in great shape either."

Tania nodded gratefully. But then she felt compelled to speak up about another matter. "Listen, about what almost happened in there..." A shade of red stole across her cheeks.

"What exactly did happen?" Bull replied, unfazed by the question.

"You're right," she said, stumbling uncharacteristically over her words while rotating her shoulders about coyly. "Nothing *did* happen..."

She was unable to complete her sentence as she was interrupted suddenly. She heard a whooshing sound behind her and whipped around to see a steel pipe coming towards her head.

She ducked out of the way instinctively. One of The Three Bears' guards who was collecting wood chips for the digester had returned with a new load. Realising they had escaped, he decided to finish them off with his bare hands.

Bull rose to his feet, as another guard appeared and reached for his machine gun. Bull tackled him to the ground before he could use it, and they rolled about for a few seconds. He punched the guard off, knocking him into digester's on switch that started up the machine again.

Tania had her hands full. Her attacker charged at her furiously like a steam train, swinging the pipe like a baseball bat. She dodged it nimbly, bending backwards. The guard bore in again with unexpected ferocity, this time intending to pound it down upon her like a piledriver. However, the tennis star was agile and athletic while her attacker was slow and bulky. In one quick motion, she side-stepped him as he bundled past. Using the guard's own weight and momentum, she sent him flying in the direction he was already travelling with a well-placed kick from behind.

With the guard still moving, Bull grabbed him and shoved him towards the top of the digester where the steel plates were opening again. The guard went over the edge, plunging headlong into it, where the giant metal blades below were whirring. A blood-curdling scream was heard with the sound of bones grinding like food in a blender. Then nothing.

Tania gasped, shaking her head in disapproval. "Why did you do that?"

"He would've killed us," Bull replied. "It's no time to pull your punches."

She said nothing, but inwardly, her heart was shrinking.

Bull grabbed the guard on the floor and shoved him against the side of the digester. "Now if you don't want to go down the same route, you'd better tell us how to get to the Operations Room."

Unwilling to lose his life, the guard began to explain frantically, before a round of machine-gun fire whizzed past, tearing into him like divots being cut out of the ground with a golf club.

"Duck," Bull cried, pushing Tania out of the way.

They left the body behind, scrambling to their feet as a battalion of guards stormed into the area, armed to the teeth.

"Let's get out of here," he shouted, grabbing the machine gun the guard had dropped in the scuffle. Bull took Tania by the hand, and led her away from the area as the guards opened fire again.

The pair fled the scene, racing desperately through the mill with the guards hot on their trail. They entered the room which Tania had previously thought was being used for a laboratory. As they hurried towards the exit, she spotted those shaped perforating gun charges marked DANGER: HIGHLY EXPLOSIVE, near the machinery with the mounted fibre optic cables and lenses she had noticed earlier.

Before she could ask what they were for, they were showered with bullets once again. The rat-a-tat of machine-gun fire filled the air. Bullets rained down where they were, as they leapt out of the way to safety. Bull returned fire.

A fierce shootout followed, with one of the downed guards stumbling back onto the machine with the fibre optics. Accidentally tripping the switch, he set off a string of red-hot, pencil-thin laser beams, firing indiscriminately in a wide burst of activity.

"Watch out," Bull warned Tania, as a ray of light fired past her. "If one of those connect, they'll fry you instantly."

The beams took out several guards, leaving them with serious, painful burns. Temporarily distracted, with everyone trying to dodge the laser beams, no-one noticed that the rays were focussing on the shaped charges before it was too late.

The temperature increased rapidly, triggering an impulse to the shaped-charge detonators. The room was filled with a massive, ear-splitting blast and a tremendous burst of energy, throwing Tania and Bull forward, and knocking them to the ground. Hundreds of fiery fragments exploded in every direction, sending several other canisters flying through the air.

The guards were also thrown back or caught in the blast, as the charges began setting off a series of further explosions, while the canisters began releasing a noxious, colourless gas.

"Get out of here," Bull yelled. "This place is going to blow."

Chapter 32

"What was that?" Medvedev demanded, hearing the blast from the Operations Room where he was standing with Rose Red and Asteria.

"No idea," one of his men who was sitting at a computer terminal replied.

"Find out. Quickly."

The man did a cursory sweep of the newly-installed security systems in the mill. "It appears to be an explosion coming from one of the pulp processing rooms."

"Where exactly?"

The man located the precise area.

"Isn't that where you imprisoned Likamolova and Bull?" Medvedev turned around with a disgusted look, glancing at both Rose Red and Asteria. "Miss Rednikova," he began. "Find them quickly. If they've escaped, they may have caused this. If we don't get this explosion under control, it will ruin everything. Make sure you don't come back unless you've taken care of them."

***

The explosions and flames from the laboratory began to spread towards a nearby room where a superheater was stored to fire up several large boilers. The force of the blasts tore through the boilers, causing the superheater to overheat and creating the beginnings of a factory-wide meltdown.

Still coughing and spluttering from the fumes, Tania and Bull took a moment to rest.

Tania took a deep breath, and then tightened her resolve again. There was still the problem of stopping The Three Bears. Any moment now, they were planning to remotely fire the perforating guns that would probably devastate Sakhalin Island. She turned to face Bull. "What are we going to do about Medvedev's plan?"

"We have to get to the control room," he informed her.

She frowned. "I have to ask. How will we stop them once we get in there?"

"Hopefully, it will be full of scientists and engineers. Between the two of us, we should be able to take them out."

"And if it's not?"

"Then we'll have to find another way. We'll cross that bridge when we come to it."

***

Abraham Hassall was on the verge of giving up on his phone call, but with few options available, he clung to this hope for as long as possible.

Suddenly, Elf piped up. "I think we've got him on the line. President Dmitry Zolkin for you, sir."

Hassall took the phone anxiously from Elvin Xiu, placing it to his ear. He took a deep breath, poising himself to speak, hoping he would know the right words to say to convince the President to use his influence to dismantle the perforating guns.

"Mr President, sir," he began. "This is Abraham Hassall from IRIS - International Intelligence. I'm sorry to bother you at this particular time."

The President was understandably suspicious. With IRIS being a covert operation he was little involved in, he began to ask a number of questions which Hassall thought entirely unnecessary under the circumstances.

"So, you need my help now?" Zolkin began, sounding unwilling to entertain any notion of co-operating with other intelligence agencies.

"President Zolkin," Hassall continued. "I don't have time to explain everything. We have an emergency situation here that concerns both you and your people. I think you're going to want to know about it since it involves a plot by The Three Bears against Russia."

Reluctantly, the President began to listen as Hassall filled him in on the details. When the IRIS Director had finished, he was hopeful that things could get moving.

To his consternation, Zolkin stated simply, "I will have my own Federal Security Service look into it."

"With all due respect, sir," Hassall said, determined not to accept the Russian President's answer. "The FSB could take a while to investigate the matter. Who knows how long? By which time, The Three Bears will be unstoppable."

Hassall continued to try to reason with him, but the Russian President was adamant that things would be done his way, without any interference from international intelligence agencies.

"That is the best I can do at the moment," Zolkin replied with resolute finality.

"But sir..." Hassall protested.

"I cannot speak any longer," Zolkin replied. "I have an urgent meeting to attend. Thank you for bringing this matter to our attention. Goodbye."

The line went dead, leaving Hassall at the end of his wits.

"Oh well, at least you tried, sir," Elf began.

Hassall shook his head. "It's out of our hands. It's all down to Bull and Likamolova now."

***

Tania and Bull hurried through the labyrinth of rooms within the mill complex. They had to get to that control room. Fast. They came to the area where the paper-cutting machines had once been, with heavy paper rolls on a sliding trolley. The controls for this machine appeared to be a small box attached to the end of a power cable that was lying on the floor. The control box had green and red on-off buttons respectively, and a series of variable speed settings. Tania picked it up out of curiosity and examined it.

"Don't touch that," Bull warned her abruptly, pulling the box out of her hand. "If you press that switch the trolley will probably shunt across suddenly and crash into you."

"Really?"

"Yes." Bull bent down and examined it. "Fortunately it was only on the slowest setting, so if it did hit into you, it would simply knock you over and wind you. But if it were on its fastest, it would probably crush you to death."

"Thanks for the warning," she replied gratefully, tossing it back onto the floor. No need for that.

As they lurched forward, suddenly they heard a whizzing noise behind them. There was barely time to see where it was coming from as the now-familiar sight of a diabolo came into view. It spun through the air towards them like a bouncing bomb. Tania gasped, ducking immediately to avoid being hit on the head.

The diabolo appeared as if it was going to crash into them, but at the last second it was snapped backwards suddenly, recoiled on a length of cord like a yo-yo. However, it tore Bull's machine gun out of his hand, sending it sprawling away irretrievably.

They both looked up to see Rose Red standing, some fifteen feet away, reining in the deadly juggling device.

"I don't know how the two of you escaped," the red-head began. "But at least one good thing to come out of this is that it will give us the chance to get reacquainted properly this time."

The assassin began sliding the diabolo on the string between the two batons, toying with it as if she were trying to decide which kind of manoeuvre she would execute next.

"I'll hold her off," Tania said to Bull. "You try to get to the control room."

"What?" Are you sure?"

"Yes, now go already." Did she just say that? She actually volunteered to stay behind and fight off this menace before her? But Jonah would have a better chance of knowing what to do, so it was probably for the best.

"Just stay out the way of that diabolo," he shouted, glancing backwards one more time before rushing off. "Don't let it hit you, whatever you do."

"I'll try." The Russian beauty rose to her feet as Jonah disappeared into the distance. She knew that the next strike would probably connect. She might not be so lucky. She began to move her feet and edge forward again.

"Don't think you can outrun this," Rose Red taunted her.

Tania ignored her words, and sprinted across the room as fast as her legs could carry her.

Rose Red flung the diabolo again. It soared high into the air, spinning like a top. Before it landed, the red-head performed a series of acrobatic moves that brought her closer to where the tennis star was standing. The

Russian moved out of the way, but the assassin had merely intended to scare her, as she caught the device again.

"I don't even need to use this to kill you," Rose Red boasted. She began a series of kicks, high towards Tania's face. The Siberian dodged and weaved, but did not wait until the red-head had finished her moves to counterattack. While the assassin was slightly off balance, one foot still in the air and her other foot moving, Tania stepped in and swept Rose Red's leg out from under her. The red-head lost balance and staggered backward. As she was falling, Tania moved in and elbowed her in the face. The red-head fell sprawling, straight onto her back. Immediately, she lost control of the diabolo, sending it rolling across the floor, pulling the two sticks attached to the string with them.

Tania bent over and picked them up. Maybe she could use her opponent's weapon against her. If she even knew how.

Still lying on the floor, Rose Red laughed derisively, seeing what the Russian was attempting. "That takes years of skill and practice, and now you expect to use them against an expert in a few seconds? You'd probably end up killing yourself first before it even reaches me."

Tania quickly looked down at it. The exotic assassin was right. She had no idea what to do. What was she thinking? But she had to try something.

In an act of desperation, the Siberian blonde flung the diabolo, attempting to emulate the moves she had observed previously. Without the right co-ordination, it was heavy and difficult to toss. It flew limply through the air, while Rose Red easily rolled out of the way.

The red-head arched her back and used her arms to push off as she sprung straight to her feet. She did not immediately go for the diabolo but moved in to fight the tennis ace instead.

"You were lucky that time," she said. "But I don't make it a habit of being swept off my feet."

She produced another series of kicks. Tania did her best to avoid them. But a strategically planted fist connected with her, straight between the eyes, sending her stumbling backwards. The Russian was in shock. She had never been punched in the face before. She began to feel dizzy. But the adrenaline and the fear of being killed kept her alert. She shook off the blow, blinking her eyes as she tried to focus on where the red-head was currently. She did not have time to see, as another blow landed on her. Rose Red kicked her straight in the chest, knocking the wind straight out of her and sending her backwards as if she had been hit by a piston. A final reverse back kick from the assassin sent Tania spinning to the ground, landing face forward next to the paper-cutting machine.

Lying there dazed, the fear began welling up inside of her as Tania watched Rose Red use that deadly weapon again. The red-haired assassin began executing a series of fancy moves, twirling her batons everywhere. The effect was dizzying but mesmerising. The diabolo travelled up the string as she flung it high into the air, easily over thirty feet.

Pull yourself together, Tania told herself. This time the diabolo was likely to find its target if she didn't move. But before she could act, she was suddenly pinned down by the red-haired assassin. *What on earth?* She had her in an aikido-like hold, pinning her arm down so she couldn't move. *No.* Rose Red was holding her there in place so that the infernal diabolo would crash-land straight on her.

She began to struggle, but couldn't move. Only mere seconds before the fateful death blow. What could she do? It was getting perilously close. In the corner of her eye, Tania saw the control box she had flung to the floor moments earlier.

It was just in reach of her free arm.

With a last act of desperation, she stretched out her hand and hit the green on-button. The machine hummed to life. It slammed into both of them, taking the red-head by surprise. As it was merely on its slowest setting, it shunted them across. Just enough so that their positions shifted, and the assassin was now nudged into the place where Tania had previously been.

Startled. For a split second, Rose Red temporarily forgot about the spinning diabolo that was now hurtling down under the force of gravity. She shrieked with panic as it plummeted towards her. With no time to move out of the way, the abrupt sound of bone cracking was heard as it crashed on top of her head, killing her instantly.

Tania shielded her eyes, shocked as to what had happened. When she eventually opened her eyes to assess the damage, she peered over and gasped. She didn't mean to do that. All she had intended was to shift herself out of the way, but inadvertently, she had brought about the red-haired assassin's demise through her own weapon.

Tania stifled a cry as she rose to her feet, trying to forget what she had just been involved in. Why did Jonah leave her alone here by herself? Oh yeah. Because she had suggested it. Hopefully she could find him. He'd know what to do. With any luck, he was probably near the control room by now.

Unfortunately, she was probably too optimistic. Jonah Bull made up a series of staircases and along a stretch of catwalk, high above the factory. The path to the Operations Room appeared to be sealed off, with a raging fire blocking his path.

Below him, the guards tore through the Pulp and Paper Mill, either trying to escape or locate the escaped prisoners as the plant was filled with the sound of a chain of explosions, scattering debris in every direction and leaving a thick cloud of smoke billowing towards him.

Bull looked around, considering his options. Medvedev was probably safely out of reach with no-one to disturb him. The only way to prevent The Three Bears' plan coming to fruition was by shutting the satellite down physically and directly rather than electronically and remotely.

But how?

Bull glanced around once more. Perhaps, after all, he should head back towards the area he had come from. There had to be another way to the control room. Besides, he had left Tania there, and she could be in trouble. However, after taking a few steps in the opposite direction, he saw her heading towards his location and rushed out to meet her.

"What happened?" she asked. "I thought you were heading to the control room to stop Medvedev."

"The path to the control room has been sealed off," Bull replied. "We'll have to shut it down another way."

"How?"

"If we can't do it remotely, we'll have to do it by sabotaging it physically. One of us will have to go on the transmission tower and disable the satellite from there. Take out the transmitter or something."

"We'll both go," Tania said. "You're not leaving me by myself again."

They doubled back on themselves the way they came as the flames began spreading a tidal wave of destruction. The power in the plant began to shut down at various locations, with the lights blinking everywhere. Tania and Bull entered a storage room where the giant paper rolls were stacked horizontally on top of each other on a ramp and held in place by the electromagnet.

"They're still coming for us," Tania wailed.

"Hurry, this way," Bull replied, pointing towards the exit at the other side.

But wait. The guards began pouring from there. Where did they come from? They were trapped. Killers on every side. Nowhere to run.

***

Medvedev stood in the Operations Room, waiting eagerly as the engineers made their final preparations, and the signal was about to be transmitted.

The other two Bears came on again over the communications channel.

"What is happening there?" Blue Bear inquired.

"Nothing that will interfere with our plans," Medvedev replied.

"I am not so sure of that," Green Bear spoke. "From what I understand, your base of operations is coming apart."

"We have everything under control," Medvedev assured them. "Trust me. Everything is in place. All the modifications have been made. Now watch as the world prepares to go into Anti-Goldilocks."

***

Tania cast an eye towards Jonah as she saw the guards move in towards them. Perhaps he would have an idea how to get out of this sticky situation. At this point, she was willing to try anything to gain the upper hand.

All out of options, they were about to surrender in order to buy time, when the electrical power short-circuited, causing the electromagnets to switch off. With the power out, the force clamping the steel cores at the centre of each paper roll in place was removed and the rolls started to move.

With all eyes fixed on the rumbling, the rolls gathered speed and came tumbling down the ramp like enormous rolling wheels thundering along, threatening to squash everything in their path.

Frozen with fear. Through sheer willpower, Tania commanded her feet to move. At the same time, Jonah yanked her arm and dragged her forward.

With the giant paper rolls snowballing towards them, the security guards forgot all about their quarry and turned in panic to save themselves. They were like stampeding horses, desperate to escape the onslaught. But the rolls kept thundering furiously, crushing several of the guards in their path.

Faster. Come on.

Tania would soon be mowed down, squashed any second now if she didn't move.

"Jump to the side," Jonah barked, seeing they were unable to outrun this relentless avalanche.

Tania dived to her right to escape the swathe of destruction, while Bull leapt simultaneously to his left. She gasped as the rolls hurtled past her, breathing a huge sigh of relief. But her heart sank as she heard the anguished cry from Bull, as the edge of one of the rolls struck him, nearly crushing his leg. He managed to pull it away in time before any further damage was done.

When the smoke and debris had settled, Tania looked around to see a number of mangled corpses flattened by the terrible devastation. Where was Jonah? That was her first concern. Her eyes darted around desperately, afraid that he might have been caught up in it, and she would be all alone. He had to be alive.

Please.

Chapter 33

Tania found Jonah lying there in agony. He was alive, but crippled. At least for the moment.

She rushed towards him, dragged him to a more comfortable location in the room, then bent over him anxiously to examine his injury.

"Are you okay?" she asked.

"No," he replied. "I think… I think my ankle may be broken. I'm not sure."

"Oh no," Tania gasped. "That can't be good."

"Not good at all," he replied ominously. "I hesitated for a second to see that you were okay, but that was all that was needed to be almost too late to escape those rolls."

"No need to explain," she assured him. "Can you stand though?"

"I'll try." Bull placed his arm around Tania's shoulder as he tried to get up. He yelped in pain. "It's no use. I can't put my weight on it properly. I can barely walk."

"Now what?"

He looked at her despairingly. "You've got to go on the transmission tower and disable the satellite yourself. You have to leave me."

"What?" Tania exclaimed. "This was never part of the deal. I can't do that."

"Of course you can. And you must, because one of us needs to get to that transmitter quickly, and I'm not about to break any speed records."

"I'm not good with electronics. There's no way I could do it on my own."

"Sure you can. It'll be just like changing a fuse."

Tania shot him a sceptical look. "Surely not."

"Look, I'll explain everything," he assured her. "You just need to stick to the plan and not panic. I'll try to hold off the others."

Tania protested. "But... I'm not ready for this."

"You might never be ready, but it doesn't matter. Don't be like the thing you called me," he continued. "A sitting bull. Now go already."

She smiled, then steeled herself for what she had to do. She gave him one last look. "Are you sure you'll be okay?"

"Yes," he lied, not wishing to give her any further cause for hesitation. "I'll be fine. Now go."

Without looking back, Tania got up and began running down the catwalk. She was hesitant at first, but then picked up her pace as she continued towards her destination.

She scuttled through the walkways, knowing each passing moment was a step closer to the destruction of Sakhalin Island and everything around.

Reaching the end of the catwalk where it met part of the latticework scaffolding for the transmission tower, she paused briefly to peer over the edge. Shooting up almost to the same level where she had to climb were the giant, vertically-stacked, twenty-ton paper rolls she had seen earlier, held in place by metal cores, one on top of the other on large turntables, each of which were designed to travel down a figure-eight-shaped track.

Also in the same room were a series of chains attached to a tow hook on one end, and a pulley on the other, mounted on an overhead track. It appeared to be controlled by one of the switches on the wall to allow it to travel back and forth. That was probably used to hoist heavy equipment. Further down below, leading to wood shredders, were trough-like conveyor belts with protective metal barriers on each side of the moving rubber belts. Fortunately, all of these machines were turned off.

She looked up, assessing the daunting task ahead of her. She had to ascend at least thirty feet to get up to the maintenance box. There wasn't a ladder she could simply mount, rung by rung. *No.* Instead, she had to work her way up the lattice scaffolding, like a construction worker, finding her footing wherever she could. No mean feat. Taking a deep breath, she began to climb. *Oh God, please don't let me fall. How on earth did I end up doing this sort of thing?* Her nerves were shot with fear, but she had no choice. Slowly but surely she made her way up, one step at a time.

She stopped to take a breath several times, urging herself on, not wishing to look down. Once up there, she found her way to a large metallic maintenance box. Protruding from it and travelling upwards were thick, electrical cables that seemed to connect to the external satellite. She opened the box carefully. Inside was a swirling mass of multi-coloured wires, intertwining with each other. A tangled bowl of spaghetti mixed with bean sprouts. What was she supposed to do? Simply disconnect them all? No. Jonah had explained to her that she needed to look for some kind of fuse box and remove any fuses. Hopefully, that would automatically shut down the mechanism for the transmitter. But where was it?

She began searching around frantically, aware that everything depended on her.

"Yes," she cried triumphantly. She had finally located a panel of three fuses arranged in series. They had been staring her in the face the whole time, but were simply hidden behind the jungle of wires. Besides, she had been looking for a fuse box, which had misled her.

Now what?

Above the row of fuses were three corresponding large, metal square buttons. They must be switches or release buttons, just like those found in a box in an ordinary house. Pressing on these would pop the fuses out. *Was that all there was to it?*

She extended a slender finger towards one of the metal squares and pushed it. The fuse refused to budge. *What the hell?* These seemed to be heavy-duty fuses, designed so that they couldn't simply be removed casually. It required greater force to eject the blasted thing. *But how?* She slammed her palms on the button, but that still didn't do it. She banged on it hard with the bottom of her fist. All that that succeeded in doing was hurting her hand. She couldn't do much more of that. An injured hand would be extremely bad for tennis.

Wait a minute. This was no time to be thinking about her sport. There were lives at stake here, and all she was concerned about was a stupid injury?

She shook her head in frustration. But even so, the force of her fists wasn't strong enough to pop those stubborn fuses out. She would have to climb up higher and kick each one of those buttons with the heel of her shoe.

***

In the Operations Room, Boris Medvedev watched anxiously as he waited for the engineers to transmit the final data to the perforating guns installed around Russia.

One of the technicians spun around from the console at which he sat. He gave Medvedev a doleful look. "Someone is attempting to tamper with the transmitter."

Medvedev looked closer at one of the view screens. The technician was right. Someone was up on the transmission tower near the maintenance box. "Likamolova," he growled. "She'll ruin everything."

"Looks like she had another ace up her sleeve," Asteria remarked.

Medvedev turned to Asteria. "Go out there. Do whatever you have to do. Stop Likamolova."

***

Tania climbed up further, clenching her teeth as her heart hammered away in fear. She had to get those nerves under control, or else she would be useless. How different could this be from playing those big points in a tennis match? So often, players would falter under pressure. She was renowned for holding her own. Having veins of ice and nerves of steel. It was simply a matter of adopting the same frame of mind here.

She exhaled deeply and counted to ten, galvanising herself for what she had to do. She would have to hold on carefully while slamming her heel into the metal squares. Hopefully, that would have enough force to push those fuses out. Only three of them. How difficult could it be? Just three or so kicks and it would be done. Then she could climb back down and be done with this.

She positioned herself above the maintenance box. Square number one. Clutching on tightly, she brought her leg up, then, with the full force of her weight, slammed the bottom of her shoe into it with all her might.

The fuse moved. *Yes.* Only a flicker, but it was a start. Maybe a few more kicks and the whole thing would come loose. She brought her leg up again a further two times and banged down on the button. Finally she heard the noise of something popping and the fuse fell out.

At last.

One down. Two more to go. But she needed to pause for a breather, because this was hard work, and her foot was getting sore. Fortunately, she had gotten the hang of it. Now all she had to do was concentrate.

***

Jonah Bull had followed Tania to the area leading to the transmission tower, where she had climbed up. Limping slowly, every step was excruciating, but he couldn't simply leave her. What if she needed his help?

From where he was looking, however, she seemed to be doing okay. Hopefully, no-one would enter the area and try to stop her. She had to be entirely focused on the task without having to worry about anyone else. That was the last thing she needed. That's why he was there, wasn't it? To hold off any potential threats?

Well, yes. But he was mostly concerned for her safety.

Suddenly, at the corner of his eye, he noticed someone approaching.

No.

It was Asteria.

She seemed to be carrying something with her. But what? *A tennis racquet?* What on earth was she planning to do with that?

He had to stop her, otherwise this could be disastrous for all concerned. And if she climbed up that tower and followed Tania to the top, then what? The beautiful Russian could soon be plummeting to her death, especially with the strength of that warrior woman.

Pushing past the pain, he struggled on across the maze of catwalks to face the giantess himself. He would willingly sacrifice his own life if that meant allowing her the chance to complete her task.

Above, Tania was entirely oblivious to the amazon's presence. She poised her foot to kick another one of those metal buttons when she heard a strident, warlike voice that she instantly recognised.

"Get away from there."

Tania barely had time to look, when suddenly, out of nowhere, a metallic projectile came flying upward through the air like a rocket. Turning around, it grazed her arm, causing her to yelp in pain. Still holding onto the lattice framework, she was forced to shrug off the pain as she turned to see where the voice had originated from.

In the distance on the catwalk below stood Asteria, brandishing a racquet in one hand, and a few steel tennis balls in the other. It looked like, any second now, she was about to launch a few more of those cannons.

But what could she do? She had to finish removing those fuses. Of course, that last cannon had hurt her arm. Asteria always did have a killer serve. The fastest one in the game. Tania had no desire to experience it again first hand. If it connected with her head at the speed the amazon could serve it, it would probably kill her.

Miraculously though, at least from her point of view, Jonah appeared, still injured, but there to attempt a rescue. What was he doing there? That fool was going to get himself killed.

Bull charged into Asteria with what strength he had left, hoping to tackle her to the ground. But the amazon's abnormal strength made her easily as strong as any heavily-built man. Quite possibly stronger. He planted a couple of jabs to her face, but she laughed it off, and swatted him away savagely with the back of her hand, causing him to lose balance. As his leg was already hurt, he stumbled backwards towards the edge of the catwalk. Pressing her advantage, Asteria let out a kick like a mule, with such force that it sent him hurtling over the edge.

"No," Tania screamed, as she watched Jonah disappear from above. As a result of the shock, and her temporary distraction, she lost both her footing and her grip on the latticework, giving a shriek as she slipped off the transmission tower.

***

A massive explosion rocked the plant Operations Room, a few moments earlier, short-circuiting some of the computers, and sending hundreds of volts of electric current into some of the employees.

"Sir, we have to get out of here," one of the scientists urged Medvedev.

"No," he barked. "We can't leave this now."

"Sir, you have to get to safety. This place is going to blow."

"No. You are ordered to stay where you are. This is not finished at all." He pointed to one of the monitors on the wall. "There, you see, my assistant Asteria has everything under control. As long as Likamolova doesn't disconnect all the fuses, the connection with the satellite won't be broken, and we can still transmit the relevant data."

But it was no use. His employees around him quickly forgot their loyalty to him and merely tried to save their own skins as they fled in every direction as the flames licked the room with increasing intensity.

***

The criss-cross latticework was a blur as she sailed downwards a few metres. Fortunately, Tania managed to grab hold of one of the metal girders, bringing her abruptly to a halt. *Ouch.* It felt as if her shoulder had been yanked out of its socket. That was likely to give her an injury that could put her out of action for months. Well at least she was alive. She pinched herself to double-check. *Yep. No question there.* Alive, even though she was dangling precariously with one hand.

But where was Jonah? He had to be okay. *Please.*

Tania peered down, dreading the worst. He had landed heavily with a thud on the stationary, trough-like conveyor belt below. Felled by the amazon. And now she was coming after her.

Hopefully, Jonah would be okay down there, because the other possibility was too horrible to even consider. He would probably want her to continue anyway, and even if he didn't, this was what she had to do.

Finding a part of the latticework to place her hand onto, Tania slowly and steadily began to climb back up the transmission tower.

But she would have to be quick, because Asteria was out for her blood, climbing up with incredible speed to meet Tania head on. And furthermore, her muscular nemesis had her racquet strapped across her back as she ascended.

I don't believe it. She's actually planning to use that against me up here.

***

The Operations Room was in complete disarray. It was too late. Medvedev would have to resume his plan some other day. For now, he needed to escape. He had a hydrofoil stored away, but had to get to it first.

Suddenly, a fireball engulfed the Operations Room, showering it with debris. Medvedev was trapped. Unless he could find an alternative exit, he would perish here with the rest of those faithful few who had stayed behind. His business plans were going up in smoke, left up to the other two Bears to carry out.

***

Tania studied her opponent carefully. Asteria had a utility belt loaded with nearly a dozen metal balls, identical to the one she had fired at the Russian earlier. All it would take would be one slip of the hand into one of those pouches and the Mohawked giantess could launch another offensive, which, from this distance could be devastating. Of course, that was provided Tania kept her balance on the latticework and managed to hold on.

Continuing her climb, Tania reached the maintenance box. *Just in time*. But would it be enough to knock out two fuses before the amazon caught up with her? She certainly would have to try. She positioned herself above the square button and gave it a good firm kick with her heel. Hard and determined. This one moved more easily than the first, but it still needed another kick for good measure.

She slammed her heel against it again. Smashing it for all she was worth. The fuse shot out of its socket, and Tania breathed a sigh of relief.

Only one left.

In theory, yes. In practice, would she ever have the chance to eject it? The amazon was upon her, grabbing at the Russian's leg, trying to yank her off the tower. Then, Asteria climbed up a few further steps so that she was level with her and tried to knock her off with a single punch.

No. She couldn't fail now. Not when she had come so far. All that was needed was a good, hard kick or two and she could be home free. Well, at least, free to fight off that monster. Dodging out of the way of Asteria's fist, Tania slammed her foot once more against the button. It budged slightly, but that was all the chance she got. The amazon grabbed her leg and pulled her towards her with one mighty swing.

The force of the tug was so hard that it almost dislodged her from the tower entirely. Asteria had the Russian's leg in her hand, and now here Tania was, thrashing about wildly, wrestling to break free. Somehow, in the struggle, she managed to land a punch on Asteria's face. Her opponent merely flinched. Why did she always seem to be fighting these big, unbeatable opponents?

Tania hung on for dear life as Asteria attempted to wrest her grip from the metal frame, prising her fingers away one by one so that she would plunge thirty to forty feet, probably to her death.

The amazon increased her attention on finishing off the young Russian. With one mighty surge of aggression, she ripped the frightened girl from her grasp, sending her over the edge.

Oh God. Desperate to grab onto anything, Tania clutched hold of Asteria's utility belt, her momentum pulling the muscular tennis player off with her, breaking her grip and causing them both to go over.

Chapter 34

Tania groaned. Her battered body ached, but the stack of giant paper rolls had cushioned her fall. Fortunately, the way they both fell had caused them to spin through the air, both landing only a few feet below. *That was lucky.* Yet she had probably sustained more injuries here than she ever had in the whole of her young tennis career. She rose quickly to her feet as her opponent renewed her attack.

The utility belt that Asteria wore had been torn off from her waist from the force of Tania's falling bodyweight when she had grabbed it in an attempt to break her fall. The amazon would simply have to hold the belt now. She picked it up and drew another metallic ball from one of the pouches as she unsheathed her tennis racquet, which miraculously, had not been broken in the fall. Unlucky for the Russian. Asteria swung her racquet upwards to serve once more. Determined not to be hit again, the blonde charged into her, attempting to move her arm out of the way to deflect the ball.

Right idea, wrong timing.

The ball fired off, going askew, and ricocheting off the master control switch for the entire machinery in the room. The turntable for the giant, vertically-stacked paper rolls roared to life and began to grind slowly in a circle. Overhead, the chains attached to those tow hooks on the pulleys began sliding across the ceiling. Meanwhile, the rolls themselves began snaking along like bottles in a bottling factory, shuffling down the figure-eight-shaped track and gradually picking up speed.

Oh no. What have I done? As if that wasn't bad enough, the master control switch had caused the conveyor belt where Bull lay unconscious to hum to life, edging forward inch by inch towards that wood shredding machine.

Now she had three problems on her hand. Not only did she have to escape that dreaded racquet and those balls, but she had to remove that last fuse if she could ever get back up there again. And to crown it all, now she might actually have to save Jonah Bull, if it wasn't too late already.

Great! As if she didn't have her work already cut out for her.

The paper rolls were gyrating at a moderate speed from the centripetal forces of the turntables, making the flat, cross-sectional surfaces unpredictable and awkward to balance upon. Near the circumference of the turntables, the speed of the rolls was faster. Tania definitely didn't want to step there, or she would surely lose her footing.

She tried to back away as Asteria swung her weapon once again in a violent whipping motion. There was nowhere to move out of the way, so Tania jumped from the top of one paper roll to the next. Landing on a faster moving part of the roll near the turntable's circumference, the horizontal force spun her round instantly and almost caused her to lose her balance as a ball whizzed past. Tania instinctively shielded herself, covering her head, her arms up in defence. Under normal circumstances, Asteria's deadly accuracy would have achieved a direct connection squarely with her target, but because the turntable's momentum had carried Tania round, it was merely a glancing blow, not fatal, but enough to bruise her forearms.

More injury.

And to make matters worse, the turntable sensors detected that the rolls were becoming congested and automatically increased the number of cycles per minute, and consequently, the speed of the whole system. The tower and the conveyor belt were getting farther away. But not all was lost. Because of the figure-of-eight design of the tracks upon which the turntables were placed, the ultimate destination of the rolls would eventually be back where they started – near the tower again. But at the speed this was going due to the increased velocity of the machinery, that might not be very long at all.

Tania tried to maintain her equilibrium as the giant rolls spun round while snaking their way down the track, weaving in and out of the bends. It was like riding a rollercoaster.

However, that was not her only problem. The flames which had started in the processing room had spread through the mill and were now in the paper storage area. The dry paper rolls had ignited from below and the flames were making their way up to the surface on which the Russian was standing. With the paper disintegrating, the struggle on top had become that much harder.

Meanwhile, the conveyor belt with Jonah Bull was edging closer and closer to the wood shredder. Bull awoke slowly, unaware of his surroundings, and of the imminent danger ahead.

The amazon looked like she was ready to attack again. Tania raced forward before Asteria could remove a further ball from her utility belt and serve another missile. She leapt onto another roll, aiming for the metal core at the centre and adjusting her step to match the speed of the moving surface under her feet. No way was she going to lose her balance again.

Asteria followed her, taking a massive leap as well. However, distracted by the flames and the heat reaching the top, she misjudged the distance. She landed on the outer edge. That was Tania's chance. As the amazon whirled out of control, the Russian pressed her advantage with a well-placed front kick. It stunned her opponent, but failed to knock her off. However, the force of the kick caused both the racquet and the utility belt to fly out of Asteria's hand, landing on top of the next roll along.

With the amazon momentarily disorientated, Tania attacked her with a series of desperate kicks to different parts of Asteria's body. Tania had to put her opponent out of action as quickly as possible. That wasn't going to be easy. Asteria had regained her equilibrium more quickly than Tania had anticipated. She blocked the Russian, grabbing her leg and throwing her backwards as if she were tossing a sandbag.

Tania crash-landed on the same roll where the utility belt and racquet lay. The latter was nearer, so Tania went for that. Picking herself up so she was standing upright again, she tried to swat her enemy across the face. However, Asteria, standing on the other roll, caught her arm. She tore the racquet away from her, and hauled her across towards the edge of the roll. The Russian nearly disappeared over the edge, but managed to keep her balance at the last second to avert the danger.

Clambering to her feet, Tania saw that she had landed next to Asteria's utility belt. There were still a number of metal balls in it. Her opponent was much bigger and stronger, and with an unbreakable will. She seemed to be completely unstoppable. What's more, Asteria now had that deadly racquet again which, in the hands of that muscular, female Goliath, could be used in itself to club the seemingly-helpless young Russian to death.

The amazon gave a derisive laugh. "You always were the underdog. What makes you think you can beat me now?"

Suddenly, Tania remembered the words of her coach. *Don't play another person's game, because it may put you at a disadvantage. Play your own game.*

The Russian blonde knew what she had to do. She couldn't beat the muscular amazon by brute strength alone. Only by skill and her ability to move more quickly. Maybe even turning a weakness into a strength. She picked up the utility belt and began whipping it around in a rapid lasso motion. The action was so ingrained into her. She had used it instinctively so many times on court. Now swinging it in this way was second nature as she began using the utility belt like a slingshot.

"Every dog has her day," Tania replied, as the makeshift, utility-belt slingshot launched one of the metal balls. It struck her opponent squarely on the forehead. "You've just had yours."

Asteria buckled, howling in immense pain. Temporarily disorientated, she stumbled backwards towards the outer circumference of the paper roll where the velocity was fastest. With the unstable moving surface, Asteria automatically lost her balance. She was spun off the roll immediately, causing her to fly over the edge.

"Who says the lasso forehand doesn't work?" Tania muttered triumphantly, as she made a cautious attempt to see where her enemy had landed.

Asteria had plunged straight down into the teeth of the wood shredder below, just in front of where Jonah Bull was currently heading. She thrashed around for a few seconds, screaming in agony as blood spattered everywhere.

Then all was silent.

Tania was sickened to the pit of her stomach when her actions finally dawned upon her. Such a bloody mess down there below. *Oh God, what have I done?* But it was all in self-defence. At least that's what she'd have to keep telling herself from now on if she were ever to sleep at night again. And better hope the tennis world didn't make too much of Asteria's absence. Maybe they'd think she simply retired. After all, lots of players did that, didn't they?

But one bloody mess could soon follow another, as Bull slid over the edge of the conveyor belt. At the last moment, he caught onto one of the protective metal barriers that formed the trough, with his feet dangling over the shredding machine. However, with the awkward shape of the metal edges, keeping a firm grasp was proving extremely difficult, and his hands were beginning to lose their grip.

"Jonah," Tania cried, ripped from her state of shock immediately.

"Tania," he urged her. "You've got to turn the machine off."

"Where?" she asked.

"Find the off switch or the emergency stop button. Hurry. Quickly."

The Russian looked around. She spotted it, but it was too far for her to reach from where she stood. She would never make it in time. There appeared to be no easy route to clamber down from the giant paper rolls without encountering the fire herself. By the time she could find a way, Jonah would be ripped to a hundred strips of flesh.

Suddenly, a warning message came blaring over the loudspeakers, giving Tania a fright: "TIME UNTIL TRANSMISSION: ONE MINUTE."

Chapter 35

"**O**h God," Tania shrieked in horror. "The Three Bears must've activated the countdown."

"Leave me," Bull shouted, assessing their priorities. "Get to the fuse."

But how could she? There would only be time enough for one activity. If she were able to climb up on the tower again and kick in that last button, it would mean that Jonah would meet the same horrible fate as Asteria. She couldn't bear to think about that one. But if she did try to save him, she could never get back in time to mount the tower and disrupt the fuse. Then not only would the entire Russian oil supply be contaminated, but worse, Sakhalin Island and the surrounding areas could be devastated. Her family gone.

What kind of choice was that? Why was she constantly faced with these insurmountable dilemmas? And why was she always having to play these games?

Come on. Think quickly. There had to be a way around this. She darted her eyes back and forth. Asteria's tennis racquet was still lying on one of the paper rolls next to her. And three remaining metal tennis balls in the utility belt too. This gave her an idea, if she could pull it off. If she were accurate enough, she might be able to hit out that last fuse from this distance with the ball. The speed of the serve combined with the density of the sphere ought to have the same effect as kicking it in. Well, in theory. It was a long shot, but it was worth a try. The problem was that the paper rolls were still rotating on the turntable and shuffling up and down the track, bringing her nearer, and then further away from the target.

She removed one of the balls. *How on earth did Asteria manage to serve with these?* If she ever thought the regular tennis balls were too heavy, this made them seem like they were made of sponge.

"TIME UNTIL TRANSMISSION: 45 SECONDS."

"What are you doing?" Jonah cried, hearing the precious moments ticking away. "Hurry. Get to the tower. Forget about me."

"Hold on," she replied.

"Believe me, I'm trying."

Tania ignored him and focused. She had executed this move hundred of times both in practice and during a tennis match, but never under these kinds of conditions.

She steeled herself as the paper rolls completed another rotation around the track, bringing her to the correct distance. This had to be timed just right.

The Russian ace took aim and served. *Come on.* She struck the ball. It lacked the power. *Too soft.* She was serving upwards at an awkward angle to which she was not accustomed. Failing to gain the proper reach, the ball merely tapped the button but the fuse remained firmly in place.

Damn. So close.

"This is no time to be practising your tennis," Bull urged.

"TIME UNTIL TRANSMISSION: 30 SECONDS."

Tania aimed again, waiting for the rolls to complete their rotation. This time she pelted it with all her might. She misjudged the angle. The ball fired from the racquet, shooting wide of the mark as it ricocheted off one of the side of the maintenance box.

Too hard this time.

"TIME UNTIL TRANSMISSION: 15 SECONDS."

She remembered her practice session involving Isabelle and that dunk tank on court back in Flushing Meadows. She had kept missing that large, emergency-stop-style target every time. Her aim had been off then, but her coach had made her practise hitting one ball after another, to no avail at the time. Would it be the same story here? But then she had been so accurate with her thundering serve when she rescued Natalya from that electric shock back at the US Open. Now, just like then, Tania had to serve with deadly precision again. No second chances. No room for error. Everything had to be just right.

The paper roll completed another rotation, but she was not ready. She had to wait for it to go round again.

"Will you hurry up?" Bull urged her.

"TIME UNTIL TRANSMISSION: 8 SECONDS."

Tania concentrated, waiting to be in position. Only one shot left. She would have to hit that button to release the fuse.

She focused. Stilled her nerves. Allowed all the pressure around her to dissipate. She had to be relaxed. Try to get herself in the zone, where she couldn't miss. Changing the angle of her service motion, she swung her racquet in a single balletic action, her eye carefully on the target, while letting out her trademark scream. The racquet connected with the metal sphere, sending it coursing through the air like a missile. This time, it hit the square metal button dead centre, with the right amount of force. The fuse sprung out immediately, and accordingly, the loud speaker warning announced a new message:

"TRANSMISSION ABORTED."

"Game over," Tania whispered as she breathed a huge sigh of relief. She did it.

But what about Jonah?

That conveyor belt was still rolling, and he was hanging with his life in the balance, rapidly losing his grip.

All out of ammunition. And still no way to get to him from the giant paper rolls. Now what? All she had was the tennis racquet.

She looked around. Those tow hooks on the end of a chain, attached to a pulley, were still sliding across that overhead track. She tied the utility belt taut around her waist with a knot, and shoved the racquet in between the gap. Taking a deep breath, she poised herself from the top of the paper rolls as they were still rotating, and leapt towards one of the chains.

Oh God.

Somehow, her hands managed to find those dangling metal creepers as it swung from side to side, carrying her along until she neared the emergency stop. She wrapped her long legs around the chain and held on tightly with both hands. When she was close enough, she released her right hand and yanked the racquet out from her belt, swinging it as if she were simply executing a ground stroke. With the extended reach of the racquet, and the momentum of the swing, the strings slapped hard against the master control switch, bringing all the machinery in the room, including the conveyor belt and shredder, and the giant paper rolls on the track to an abrupt halt.

"Thanks," muttered Bull, as he attempted to haul himself back up onto the now-stationary conveyor belt, taking a few moments to catch his breath.

"Don't mention it," Tania replied, equally as relieved. She had done it. Her skills, honed in the heat of battle, came together when it mattered. The problem she now faced was dismounting safely from the chain, with the fire rising rapidly from below. There appeared to be no way of escape without encountering the raging blaze.

"How do I get down now?" she wailed, still swinging about in mid-air near the emergency stop, while holding onto the racquet.

"Just wait, I'll be there in a few seconds."

"I don't think I'm going anywhere, anytime soon," she replied.

"Don't worry," he assured her. "I'll be there to catch you."

But what could Jonah do? And what was *she* supposed to do? Take a leap and land in his arms? Would he really be able to support her, cushion her landing, especially with his injured leg? And don't even mention the fire.

No. She would have to save herself.

But how? Think.

A light bulb went on in her head. It was a crazy idea, but she had to try it anyway. "Jonah," she began. "You've got to get on one of those chains."

"What?"

"Trust me," she assured him, recognising that same expression of disbelief she had displayed so many times before when he would suggest something similar. "Jump."

Probably easier said than done. Especially with his leg. But there wasn't much of a choice. And how many times had he asked her to trust him? She wasn't even sure this would work.

With the strength he had left, Jonah leapt off the conveyor belt. He caught on just as an explosion followed, which threatened to blow them to pieces. However, Tania swung her racquet once more, reactivating the master control switch. The machines hummed to life again, and the chains began moving swiftly across the overhead rail towards a safer area, unaffected by the blaze.

Disembarking before the whole rail system went round again, taking them back to where they were, they landed with a bump. The height of the drop meant they crashed to the ground, with the Russian landing on top of Jonah, knocking the wind out of him. But at least they were safe.

Tania groaned as she picked herself up off the floor, disentangling her limbs from his. "Are you okay?"

Bull crawled out from under her. "I'll live." He tried to stand, but his leg was still hurting. He gave a sigh. "So was this your idea of the princess in the tower waiting for her prince to climb up and save her but then needing to save herself instead?"

"Perhaps," she replied, a smile beginning to flicker across her face. "I just thought it was time I became a player."

She was right. Bull looked at her, as if for the first time, seeing how this Russian Goldilocks had blossomed into this beautiful, young woman who was now fully aware she was in the game, and not the naïve girl who didn't, or had unwittingly become the game herself. She had managed to defuse the transmitter, avert disaster, as well as save his skin. He wanted to hold her in his arms, thank her even, and kiss those oh-so-sweet lips of hers that had now parted to flash a brilliant smile. However, all he said was "You did it. Well done."

"Thanks," she replied modestly, feeling a touch of red rising in her cheeks. "But what about Medvedev?"

"I don't know." He shook his head, unable to provide a definite answer. "He was in the control room when it exploded. I don't see how he could've survived. But you stopped his plan. You did it, and for the moment, that's all that counts."

That much was true. By disrupting the satellite, Medvedev was unable to transmit the data to the oil perforating guns that would contaminate the Russian oil supply and thereby achieve his global bear market. The destruction of their base of operations would ensure that it remained that way for the foreseeable future, allowing the relevant authorities in the meantime to check any technology employed in oil exploration and take counter measures against any would-be threats. Most importantly, Tania had prevented a disaster of cataclysmic proportions around Sakhalin Island. But could it really be said that Goldilocks had beaten The Three Bears at their game or was it merely a stalemate? After all, they were still at large, even though their immediate plans had not come to fruition.

"You never know," she responded sceptically. "Sometimes bears are only hibernating until the winter has passed."

"Well, hibernating or not, we've got to get out of here. This place is going to blow."

"How?" Tania was less than hopeful.

"Well if we can get to it, there's a ride waiting for us by the lake."

Tania slung his arm around her shoulder, helping Jonah to his feet as she began dragging him through the mill to find the exit. As they fled frantically through the huge complex, the smoke and fumes threatened to overwhelm them several times, but swiftly and surely, they forged a way out.

Finally, they emerged through the troughs where she had entered before, scrambling down the rocky terrain towards the lake.

"Over there," Bull said, pointing to Hawk Eye in the distance. "That's our ride."

Tania looked into the horizon, near the edge of Lake Baikal, to see that strange, hybrid helicopter-plane, or whatever it was, sitting there. No time to inquire about it. She had seen enough strange things lately to know better. She continued to run with Jonah down the hill, bearing his weight like a crutch to compensate for his broken ankle, as a final blast hurled them forward. They began rolling down with speed, snowballing before they landed on a flat surface at the bottom.

When they reached Hawk Eye, Tania and Bull clambered into the cockpit as the last remains of the mill began to collapse.

"Are you sure you can fly in the condition you're in?" she asked.

"Well, unless you'd like to give it a go?"

"No," she said, nodding resolutely. "I've had enough of trying out new things to last me a whole year."

Bull started up the engine. Slowly, the blades began to turn, picking up speed and rapidly reaching 425 rpm. This time he had the hang of things. He pulled the collective up first time, as the aircraft lifted steadily off the ground.

Tania took a moment to glance behind her, almost as if she were wishing the place a last farewell. This mill had once been a site of much ecological controversy with all the pollution flowing into the lake. What would happen now with all the devastation that had occurred?

Time was short, leaving no room for such ruminations. IRIS or someone else would probably have to come in and do some sort of damage control later on. It would be interesting to see them explain that one.

Hawk Eye rose up vertically, banked around for a few seconds, before climbing rapidly into the air. Within moments, they were hurtling away, leaving the thunderous sound of a sonic boom in their wake as they began their long flight home.

Epilogue

One week later.

The sand felt good between her toes as Tania stood on the beach of the tropical island paradise of Key Biscayne, basking in the warm Florida sunshine. Wearing a sleek white bikini with a short, diaphanous white Polynesian pareo tied around her waist like a skirt, and a pair of *Gucci* sunglasses, she gazed pensively towards the ocean. The glittering waters seemed to have a hypnotic effect on her as she watched a number of yachts and kite surfers with child-like fascination. She smiled as she took in the fresh, Atlantic sea air, allowing the gentle breeze to blow through her sun-kissed, golden hair. Picking up a smooth, flat pebble, she skimmed it across the water, watching it bounce gently across the surface, until it disappeared beneath a small ripple.

It was good to be home again.

Jonah Bull remained a furtive figure. Currently assisted by a cane, he limped slowly past a cluster of coconut trees, towards the foam-filled shoreline where Tania stood, observing her from a distance.

She seemed a happy and carefree girl now, as if all the burdens of the previous week were but a distant memory. She was at her most enchanting when she was neither weighed down by the competitive pull of professional tennis, nor the glamour of being a celebrity superstar. Instead, she was simply an ordinary, albeit beautiful girl-next-door once again, full of youthful exuberance, playing contentedly in the surf.

He approached her cautiously, unsure of how she would respond. Upon drawing closer, he noticed there was now a certain aloofness about her, as if the light he had previously seen in her had dimmed a little.

"Hi Tania-rhymes-with-Narnia," he began, trying to find something humorous to say to break the ice. "I was told I might find you here."

She looked up to acknowledge him, and immediately she beamed with a radiant smile that melted his heart. However, there was now an incongruous hint of melancholy in her eyes that had not been present before. Had her association with IRIS taken its toll on her? Had she lost a part of her innocence?

"Hello," she began, somewhat casually, as if she was not at all surprised to see him. "I sometimes like to come here after a tournament, just to be alone and watch the ocean. I find it very therapeutic. How's your leg by the way?"

"Well I won't be auditioning for the part of Long John Silver any time soon," he replied, lifting the cane and making light of it. "The doctors say I'll recover soon enough. How was your match in Beijing?"

"Oh, I lost," she said, with a passing stab of sadness in her voice. But then she quickly perked up again and giggled. "It wasn't much of a contest actually."

"You don't seem overly bothered suddenly."

"Oh no, I am," she clarified. "Don't get me wrong. I still love tennis, but perhaps in the last few days I've learnt that there's more to life than that. Certainly more than being the World Number One."

"I'm sure you'll get there eventually."

"Yeah," she agreed wistfully. "*Eventually*."

"And your coach?"

Tania gave him a pained look, and her sunny disposition disappeared temporarily behind a cloud of concern. "Well you know. It's as to be expected at this stage. I had him flown here and he's getting the best medical care available now. I won't know for a while, but hopefully he'll recover and pull through."

"I'm sorry to hear that," Bull replied grimly. "I hope he makes it too."

"Thanks. All we can do is wait now. And pray."

"Yeah. I guess so. What about your friend, Isabelle, is it? You had some problems with her, didn't you?"

"Oh, that's all sorted out," she replied, waving her hand as if to dismiss it already. "She's forgiven me long ago for missing her birthday. Yet again. But we had our own private celebration later on."

Bull smiled. "She sounds like a good friend."

"Mmhmm." Tania nodded in agreement, picking up another flat pebble as she skimmed it into the ocean. "You have no idea. She's a very, very good friend."

"I don't think I ever got the pleasure of meeting her."

"I'll have to introduce you two another time. Though I'm not sure what I'd tell her about how I know you." She began to giggle, her face brightening again. "Maybe I'll say you're some kind of groupie or something."

Bull's expression turned sombre. "You know you can't tell her or anyone else about what happened."

"Yeah, I know," Tania sighed, slightly troubled by the fact that she may never be able to fully confide in her best friend, and worse than that, would probably have to lie to her the whole time. "Spy confidentiality or whatever you call it."

"Yeah. Listen," he began, somewhat tentatively. "There's something I've been meaning to talk to you about."

The look she gave him was one of unstudied curiosity, as if she hadn't the faintest notion what the subject might be. "What's on your mind?"

"About what happened when we were in that grinding drum in Lake Baikal…"

She blushed and lowered her eyes. "I thought we agreed that nothing *did* happen." She gave him a shy, but disarming smile to assure him that everything was fine between them. "And it's probably best that it didn't."

"Well, actually I was thinking…"

"Yeah, me too," she interjected. "You're probably still grieving the death of Felissia."

"Uh, yeah," Jonah agreed, although his expression seemed to suggest that perhaps he had something else he wanted to say. "I was thinking the exact same thing. And you're probably still getting over your betrayal by Piotr."

"Right."

"Besides, we lead such different lifestyles, you with your tennis, me with my work at IRIS…"

"Hey, forget it. I already have. But something tells me you didn't come all the way out here today just to discuss that. Or am I completely wrong?"

Jonah shook his head. "No. You're right. Hassall wanted me to come and thank you personally for all your help in this matter."

"I don't know how much help I was."

"We couldn't have done it without you."

"Well if you say so." She smiled, but was unconvinced. "Where's Hassall though? Why didn't he come in person?"

"He thought he'd obstructed you enough from playing your tennis."

"And you had no such qualms, flying out here to Miami-Dade County with your injured leg?" She giggled with a girlish lilt in her voice.

"Actually I wanted to come and thank you myself."

She raised her eyebrows in surprise. "For what?"

"For giving me a new perspective on things. For helping me to start to live life again."

Tania's cheeks turned a rosy shade again, as she shrugged her shoulders in abashment. "That's really sweet. But I think I should thank you. For flying to my rescue in Lake Baikal. And for challenging me to learn to deal with life's hot and cold, less-than-perfect situations."

"Well, I think you mainly helped yourself," he replied. "You already had it in you. You just needed the right circumstances for it to come into play." His expression grew more serious. "But there's something else Hassall wanted me to communicate to you."

Tania's expression darkened accordingly. "Oh no. What's that?"

"Well, you don't have to answer this right now, just think about it. Hassall says we could always use an operative within the tennis world."

"Oh no," she groaned. "You know how I feel about the whole spy game. Okay, maybe I'm not as weirded out by the concept as before, but it's not something I'd do out of choice. I think I'll stick to my own game of tennis, if that's okay."

"Well hear us out. It's not any kind of dilemma like before. On the contrary, it's all subject to your approval."

"My approval?"

Bull nodded. "Yes. It would only be in a part-time capacity. You'd still get to lie dormant and play your tennis the rest of the year round, but you'd get a wake-up call every now and then whenever we needed you. We would, of course, ensure you were trained properly."

Tania shook her head resolutely. "And what would I do when it comes to actually competing in tournaments? Tell them I have to pull out because of an 'injury'? How long will that story fly?"

"Hey, whatever works."

"Hmm…" Tania gave a scowl of mock irritation before allowing her expression to lighten again as the cogs began turning in her head. "I suppose it would give me an excuse to miss the dreaded clay court season."

"Well there you go," Bull agreed, pointing towards her with an open hand, as if his powers of persuasion were finally working on her.

Tania shot him a clearly discernible, fake-smile, then laughed. "I was just joking."

"Well, think about it. The Three Bears are still out there, and we still need our Goldilocks."

Tania frowned with a look of concern. "If I recall correctly, in the story The Three Bears returned to their cottage without warning while Goldilocks was fast asleep."

"Which is why we'd want you as a sleeper agent. You'd get the protection of IRIS so you can sleep soundly at night, and you'd get to do what you love doing as well. What could be better than that? What do you say, Tania-rhymes-with-Narnia? Are you game?"

Tania thought for a moment about the implications of his words. She had to admit that it would be good to have that added protection, even more than her regular bodyguards could provide. Furthermore, there was no denying that, in the end, it was a thrill to be involved on that mission with IRIS, even though it had her scared out of her wits on more than one occasion. But she felt alive. And that's what counted.

"Tell you what," she said with a sly grin on her face. "Why don't you let me sleep on it?"

www.ingramcontent.com/pod-product-compliance
Lightning Source LLC
Chambersburg PA
CBHW060416030726

47495CB00003B/604